THE PROSPECTOR

WALSTINE G. JONES

iCrew
digital publishing

Chula Vista • Columbus

ISBN: 978-1-946739-09-4

Printed in the United States of America

Cover design by DJ Rogers
justwritedesign.com

Published by iCrew Digital Publishing

Chula Vista • Columbus

Website: icrewdigitalpublishing.com

e-mail: icrewdigital@gmail.com

iCrew Digital Publishing is an independent publisher of digital works. We support the efforts of author-publishers in the digital world.

❀ Created with Vellum

CONTENTS

FOREWORD

The author, Walstine Grafton Jones, my father, was born on December 31, 1913. Unusual name you say?

The Author (lower right) with son, Michael, and wife, Ruth, 1970

Indeed! He was named by his Dad, John Sidney Jones Jr., after his Mom, Rosa, named the other siblings, perhaps a "thank you", to the Mayor of Hubbard, Texas, named "Walstine", & the Pastor, named "Grafton". My Dad always had a penchant for learning about things, as well as history. He expressed his many thoughts on events, both past and current. "Wally," as he was known, was a voracious reader, and seemed to have a memory of events, far better than myself. To sit down and talk with him could almost be intimidating because his knowledge was so vast. Dad didn't really start writing short stories, the family history, and The Prospector, until after he retired from 30 years with Civil Service, among other jobs he had when younger, in addition to serving in World War 2, meeting and marrying my Mom Ruth, in 1938. Now, to the Mojave Desert, where this book is based, and where he really grew up.

At three years old, Wally was transplanted with his parents, from Hubbard City, Texas, his birthplace, to Kramer Junction, in the Mojave Desert. He started school in the 2nd grade, at the age of nine. For many, this would have been a detriment to his education. Far from it! Dad made up for it, probably because he loved to read and learn, besides pestering his parents and anyone who would answer his questions, about life in the desert, what mining was all about, where were the trains going-how did they work, what was going on, outside of the booming mining towns of Atolia, Randsburg, Kramer Junction, Red Mountain, Daggett, Hinckley and Barstow, back about 1916 to 1927, or so era.

While Wally's Dad worked on the railway lines, his Mom made sure the section hands of the railroad and their families, were fed and had living quarters, & was also the local nurse. The early years of his life in the desert were difficult. Transportation was mainly by rail, pulled by steam engine locomotives. Wally rode the trains, to get back and forth to other towns, with his parents. Grandpa Jones, whose job was to maintain 24 miles of railroad tracks, even had a small motor car, which ran the rails. This was used for work, as well as notifying the local Dr. Denton, in Randsburg, of someone's emergency ills. The Model T Ford was used by those fortunate enough to have one, including the doctor and the sheriff. The older kids from this area, traveled to Barstow to high school, while the younger ones attended, the small school in Daggett.

Kids being kids, Dad included, all managed to get into various troubles. They fired rocks off their slingshots, swam in the canals and water pools, and got bloody noses in fistfights ... or worse. Playing with the lizards and avoiding rattlesnakes in the greasewood brush, around the area, was all part of the fun, besides gazing at the moon and the vast galaxies of stars at night.

Days were hot in the summer, and downright cold in the winter, with the periodic snowfall, which made traveling for supplies, even more tricky, in the Model T cars and trucks. Luckily, a lot of provisions needed, came by rail, with trains coming through a couple of times per day. According to Dad, that was the highlight of the day. When the railroads came rumbling through, the children ran out to greet the engineers and crew. The trains would then head to the mines, and ore would be loaded for transport back to the various destinations. Suffice it to say, Wally lived the desert life for many years, and always had vivid memories, as a kid, of what went on and how things happened.

To give the reader some insight, The Prospector himself is Wally's fantasy deep down. Had he had the opportunity, he just might have become a miner, like his childhood friend Don Kinney. Don lived in the desert for years and continued to mine-and had claims filed-even when Dad and I went out to Atolia, and I met him in 1991.

Dad and Don stayed up for hours at Don's home, after I bedded down for the night. They likely talked about their youth together, their relatives, friends, the gold, silver, tungsten mining industry. In his research & recollections, that's where Dad got a lot of information about people and events for this book, about times and places, now nearly non-existent. In Randsburg, there is still ore to be extracted. I still have pictures of that trip, and a later one, in 2000, after Dad had his massive stroke. It was to be his last trip to the Mojave Desert, and all those towns. Dad passed away at age 88, in 2002, as did his other friends I had met, a year or two later, but the old memories remain. Dad was an old west buff, but he also liked mystery, romance, and all of the things that make up a book about life in the desert. including bootleg moonshine, gunfights, love, and skulduggery included!

So, settle back, for a trip back in time, to the early 1900s, to the Mojave Desert. As you read The Prospector, you will smell the yellow Asters in bloom, hear the grinding of the equipment at the mines, feel the booms of dynamite going off, and feel the warm wind. From the summer heat to the winter cold, from the billowing smoke of the steam engines to the jackrabbits jumping and the coyotes howling, watch the black buzzards circling the mines.

Oh, and here's Grandma, telling Dad to stop playing, get cleaned up, calling Wally into dinner-for fresh plucked, fried chicken, mashed potatoes, gravy, and fresh-picked green beans. Can you smell it? Remember, this is fiction, combined with the firsthand experience of my Dad's life in the desert, all which make this book possible. This book was over six years in the making, with Dad taking care of my Mom Ruth as well, 63 years of marriage, with both having various serious ailments. So, finally, after nearly 20 years, here it is!

I hope you enjoy The Prospector, as much as Dad, Mom, my former wife Celeste, and I, along with a few others enjoyed editing and helping Dad put it together!

Happy reading!
Michael S. Jones
Son of Walstine G. Jones October 5, 2019

1

THE CLAIM

Buzzards circled high in the clear desert sky. Their keen vision gave them a panoramic view of all things and all places. Had they been so inclined, they could have seen the mining town of Randsburg twenty miles to the Northwest; had they looked in the opposite direction, perhaps they would have noticed the smoke rising from the trains arriving and leaving the town of Barstow thirty miles to the Southeast.

For the moment, however, their attention seemed to be focused on two objects, far down below, creeping across the barren desert. Perhaps some instinct had kindled their interest. If so, their interest may not have been totally unjustified. Bleached bones scattered across this arid land provided ample evidence and a constant reminder of the peril all animals, including man, faced each day and each night in this vast wilderness called the Mojave Desert which extends from the Tehachapi Mountains to the Colorado River and from Death Valley to the Mexican border.

Down below, the old prospector leading his burro, paid little attention to the scavengers. Buzzards always seemed to be somewhere in the desert sky soaring or circling and dipping now and then as if to break the monotony of the soaring and circling. Buzzards, like the coyotes that roam the desert, are always searching for food, an endless quest. The buzzards search by day, the coyotes hunt both day and night.

The weather was exceptionally warm for mid-November as the old prospector led his burro down a dim trail. The trail was called many names but was generally referred to as the Old Indian Trail. Smaller trails used for centuries by Indians living along the eastern slopes of the Sierra Nevada Mountain Range merged to form the Old Indian Trail. It traveled south passing through Owens Valley and Indian Wells Valley, then continued south towards Randsburg. Before reaching Randsburg, the trail turned in a southeasterly direction and moved north of Johannesburg and continued its southeasterly route passing east of Fremont Peak to the Mojave River, near Barstow, where it joined the Mojave River Indian Trail.

The Mojave River Indian Trail ran the length of the Mojave River, a strange and mysterious river that flows underground, surfacing only now and then while making its 200-mile underground journey across the Mojave Desert. Waters from deep snowpack's in the San Bernardino Mountains, which sometimes melt too quickly flood the converging streams, sending torrents of water rolling over the underground river's route destroying bridges and other manmade structures in its path. In two or three weeks the flood waters begin to recede and then disappear into the mysterious underground channel leaving only the white dry sands of the riverbed as evidence of its brief but awesome surface appearances.

Most of the Old Indian Trail had disappeared under the churning wheels of mule and horse drawn wagons traveling to and from northern Nevada and southern California while following the route of the Old Indian Trail.

Eventually, the route became known as California Route 395. Route 395 left the Old Indian Trail a few miles north of Randsburg and continued south and hooked up with Route 66 west of Victorville. Those who traveled by foot or horseback, including Indians and prospectors, continued to use the Old Indian Trail since it was the shortest route between Randsburg and Barstow, that is, until the arrival of the Model T Ford.

The Model T Ford touched just about everyone's life. The Indians decided the Model T and the reservation offered a better way of life than their nomadic heritage. Those who traveled by horseback sold their horses and bought Model T's. Why, they argued, should a person spend two days in a saddle riding to Barstow when he could crank up a Model T, take 395 to Kramer Junction, turn left and be in Barstow in a matter of hours? And those who walked could bum a ride or take the once-a-day train over the newly built rail line. The prospectors, who had used burros to search for wealth since the beginning of time, switched to Model T's for greater mobility.

But some of the old timers, like Jim, the old prospector leading his burro down the Old Indian Trail, refused to change. Using prospectors' common sense, the old timers knew that a Model T might travel faster, but it could not go to places you could lead a burro. And what if the darn contraption broke down out in the middle of nowhere? Besides, a burro can be a lot of company in the lonely desert. And you can talk to a burro, but who wants to talk to a Model T Ford?

The old prospector looked tired and his aging body had

begun to feel the same way. He had walked the twenty miles from Randsburg during the heat of the day and still had five miles to go before he reached his claim. He was in excellent health for a man in his mid-seventies, but he lacked the stamina of his youth. Twenty years ago, he had walked the twenty miles stopping only a couple of times along the way to rest his pack animal. Today, he found excuses to rest the animal every four or five miles.

The old prospector and his burro were a mile north of Fremont Peak when he paused, pushed back his broad brimmed hat, and glanced at the sun. Dust disguised the color of the old Stetson; it could have been brown or grey. Years of sweat seeping through the headband and years of wear gave it a look that seemed to be asking for respect, respect because it had withstood the rigors of mountain winters, hot desert summers, and sand storms that peeled the skin off a man's face, and it still managed to survive as an essential part of the old prospector's meager wardrobe.

The hat shaded the old man's fair skin and eyes, eyes as clear and as blue as the desert sky, eyes still sharp enough to hit a quarter at fifty paces with the .22 caliber rifle he carried in the scabbard hanging from the pack saddle.

Although the broad brimmed hat helped to protect the old prospector's eyes and exposed skin around his neck and face, the hot desert winds and cold winters, combined with hard work and passing of time, had taken their toll. Deep seams spread from the corners of his eyes upward to his temples and downward to his cheekbones like erosions through the sands of a dry river delta. Sunspots, some large, some small freckled the backs of his hands and the areas of his face where the sun sneaked around his hat and his neatly trimmed beard, a beard now white, once red.

After glancing at the sun, the old prospector pulled a dollar Ingersoll from his Levi's. He noted the large hand pointed at twelve and the small hand at three. He glanced at the sun again and simultaneously rubbed his beard with his left hand. The seams in the corners of his eyes deepened even more and the corners of his lips curled ever so slightly as he nodded his head with satisfaction. The sun and the watch agreed on the time of day. The old man knew he didn't need the watch, especially during the daylight hours, but he enjoyed playing the game. He held the watch to his ear for a moment before returning it to his watch pocket.

The old prospector turned to the burro and said, "Well Suzie, let's take a short rest. About five more miles and we will be there."

While talking to his burro, he began removing the heavier items of the 300-pound load.

"You will be able to rest more comfortably with some of this weight off your back," he said. "I'm only going to remove the heavy items. If I take all of them off, you may decide this is the end of our trip and lie down on me."

It took only a few moments for him to untie and unload the fifty pounds of hard rock drills, the hundred-pound sack of oats, and the two gunny sacks containing his food supplies. For a man of his age, and of medium height and weight, he handled the heavy cumbersome items with ease. Old timers who knew him when he was a young man said he was as agile and strong as a circus trapeze performer. One old timer told about the time he had watched him climb a thirty-foot rope ladder up a mine shaft, hand over hand, without using his legs or his feet.

The old prospector finished unloading the supplies and loosened the pack saddle cinch straps. Then he filled his hat with water from one of the canteens and offered it to the jenny.

While he had been unloading the supplies and tending to the burro's needs, he kept the lead rope looped over his wrist indicating he did not totally trust the jenny. Perhaps, at one time in the past, a burro had bolted on him and left him stranded.

He finished watering the jenny and sat down on a nearby rock. While sitting there resting and watching the jenny, he thought how lucky he had been to find and to acquire such an excellent animal. Most stables kept only two or three burros because of the limited demand. Bill Cole, who owned the stable in Randsburg, had three in the corral at the time he had bought the jenny. He had walked up to the corral and had his arms draped over one of the fence posts looking over the stock but had only been there a minute or two when Bill Cole strolled out of the barn chewing on a piece of straw.

"Hi, Jim," he said, "when did you get into town? I haven't seen you in quite a spell."

"I've been up north, Bill," replied the old prospector while shaking hands through the barbed wire fence. "I just got into town a couple of days ago."

"Are you staying in town for a while or moving on?" asked Cole.

"I'll be here for a few days while I get some supplies together, and then I'll head out for the claim near Fremont Peak I've been developing. Because of personal problems, I haven't been able to do much with it for the past 20 years, except the assessment work, and I haven't done that in two years. That's why I came over, Bill, I'm looking for a pack animal. What have you got that might interest me?"

Jim had already decided, that of the three burros in the corral, he wanted the big jenny, but he didn't want to seem too anxious. After all, he thought, buying and selling livestock has always involved a certain amount of liars' poker, and I don't want to give my hand away. Bill is an honest man, but horse traders are horse traders and you can't change them.

"I don't have many to choose from, Jim, but the ones I have are good healthy stock. Come on inside the corral where you can have a closer look."

They walked together, one inside and the other outside the fence, to the gate next to the barn. Cole opened the gate and Jim stepped inside the corral.

As Cole closed the gate, he asked, "Are you interested in a pack horse, a mule, or a burro? I have one pack horse, no mules, but if you want one, I can get it, but it will take a few days, and I have three burros."

The old prospector always used burros and Bill Cole knew it. He had been buying and renting pack animals from him for over thirty years, but he did not argue the point of Cole's feigned ignorance.

"I think I'll look at your burros, Bill," Jim said. "It's been a dry winter and the feed may be light out around Fremont Peak. Burros don't need as much feed as horses and mules, but you know that, I don't have to tell you."

Momentarily a slight frown creased Cole's forehead. But Jim saw it and he knew Cole had just envisioned the old prospector selecting the smallest burro in the corral. Jim didn't blink, he said, "Let's see what you've got."

Bill Cole walked over to the big jenny and said, "This is a fine animal, Jim. I don't think you will find a better one this side of Reno."

Jim, busy examining the smallest of the three burros, pretended he didn't hear Cole. When he thought he had Cole sufficiently concerned, he walked over to the jenny where Cole was still standing and began examining her.

Cole repeated his earlier statement and said, "She's a fine

animal, Jim."

The jenny stood three hands taller than the other two burros and Jim was impressed with her strong legs and broad back. He asked, "Where did you get this animal, Bill?"

"I picked her up at an auction in Bishop," replied Cole. "She belonged to a freighter who owned a string of pack animals and used them to haul supplies to small logging and mining camps up the Sierras. From what I heard, he got into a drunken brawl one night and someone stuck a knife between his ribs, and he died. He owed his supplier, who lives in Bishop, quite a sum of money so the supplier claimed the pack animals and auctioned them off."

While examining the jenny, the old prospector ran his hand over her shoulder and her skin quivered. He looked closer and saw long thin scars running parallel on her neck and shoulder. "I wonder what caused these scars?" commented Jim, without really expecting a positive response.

"It's hard to say," Cole said. "It may have been a cougar. There are plenty of them up in the Sierras. One may have attacked her during the night, or they might be marks from a quirt. I heard the freighter who owned her was a mean bastard, he may have cut her up. It's too bad the jenny can't talk, I'll bet she has a lot of stories she could tell. Jim, I'll tell you what I'll do. If you are interested in her, I'll give you such a good price you can't refuse."

Finally, after discussing the jenny, the price, and the weather, Jim agreed to give Cole five dollars more for the jenny than he was asking for each of the other two burros. Cole also agreed to board the jenny for fifty cents a day until he was ready to leave for his claim.

The old prospector sat on the rock resting, with the lead rope looped over his wrist, admiring the jenny and congratulating himself on the deal he had made with Bill Cole.

"Suzie," he said, "I admired you so much at the time I dickered for you, I would gladly have given Bill an extra five dollars to get you if I had to. But as it turned out, it wasn't necessary. You may not know it, but you are a true daughter of the desert. Your color is that of the sands, and those small round patches of brown along your neck, shoulders, and rump, make you blend with the desert like the other animals of the desert do."

"Well, Suzie," he said, "it's time to stop admiring you and congratulating myself and get moving. If we don't, we will be spending the night here."

The old prospector rose slowly to his feet, rubbing the lower part of his back with the knuckles of his right hand. He walked over to the jenny and patted her on the neck before reloading the supplies. When he touched the scars on her shoulder, her skin quivered and he wondered again about the scars.

They started down the trail and the old prospector looked over his right shoulder at Fremont Peak. It rose about 4500 feet above sea level dwarfing the smaller hills in the area. "Someday," he said aloud to the jenny, "you and I will hike over here and see what we can find in that pile of rock. There's bound to be some kind of mineral buried in there somewhere, and I'll bet we won't be the first prospectors who have climbed over it to see what they could find."

The jenny, beginning to tire from carrying the heavy load, ignored his comments.

The sun turned from white to gold as they moved along the

trail toward the old prospector's claim. He thought of the claim and suddenly realized he felt as if he were returning home, a strange feeling he could not recall experiencing since the time he had left home almost 60 years ago. Since then he had never settled down in one place, nor had he ever married, nor did he refer to any one town as being his home including Virginia City, Nevada, where he had worked in the Comstock during the Civil War. Perhaps, he thought, it's because I've sold all of my other claims. But I really don't know.

He was still a young man when the War ended. A short time later he quit the Comstock and began prospecting. I never found anything big, he thought. Consequently, when I ran out of money, I had to return to the mines. As soon as I had saved enough, I bought supplies and a burro and took off again. He prospected throughout California, Arizona, and Nevada. He became known as a quiet but hard-working man who moved from job to job and back again without having to explain why he was leaving or why he had returned. On occasions he might mention his experiences at the Comstock, the Silver King near Daggett, California, the tungsten mine in Atolia, and among others, the copper mines in Arizona. The Yellow Aster, in Randsburg, had always rehired him.

Unfortunately, the Comstock, the Silver King, and the Yellow Aster had reduced their operations, for various reasons, to a minimum. The old prospector's arrival in Randsburg from northern California coincided with the signing of the Armistice. Just before he had left Randsburg, rumors were flying thick and fast the tungsten mine and mill in Atolia were about to shut down because of the drop in the price of tungsten as soon as the War ended. When he had passed by Atolia earlier in the day he could hear the roar of the mill grinding the tungsten ore and he knew, that at least for the moment, the mine and mill were still operating.

An era is passing, the old prospector thought, as he considered what day might be the last day the mine and the mill would operate. All the other big mines where I have worked have closed down or have limited operations. It's a nice feeling to know I was a part of that golden era. I can no longer muck, or buck compressed air drills weighing 100 pounds, eight to ten hours a day, that is a young man's job. But I still have my health and that is the important thing.

The old man's work world had been reduced to that of night watchman, handyman, caretaker, or any other odd jobs he could pick up. My pride has been hurt, he thought, as he remembered the many different jobs he had held. But I can't let that bother me. The work helped me provide assistance to my mother before she died, and the means to continue the assessment work on my claims. And by being thrifty I have saved enough, I hope, to prove this claim. I can't go on working forever because time is running out. If I don't strike something good within the next two or three years, I'll be spending the rest of my life in the poorhouse.

The old prospector turned to the jenny and said, "We'll reach the claim in another half hour, Suzie."

He turned his attention back to the trail but continued talking to the jenny as if she understood every word he said, "This claim may be the answer to our future. The ore samples have looked better each foot I have advanced the tunnel. If I could have found more time to work it, it might have been worth something by now."

He discontinued his one-way conversation with the jenny but continued to think about the claim. I have enough supplies and money to keep me going for at least six months, and maybe longer, if I'm careful how I spend each dime. If I go broke before I can prove the claim is profitable, I'll find a job and save until I can come back and work it again. I'm going to bet all of my few remaining years I will find gold in that hill because I am getting too old to look for another prospect and develop it.

The old prospector realized he had spent most of his life moving from one town to another as he moved from claim to claim and from job to job. Because he had never established roots at any one place, some people considered him unstable, irresponsible, and unwilling to settle down and accept social responsibilities. But the old prospector never thought of himself as being antisocial. Yes, he was a bit shy, and had been most of his life. And sometimes he preferred his burro to being around people, especially when they began quarreling or bickering about something he considered inconsequential. But antisocial? No. When he arrived in town from one of his claims, his first stop was one of the saloons. He ordered a drink and sometimes two, listened to the local gossip, and then looked for a room. He bathed, changed his clothes, and headed for the barber shop. While getting his hair cut and his beard trimmed, he questioned the barber for additional news and happenings around town since his last visit. He listened more than he talked, except to inject a question now and then to steer the conversation in the direction he wanted it to go.

That evening, after supper, he usually strolled back to the saloon to renew acquaintances and hoping, too, he might run into one of his very few friends. Nearly everyone who met Jim seemed to like him. Perhaps it was his quiet, yet friendly disposition. But very few people got to know him and maybe that was the reason some people thought of him as being secretive and unsociable. Nor was Jim much of a drinker. When he sat with others who were having a drink, he ordered one. Later in the evening he might visit his favorite prostitute.

When prospecting or working one of his claims, Jim always carried with him two quarts of whiskey, switching to bootleg after Prohibition. When asked about the whiskey and the large bottle of aspirin he also carried, he always replied, "They are both for medicinal purposes. A man can never tell when he might be bitten by a rattlesnake." But the real reason, he thought, is to show my hospitality to fellow prospectors or visitors who might drop by, by offering them a drink and a bite to eat.

As the old prospector and his burro trudged along the trail, the sun dipped lower and lower towards the horizon. Now he could see the ore dump as they drew near the trail leading to the claim.

"Only another half mile to go, Suzie, but it will be dusk before we get there. I'm tired and I know you are too. The sooner we get there, the sooner we can both rest. I'm older than you but you've been doing all the work, and I'll remember that when I'm dishing up the oats this evening."

The squat oval shaped sage bushes and the long slender branches of the greasewoods cast ghostly shadows as the sun, now a huge orange ball, hung on the brink of the western horizon ready to disappear and plunge the desert into darkness. The old prospector's shirt, wet from sweat where the heavy suspenders ran over his shoulders and crossed in the middle of his back, turned white from body salt as the air cooled quickly and the sweat evaporated. They came to the dim but still visible trail leading to the claim and followed it to the ore dump.

"Well, Suzie, we made it." The old prospector patted her on

the neck and began removing the supplies, starting with the saddlebags containing the two quarts of whiskey and his personal items. When he finished, he lifted the pack saddle from her back and rubbed her down with the saddle blanket and replaced the lead rope with a tether. He watched as she dropped to her knees and rolled over on her back then rubbed her back in the sand, moaning and groaning with pleasure with every twist of her body.

"You may not know it, Suzie," he said as he watched her, "but I kind of envy you. I wish I could take off my clothes and roll in the sand like that. But what would people think? You enjoy yourself while I hunt for a pan to water and feed you." The jenny snorted as if she understood and kept on rolling.

The old prospector secured the tether to a tough grease-wood bush and walked up the rock ramp to the entrance of the tunnel. The tunnel entrance opened eight feet above the base of the hill, and he had constructed the rock ramp to reach it. Just inside the tunnel entrance he found the old galvanized pan he had used to water and feed his other pack animals. He hadn't bothered to hide the pan because he didn't consider it worth stealing.

He carried the pan down the ramp and scrubbed it with sand before rinsing and filling it with water. After watering and feeding the jenny, with the extra ration of oats he had promised her, he drove a metal stake deep into the ground and tied the tether to it.

The sunlight faded rapidly while he was sorting and carrying the supplies up the ramp and into the tunnel. By the time he had finished, only a faint glow hovered over the western horizon. Now, he thought, I'll check on the supplies I hid in the back of the tunnel. Assuming nothing has been disturbed, I'll dig up the cot and the lantern and worry about the rest tomorrow.

The old prospector looked through the equipment he had packed in and located his carbide lamp. He checked the carbide and filled the water receptacle, then let the gas generate for a few seconds before lighting the gas jet. The bright light from the lamp flashed through the tunnel entrance into the depths of the tunnel creating dancing shadows among the jagged rocks protruding from the tunnel walls and ceiling. As he moved slowly toward the rear of the tunnel, the hollow echoes from his footsteps and the loose rocks, accidentally struck by his heavy shoes, added to the eerie mood of the tunnel.

He directed the light along the ceiling, the walls, and the floor. Rocks that might break loose from the ceiling and the walls concerned him the most, but at the same time he had to be wary of rattlers that may have crawled into the tunnel to hibernate for the winter. Rattlesnakes, the old prospector thought, also enjoy the cool temperature of the tunnel during the summer. A man can't be too careful entering a tunnel winter or summer. I appreciate the rattlers' ability to keep the mouse and rat population under control, but I would prefer they do their hunting outside and not inside the tunnel.

His cautious walk brought him safely to the head of the tunnel. Nothing had been disturbed. He removed the rock and gravel that hid the equipment and selected what he needed. He set the lantern and the cot aside and then carried them to the front of the tunnel.

The old prospector filled the coal oil lamp and lit it, then set up the folding cot and spread the blankets over it. Now, he thought, I'll fix something to eat. I'm too tired to be hungry and too tired to fix a hot meal. A can of beans and a couple of those biscuits I saved from breakfast this morning should carry me over until tomorrow morning, but I think I will fix some hot coffee. It's going to be chilly this evening and the hot coffee will make the cold beans and biscuits taste better.

The old man finished eating and walked down the ramp to check on the jenny before going to bed. The burro was lying down and did not get up when he drew near. "Well, Suzie," he said, while reaching down to pat her on the neck, "I don't blame you for not getting up. You've had a long day and I know you are tired. You get a good night's sleep because the first thing tomorrow we're going out to the spring to see if we have a water supply." He patted her on the neck again, told her goodnight, and turned toward the ramp.

As he walked up the ramp, he pulled out his watch and wound it, then held it to his ear for a moment before returning it to his pocket. When he reached the top of the ramp, he picked up the lantern he had left by the stove and carried it inside the tunnel and set it on an empty dynamite box by the cot. He stretched for a moment, rubbed his lower back, then sat down on the cot and removed his shoes, socks, and Levi's. He rolled his Levi's into a pillow without removing his watch, blew out the lantern, and lay down. The old prospector could hear the watch ticking as he dropped off into a deep untroubled sleep.

The old man woke up just before dawn. While putting on his clothes, he said aloud. "Jim, winter is not too far away. You can feel the nip in the air." A slight chill ran up his back. He slipped on his mackinaw and began blowing on his hands and rubbing them together. A fire will feel good, he thought.

He had constructed the stove with rocks near the tunnel entrance. It resembled a fireplace except he had extended the walls of the firebox three feet to support a piece of sheet iron that served as the top of the stove, which stood three feet high.

Another thing I'll have to do today, he thought while starting the fire, is to get some wood. I have enough to fix breakfast and supper but that will just about clean out what I had left from my last trip. I guess I'm lucky someone didn't come along and use it.

As the flames grew and licked out of the firebox and over the edge of the sheet iron, the old prospector stretched his hands, palms toward the fire, and rubbed them together. Then he turned, holding his hands behind him, and warmed his backside. After enjoying the warmth of the fire for a few minutes, he picked up the coffee pot and added coffee and water to the leftovers and put it on to boil. Before leaving to check and move the burro, he bent over and added a couple of sticks of wood to the firebox.

The jenny had been nibbling on the tips of a sagebrush but raised her head and cocked her ears in his direction when she heard the old prospector walking down the ramp.

When he drew near, he said, "Good morning, Suzie. Did you have a good night's rest?" He patted her on the neck and continued talking to her as he replaced the short tether with a longer one. Then he led her to an area near the claim where small patches of bunch grass grew.

"I'll bet you are hungry. And are we lucky, your relatives haven't been around to eat everything in sight."

I am, indeed, lucky, he thought. None of the wild burros roaming the Mojave desert have been in this area. Of course, that doesn't mean they won't discover this spot tomorrow and move in on us.

The old prospector recalled the stories he had heard of the origin of the wild burros. When the prospectors, freighters, and others began using Model T's and varied motorized equipment, they released their burros to roam and fend for themselves. Since jennies and gelded males, only, were used, the release of the burros did not cause any particular problem. However, the mule breeders in Owens Valley soon found out that cars and trucks had also killed the demand for mules. Consequently, if one of their jacks escaped, little or no effort was made to find him. It didn't take the jacks long to find the jennies and start a burro population explosion.

Wild burros have stolen jennies from prospectors in the past, thought the old prospector, and it could happen to me. There is no point in being careless. I'll tether her at the foot of the ore dump at night and move her out to graze during the day. It might be a good idea to string up some tin cans around the ore dump to alert me to any disturbances that might occur during the night. I don't like the thought of being stranded in the middle of the desert if I can avoid it.

He drove a stake deep into the ground and attached the tether to it and tested it to be sure it could withstand a sudden shock if the burro became frightened. Then he stood and walked up to the jenny and patted her on the neck and said, "While you're having your breakfast, I'm going back to the tunnel and see what I can stir up for mine. After breakfast we'll walk over to the spring and see how it looks." The jenny had started grazing and ignored his comments.

The aroma from the boiling coffee drifted down to him before he reached the ramp. "Jim," he said aloud, "that's just what a man needs on a frosty morning like this." But, he thought, the air is too dry for any frost. If it wasn't so dry there would be frost, so at least I'm half right.

When he reached the cooking area, he selected a clean cup, and using a towel to protect his hand, picked up the pot by its metal handle and filled the cup. The old prospector took a few noisy sips and set the pot on the stove to keep it warm and set the cup on the wooden table. I'll let the coffee cool down for a few minutes, he thought, while I bring the rest of the equipment up from the back of the tunnel.

He relit the lantern and made his way to the back of the tunnel. Two trips to the face of the tunnel and back were all that he needed to move his cooking and eating utensils, and the remaining miscellaneous items, to the front of the tunnel. The old man wiped the dirt and dust off the utensils and then rinsed them and set them on the makeshift table he had nailed together from salvaged lumber.

There's no big rush to get to the spring, he thought. After that skimpy meal I had last night, I'm hungry and in the mood for a big breakfast. I'll slice some bacon from one of the slabs I brought, stir up a batch of biscuits, and try out the new Dutch oven. I'll also slice some potatoes and fry them in bacon grease.

"It would be nice if you had some eggs, Jim," he said aloud. "But past experience has taught you eggs don't travel well on a packsaddle."

He finished his breakfast and belched. I really enjoyed that, he thought, even if I did fix it myself.

Then he said aloud, "Careful there, Jim, someone might hear you and accuse you of bragging on your own cooking."

The old prospector refilled his coffee cup and began cleaning the cooking and eating utensils.

When he finished his chores, he picked up the packsaddle, blanket, and rifle and carried them down to the foot of the ramp. After dropping them off he walked out to the grazing area and led back the jenny, cinched on the packsaddle, tied on a shovel, axe, mattock, some gunny sacks, hooked the strap of a full canteen of water on the saddle-tree, then picked up his rifle.

When they started down the trail to the spring, the old prospector pulled out his watch and checked the time and then glanced at the sun. No one ever knew if he checked his watch against the time the sun indicated, or if he tested his own skill at telling time by the sun. Again, the small smile appeared briefly. Both the sun and the watch confirmed the time to be 9:35.

The old prospector and the burro followed the trail he had made to the spring shortly after he staked out his claim. Dust storms over the past two years had left it barely visible. It would have made little difference, since he had traveled the mile so many times, he knew he could travel it at night by the light of the stars if necessary.

"Suzie," he said, "it's going to be another beautiful day. Let's hope this weather lasts through Thanksgiving. That's about the time the first snows hit the Sierras and we can expect just about any kind of weather after that."

The old prospector used the plural "we" to include the jenny as if she were another person. All of the other prospectors he had known talked to their burros and people who had lived around prospectors most of their lives considered talking to a burro the normal thing for a prospector to do. They figured living in the middle of the desert for two or three months at a time was reason enough for a man to start talking even to a sage bush.

The old prospector continued his one-way conversation with the jenny. "It may get cold down here, but it can never be as miserable as the last two winters I spent in northern Nevada and in the mountains along the American River above Sacramento."

The jenny raised her head for a moment then cocked one ear forward as if she understood, then dropped her head and resumed the effortless task of following the lead rope.

As the sun climbed higher, the desert sands warmed, and the small creatures of the desert began to crawl from their shelters and appear along the trail. The old prospector kicked a dead sage bush branch from the trail, and it landed near a lizard sun-bathing on a rock. The surprised lizard jumped from the rock and scurried ahead to another rock lying near the trail. The lizard turned and looked at the two strangers, its white throat and belly glistening in the sunlight. When the strangers drew near, the lizard did a few push-ups and suddenly darted, with its tail curled over its back, through the bushes toward home.

Desert chipmunks, never too far from their burrows, sat up on their hind legs when they heard the old prospector and his burro approaching, their heads swiveled in the direction of the noise. Suddenly, the old man and his burro appeared from behind a large greasewood bush. One of the chipmunks chattered, and as if by command, each one streaked for its own respective shelter.

The two travelers continued their leisurely trip along the trail until the old prospector stopped the jenny to watch a horned lizard squatting on the edge of an ant hill licking up any ant coming within reach of its tongue. Other ants, frustrated by the tough skin of this tiny descendant from the dinosaurs, scampered over the horned lizard's body trying to find a vulnerable spot.

The old prospector, like other people who lived on the desert, called the horned lizards, horned toads, and no one knew why. They didn't look like toads, but on the other hand, they didn't look like lizards. Their looks and characteristics were all their own.

They left the horned toad and the frustrated ants and continued their unhurried pace toward the spring. The old prospector had heard many strange stories about these interesting little reptiles. A Mexican from the Sonora Desert told him snakes seldom included horned toads in their diet because, when swallowed, the horns protruding like a crown from the top half of the back of their heads, punctured the snake's stomach with deadly results. He had also heard when a horned toad becomes frightened, bloody tears form in the corner of their eyes.

"Suzie," he said, "our immediate problem is not horned toads, it's water. I think you will agree, won't you?"

The jenny raised her head for a moment as if to say, "That is a pretty dumb question."

But a frown appeared on the old prospector's face. I haven't seen a rabbit since we left the claim, he thought. And now that I think back, I don't recall seeing more than two or three during our trip from Randsburg to the claim. Usually, I see at least a dozen. Maybe it's just a coincidence. They are probably out there, and I didn't see them. I hope so, because I had planned on having a rabbit supper about once a week. And then he thought, it's been a dry year, if the rabbit population is down and we have a long winter, we may have trouble with the coyotes because the coyotes depend on the rabbit population for their primary source of food. If they can't catch rabbits, they may start traveling in packs and look for bigger game. If they are hungry enough, they may try to attack the jenny. It's something I have to think about.

He dismissed the problem and concentrated on getting to the spring.

The Old Indian Trail passed approximately a hundred yards west of the spring. During his many trips to the spring, the old prospector had found flint arrowheads and flint knives, and other Indian artifacts in or near the surrounding area. He tried to guess how long the Indians had used the spring as a rest area when traveling to and from the Mojave River. Perhaps a thousand years or more, he thought.

When they reached the spring, he found the water in the basin covered with a thick scum of green moss. Two field mice and a kangaroo rat lay dead on top of the moss, victims of the lifesaving spring. He looked at the rodents and thought, they got their feet tangled up in the moss and drowned trying to get out.

He removed the dead rodents and then began carefully removing the moss to avoid stirring up the slime lying in the bottom of the basin. After completing the task, he led the jenny to the basin to drink then staked her out to nibble on sage brush while he finished cleaning the basin.

The water from the spring trickled into the basin located at the foot of a low hill which ran parallel to the Old Indian Trail. Nothing unusual marked the location of the spring, except if one looked closely, he would have noticed the sage and the greasewood bushes near the spring were larger and greener. Someone, perhaps another prospector, no one knew for sure, had been thoughtful enough to dig a washtub size hole beneath the rocks from which the water dripped and line it with cement to keep it from vanishing in the desert sand.

As the old prospector cleaned the basin, his thoughts turned to the source of the water that fed the spring. He stopped working and watched the water drip into the basin. It's a fast drip, he thought, but far short from being a stream. I've sat here before and tried to figure out where it comes from.

Does it come from the Tehachapis, the southern tip of the Sierras, or the Mojave River? He continued to watch as if slightly mesmerized by the dripping water.

Hundreds of springs are scattered across the Mojave Desert, he thought, some in places people would never think to look. Even Death Valley has its share of springs, quite a variety, too, hot, cold, and poisonous. Most desert springs dry up in the summer, but this one doesn't. Maybe it flows along a fault that crosses the underground river some say exists below the dry Mojave Riverbed and rises here to feed this spring. If my theory about the fault is correct, it could continue on and be the same fault that cuts through my tunnel. If it is, I'm lucky the water surfaces here and not in my tunnel.

The old prospector sighed and said aloud, "You are not a geologist, Jim, and you have done enough wool gathering for the day. Now get busy and clean this basin so you and Suzie will have a supply of fresh water."

His eyes crinkled and a small smile touched his lips. If people heard me talking to myself as if I were another person, and heard me talking to the burro, too, their eyes would roll while they whispered among themselves about me being ready for the coo-coo house. It may bother people, but it doesn't bother Suzie.

Then, he said aloud, "It doesn't bother you, does it, Suzie?" The jenny raised her head, cocked one ear in his direction, and returned to nibbling on the sagebrush.

The old prospector finished cleaning the basin and rose slowly to his feet, rubbing his lower back, he said aloud, "Jim, if your lumbago gets any worse, you may have to invest in a bottle of Sloan's Liniment."

He looked at the basin. It will take two or three days for the basin to fill but it is nice to know we have water, he thought. In the meantime, I have enough water for my needs, and I can bring the jenny to the spring.

The old prospector picked up the canteen of water and the shovel, then he walked over to the jenny and replaced the tether with the lead rope. After checking the pack saddle, he pulled out his watch and glanced at the sun. "Eleven-ten," he said aloud. A dozen or more buzzards soared in a tight circle two miles to the Southeast in the direction of Barstow. They must have found something, he thought. He shook off a disturbing vision of the find and turned back to the jenny.

"Well, Suzie, now that we know we have water, let's gather some wood." They turned north on the Old Indian Trail and followed it to an arroyo that originated on the East side of Fremont Peak. The arroyo carried the run-off from the winter storms and summer cloudbursts east, from Fremont Peak and the nearby hills, to a lake fifteen miles away. The lake sometimes remained dry for years waiting for a truly wet winter or local cloud burst.

Mesquite bushes grew in the arroyo and the limbs from the mesquite had been used for firewood by the Indians for centuries. Since the Indians no longer travel the Old Indian trail, the old prospector thought, I'll never have to worry about firewood.

The old prospector led the jenny down the middle of the arroyo until he found a large dead mesquite bush.

"This is what we are looking for, Suzie, but before I start swinging an axe, I'm going to eat a couple of biscuit and bacon sandwiches I hung on the saddle. I'll stake you out, and if you're not too fussy, maybe you can find something to eat, too. I've heard the Indians eat mesquite beans, so you might try some and see how you like them."

He staked out the jenny and ate his lunch with an occasional drink from the canteen then stretched out on the sand to rest.

In the meantime, the jenny seemed to be totally familiar with mesquite beans, picking and chewing them with what seemed to the old prospector, special delight.

"Well, Jim," he said aloud, after a short rest, "mesquite is tough stuff. It won't get cut lying here." He looked at the jenny and asked, "Will it, Suzie?" The jenny looked in the direction of the old prospector for a moment but never stopped chewing on her mesquite bean.

Two hours of hard work with the axe and he loaded the limbs on the jenny. Then he turned his efforts to digging up dead sage bush roots. Three or four well placed strokes with the mattock brought the roots to the surface. Digging up dead sage bush roots, he thought, sure beats chopping mesquite branches, even with a sharp axe. He used the sagebrush roots to supplement the mesquite wood. Both gave off a pleasant aroma, but he preferred cooking with mesquite and using the sage roots to keep the fire going in the evening while smoking his pipe. When I toss a sage bush root on the fire, he thought, it means I'll have one less piece of mesquite wood to cut.

"This load should last us about a week, Suzie, then we will have to come back and do some more chopping and digging," he commented as he loaded the gunny sacks on the jenny. "It may be a long winter and it's a nice feeling to know we don't have to worry about running out of wood. What do you think, Suzie?"

The jenny felt a fly light on her ear and shook her head from side to side. The old prospector accepted this as a negative response and decided against pursuing his conversation further.

The old prospector pulled his watch from his pocket,

checked the time and glanced at the sun. He noticed the buzzards had moved and were circling a mile to the northwest of Fremont Peak.

As the old prospector and the jenny headed out of the arroyo, a frightened cottontail jumped from beneath a mesquite bush and darted away.

"Jim," he said aloud and with a bit of disgust in his voice, "you are not only tired, but more important, you are getting too old to react. You didn't even raise your rifle."

He turned to the jenny and said, "At least there is some consolation in what we have learned from this experience, Suzie, we know there are a few rabbits around."

He turned his attention back to the trail but continued his one-way conversation with the jenny, "I had kinda planned on having rabbit for supper this evening, Suzie. Now I'll have to wait for another day. And the next time, we will try to be ready."

"We've got four miles to go, Suzie, and we aren't going to get there by thinking what might have happened."

The jenny didn't need any encouragement. She knew they were heading back to the claim, and she was as anxious as the old prospector to get there. Perhaps she visualized a pan of oats waiting for her.

The day has been well spent, the old prospector thought.

Tomorrow we will return to the spring and find out how fast the basin is filling.

It was after four o'clock when they arrived at the claim, too late to stake out the jenny to graze. The old prospector tied her to the tether near the ore dump, removed her load, and rubbed her down, then gave her a ration of oats. I'll wait 'til morning when I'm rested to carry the wood up the ramp, he thought.

He patted the jenny on the neck before starting up the ramp to fix supper.

The old prospector decided to substitute a can of corned beef fried with potatoes for the rabbit he could still see dashing away through the brush. He consoled himself by thinking that corned beef hash, hot biscuits, with canned peaches for dessert, and hot coffee, should be enough to satisfy any hungry man's stomach.

After finishing his meal, he cleaned up the eating and cooking utensils and then poured some red beans from a cloth sack into the Dutch oven to soak overnight. By the time he had finished his chores, the first stars began to appear, the old prospector's favorite time for relaxing. He placed an empty dynamite box outside the tunnel where he could lean against the shoring. Before sitting down, he lit his pipe and filled his tin cup with coffee.

Sitting on the wooden box, sipping the hot coffee and puffing his pipe, he watched the Milky Way emerge. As the clear sky darkened, more and more stars became visible. Hundreds, thousands, then billions filled the heavens with a golden glow across the desert sky from horizon to horizon.

The old prospector watched and marveled as he had many times before. The stars seemed so near, but he knew they were far away, so far away he could not comprehend the distance. An occasional shooting star added to the magnificence of the spectacle. And each time he looked upon this awesome but glorious scene, he experienced the feeling of being as close to God as he ever did during any moment of his life.

A slight shiver ran up the old man's back. Prospecting is a lonely job, he thought. But I seldom feel the loneliness some do who live alone. I have never felt alone while prospecting. Perhaps that is one of the reasons why I enjoy it. Other prospectors have told me their thoughts are similar to mine. I wonder if that's why people think prospectors are a bit different.

The old prospector continued sipping his coffee and smoking his pipe long after the coffee had become cold. He thought of the places he had been, the people he had met, and his experiences. Finally, he sighed, knocked the ashes from his pipe, put the pipe in his shirt pocket, and set his cup aside. Then he put his hands on his knees, pushed himself up, and stood for a moment rubbing his lower back, stretched, and walked through the tunnel entrance to his cot.

I didn't realize how tired I was until I stood up, and tomorrow will be another busy day. He wound his watch and returned it to the watch pocket in his Levi's before sitting down. After removing his shoes and his Levi's, he rolled his Levi's into a pillow. He lay down with his head on the pillow and listened to his watch ticking. The lines in his face relaxed and began to soften showing his feeling of contentment, sleep followed a few moments later.

The old prospector awakened in his habitual way at dawn.

He dressed, started a fire and put the coffee on to boil, then walked down the ramp to check on the jenny and led her out to graze.

After fixing and eating breakfast, he cut a piece of rind from the bacon slab and added it to the beans and put them on to cook. He finished his chores and began the task of assembling his mining equipment. He knew when he left the claim he might be gone for a long period of time. Accordingly, in addition to hiding part of his supplies in the back of the tunnel, he had buried the larger items and the explosives in the sand near the ramp. It was not unusual for prospectors to hide their equipment when they knew they were going to be gone for a month or more. Hauling in equipment on a pack animal is not an easy task, and there are always a few who are not above stealing the equipment, or even jumping prospectors' claims if they think they can get away with it.

He used a short-handled shovel he had hidden in the back of the tunnel to do the digging. It will take most of the morning, he thought, to dig up all the equipment I've hidden here. It's a lot easier to dig a hole and bury things than it is to dig it up and clean it, especially the wheelbarrow.

While digging up the equipment, the old prospector's thoughts returned to the time when he discovered the claim. It had been over twenty years ago, he couldn't remember the exact date, because he and other prospectors had been prospecting the area around Randsburg and Atolia, and between Randsburg and Barstow, before the time gold was discovered at Randsburg and when Barstow was called Waterman Junction. The more I think about it, he thought, the more I'm amazed someone didn't find it sooner.

It reminds me of an old saying I heard years ago, 'Sometimes you look but you don't see.' I'll bet a dozen prospectors looked right at that quartz outcropping and never saw it.

When he discovered the claim, he had been walking southwest around the end of a hill he estimated to be between two and three hundred feet high. He noticed what appeared to be quartz about fifteen feet above the base of the hill, but he couldn't be sure because the object of this curiosity was partially concealed by brush and dust. If the sun had not been shining directly on it, he thought, I would never have noticed it. I decided it was worth checking. I tied the burro's lead rope to a greasewood bush, pulled the shovel out of my pack, and climbed the hill for a better look. And sure enough, he recalled, when I cleared away the brush and examined the formation, I identified it as quartz, and a much larger outcropping than it appeared to be from below. More important, it was the kind of quartz associated with gold bearing ore.

The old prospector continued his thoughts about the claim while digging up the equipment and removing the oiled canvas he had used to wrap each piece to protect it. I climbed down and spent the next two weeks staking out the boundaries of the claim, registering it, setting up camp, and hauling in supplies. When I started working the claim, the quartz vein led directly into the hill. As I drove the tunnel deeper into the hill, I thought, will the vein continue, or will it peter out? It didn't peter out and it began to look promising. Then the samples began showing a little color. Not much, just enough to keep my hopes alive.

The old prospector recalled how he had advanced the tunnel twenty-five feet through solid rock when he ran out of money which turned out to be merely the beginning of his many problems.

I had a plan, he recalled. Since I had to have money to continue developing the claim, I decided to stop work on the claim, bury my equipment and supplies and go back to work in the mines. While working, I planned to contact some of the mine owners and try to sell some of my other claims. I figured I should be able to return to this claim and begin working it again in about a year. I also considered finding someone to grubstake me. But, I thought, I've always been too darn independent, and whoever paid for the grubstake, might try to tell me how to run my operation which would be something I could not handle.

Although Jim was in his mid-fifties, the Yellow Aster Mine hired him and he went to work the next day. The Yellow Aster, the heart and soul of Randsburg, worked three shifts, seven days a week, mining and milling gold ore. He worked at the mine for over a year, and by being frugal, he saved and banked a sizable sum from his paycheck. During the same period, he sold a couple of his claims, adding to his savings. One day Jim did a little arithmetic and decided he had saved enough to finance another try at developing his claim near Fremont Peak.

Any plans he may have considered had to be dropped when he received a letter from his mother telling him his sister had tuberculosis and had entered a sanitarium in Phoenix. She also told him she did not know how long his sister could remain in the sanitarium because of her limited finances. The following morning Jim went to the bank and withdrew part of his savings and sent them to the sanitarium. Thereafter, he sent her monthly sums. She lived four years. Jim paid the bills and the funeral expenses.

Jim continued to work at the Yellow Aster. He took time off to do his assessment work on the claim near Fremont Peak and the more promising of his other claims. But, Jim discovered, bad luck sometimes follows bad luck. Shortly after his sister died, he received word his mother had entered a hospital with a broken hip. Knowing she could not care for herself when she was released from the hospital, Jim arranged to have her placed in a convalescent home. She recovered and lived to reach the age of ninety. How lucky I have been, Jim thought. I have been able to keep my health and provide for her during her final years. I have no other living relatives (then he recalled the letter from Alice) except, perhaps, a son or a daughter somewhere.

Jim remembered, too, during those difficult years, when he returned to the Yellow Aster from doing his assessment work, the boss apologized then told him he could not rehire him because he was too old to work in the mines.

The old prospector's thoughts returned to the present. He examined one of the drills he had wrapped in oilcloth and said aloud, "Twenty years and only forty feet. Not much to show for twenty years." But, he thought, I had to do my assessment work on my other claims, too, or I would have lost my title to them. And I don't regret what I did for my family, the small bit of comfort I provided for them is more important to me than •all the gold this claim, and all my other claims, might have produced at some future date. I only regret I did not keep my promise to Alice.

Now, he thought, I must put all of that behind me and find out if my hunch is correct and prove gold is buried somewhere in the bowels of this hill. Since I've sold all my claims except this one, I have no worries other than to confirm it is worth the time and effort I've spent on it and the time and effort I've committed myself to spend on it in the future.

He continued examining the drills as he removed them from the oilcloth and found three, although used, sharp enough to drill a few more holes. When I go into town for supplies, he thought, I'll have quite a collection for sharpening. Then he added, but it's cheaper than buying new ones.

He finished digging up the equipment, including the wheelbarrow, then turned his attention to the explosives he had buried separately. He lifted the partially filled wooden box then removed the box of caps and the role of fuse he had wrapped in oilcloth and buried near the dynamite. After prying the lid from the dynamite box, he examined each stick. He had purchased the dynamite two years before along with the other supplies he needed to do his assessment work and had buried it when he left. He had only used eight sticks, but he knew from experience dynamite becomes unstable with age and his examination was one of precaution. After checking each stick, he decided the dynamite was safe.

He reburied the explosives to keep them cool, then loaded the wheelbarrow with picks, shovels, and drills, and pushed them up the ramp. The old prospector spent the rest of the morning sorting and cleaning the equipment and sharpening the picks and shovels. Then he fixed a light lunch and stretched out on the cot to rest.

It was shortly before two when the old prospector got up, put on his hat, picked up the pack saddle, saddle blanket, and rifle, and carried them down the foot of the ramp, dropped them off, and walked out to get the jenny.

The jenny raised her head and looked up at the old prospector from the clump of bunch grass but continued chewing. He patted her on the neck and said, "You seem to be enjoying this grass, Suzie, but I'll bet you would like a nice cool drink of water even better."

He unfastened the tether and attached the lead rope. "We're going out to check the spring and see how much water we have, and you can refill your water tank. My guess is, the basin should be about half full by now."

He led the jenny back to the ramp and cinched on the pack saddle, tied on a shovel, an axe, and an empty canteen. When he picked up his rifle, he thought, I'm going to try to be more alert today and be ready, if we are lucky enough to see another rabbit.

They arrived at the spring and found the water line in the basin close to the halfway mark. The old prospector filled the canteen and then let the jenny drink.

"Well, Suzie, that's another worry we can set aside. We've got plenty of water. I may even do my laundry one of these days, and if it doesn't get too cold you may even see me taking a spit bath. But don't bet any money, or maybe I should say, oats on it." The old man smiled at his own simple joke.

As he turned to lead the jenny from the spring, he said to her, "I had a notion about getting some wood today when we started out, but it turned out to be only a notion. I'm too weary. Let's get back to camp and I'll rest and be ready tomorrow to get started on the job of trying to find that gold I'm convinced is somewhere in the heart of that hill."

They had walked about two hundred feet from the spring when a young jack rabbit jumped from beneath a bush in front of them. The second the old man saw the rabbit, he whistled sharply several times. The rabbit slowed, then stopped. He flipped the rifle to his shoulder and fired. This isn't the way a sportsman would do it, he thought, but I'll have rabbit for supper this evening.

The jenny, momentarily startled by the rifle shot, threw back her head jerking the lead rope looped around the old prospector's wrist, interrupting his pleasant thoughts. He walked up to her while holding on to the lead rope and gently stroked her neck until she relaxed, then slipped the rifle into the scabbard.

"Now, Suzie, let's go pick up the rabbit."

He led the jenny to where the rabbit lay and reached down to get it, but when he attempted to tie the rabbit on the pack saddle, she began backing away, rolling her eyes and dragging the old prospector. He dropped the rabbit and grabbed the lead rope with both hands and dug his heels into the sand until she stopped. Then pulling himself hand over hand until he reached the halter, he grabbed it and began talking to her. "What frightened you, Suzie? You may still have been skittish from the rifle shot but something else scared you, too. I don't think my attempt to tie the rabbit on the pack saddle caused you to panic because you are used to carrying loads. Could it have been the smell of blood? I've known pack animals to shy and bolt when hunters tried to load freshly killed game on them."

The old prospector continued to talk to the jenny while holding on to the halter. "Easy now, Suzie, nothing is going to hurt you. I don't know what scared you. If it was the rabbit, don't worry about it. If you don't want to carry the rabbit, I will."

While holding her by the halter, he noticed the leather straps had worn thin from years of use, especially the leather loop around the steel ring holding the neck strap. This strap is going to break one of these days when I least expect it, he thought. It could have happened today. The next time I go to town, I'll have it replaced.

His thoughts returned to the cause of the jenny's fright.

"Suzie, do those scars across your neck and shoulders have anything to do with you being frightened by something? I wish you could talk. I'll bet you would say, 'Yes', and I'll also bet they are quirt marks."

The jenny had calmed down, so he led her to the rabbit and stood by it. She watched him but without the concern she had shown earlier. He picked up the rabbit and carried it by its hind legs back to the claim.

When they reached the claim, the old man tossed the rabbit on the foot of the ramp and unsaddled the jenny. He looked at the long thin scars again, and out of sympathy, unconsciously reached over and gently ran his hand over them. Her skin quivered. I wish Suzie could talk, he thought once again.

He looked at his watch, checked the time, and glanced at the sun. "It's a little after three, Suzie. You can graze for about an hour while I clean the rabbit and clear some of the loose rocks from the tunnel. Then I'll come and get you and you can bed down for the night."

Flies were buzzing around the dead rabbit by the time the old prospector returned. He quickly skinned and cleaned the rabbit and buried the unusable parts, then cut up the rabbit and put the parts in a pan of saltwater to soak. Now, I'll rekindle the fire, he thought, and start the beans cooking again. He stirred the beans and looked down at the rabbit. It's been quite a spell since I tasted fried rabbit. It should go great with these beans and some hot biscuits.

He used the remaining time to clear the loose rocks from the tunnel floor that had fallen during his two-year absence. He completed the task and picked out the tools he would need for the following day, loaded them into the wheelbarrow, and wheeled them to the rear of the tunnel. Now, he thought, I'll walk out and lead Suzie in and get her settled down for the night before I start supper.

While frying the rabbit, the old prospector's thoughts flashed back to the earlier years when he had been working the claim. One afternoon, after the dust had cleared from a round of shots, he returned to the heading to inspect the blasting results and found he had uncovered a fault intersecting the tunnel. During several subsequent trips to the claim to do assessment work, he had tried to work around it but without much success. Every time I would blast, he recalled, the vibration jarred rocks loose in the fault area. I worried about rocks falling on my head, and even worse, a possible cave-in. I decided to stop all digging and blasting in the tunnel until I could install shoring. And I decided that while I was at it, why not shore up the entrance to the tunnel to keep rocks from rolling down the hill into the cooking area.

The old prospector knew of an abandoned mine shaft about

twenty miles to the northwest in the direction of Johannes-burg. The last time he had passed the abandoned mine, the timbers in the mine shaft were still intact. Since my funds were limited, he recalled, I decided to rent an extra burro and salvage the lumber from the mine shaft to do the shoring. And while I was at it, I decided to salvage enough for an extra load as insurance for any future needs. I estimated it would take about a week to remove the timbers and haul them to the claim.

Well, he recalled, I ran into problems I hadn't anticipated.

I didn't have any problems renting an extra burro from Bill Cole, but if I had tried to climb down that ladder in the mine shaft before fixing it, I'd probably still be at the bottom. I also had to install a hoist so I could use one of the burros to pull up the lumber. It was a bad guess; it took me two weeks.

That's all behind me now, he thought, while stirring the beans. He turned and looked at the shoring around the tunnel entrance and visualized the shoring under the fault. "And not a bad job either," he said aloud while smiling.

He began drilling the next morning. The carbide lamp attached to his miners' cap lit the surface. He carefully marked the heading where each hole was to be drilled, then he picked up one of the shorter drills and began striking it with a four-pound hammer, giving the drill a quarter turn after each blow. The drilling, he thought, will take two to three days. Setting the explosives and cleaning out the tunnel after the blasting will take another two days. If I were younger, I might shave a few hours. Since I'm not, I'll have to just keep plug-ging away.

The old prospector continued the laborious and monotonous job of drilling, changing to longer and longer drills, until the hole was twenty-four inches deep. When he finished the first hole, he took a breath and said aloud, "Jim, it would be nice if you had a compressor." The old man smiled and picked up the short drill to start the second hole.

An hour later and the old man laid down the hammer and drill and muttered to himself, "Working a single jack has never been easy and each year it seems to get a little bit tougher. A check on the jenny is as good of an excuse as any to take a break and rest for a few minutes."

He stopped at the tunnel entrance and took a swig of water from one of the canteens and replaced his miners cap with his old Stetson. When he reached the grazing area, he patted the jenny gently on the neck. "You seem pretty contented, Suzie. But I'm going to move you to another spot. If I don't, you'll eat the grass down to the roots and it will die. And we don't want it to do that, we want it to keep growing so we can have feed for you in the days ahead."

After moving the jenny to another location, he returned to the tunnel and rested for a few minutes then returned to the task of drilling. Another two hours drilling, and he stopped for a cold lunch of rabbit, beans, biscuits, and warmed-over coffee. After lunch, he stretched out on the cot for a short nap then went back to drilling. Another two hours and he decided to quit for the day. I haven't worked this hard for years, he thought, if I don't quit now, I'll be so stove up, I won't be able to get out of bed tomorrow. Besides, it's been pretty warm today and the jenny must be thirsty.

The old prospector led the jenny to the ramp and cinched on the pack saddle. After tying on two canteens, he added an axe and a shovel, picked up his rifle, looped the lead rope over his wrist, and started toward the spring.

As they walked, the old man said aloud, "Six or seven hours of drilling a day is about all I can handle, Suzie. My arms and legs get tired, my back begins to hurt, and my muscles begin to cramp. Old age, I guess. We could haul enough water in one trip to last us a couple of days. But if we walk out to the spring and back every day, it will do us both some good. The walking will loosen up my muscles and it will do you a lot of good, too. If you don't get at least a little exercise, you will get so fat and lazy, you won't ever want to work. Don't you think it's a good idea?"

The jenny's head, bobbing up and down as she followed the lead rope, gave the impression she agreed with the old prospector.

The old prospector continued his one-way conversation.

"Let's hope our hard work pays off and we strike something good. Then if we can sell the claim for a decent price, we'll buy three or four acres near Victorville where the Mojave River surfaces and put up a three-room house with a parlor, bedroom, and kitchen. We will also build a small barn for you and maybe a chicken house. I always did love fresh eggs. And we'll drill a well, too. Then we won't have to haul water up from the river. But that doesn't mean if and when we get all of these nice things, we will give up prospecting. What it means, Suzie, is when we go prospecting, if we don't find anything, we won't have to worry about it. We don't want to lie around and —"

The old prospector never finished the sentence. The jenny had stopped suddenly and thrown back her head jerking the old man's arm holding the lead rope causing him to miss his stride.

At that very moment he heard the buzz of the rattler and felt the strike on the sole of his shoe. The jenny snorting and her eyes rolling, backed away, the old man dropped the rifle and grabbed the lead rope with both hands. She stopped but continued to express her concern with flared nostrils and arched neck and ears cocked forward while looking nervously in the direction of the diamondback. The old prospector got his first good look at the snake as it moved its thick body from the trail toward the shelter of the sagebrush.

"That was a close one, Suzie." He held the halter and stroked her neck. "If you hadn't jerked me back, it would have got me for sure. I would have stepped right where the rattler lay."

The jenny replied with a short half snort, half whinny, but continued to direct her attention to the spot where the snake had disappeared into the brush.

"No, we aren't going to kill it. Rattlesnakes are great mousers and they also help to control the rat population. Besides, he has as much right to this trail as we have. If I had been paying attention instead of daydreaming, I would have seen it. It was big enough. That rattler is as big around as my wrist and must be carrying ten or more rattles. My guess is he must have been asleep, or we would have been warned sooner. Most rattlers should be hibernating by now, but this fellow must have decided to catch a few more mice and maybe a rat or two before crawling info his den for the long winter sleep."

The old prospector's long discussion about the snake, using a low assuring voice, had calmed the jenny. She stood relaxed with her head drooping slightly and her long ears pointing in opposite directions.

"That's an experience I won't forget for a while," he said aloud. "I owe you, Suzie. Now are you about ready to move along?"

They started up the trail toward the spring. "If that rattler had hit me above the shoe top instead of on the sole of the shoe, you would be lugging me back to the claim and I would be wondering if we were going to make it. A diamondback that big can pump a lot of poison into your leg. You don't last long when one that big strikes you. And it wasn't very smart of me to leave my snake bite kit all wrapped up nice and neat back at the claim, was it? Well, when we get back, we'll tie it on the pack saddle. Then the snake bite kit will go wherever we go, even if this is the time of year when no snakes are supposed to be around."

When they arrived at the spring, the old prospector found the basin three-fourths full. He filled the two canteens and let the jenny drink. When she finished, she raised her head and cocked her ears forward and looked off into the distance in the direction of the railroad tracks some eight to ten miles away. Then she lowered her head and nuzzled the water with her upper lip as if to enjoy a final taste before leaving.

While the jenny had been drinking, the old prospector had removed his left shoe, avoiding any contact with his sole.

He looked at the place where he had felt the snake strike and saw the green venom stain on the edge of the sole. Looking closer, he found the fang he was searching for, imbedded and broken off, in the top of the leather sole.

Wow, he thought, while looking at the fang, an inch higher and he would have struck my little toe. Fortunately for the rattler, he will grow another fang. But if my little toe had to be amputated, I would have to get along with one less toe.

"Thanks to you, Suzie," he said aloud, "I can joke about it now."

As soon as I get back to the claim, he thought, I'll remove the fang and scrub off the venom. If I don't, I could join a sizeable group of people who have scratched a hand or a leg on a fang broken off in a shoe or a boot, and later wondered what caused the infection.

The old prospector did not finish drilling the first set of

holes until noon of the third day. After drilling the last hole, he loaded the wheelbarrow with the tools and rolled it outside the tunnel.

Preparing the charges and loading the holes is such a tedious job, I'll fix lunch and rest before I start, he thought.

After lunch and a short nap, the old man dug up the dynamite, caps, and fuses and carried them to the mouth of the tunnel. Sitting on an empty dynamite box, he cut the fusers into different lengths so no two lengths were the same, then he crimped a cap on one end and split the other end of the fuse. Next, he cut the sticks of dynamite in half to reduce the shock waves from the explosions that might loosen rocks in the unshored parts of the tunnel. The old prospector then inserted a cap and fuse into each of the half sticks and carried the assembled charges back to the heading and began the dangerous task of loading each of the holes with one of the charges.

After loading and tamping the holes, he moved his bed and his supplies outside the tunnel to protect them from flying rocks and dust. Then the old prospector picked up the box of dynamite, the caps, and fuses, and carried them down the ramp and reburied them.

Now, he thought, comes the payoff. He returned to the heading, removed the carbide lamp from his cap, lit each one of the fuses, and headed quickly for the mouth of the tunnel.

While the old prospector waited at the side of the ramp, it seemed an eternity before he heard the dull thud of the first explosion. When he counted the last one, he sighed. What a relief that is, he thought. When a miner counts explosions and hears the last one, he knows he won't have to return and dig to look for a dud. I'll always remember a miner I knew who accidentally stuck his pick into an unexploded charge. It wasn't a pretty sight.

He watched the dust billow from the mouth of the tunnel.

It will be hours before I can go in, he thought. The Jenny needs water and I need to walk and relax. When they returned from the spring, the old prospector considered checking the results of the blasting, but it was getting late and he decided to wait until morning.

He woke up at dawn, lit the lantern, and put on his clothes and mackinaw, then lit the carbide lamp and attached to his cap. Now, he thought, to see what happened. He picked up the lantern and his prospector's pick and began working his way slowly toward the heading, checking the walls and the ceiling for rocks that might have been jarred loose by the explosions. When the old prospector reached the heading, he nodded his head in approval as he moved the lantern over the fractured face of the heading, "Jim," he said aloud, "you haven't lost your touch."

He moved the lantern over the shattered rock once again before returning to the mouth of the tunnel. Now, he thought, to get a fire started for the coffee and stake out the jenny.

I'll clean out the tunnel after breakfast and then work on the heading. Looking behind each round of shots is what keeps a prospector prospecting. You never know what might show up.

Maybe I'll find what I'm looking for.

He began clearing the tunnel after breakfast and completed the task by noon. The old prospector ate lunch and took a short nap. Now, he thought, to tackle the heading. Using a pick, he began digging the fractured rock out of the heading and removing it from the tunnel to the ore dump with the wheelbarrow.

All of the rock I've cleared from the tunnel floor, plus the two loads I've dug out of the heading and pushed to the dump, is enough work for the day, he thought. Each load seems to get heavier as the tunnel gets longer. Besides, it's three o'clock and time to go to the spring and water Suzie.

The next morning, he tackled the heading again and began selecting samples from the ore. At noon he examined them with a magnifying glass. Looking better, he thought. After lunch I'll grind some of the samples in the mortar and see what I get.

Using the steel mortar, he ground the ore into tiny particles and emptied the ground particles into a clean frying pan, added water and stirred the mixture with his forefinger until the smallest particles settled to the bottom. Then he began rocking the pan back and forth, washing the larger particles over the edge.

He continued this process, adding water when necessary, until the remaining particles formed a small steak of quartz crystals and minerals, about two inches long, in the crevice of the pan. He rocked the pan a few more times and then rolled the pan slightly, running the water over the sediment. As the water moved over sediment, it carried the quartz crystals and the lighter minerals with it, leaving a few tiny specks of gold at the upper tip.

He looked at the gold specks with his magnifying glass and said aloud, "Jim, just as you said before; 'It's interesting, but no bonanza.'"

Well, he thought, at the very minimum, it shows there is gold in this hill. How much and where? Those are the questions. But, he thought, all the signs look pretty good.

The old prospector pursued his daily routine of drilling and blasting and examined them in the same way he had examined the first batch. The gold content appeared to be increasing with each examination.

He made slow but steady progress. The rock on each side of the quartz vein had to be drilled and blasted loose to provide a passage sufficiently wide enough to work in. The granite dulled the drills and the drilling chewed up time, and the farther he advanced the tunnel, the farther he had to push the wheelbarrow to reach the dump. By the middle of December, he had advanced the tunnel only an additional twenty-five feet. Nevertheless, he was pleased with his progress.

I know, he thought, twenty-five feet in thirty days is less than a foot a day, but I'm not as young as I was thirty years ago. He smiled at his thoughts.

The old prospector continued to break the monotony of his work schedule by walking the jenny to the spring each day. He also had to cut and haul wood, and on Sundays he hunted and prospected. Twice he had bagged a couple of doves. He wasn't particularly fond of the taste, but he welcomed the change in his diet.

Food and other supplies were getting low and the drills needed sharpening. So, he decided to make a trip to Barstow the following week. While there, he also planned to have some of the ore samples assayed. I can sell the claim now without further development, he thought, but I know I can't get what it is worth. If for some reason I'm forced to sell, the results of an assay may help.

The old man's plan included spending Christmas in Barstow.

It will be interesting, he thought, to find out what has been happening around the country since the War ended.

The few remaining days in the week seemed to slip by faster than usual. By mid-morning on Monday, the old prospector finished drilling the last hole and began moving the tools and equipment from the tunnel. When he completed the task, he lay down on the cot outside the tunnel to rest before preparing and setting the charges. I'll get everything ready this evening and tomorrow, he thought, then we can get an early start Wednesday morning. A change in the scenery, and seeing and talking to people, should rejuvenate me a bit. Talking to a burro for six weeks is neither informative nor a very interesting way to carry on a conversation, even though she is a nice lady.

Well, he thought, stretching out on a cot and resting for a few minutes, sure does the old bones a world of good, but it doesn't get the job done.

The old prospector got up from the cot and began preparing and setting the charges. When he finished tamping the last one in the hole, he made a final check to insure all was in order and he had not miscounted the charges, then he lit the fuses. Outside, and a safe distance from the tunnel, he listened for the dull thud of each explosion, and as always, counted each one. After watching the dust roll from the tunnel for a few minutes, he began walking up the ramp. It's time to fix a bite to eat and walk Susie to the spring, he thought.

As they drew near the spring, the old man thought about the increase in the number of coyote tracks and stools he had noticed during the last ten days. This much sign, he said to himself, indicates they are traveling in packs. It's been a dry year; food must be scarce, and they are stalking everything that comes near the spring. I told myself a month ago to string up tin cans to warn me of any attack on the jenny, now it's a must. I'll string them up as soon as I get back from Barstow.

An hour of light remained when they reached the claim. He staked out the jenny and let her graze while he cleared the rocks from his sleeping area blown there by the explosions, then he moved his cot and other equipment back into the shelter of the tunnel.

The old prospector started supper, then led the jenny back, and tethered her next to the ore dump. After eating and doing his chores, he began packing his only clean pants and shirt, and the essentials he planned to take on the trip. Tomorrow, he thought, I'll select the drills and other tools that need sharpening and pick out the ore samples I want assayed. He completed the packing and decided he had done enough for the day. Now, he thought, I'll pour some coffee and sit outside and sip it while I smoke my pipe.

While sitting on the wooden dynamite box thinking about the trip, the sky grew lighter. The moon is rising, he thought.

It will be a full one tonight, but I won't be able to see it before I go to bed because of the hill. The old prospector sucked on his pipe and sipped his coffee while watching the stars dim and the sky grow brighter as the moon climbed toward the heavens. Ghostlike shadows of the sage brush and the greasewoods began to appear. Suddenly, the sound of yipping and howling coyotes cut through the cold night air. The old man pulled his mackinaw tighter. There must be a half dozen over by the spring, he thought, but you really can't tell, sometimes two can make as much noise as a dozen.

He sat and listened for a few minutes then knocked the ashes from his pipe and stood up. I should have strung up those tin cans this afternoon when there was plenty of light but it's too late now. I can't go stumbling around in the moonlight looking for tin cans at my age, he thought.

He set the empty cup on the corner of the stove and walked into the tunnel. Before going to bed he moved the cot near the entrance and placed the rifle within easy reach.

The night passed without incident. The next morning the

old prospector moved his cot and equipment outside the tunnel and began removing more loose rock from the tunnel. I'll work my way to the heading and dig out a few more samples to take to Barstow, he thought.

By noon he had cleared the tunnel to within a few feet of the heading but decided to have lunch and rest before taking the samples. He rekindled the fire and made a fresh pot of coffee. While waiting for it to boil, he moved his cot and other equipment back into the shelter of the tunnel. Then he walked out to the grazing area and led the jenny to the tether at the foot of the ore dump. I'll take Suzie to the spring he thought.

When he reached the top of the ramp, the coffee was boiling.

He fixed and ate a light lunch and lay down and napped for a half an hour.

As usual, he felt refreshed after the short rest. He got up and pulled out his watch while walking out to the edge of the ore dump. He glanced at the sun and looked at his watch.

"1:35," he said aloud. His eyes shifted toward Fremont Peak where the buzzards were circling. They seem to be moving this way, he thought. I wonder what poor animal's bones they intend to pick. For some reason I get the heebie-jeebies when I watch them, and I can't explain why. Maybe it's their bald heads or the smell of death they carry, or perhaps it's because they only eat the dead. Black has always been associated with death and that could be a reason. I guess it is a combination of all those things.

The old prospector sighed, turned and entered the tunnel.

He put on his miner's cap and lit the carbide lamp, selected a pick and shovel from those leaning against the wall, then picked up a gunny sack for the ore samples and began walking to the back of the tunnel.

When he reached the heading, he removed the lamp from his cap and examined the fractured heading, then moved the lamp close to the quartz vein. Better than I've seen so far, he thought. Maybe I'm getting close. The next round of shots might do it.

Again, he attached the lamp to his cap and selected some of the loose quartz crystals showing tiny gold specks from the vein and dropped them into the gunnysack. Next, he attacked the heading with his pick. Spotting an excellent specimen, he drove the pick into the fractured vein of the heading, concentrating on the spot where he wanted the pick to strike.

He heard it before he saw it, a noise from above like a shot from his .22 rifle. The old prospector had heard the sound before and he tried to step back but slipped on loose rock and gravel. Before he could regain his balance, a jagged rock, as large as a water pail, broke loose from the top of the heading and struck his left leg between the knee and the hip driving him to the tunnel floor.

His head struck the rock floor knocking off his cap and the attached carbide lamp. He lay there several seconds before recovering his senses. He tried to get up, but his left leg refused to function. Then he remembered that peculiar cracking noise and the falling rock. Instinctively, he moved his hand down his left leg to the wound and felt the wetness of the blood seeping through his underwear and Levi's. He knew then his leg had been slashed by the sharp edge of the falling rock. His head throbbed, and when he tried to draw up his right leg, his ankle felt numb. I must have sprained it when I slipped on that loose gravel, he thought.

Having fully regained consciousness, the old man began to realize the problems he faced. Fortunately, the carbide lamp was still burning. He reached back over his head and found he could reach the cap and grasp it, and pull the cap with the lantern attached, toward him.

The old man pushed himself to a sitting position. I've got to get to the tunnel entrance and find out how badly I'm hurt, he thought. He started to put on the miner's cap but began feeling dizzy and lay back down again.

"Don't faint on me, Jim," he said aloud. "You've been hurt before. Faint now and you could bleed to death and never know it."

He lay on his back until the dizziness passed, then pushed himself up again. I can't wait any longer, he thought. The old man put on his miner's cap and turned over on his stomach. Pulling with his hands, forearms, and elbows, and pushing with his right knee, he began his slow struggle to the entrance. He knew he was leaving a trail of blood, but he had to stop and rest every five or six feet or pass out.

Exhausted, he reached the front of the tunnel and his supplies. He opened one of the bottles of whiskey and took a long swig. Weak, and trembling from the exertion, he rested for a minute or two and took a few deep breaths, then took another swig. The old man put the bottle down, removed the knife from his pocket, and began cutting and removing the bloody cloth from the wound. When he completed the task, he pulled one of the canteens leaning against the tunnel wall to his side, unscrewed the cap, and began washing the blood and grit from the wound. As the caked blood washed away, the old man saw what he dreaded most, the shattered bone beneath the mangled flesh.

Suddenly, he felt loneliness and fear, feelings he had never experienced before. A strange thought crossed his mind. I can't ever recall talking to a prospector about being seriously injured while alone in the desert.

Shivering from the thought and the shock from the injury, the old prospector reached for the bottle and took another drink. He relaxed for a moment and then poured whiskey into the deep gash and watched the blood color the whiskey and trickle over the side of his leg. I guess I should consider myself lucky I didn't cut an artery, if I had, I could have passed out and be dead by now.

He poured more whiskey into the wound and then bound it with a clean towel. I hope the whiskey will sterilize it and keep me from getting infection until I can see a doctor, he thought.

Exhausted from the effort of treating the wound, he leaned back against the cot. He looked at his leg and watched the blood slowly seep through the bandage. I'll rest for a few minutes, he thought, and give the blood a chance to clot. And while I'm waiting, maybe I can think of the best way to get out of this mess. Whatever I do, I must act quickly before the pain sets in and saps my strength. He pulled a blanket from the cot, rolled it up and used it for a pillow and then lay back on the rock floor of the tunnel.

The old prospector rested for only a few minutes and decided not to wait. Another couple of hours, he thought, and the sun will be setting. He dug through his supplies and found the large bottle of aspirin he carried. He shook three from the bottle and washed them down with water. Then he looked over at the small pile of lumber left from shoring the fault as a possible source for splints.

He worked his way to the lumber and selected pieces he considered suitable and began binding the boards to his leg with ropes located near the lumber that he used for lashing supplies to the pack saddle. Crude, he thought, but maybe it will hold the bone in place.

Next, he examined his ankle. He decided it was sprained

but not broken. I'll bind it with a towel without removing my shoe, he thought. The towel will help cushion the injury when I move or bump it.

The old prospector sighed and lay back down again. Now that I've got myself patched up; the next step is to figure out what I can do to get help. The nearest inhabitants live-six miles to the west at Fremont Railroad Station. My best chance of getting help will depend on my ability to get on the jenny and guide her in that direction. And, he thought, glancing at the sun, I've got about an hour and a half left before sunset.

The old man pushed himself up to a sitting position and reached for the whiskey bottle. He took a long swig and put the cork carefully back into the bottle and set it down. Then he began the long painful task of dragging himself down the ramp.

While working his way down the ramp, he thought about how lucky he had been to have decided to bring the jenny in early from the grazing area.

The old prospector did not notice the strange scraping noises the wooden splints made as he dragged his broken leg down the rock ramp. The burro, tethered behind the dump, heard the unusual noises but could not see what was making them. She raised her head with her ears cocked forward and looked with some concern in the direction of the strange noises.

The old prospector continued his slow but steady half crawling half dragging movement down the ramp and around the base of the ore dump. When the burro saw him working his way toward the tether, she began to back away. She did not recognize this strange creature moving toward her as if to attack her, nor did she recognize the strange noises the creature made.

The tether, now taut as she strained against it, vibrated from the tension, and her eyes began to roll showing her fear.

He reached the tether and tried to pull the jenny to him, but he was too weak. Then he tried to calm her by talking to her, but his voice trembled and cracked under the stress.

The afternoon breezes had begun, and a whiff of the combined odor of the whiskey and blood drifted into the flared nostrils of the jenny. The smell suddenly reminded her of the bleary-eyed man who held her by the halter and beat her across the neck and withers until the blood trickled down her shoulders.

The smell, and the unknown creature pulling on the tether, caused her to panic. She reared on her hind legs and jerked back her head. The worn halter snapped, and she fell on her back, her hooves pawing and kicking the air as she wriggled on her back trying to get up.

The old prospector peering through the swirling dust saw her flip on her side and seemingly spring in the air and light on her feet in one motion. With her head down and her ears laid back, she ran from the ore dump in the general direction of Randsburg, bucking and kicking right and left with both heels.

The old prospector tried to yell at the burro but the emotional shock and the consequences of the sudden and unexpected turn of events closed his throat. While pounding the desert sand with his fists, he suddenly realized he still held the limp tether. He watched with frustration and despair as the burro blended with the desert then disappeared among the sage and the greasewood bushes.

He lay in the sand agonizing and trying to think while looking in the direction the burro had disappeared and hoping, perhaps, to catch a last glimpse of her. What are the chances of her reaching Randsburg and alerting people that something is wrong? he thought. Fifty-fifty, maybe. Burros are strange creatures. She may decide to wander in the desert until she finds other burros to join. There is even a remote possibility she may return, but I don't have the time to wait and find out.

The old prospector sighed and began the slow and torturous task of dragging his aching body up the ramp and to the tunnel.

Although he tried to concentrate on his struggle to get back to the tunnel, he could not block out thoughts about the future. What is the solution to your predicament, Jim? Is it, hopeless, or should you try to reach Fremont Station on your own? It's a possibility but it's too late to try today. The winter days are short, and the sun will be setting in less than an hour, and it has been getting so cold at night the water has been freezing in the coffee pot. Being that cold, Jim, the loss of blood could cause you to freeze.

The coyotes, he thought, are also a worry. If they pick up the scent where I've crawled, they will follow me. Coyotes attacking human beings is unusual, but it has happened, more often when the individual was wounded, and the coyotes were hungry and traveling in packs. And from the signs I saw around the spring, they are traveling in packs.

He decided to postpone further thoughts about the subject until the following day.

The old prospector reached the mouth of the tunnel and lay prone for several minutes before dragging himself inside where he could reach the whiskey bottle. Wet with sweat and wracked with pain, he uncorked the whiskey bottle and gulped down two swallows before setting it aside. Then he shook two aspirins from the bottle into his hand and washed them down with water. Now, he thought, I'll rest a few minutes and let the whiskey and aspirin start working. If I can get a fire started and warm up some coffee, a cup or two will help calm me down so I can think.

His hands, elbows, and right knee were scratched and sore from crawling over the rocks. While waiting for the whiskey and aspirin to take effect, he tied a towel around his right knee to protect it.

Feeling some relief from the pain after taking his limited medication, he worked his way to the stove and rekindled the fire.

I'm not hungry, he thought, but I've got to eat. If I don't, I'll get weaker and weaker. Maybe, I can eat a piece of that cold rabbit and a biscuit I had planned to take to Barstow. I hope it doesn't make me sick. If it does, I'll feel worse than I do now.

He lay by the stove until the coffee began to boil. After he had finished drinking one cup, he poured another. Pushing the cup in front of him, he inched his way back into the tunnel to his food box and unwrapped a piece of rabbit and a biscuit. The coffee tasted better than the food.

As soon as the sun dipped below the horizon, the temperature dropped rapidly. The old prospector selected some of the larger pieces of mesquite and tossed them into the fire box hoping a little of the heat might work its way into the tunnel.

Now, he thought, what about sleep tonight? It will take too much energy to get on the cot, and I don't think I could make it even if I tried. If I spread a piece of canvas on the floor and add the saddle blanket, plus two other blankets, and use the other two for cover, I should be fairly comfortable. Another piece of canvas over the blankets will also help. And, he thought, everything I need is on the cot, or near it, so I won't have to drag myself around the tunnel to get what I need.

When he had completed putting the pallet together, he filled the kerosene lantern, lit it and turned it low, then placed the whiskey, aspirin, and a canteen of water within easy reach.

He wound his watch, laid it on the head of the pallet, and rolled his mackinaw into a pillow and laid the pillow over the watch.

He groaned and then sighed with relief. After struggling between the blankets, he immediately dropped off to sleep.

He slept for about four hours before the pain awakened him.

He had been dreaming, and in the dream a large timber from a mine shaft in which he was working, broke loose from a cave-in and pinned his leg against the wall. He had been trying to pull his leg from beneath the timber when he awakened. After shaking off the nightmare, he reached for the aspirin and the bottle of whiskey. He thought about adding wood to the fire but only for the moment before he felt the sharp pains in his leg when he tried to move it.

As the aspirin and whiskey dulled the pain, he began to relax and dropped off to sleep again. He slept quietly until the drugs began to wear off, then troubled dreams of coyotes and buzzards disturbed his sleep. Coyotes attacked the jenny and buzzards circled overhead waiting. He woke up wet with sweat and with his leg throbbing. He pulled the blankets up under his chin to keep from chilling and waited for his body to cool before taking more medication. He dropped off into another restless sleep, awakened again and again by nightmares, but each time he managed to slip back into his fretful sleep.

He was fully awake before dawn but lay in bed after taking more aspirin and waited until the sun had risen high enough to warm the outside air and ground.

When he threw off the blankets to pull himself off the pallet, he saw his leg had swollen during the night. Since he had not removed his shoe when he had bandaged his leg, nor had he removed it when he had gone to bed, the lower leg, ankle and foot were also swollen. The shoe is cutting off the circulation, he thought. If I remove the shoe, I'll never get it back on again. I think my best bet is to leave the shoe on and cut the laces.

The simple task of bending forward to cut the laces caused him to feel nauseated. He lay back down again until the feeling passed and then reached for the whiskey bottle. Adding the whiskey to the aspirin will help settle my stomach, he thought. Maybe the concoction will also help to ease this sore and aching body of mine.

The whiskey combined with the aspirin began to make him feel better. He sat up and looked at his watch. It was 8:30. The old prospector held the watch to his ear for a moment then slipped the watch into his shirt pocket. After unrolling his mackinaw and struggling into it, he rested for a few minutes. Time is slipping away, he thought, and I don't have any to waste. I've got to figure out how I'm going to get to Fremont Station.

Although the aspirin and whiskey had dulled the pain, his body stiff and sore from the injuries, hurt as he turned over on his stomach and tortured him as he inched his way out of the tunnel, pulling a canteen of water and pushing a can of coffee.

Outside the tunnel he noticed a slight breeze blowing from the northeast and the breeze felt warm. Jim, he thought, in addition to the many problems you now have, you are in for a desert windstorm, and it could be a bad one. It may last three days but the nights will be warmer, if that's any consolation. Then he thought, if my prediction is correct, even if the burro reaches Randsburg, the storm will discourage any effort by the people I know to search for me.

The old prospector started a fire, rinsed out the coffee pot, and prepared a fresh one. The stove began to heat up and the old man sat by the stove and enjoyed its warmth for a few minutes before returning to the tunnel.

Inside the tunnel, he began removing the splints from the broken leg. When he tried to remove the bloody towel from the wound, he found it had stuck, and had to be soaked with water to loosen it. After removing the towel, he examined the wound. It appeared puffy on both sides of the gash which added to the grisly look of the swollen and discolored leg. It's best not to disturb the clot, he thought. I'll pour some whiskey over it to cut down the possibility of infection and rebandage it. He picked up the bottle of whiskey and tilted it slightly to let the liquid trickle into the wound. This is going to burn, he thought, then, "Wow," he said aloud. "It feels like someone stuck a red-hot branding iron to my leg."

The burning subsided and he rewrapped the wound with a clean towel and tied the bandage in place. He replaced the splints and then pressed his right foot against the tunnel wall to test his sprained ankle. Sharp pains radiated up his leg from the swollen ankle. I hope I didn't break any bones, he thought. A bad sprain can hurt just as much. But I'm not going to worry about rebinding it since the circulation seems to be OK.

The old prospector worked his way back toward the stove.

It will be impossible for me to drag this body of mine ten miles to Fremont Station, he thought. I'll have to rest every hundred feet, and each additional hundred feet will require a little more rest. Even if I tried it, it would take twenty-four hours to get there, if the coyotes get on my trail, I'll need my rifle. Unless the ankle improves, I'll have to depend on the burro reaching Randsburg. But it's hard to figure out what she will do in this windstorm.

He spent the rest of the day lying in the sun protected by

the hill. He kept the fire going and coffee hot, lacing the coffee with whiskey and taking aspirin to dull the pain.

The old prospector made a fresh pot of coffee and opened a can of tomatoes before the sun dropped below the horizon. I'm not hungry, he thought, but I've got to force myself to eat.

I wish I had some scrambled eggs. I always did have a craving for scrambled eggs when I felt under the weather. I don't have them so I'll have to settle for what I've got, a couple of biscuits and a can of tomatoes. He finished his meal and crawled back into the tunnel and into bed.

He slept soundly for several hours before the pain awakened him. He took his self-prescribed medication and when the pain subsided, he dropped off into a disturbed sleep. He dreamed he and Suzie were walking up a canyon with steep walls on each side, when suddenly the canyon ended. He tried to turn the jenny around, but the canyon was too narrow. Then he tried to climb the steep slope at the end of the canyon and help the jenny by pulling on the lead rope. But each time they climbed a few feet, the jenny lost her footing and slid back. He decided to rest a few minutes before making another try. Then he heard the yip of coyotes on their trail. The jenny became frightened and tried to leap up the steep slope and fell on his leg. The pain awakened him. He felt hot and dry and knew he had a fever.

He turned up the lantern and reached for the whiskey and aspirin. Then he lay back again and struggled through a feverish night of dreams and nightmares. Pain woke up the old prospector before dawn. He took his simple medication and lay in bed until he could see from his pallet the sunlight shining beyond the shadows of the hill. Then he unrolled his mackinaw, struggled into it and made his way to the stove.

The winds had subsided during the night to a warm breeze.

But the old prospector knew from experience they would return and be more violent. Today, he thought, the storm will reach its peak and begin tapering off tomorrow. Although the weather warms during these storms, the warming will not help me if the dust is so thick, I'll get lost. I've even heard of men choking to death. Desert sandstorms are always treacherous and miserable under any circumstances, and mine couldn't be worse.

This is Christmas Eve, he thought while fixing his coffee.

I should be in Barstow enjoying the festivities. But here I am with a broken leg and with no way of knowing what will happen the next few days. But I won't give up, I'll begin working on a pair of crutches as soon as I have had something to eat. The fever seems to have dropped and I feel better. The aspirin and the whiskey do help. This warm weather is probably helping too. I'll fix some oatmeal and open a can of milk. The hot oatmeal warmed over biscuits, and hot coffee should give me the energy I need. If necessary, I must force myself to eat.

While leaning against the tunnel entrance shoring, eating his oatmeal, the old prospector thought of his mother and remembered her saying, "Jim, you can't leave this table until you have finished your oatmeal. It's good for you and you eat every bite of it."

It is strange, he thought, that I should think of Mother when I am so desperately in need of help.

The old prospector finished eating and struggled back into the tunnel. He leaned against the tunnel wall and watched the velocity of the winds gradually increase. Dust clouds began to form as the speed of the winds accelerated. And while he watched, the clouds grew larger. The winds scooped dirt and sand from the desert floor and threw it high into the air until the clouds extended for miles. Sage bushes and tumble weeds, uprooted by the force of the storm and pushed by the relentless winds, rolled across the desert jumping and skipping over the sagebrush like elves in a fantasy dream. He watched the struggle between the winds and the long wiry limbs of the greasewood bushes. The winds forced the limbs to bend until their green tassels swept the ground, but they refused to break.

I wonder where the jenny is? he thought. All animals look for shelter when the winds blow this hard. Maybe she made it back to Randsburg. If she did, will someone become concerned and start looking for me after the storm? Lots of questions, but no answers.

Dust began drifting into the tunnel, I'm protected from the storm by the hill, he thought, but it doesn't protect me from the dust. I'll be better off if I can move my pallet and supplies deeper into the tunnel. Now that I think of it, if I had watered the jenny the morning of the accident, I would be out of water by now. If I'm careful and don't waste any, I've enough to last three or four days.

Now, he thought, what is the easiest way to move the pallet, water, and the other supplies? He began by tying a rope around the pallet. Pushing the coil of rope ahead, he dragged his body along the tunnel floor until he lay directly under the shoring supporting the fault. This should be the safest place in the tunnel, he thought. And it should be far enough from the entrance to give me some protection from the dust. He pulled the pallet to his side and untied the rope, then smoothed the pallet. I'll rest a few minutes before I make another trip.

After resting, he rolled off the pallet and worked his way to the front of the tunnel, pushing the rope before him. An empty dynamite box will hold the things I need, he thought. The old prospector tied the rope around the box and loaded it with a canteen of water, the unopened bottle of whiskey, his aspirin, a box of matches, and his last clean towel. Now, he thought, I'll fill the lantern and drink the last of the whiskey in the bottle and begin my struggle back to the pallet. It's only 30 feet but it will seem like 300 yards.

He pushed the lantern and pulled the end of the rope back to the pallet and then pulled back the dynamite box with the supplies. If I leave the supplies in the box, he thought, they won't get scattered and I can find them easier at night. Sweat trickled from his chin as he sat on the pallet with his eyes closed and his head bowed, waiting for his strength to return. I'm tired and worn out, he thought. I'll take some aspirin and rest before I try to do anything else. He rolled his mackinaw into a pillow and lay down on the pallet, pulled a blanket over his shoulders and immediately dropped off to sleep.

When the old prospector awoke, he felt feverish. He raised up and looked out the tunnel entrance. It's lighter in the tunnel now, he thought, and it will continue to get lighter as the sun drops closer to the tunnel entrance. The sunlight and the lantern will provide enough light to change the bandage.

He began removing the splints and the towel, but the final turn had to be dampened before he could work it loose. Then he lifted the lantern and examined the wound. Infection is what is causing the fever, he thought, and whiskey is the only antiseptic I have to fight it. Pouring whiskey on a raw wound makes me feel like a coward. He put down the lantern and uncorked the bottle of whiskey. Then picking up the lantern and taking a deep breath, he tilted the bottle, hesitated for a moment, then watched while the drops of whiskey seeped slowly into the wound. For the first few seconds the bruised and benumbed flesh prevented the old man from feeling the pain, and he kept the trickle flowing. Then the raw whiskey penetrated to the unprotected nerves. He wanted to yell but vented his suffering on the neck of the whiskey bottle, squeezing it until his knuckles turned white, while he rocked back and forth hoping, perhaps, the effort might ease the pain.

The agony passed, and the old prospector rebandaged his leg and replaced the splints. The infection is spreading, he thought. Now, I can add that to my worries. If I don't get out of here by tomorrow, I won't be able to make it. By evening, tomorrow, all of my whiskey and aspirin will be gone, and I'll have nothing I can use to control the pain and the fever. This is a miserable situation, he thought, and the crutches are the only means I can think of to get out of it. I can't wait any longer.

The old prospector picked up the bottle of whiskey, took a hefty drink, grimaced, and set it down. Then he drank from the canteen and used some of his precious water to wet a soiled towel. The old man wrapped the towel around his face, covering his mouth and nostrils. He took a deep breath and began his struggle, pushing the rope in front of him. His eyes burned as he worked his way through the dust swirling around the tunnel entrance to a pile of mesquite limbs lying near the stove. It's a good thing I didn't chop all of these branches into firewood, he thought.

Now to find two I can convert into crutches.

The search turned up two good possibilities, each with a fork in one end. I can trim these, he thought, and with very little effort pad the forks to protect the muscles and skin under my arms. He pulled the branches into the tunnel and tied the rope around them, selected tools he needed, and put them in a gunny sack. Next, he thought, I'll throw in a couple of dirty towels for padding, tie the sack on the rope, work back to the pallet, and get started. When he reached the pallet, he drew in the sack and the branches and looked out the tunnel entrance.

In another hour, he thought, the sun's rays will drop below the tunnel entrance. But in the meantime, it will help me see what I'm doing.

By the time he had finished, only a faint glow from the setting sun penetrated the dust storm and appeared like a distant campfire to the old prospector.

The old man turning the crutches over and over said aloud, "They aren't much to look at, Jim, but they will do the job."

He laid the crutches aside and stretched his arm and back muscles. I didn't notice it while I was busy but now, I feel weak and tired, I guess it's the fever, he thought. And my leg is killing me. He downed three aspirin with the help of several swallows of water followed by two tilts from the whiskey bottle.

The old man thought of food, but only for a moment. I need rest more than I need food, he thought. He blew out the lantern and lay back on the pallet, then he covered his eyes with his left forearm and immediately fell to sleep.

The old prospector slept several hours and then began to moan and jerk his head from side to side as nightmares began disrupting his sleep. A huge coyote, as large as a timber wolf, stalked cautiously up to the tunnel entrance. He sniffed the air and slowly lowered his head, his glowing eyes fixed on the back of the tunnel. With his head lowered and his nose close to the ground, he began slowly walking from one side of the tunnel to the other. With each turn, his body swiveled but his head remained low and fixed, his phosphorescent eyes continued to focus where the old man lay.

The old prospector's moans grew louder. Suddenly, he pushed himself up on his elbows and began yelling. He awakened and realized he had been dreaming. Sweat saturated his clothes, his leg throbbed, and his head ached. No light came through the tunnel entrance and he could not see the tunnel walls which were only three feet away. He felt like they were closing in trying to suffocate him. He fumbled in the box for matches, struck one and lit the lantern. The light broke the spell. Holding his watch near the lantern, he could see it was after nine o'clock.

He began shaking and mumbled aloud, "First fever and now chills." He reached for the aspirin bottle and dropped it twice before he could unscrew the cap. He poured three into the palm of his shaking hand and put one at a time in his mouth. After a drink of water, he picked up the whiskey bottle and uncorked it. It slipped from his hand and lit on the edge of the pallet spilling a third before he could recover it. Still shaking, he took a drink, recorked the bottle, returned it to the box, then lay back and pulled the blankets over his body.

Now, he thought, if I can get warm, maybe I can get some more sleep. He stopped shivering but sleep eluded him. Perhaps, he thought, I'm worried about the return of the coyote.

As he lay there, the old prospector's thoughts turned to the past and to the small mining town in California where he grew up but left at the age of sixteen. He thought of his mother and how she held his hand as they walked down the boardwalk past the saloon to the only grocery store in town. And he recalled his father, who was also a miner, coming home from work each night tired and dirty. His sister, three years older than he, always seemed very special. She wore her long blond hair in two braids that hung down her back, and sometimes he would touch them and feel their softness. When he started to school, she walked with him to the one room schoolhouse and watched over him. He remembered how her soft blue eyes turned icy when older children tried to tease him.

He thought about the last time he had seen his sister. She was in a sanitarium in Phoenix and he had gone to see her. That was sixteen years ago. He knew she was ill, and he had been sending her money, but when he saw her lying in bed, he barely recognized her. She was so thin, and she had faded so since the last time he saw her. These thoughts flashed through his mind as he walked from the screen door over to her bed. He felt guilty and ill at ease standing beside her knowing she was dying, and also knowing he had made no great effort to see her more often, nor to inquire about her health.

As he stood by her bed trying to smile, she held up a thin transparent hand and said, "It's good to see you, Jim. Thank you for coming. But I don't know how to thank you for all the help you have given me. I don't know what I would have done if it hadn't been for you."

Her voice, weak from the lung disease, barely reached his ears, and he had to bend down to hear what she was saying. Her white colorless skin, marred only by the dark circles around her eyes and her feverish red cheeks, told him death was near. He tried to comment and heard himself mumble something unintelligible. He regained control and leaned down and kissed her on the cheek. While still holding her hand, he sat down in the chair next to her bed.

They talked. They talked about their childhood and their mother and father and mutual friends they had known when they were young — but not about her health. Jim carried most of the conversation. His sister started coughing when she tried to talk for more than a few seconds.

After a half an hour, he saw the strain of trying to talk and be attentive had begun to tire her and he decided to leave. He leaned over and kissed her on the cheek and told her goodbye.

She took his hand and said, "Thanks for coming, Jim." She dropped his hand and closed her eyes.

Jim walked to the screen door and turned toward her, "I'll be back tomorrow—," he had started to add "Sis", but his voice trailed off. I don't think she heard me, he thought.

It was late spring and warm in Phoenix, he recalled, while walking back to the hotel with his coat thrown over his shoulder.

When I arrived at the hotel, I went directly to my room. After hanging up my coat and removing my shoes, I lay down on the bed with my fingers locked together behind my head watching the long wooden blades of the ceiling fan turning slowly, giving off a swishing sound as they pushed down the air. I watched the fan, but it faded into my sister's haunting blue eyes framed with dark circles, and her white face rouged by fever.

What can I do? I thought. And how can I best serve her?

How long will she live, six months, or perhaps as little as three months? I wish I could stay with her, but if I did, I couldn't continue to help her. She is receiving good care in the sanitarium and the people who work there are taking better care of her than I can.

The next morning Jim returned to the sanitarium. He had come to tell her goodbye. Again, he stayed until he saw she was beginning to tire. He kissed her on the cheek and said he would return in a few weeks. Both knew, even though neither voiced their inner thoughts, it was doubtful they would see each other again.

Six weeks later, his sister died. Jim did not return for the funeral, but he paid the bills.

The old prospector lay on the pallet thinking about his sister's death and pondered whether or not he could have done more. His last visions of her faded and his thoughts turned to the Civil War and the problems it created in Virginia City.

He remembered the vicious fights, some deadly, which occurred almost daily between Northern and Southern sympathizers. He avoided trouble by not choosing sides and keeping quiet. He was not asked to join the military because the North needed the silver and gold pouring from the Comstock more than it needed bodies. And the miners, like Jim, were the only ones who could keep the Comstock at peak production. Because he was a miner, he remained at the Comstock until the Civil War ended.

Jim, he thought, you, nor anyone else, will ever see that much silver again.

He recalled the Silver Lady Saloon. The proprietors had attached silver dollars to one of the walls to form a lady wearing an ankle length evening dress. She appeared to be ten feet tall. The Silver Horseshoe Saloon, not to be outdone nailed silver horseshoes on the wall in back of the bar to demonstrate to its customers and to the world the wealth of Virginia City.

As always, when the old prospector's thoughts returned to his years in Virginia City, they included Alice, the only girl he had ever loved. Tonight, his recollections of her seemed more vivid than usual. It's the loneliness, he thought. Fifty-five years have slipped away since the last time I saw her.

I met Alice quite by accident, he recalled. I had taken two weeks leave from the Comstock to visit San Francisco and to buy Christmas presents for my parents. While shopping in San Francisco's largest department store, I turned away from one of the counters and stepped directly into a young lady with both arms loaded with packages and sent her sprawling. Immediately, I dropped down on my knees, mumbling apologies, and knowing my face was quite red, began picking up her packages. Apparently, she saw how upset I was with myself and dropped down beside me.

"Let me help," I recall her saying. "If I hadn't been carrying so many packages, I could have seen where I was going."

Her steady blue-grey eyes held mine during her apology.

"It wasn't your fault it was mine," I said. "This store is crowded, and I should have been watching where I was going."

As we picked up the scattered packages, I began to recover from my embarrassment and suddenly realized I had never met anyone so beautiful. Her blue-grey eyes, he thought, match perfectly with her fair skin and auburn hair. Very kissable lips, too, a nose that verges on being haughty, and a chin indicating she probably could be very stubborn and possess a mind of her own.

When standing, I could not help but notice her well-proportioned body, and stood almost as tall as I.

We finished picking up the packages and each held half.

"After all the trouble I've caused you," I said, "the least I can do is help you with these packages. Do you have transportation?"

"Yes," she replied, "I have a carriage waiting outside. And I think I would like your help." She gave me a smile that made my heart double pump and skip a couple of beats.

A heavy mist was falling as we walked along the boardwalk lined with assorted buggies, carriages, and wagons belonging to the busy Christmas shoppers. Everyone seemed to be in a hurry except the two of us. Neither of us seemed to mind the rain nor shoppers who bumped us on the crowded walkway.

When we reached the carriage, the driver jumped down from his seat to help with the packages, then she turned to me and said, "It isn't very pleasant in this rain. After being so helpful, please let me drop you off at your next destination."

I looked at the beautiful girl and thought, I have never been so lucky. Then I replied, "I can't think of a single reason or excuse to say, 'No.'" I gave the driver the name of the hotel and helped her into the carriage.

We introduced ourselves while the horses pulled the carriage over the cobblestone streets toward my hotel. Even though we were strangers, conversation flowed easily between us. Her name was Alice and her father was the head of a law firm in Boston. Her father had come to San Francisco to resolve some legal problems concerning the construction of the intercontinental railroad construction which had started in the spring. She and her mother decided to come with her father to share in the adventure and see the West. They traveled by train to Omaha, and then by stagecoach, and again by train. They arrived in October and planned on leaving in the spring.

The old prospector recalled how he had told her about his family and their simple life. They had come West during the days of the Gold Rush, but his father had not been as fortunate as some and eventually, he had to start working in mines owned by others to support his family. He told about the fabulous wealth of the Comstock, and how, because of the War and the North's need for the bullion being produced by the Comstock, the miners could be considered conscripts. We continued our conversation until we arrived at the hotel. Feeling quite bold by this time, I turned to her and said, "I know I'm pushing my luck, but would you be so kind as to have a cup of hot chocolate with me in the hotel restaurant? It should taste good in this miserable weather." Apparently, she saw the pleading look in my eyes, I recall, because she hesitated only for a moment before she agreed. She instructed the driver to park the carriage and wait for her in the hotel lobby. When we walked into the restaurant, I signaled the head waiter and we followed him to a table. When I helped her with her coat, I noticed the cut, and knew by the feel, it was made from the finest woolen cloth. I thought of my own store-bought suit, Alice, however, did not seem to notice my clothes.

I recall the half hour we spent drinking our chocolate and how it seemed to have slipped by in minutes. I learned during our conversation she planned to enter one of the colleges for women when they returned to Boston.

Suddenly, she seemed to become conscious of the time.

She looked at the gold watch pinned to her dress and said, "I must be going. I hadn't planned on being out this late and my parents will be worried."

She started to get up and I rose quickly and helped her with her chair. While helping her, I said, "Never in my entire life has the time passed so quickly, and never have I enjoyed talking to anyone as much as I have you. I feel very uncomfortable about the way we met. If, however, it was the only means fate could provide for us to meet, I can't say that I am sorry."

She gave me a warm smile and said, "I'm not accustomed to all this flattery, but I like it, and thank you. I've enjoyed meeting you, too."

Encouraged by her response, I asked, "Is there any possibility of seeing you again?"

I knew I was begging but I could not keep the longing from creeping into my voice.

"Perhaps we can have lunch together tomorrow," she replied, "if that is agreeable with you. I'll bring the carriage and you can meet me in front of the hotel. If you have time, we can go for a drive before lunch."

The old prospector remembered her reply and how he felt like a little boy who had just discovered the present he had wished for under the Christmas tree. He wanted to grab her hand and hold it, but he was afraid he might frighten her.

"I'll be waiting for you when you arrive," I said, and I gently took her arm and guided her to the lobby where her driver waited.

We walked to the carriage and I helped her in, and we said goodbye. I watched while the carriage pulled away and disappeared into the misty darkness.

I closed the door to my room and walked over to the window and looked below at the wet cobblestones, and how they glistened from the hotel lights and the flickering street lamps, but my thoughts were with Alice. This is the most amazing thing that ever happened to me, I thought. I have strange feelings I have never experienced before. I wonder if I'm in love.

We met the next day, and the next, and the next. Each day our conversation became more personal and finally, we declared our love and decided to marry.

Then came the day Alice didn't come to meet him. The old prospector remembered his anxiety and how he worried, and how helpless he felt because she had not given him her address. His leave expired in three days; consequently, he must leave for Virginia City the morning of the third day.

I began making inquiries hoping to turn up a lead that would help me to locate her. The next morning, I continued my search and did not give up until evening. When I returned to my room, I felt tired and despondent. I closed the door and my thoughts began to run wild. Had she decided I was not the man she wanted to marry? Had she decided not to return because she did not want to tell me she found she did not love me? If she had come to that conclusion, I couldn't fault her because it was evident from her manners, her clothing, and her conversation, her family enjoyed considerable wealth, and I a lowly miner, had very little to offer her. No, I thought, Alice is too honest. She could never treat me that shabby, something else has happened.

I stood by the window looking down at the Christmas shoppers trying to figure out what may have happened when an unexpected knock on the door startled me. The bell boy, I thought, and walked to the door and opened it. There stood Alice.

Momentarily shocked, I stared at her, and then I opened my arms. I held her and we kissed, and I stroked her beautiful hair. I told her how I had worried and how much I loved her.

Together, we walked to the bed and she lay in my arms while she related her story. "I told my mother about you, Jim, and how much I loved you and how we planned to marry. My mother appeared to be annoyed but did not comment. Instead, she made her reservations known to my father. My father confronted me and wanted to know all about you, Jim. When I told him you were a twenty-year-old miner who worked for the Comstock Mining Corporation, he became irate and told me he would not permit me to marry an uneducated man who, probably at the maximum, earned three dollars a day. And he added, I was not to see you again, ever, even if he had to lock me in my room."

"It wasn't until the next morning," she continued, "when I heard my parents discussing plans to go to dinner, and then to the theatre, that I saw an opportunity to slip away from the apartment and come to see you, Jim. They asked me to come with them, but I pretended I had a headache and declined. As soon as they left, I changed my clothes and hired a carriage to bring me here. Jim, dear, I'm not proud of how I lied to my parents, but I knew you would be worried."

"Don't try to explain or apologize, Darling. Had the circumstances been reversed, I would have done the same thing." While talking to her, I gently stroked her beautiful hair and kissed her trying to soothe her. "I felt miserable and lost, and I tried to find you, but I didn't have your address. Trying to find you among San. Francisco's population of 200,000 proved to be an impossible task. But we are together again, and that is my only concern. You see, Dear, I love you very much."

We lay in bed and talked and made love until Alice had to leave so she would arrive home before her parents.

We pledged our love again, and I made a vow to her, I would ask for additional leave as soon as I arrived in Virginia City, and when I returned, we would marry. Before leaving the room, we held each other tightly and kissed for the last time. Then we walked down to the carriage and said goodbye. I waited and watched the carriage until it disappeared into the darkness, then I turned and walked slowly up to my room.

When I arrived in Virginia City, I went directly to the mine boss and explained my need for additional leave. The mine boss explained that he could not spare me, he had other men on leave and others scheduled, the War had reached a critical stage, and the North was pressuring for more bullion produc- tion to support and end the War as quickly as possible. That means, he told me, no more leave for at least two months.

The old prospector recalled as he lay on his pallet, how he had agonized over his plight. He had written to Alice explaining his predicament but had received no replies. He kept writing, Six weeks passed, and each day seemed like a week. Then a letter arrived. He recalled how he looked at it. His hands trembled and he began sweating in the cold after- noon weather. He returned to his room and sat on his bed and opened it.

My dearest Jim,

I know you have written but I have not received any of your letters. My father found out about my visit to your hotel and has not permitted me to leave the house alone. I am sure he intercepted your letters and destroyed them. When I tried to write, he refused to let me mail my letters, and he said that if you ever returned to San Francisco, he would have you thrown in jail. And I'm sure he will. He has many friends in high places.

My father is so angry with me, he has cut his business trip short. In lieu of waiting until spring and traveling overland, he has booked passage on a ship and we are leaving a week from today.

(Jim lowered the letter for a moment and thought, She is leaving today and what can I do? Nothing. He raised the letter and continued reading)

Darling, I know you will be shocked when I tell you that I think I'm pregnant. But please don't do anything foolish. If I am, I shall be happy and proud that someday I'll be the mother of your baby. And please don't try to follow me. Because, if you are around when he finds out, he will have you put in prison or, even worse, he may hire someone to kill you. Father forgets that I'll be eighteen in a few months but as you know, I'm an only child and parents think differently under such circumstances.

So again, My Love, I beg you, please don't try to follow me. It's better this way. I'll write when I can and someday, we will meet again.

Take care of yourself, and remember I love you and always will. Goodbye for now, All my love, Alice.

I sat there for an hour without moving, he recalled, and I did not go to supper that evening. I lay awake until two o'clock before dropping off to sleep. I went to work the next morning, and the next. People asked if I were ill. A week passed before I began to recover from the shock. Then, slowly, I began to develop a plan. I decided to quit the Comstock as soon as the War ended and go out on my own. I was positive plenty of gold and silver remained undiscovered, and deep in my heart; I knew Alice's father was right. I could not provide Alice the kind of life she had been accustomed to on three dollars a day.

The War ended in April. That same month, I celebrated my twenty-first birthday by quitting the Comstock and setting out on my prospecting adventure. I continued writing to Alice but gave up after three years when I did not receive replies.

It is futile to write, I thought, when I'm sure her father is intercepting the letters. As soon as I make my strike, I'll head for Boston.

The old prospector lay on the pallet and thought; In my search for the big strike, I never acknowledged defeat. Rich ore deposits were being found in California, Arizona, and in Nevada, and I knew it was only a question of time until I found mine. If I did not find it one year, I would find it the next, and now that I may have found it, it is too late. She may have passed away, or at the very least, she has built a new life for herself.

He thought about the leather saddlebags leaning against the tunnel wall near the entrance. They held all of his meager personal possessions. One pouch contained a metal box. Inside the metal box, carefully wrapped in oilcloth, lay the fifty-five-year-old letter from Alice. The box also contained a simple will leaving all of his material possessions to Alice, and subsequently to her first born, and then to any children she may have had thereafter. The only other items in the box were documents showing the registration of his claims and proof of the assessment work.

He thought about removing the letter and reading it once more. But, he thought, I'm too tired, and I know the letter by heart.

While lying on the pallet thinking of Alice, his fever had

been rising. He closed his eyes and began to doze, and his feverish mind began to wander. His dreams carried him to mines where he had worked and places where he had lived. Shadowy figures of fellow miners and people he had known appeared and faded. Now and then he heard himself speaking aloud to one of them.

His throbbing leg brought him back from his dream world.

He looked at his watch. Three hours had passed since he had taken his pills. His leg felt hot and dry when he touched the skin. He counted his aspirin. Eight were left. He poured out the usual three. Then he picked up the whiskey bottle and held it in front of the lantern. About three inches remain, he thought.

He sloshed the whiskey around in the bottle a couple of times and took two big swigs.

Feeling warm, he removed the mackinaw from his bed covers and rolled it into a pillow. Now, he thought, I'll be a little more comfortable. He mumbled aloud. "Perhaps, I can get some more sleep."

He could feel his body relax and he soon became drowsy and dropped off to sleep again.

The old prospector slept several hours then the huge coyote reappeared. He looked into the tunnel and raised his nose to sniff the air then lowered his head. With his nose barely above the tunnel floor and his phosphorescent eyes directed toward the pallet where the old prospector lay, he began his slow deliberate walk back and forth across the entrance. Then a buzzard sailed down and lit on the stove chimney in front of the tunnel and looked into the tunnel where the old prospector lay. Keeping one glowing eye on the old prospector the buzzard stood on one leg and extended a wing and began preening his black oily feathers.

Then he stood on the other leg and preened the feathers on the other wing. His bald head and hooked beak, mounted on his long scrawny featherless neck, turned to do the preening but kept one eye always focused on the pallet.

Another buzzard landed on the shoring above the tunnel entrance. As it balanced on the wooden beam, he extended his black rubbery neck and bald head down and under the shoring, looking upside down where the old prospector lay. The buzzard's bald head and neck began swinging back and forth as if in cadence to some rhythm.

The old prospector raised up, his eyes glazed with fever and sleep, shouting, "Get out!" before becoming fully awake. The he realized he had been having a nightmare.

He lay on the pallet for a few minutes then said aloud, "I can't go on like this,"

His skin felt hot and dry and his eyes burned as he looked out the tunnel entrance. Dawn is breaking, he thought, in another twenty minutes the sun will be shining.

His leg throbbed and the pain radiated up his leg to his hip adding to his misery. He looked for a moment at the five aspirin tablets remaining in the bottle and took all five washing them down with whiskey. He waited for a few minutes for the pain to subside, then pushed the blankets aside and maneuvered his body so he could reach the tunnel wall with his right foot. When he pushed his foot against the wall, shock waves shot up his leg to his knee, he jerked back his foot and winced at the same time.

I've got more than a sprained ankle, he thought. I must have broken one of the small bones in my ankle or foot. Then he said aloud, "I wonder what else can go wrong. If I have a broken bone in my right ankle or foot, too, I can forget about the crutches." The old man eased his foot against the wall, again putting pressure on the foot. It feels like a hundred needles sticking in my ankle bone, he thought. If I try the crutches, I can stand the pain. But, being that badly injured, when I walk, the muscles will start cramping. I've got to figure out some other way.

He slipped on his mackinaw and began working his way to the front of the tunnel, pushing the bottle of whiskey in front of him. During the night the winds had died down, but the warm air warned the old prospector they would return. He reached the stove and slid the coffee pot off and looked inside. About three cups left, he thought, that should be enough. He set the coffee pot back on the stove and started a fire. An empty dynamite box lay within reach. He stood it on end against the stove and used it as a back rest. Then he began removing the splints and bandages from his leg.

The stench of rotting flesh forced him to turn his head. He examined the wound and found tiny puss pockets had formed around the inner edges of the bruised flesh near the bone.

The old prospector seemed to have anticipated what he had seen and calmly replaced the bandages and the splints then poured the hot coffee into his tin cup and added half the whiskey. Leaning back against the box, he began talking to himself as if advising a friend.

"Jim," the old man said in a low voice, "you've run out of time. You've used all your medication and you are running out of water. The infection in your leg is so bad, it is doubtful a doctor could save it. And those are not your only problems. It is very likely you will get blood poisoning and die. In the meantime, the fever may cause you to lose your senses. And if you do, you could wander out into the desert, and then who knows what might happen. I know dying has not been your number one concern, especially now that you have grown older and passed the prime years of your life. With few exceptions, you've enjoyed a good life and a healthy one. True, you did not accomplish some of your major goals. But how many in their lifetimes have? Consequently, with the problems you now face, death should be welcomed and not feared."

The old prospector continued to ponder his fate and the possibility he might lose his senses and wander into the desert. I don't mind dying, he thought, but I keep thinking about the coyotes and buzzards that disrupted my dreams causing me to have nightmares. I know they are as much a part of the desert as the sand, cactus, and the sagebrush, but I can't help it if I dislike them. I can't tolerate the thought of crawling around the desert, not knowing who I am nor what I'm doing, and have a pack of coyotes attack me and scatter my bones across the desert for the buzzards to pick clean. No, he thought, I can't let that happen, there is a better way.

Then he said aloud, "I hope I have the strength to carry out my plan before the aspirin stops working."

The old prospector drank the rest of the coffee and began working his way down the ramp pushing a short-handled shovel in front of him. When he reached the location near the side of the ramp where he had buried the explosives, he dug up the dynamite, caps, and fuses and removed three sticks of dynamite from the box. Three sticks are more than enough, he thought. But I'd rather have the charge on the heavy side for this job than have one that is too light.

He tied the three sticks of dynamite together with a piece of fuse and put the dynamite cap in his pocket, then reburied the box of dynamite and the caps and fuses.

Now, he thought, getting back up the ramp without passing out is going to be the toughest part of the whole scheme.

Pushing the dynamite ahead, he began the slow process of getting back up the ramp.

The old prospector did not pass out as he continued his struggle until he reached the stove. He lay beside the stove exhausted and wet with sweat. After regaining some of his strength, he sat up and filled the tin cup half full of coffee and emptied the whiskey bottle into it. He gave the hot mixture a quick stir, drank half of it, and waited for it to start working.

Now, he thought, it's time to get started. Using his pocketknife, he cut a twelve-inch length of fuse from the piece he had pushed up the ramp and slipped the dynamite cap on one end of it. Since his crimping tool was in the tunnel, he crimped the cap on the fuse with his teeth. That's something I haven't done in forty years, he thought.

He picked up one of the sticks of dynamite, opened the end of it with his knife, and pushed the cap with the fuse attached, into the open end and closed the end tightly around the fuse. Then he split the other end of the fuse to insure it would light quickly. Next, he tied the other sticks of dynamite to the one loaded with the cap and fuse and laid it next to his leg.

The old prospector wiped his hands on his shirt and looked at the explosives. That takes care of that, he thought. He reached for the mixture of coffee and whiskey and drained the cup. He set the cup back on the stove and pulled out his watch. The hands showed the time to be ten minutes past ten. Since he could not see the sun from where he was sitting, he checked the shadows and returned the watch to his pocket. He looked out across the desert. The winds are increasing, and the dust clouds are beginning to rise, he thought. The buzzards will not venture from their roosts today, but this should be the last day of the storm. I wonder if the jenny made it back to Randsburg. She was a good friend and a great pack animal.

"I'm sorry I spooked you, Suzie," he said aloud. "I don't blame you for running away."

He turned away from the desert and looked at the tunnel entrance. He took a deep breath and the determination that had carried him this far showed on his face.

"Well, Jim," he said aloud, "let's finish the job."

Pushing the explosives ahead, and pulling his body with his hands and forearms, he struggled to the tunnel entrance. Just inside the tunnel entrance, he stopped to rest for a few moments and to pick up his prospector's pick. Then pushing the prospector's pick and the explosive charge ahead, he worked his way back to the pallet.

The lantern had died down. Tunnel entrance light lit the tunnel to the area around his pallet but not enough to provide the light he needed. The old prospector lit the carbide lamp, adjusted the flame, and began digging a small depression, about a foot in diameter and eight inches deep, directly under the shoring. This basin, he thought, will act like a mortar and direct the force of the explosion upward. If my judgement is correct, the explosion will tear out the shoring and blow all the loose and fractured rock from the fault, and that should be enough to bury me.

He finished digging the basin and tossed the pick over by the tunnel wall. Then he arranged the pallet with the head next to the lower edge of the basin and placed the lamp and the explosives near the pallet where he could reach them. He struggled into the pallet and made himself as comfortable as possible, then he picked up the lamp with one hand and the explosives with the other. While holding the lamp and the charge, the old prospector looked out the tunnel entrance. The weary look left his eyes and his face began to soften. "Alice," he said in a low voice, "I never forgot you. I always believed someday we would be together again, but things didn't work out the way I wanted them to. I never stopped loving you. Please forgive me."

The weary look returned to the old prospector's face and he turned his attention back to the explosives. He moved the flame of the lamp toward the dynamite charge until the flame enveloped the split end of the fuse. The fuse sputtered and then began hissing. He set the lamp on the tunnel floor and placed the dynamite in the basin. Then the old prospector lay back with his neck over the explosives and pulled the blankets up over his chest. Then he folded his arms beneath the blanket and closed his eyes.

2

THE OLD INDIAN TRAIL

Finding the Reese Boarding House in Randsburg was not difficult. The white two-story building could be seen from almost any place in town. It stood on the side of the hill just west of the dusty road leading to the Yellow Aster Mine and overlooked Butte Avenue. Butte Avenue housed most of the business activity in Randsburg.

Mrs. Reese had converted her two-story, three-bedroom home into a boarding house shortly after she lost her husband, a shift boss working for the Yellow Aster Mine. He had been killed when the timbers collapsed in one of the mine tunnels. Unfortunately, the accident had occurred only a year after they had married. The couple had built the large home on the assumption they would raise a large family, and she had considered selling the house after the accident and returning to Pittsburg, her hometown.

But after the shock had passed of losing her husband, Mrs. Reese decided to remain in Randsburg where she had buried her husband and where she had cultivated many friends. The thought, too, of giving up the clean desert air for the smoke, grit, and grime of Pittsburg helped her decide to stay. Now, sixteen years had passed since the accident and fifteen years since she had used the money she had received from the accident to pay off the mortgage and establish the Reese Boarding House.

Mrs. Reese made good use of the two extra bedrooms. She rented one and let the married couple who helped her use the other. The number of boarders and visitors varied from ten to fifteen, but it wasn't unusual for her to feed twice that many if something special was going on in town. The number also varied from meal to meal for the three meals she served each day.

This evening, or late afternoon, some might say, because Mrs. Reese began loading the table, family style at four-thirty, she fed a total of thirteen. Eight of the thirteen boarders had finished their meals and left. The five remaining at the table were drinking coffee, smoking, talking, or listening. The oldest man in the group, John McKay, had the best stories to tell and consequently, did most of the talking.

For the moment, however, George Summers had the group's attention. George's drawl identified him as a Texan, and he was telling a story about a subject of mutual interest to all, the weather. "I've lived in this area for fifteen years, and this winter has been the worst I've ever seen. We've had just about every kind of weather ever invented. We all know that wind isn't unusual, but when it's mixed with rain, sleet, snow, and bitter cold, that's something else. It wouldn't have surprised me if a cyclone had shown up. And if it had, I would have felt like I was right back home in East Texas. One morning in January, I walked over to my neighbors to draw a pail of water for my shack. A couple of days before, ten inches of snow had fallen, and the next day the winds started blowing down from the Sierras. During the night, the cold winds had frozen a crust of ice over snow an inch thick. Between the wind and the ice, I had a heck of a time trying to walk and stand up. When I finally reached my neighbor's house, he told me his water pipes had frozen during the night. Working together, and using a blow torch, we got the pipes thawed out. I filled my pail and started back. But that wasn't all. By the time I reached my shack, a half-inch of ice had formed on the top of the water. Man, that is cold."

Everyone around the table smiled and began exchanging remarks about his own experiences. Then John McKay spoke up, McKay always drew attention when he talked. If for no other reason, people wondered how such a small thin man could have such a low, deep, voice, everyone could hear without straining. "It's been a bad one, for sure," he said. "One of the worst winters I can recall during the thirty years I've been around here, and it has also been one of the wettest. The weather seems to run in cycles, so it's possible we may have another one this winter. I've seen some years when it seemed all we had were wind and dust storms, and as you know, we never get a lot of rain around here even during the winter months. But when we do, it sure changes the looks of this desert of ours. The other day I drove over to Johannesburg and took the road out toward Trona to the place where it crosses the Old Indian Trail. I parked the Model T and walked down the Old Indian Trail to about a quarter of a mile past Red Mountain. I have never seen anything more beautiful in my life. Red Mountain is covered with desert asters from the bottom of the south slope to halfway up the mountain. The desert asters aren't the only flowers Mother Nature uses to show off her desert glory. Many other kinds are blooming, and many more will be in the next two or three weeks. It's Mother Nature at her best, and she only puts on her best shows when we have double the average rainfall we usually get during the winter months."

McKay continued, "I might add, too, for the benefit of those who are not familiar with the story, there used to be a lot of asters around here, that's one of the reasons they named the big mine the 'Yellow Aster.' I never did find out what the 'Yellow' part stood for. It may have been that the center of the aster is yellow, and it matched the gold color of the mineral they were mining, or it could have been for some other crazy reason. Mines sometimes receive strange names, and few ever know the true reason why. The point is, the asters around here have disappeared, probably trampled to death by the 4,000 people who lived in Randsburg during the boom days."

"You spoke of the Old Indian Trail," commented Dan Sanders, "I've only been here a couple of weeks, and this is the third time I've heard it mentioned. Does it get much travel?"

"No, not really," explained McKay, "it was probably a coincidence. The Old Indian Trail isn't used more than once or twice a year if that often. I doubt if more than two or three dozen people around here even know it exists."

"I assume from what I heard, and I haven't heard much, that it truly is an old Indian trail. Do you mind telling me a little more about it?" asked Sanders.

"I'll be glad to tell you what I know, and it won't take long because I know very little, and what I do know, is all hand-me-down based on a lot of legend and very few facts. Yes, it is an old Indian trail, but most of it has vanished. It started somewhere west of Owens Valley. Apparently, many lesser trails used by small bands of Indians belonging to tribes living in or near the Sierras led into the main trail we now call the Old

Indian Trail. We believe Route 395, running down from Reno, followed the Old Indian Trail from Owens Valley south, and in the process, destroyed the original trail as far south as Johannesburg. Traces, however, are still visible where it crosses the road connecting Trona and Johannesburg, and it can be followed to the Mojave River, a few miles west of Barstow."

"For what purpose did the Indians use the trail?" Sanders asked.

"For trading," replied McKay. "The Old Indian Trail joined the Mojave River Indian Trail where it meets the Mojave River near Barstow. The desert Indians traveled up and down the Mojave Riverbed from one end to the other, and some say clear down to the Colorado River, trading among themselves and with other Indian tribes. I've also heard they crossed the mountains from the headwaters of the Mojave River to reach the Pacific Ocean. Seashells worn by some of the descendants of the Indians who traveled the Old Indian Trail seem to bear out that theory."

Sanders continued his probing. "John, you indicated earlier, the trail is seldom traveled these days. Is there a reason?"

"It is easier and quicker to get to Barstow by car, or you can take the train. The Indians, who in earlier times walked, and later rode horses, or used horses to pull travois, began using 395 when they switched to wagons and then to cars. Even though the Old Indian Trail is between five and ten miles shorter, you can't travel it with any kind of vehicle that uses wheels because of the hills, gullies, and loose sand the trail crosses. Consequently, about the only people who use it these days are prospectors, or an Indian or a Mexican who doesn't have train fare and can't bum a ride." Then he added, "And rarely a horseman."

"Speaking of prospectors," injected George Somers, "do you remember the old prospector we called Jim? He is the only person I can recall whoever traveled the Old Indian Trail, on what some might call, a regular basis. He told me he had a prospect a few miles southeast of Fremont Peak and he used the Old Indian Trail to get to his claim. He said if you looked about a half-mile to the east, you could see the ore dump from the trail. Now that I think back, I can't recall seeing him around for quite some time."

"Sure," replied McKay, answering for the group, "I remember Jim. He and I are about the same age. I always liked Jim. He never has much to say, but he is a good listener. Very few people know much about Jim or his past. He has claims scattered all over the country, and he spends most of his time working them or prospecting for more. He comes to town when he needs supplies or to find work when he runs out of money. As soon as he has earned enough to buy supplies, he takes off again."

McKay continued, "I believe the last time I saw Jim was about the time the Armistice was signed a couple of years ago. He had just returned from up north and was down at the stable dickering with Bill Cole for a jenny Bill had in the corral. Jim told me he was getting ready to leave for the claim he was developing near Fremont Peak. I'm sure it's the same one you mentioned, George. I saw the claim fifteen, maybe, sixteen years ago. It was the last time I traveled the Old Indian Trail. As I recall, Jim was doing assessment work on the claim. He showed me some ore samples, and they looked pretty good. He said if he could run the tunnel into the hill another twenty-five or thirty feet, he had a good chance of hitting pay ore. Unfortunately, he ran into a fault that cut through the tunnel. When I left, he was busy trying to shore it up. I intended to ask, the last time I saw him, how he made out with the shoring, but I forgot. And, George, I wouldn't be too concerned that you haven't seen him recently, he spent two years up around Placerville and the American River area before he showed up here. He may have taken off for Arizona or Nevada, or he may have returned to northern California. You never know where he will show up next."

Ed Reilly and Joe Sims, the other two men in the group, had been listening but had not participated in the conversation.

Ed, who had been trying to make points with Mrs. Reese, without much success, though he saw an opportunity to score a couple by cutting off the discussion. "I'm sure we are all enjoying this interesting conversation," he said, in a voice loud enough he hoped could be heard in the kitchen, "but if we don't cut it off, Mrs. Reese may ask us to. I'm sure she would like to get the dining room cleaned up and have it ready for breakfast tomorrow morning."

Heads nodded, and mumblings of agreement spread among the boarders as they pushed their chairs back from the table and prepared to leave.

Dan Sanders rose from his chair with the others and walked to the door with them but did not leave. After wishing each person a pleasant evening, he left the dining room and walked into the parlor. Dan, a young mining engineer, had arrived in Randsburg two weeks before from San Francisco. His employer, a San Francisco mining engineering consulting firm, had sent Dan to Randsburg to study the feasibility of extracting gold from the huge ore dump that marked the location of the Yellow Aster Mine.

The superintendent of the skeleton crew working the Yellow Aster was waiting for Dan in Johannesburg when he arrived at the train station. During their drive back to Randsburg, the superintendent suggested Dan stay at the Reese Boarding House. He said the food was good and the spare room Mrs. Reese rented was available. The alternative would be to stay at the only hotel in town, which was less convenient, and eat at the Chinese Restaurant. Dan had readily accepted the superintendent's recommendation.

Dan strolled to the parlor window overlooking the business district. Dusk was setting in, and as the area grew darker, electric lights began to flicker on in the stores and shops.

Lights from kerosene lamps and Coleman lanterns also began to glow through the windows and doors of the houses and shacks scattered along the hills above and below the business district. As he watched, an embryo of an idea began to form in his mind. Preoccupied with his thoughts, he did not hear Mrs. Reese enter the parlor, and when she spoke, the sudden interruption of his concentration slightly startled him. "I'm sorry I startled you, Dan," she said. "Whatever your thoughts, they must have been serious." He quickly regained his composure, but she saw a sheepish grin on his face when he turned toward her. "I was thinking of our discussion this evening about the Old Indian Trail. In school, I became fascinated by stories and artifacts that had anything to do with the American Indians. The reason, I might add, my great grandmother was a full-blooded Cherokee. My great grandfather married her while hunting and trapping in the Indian Territory, a part of which later became the Oklahoma Territory."

"I'm sorry, Mrs. Reese, I know you are busy, and here I am yapping away about something which you probably are not the least bit interested."

Dan had barely finished his apology when, in a very positive voice, she said, "You are not wasting my time, and I am enjoying every bit of your very interesting story. I want to hear more."

"Thanks, Mrs. Reese, you are a very nice person. As you can probably guess, both of my great grandparents died before I was born. Consequently, I never had the pleasure of hearing directly from them the stories of their adventures. My grandfather tried to get me interested, but I suppose I was too young. He died when I was thirteen. My interest finally surfaced during my sophomore year in high school. During my class in American History, I received an assignment to research the history of Oklahoma. While doing the research, I kept thinking about my great grandparents, and the bits of information I had absorbed from the stories I had heard and the tales my father enjoyed telling about his grandparents. It suddenly dawned on me my great grandparents were a part of that history, and the American Indian was a significant part of my heritage."

"I know you must be very proud of the pioneer and American Indian blood that flows in your veins. And if I'm not being too inquisitive, would you mind telling me what they did for a living after they married?"

"They continued living in the Indian Territory, hunting and trapping as my great grandfather had before they married. She worked beside him, helping with the traps and doing chores she could physically handle. They continued living off the land until the arrival of the buffalo hunters. The settlers followed the buffalo hunters and my great grandparents had to give up their nomadic way of life. My great grandfather then went to work as a teamster for a freight company and later started his own freight hauling business. My father told me my great grandparents were very happy together. They raised two girls and four boys."

"Perhaps now," continued Dan, "you have some inkling of

why my thoughts had slipped back in time to the days when the Indians traveled the Old Indian Trail. I'm amazed that I was so deeply engrossed in my thoughts, I did not hear you enter the parlor. Mrs. Reese, are you familiar with the Old Indian Trail, and have you heard any stories, or do you have any information that might further my knowledge?"

"I don't think I can add anything to what you have already been told. If you've talked to John McKay, you have talked to the best authority I know on the subject." Then she added, "Do you have something else in mind besides listening to stories about the Old Indian Trail? It's none of my business, but I think your thoughts are running deeper than that."

Dan gave her a curious look. "You must be psychic," he said, and without waiting for a reply, he continued. "Yes, I have been thinking of something else. I've been thinking crazy thoughts about hiking the Old Indian Trail from Johannesburg to Barstow. It sounds kind of stupid, doesn't it?"

"No, not stupid, just kind of odd. Odd, because you seem willing to risk encounters with rattlesnakes, scorpions, the heat, the cold, and the possibility of an accident, with no one around to help you when we have a perfectly good train you may ride. Strangely though, I have the feeling you have already made up your mind."

"Almost," Dan replied with a grin, "but I have a lot of checking to do before I decide."

"Since you are a city man working behind a desk most of the time, I would guess, do you think you have the stamina to carry a pack with all of the things you will need across a barren desert for fifty miles?" As she asked the question, Mrs. Reese stood in front of Dan with her hands on her hips, and her head cocked slightly to one side as if she were talking to a young son instead of a young man she had known for only two weeks.

Her black hair streaked with gray and pulled loosely back and wrapped in a bun at the back of her neck, framed her fair complexion and blue eyes. Her slight brogue suggested Irish parents.

"I feel quite confident on that point," Dan replied. "I spent six months in France building and blowing up bridges, and sometimes we had to march twenty or thirty miles carrying a fifty-pound pack. I realize that it's been over two years, but I have continued to exercise, and I feel I'm in pretty good shape."

She smiled and said, "If I were your age, I think I would give it a try. The desert is beautiful this time of year, and this year it is especially beautiful. I would try it for that reason alone, and you have additional reasons."

"Thanks, Mrs. Reese, you don't know how much I appreciate your encouragement. You've helped me make up my mind. Now let's hope I don't run into problems I can't foresee at the moment. By that, I mean, I want to check with John McKay again to find out if he has any words of wisdom or opinions that could cause me to change my mind."

"If you do leave the day after tomorrow, as you are anticipating, you don't have much time to change directions, do you, Dan?"

Dan smiled, "Now that you have talked me into it, I guess I don't when I think about it. And if I do make this trip, I have a thousand things to do, give or take a hundred, before the sun sets tomorrow evening. The most important is to get a telegram off to my boss telling him I'll be a couple of days late and making arrangements to send my personal gear and the ore samples to San Francisco by Railway Express."

Mrs. Reese watched with amusement as the excitement of the coming adventure began to show on his face and creep into his voice. "If I were twenty years younger, Dan, I would be tempted to go with you."

"That's about the nicest compliment a man can have, and again, I thank you. I mentioned earlier that I wanted to talk to John McKay again. Do you know the most likely place he might be where I might locate him early tomorrow morning?"

"John does carpenter work and odd jobs around town, so you never know exactly where he will be. My best guess is the stable. He usually drops by every morning to visit with Bill Cole, who owns the stable, and pick up the latest gossip. Business is pretty slow now that practically everyone owns a car, but he still keeps a few horses and a burro or two to rent or sell. Bill has a lot of time on his hands, and John does, too, and they are both great talkers. I think that is why John hangs around there so much. Of course, good talkers attract people, and from what I've heard, quite a congregation of old-timers gather there to swap yarns. Well, I know I've gone around the bush a couple of times to answer your question, but I thought you might be interested in knowing a little more about what goes on in our town."

"Now," Mrs. Reese concluded, "four-thirty comes pretty early, and I've got to make sure everything is ready for breakfast. So, I'll say goodnight, and I'll see you in the morning."

"Goodnight, Mrs. Reese, and once again I want to thank you for the help and encouragement you have given me on this, perhaps, not too bright a trip I'm planning."

After Mrs. Reese left the parlor, Dan returned to the window and watched the shoppers and strollers as they walked in and out of the lights shining through the doors and windows of the stores down below. While he watched, he mentally prepared his agenda for the following day, then he left the window and climbed the stairs to his room.

He sat down at the small combination lamp and writing table located next to the bed and drafted a telegram to his San Francisco office. Tomorrow, he thought, I'll hire someone to haul the ore samples and the personal things I won't need to Johannesburg and arrange to send them ahead by Railway Express. At the same time, I'll get this telegram on its way. Now, I'll get busy and sort out the things I'll need and pack the rest, that will be about all I can do this evening. If the plan falls through, it will be easy to repack everything and take the train.

Dan woke up early the next morning. Since McKay ate only his evening meal at the boarding house, Dan left for the stables as soon as he had finished breakfast. Dan found Bill Cole grooming one of the horses and asked if he had seen McKay.

"No, I haven't," replied Cole, "but I expect he will show up shortly. He usually drops by every morning to find out if I have heard any news or gossip he may have missed at one of his other stops. You may have heard he does odd carpenter jobs, and if he isn't working, he may spend an hour or so swapping yarns with me or some of the other boys that might come by. Can I help?"

"Perhaps," replied Dan. "I've finished my work at the Yellow Aster, and I'll be leaving tomorrow. I have been giving some thought to following the Old Indian Trail to Barstow in lieu of returning by train. I want to get McKay's opinion on the idea before I go off halfcocked. What do you think? Will it be worth the time and effort?"

"It sounds like a great idea to me, and you couldn't have picked a better time of year. It is not too hot, and it is not too cold. You look strong and healthy, and I might add, if this is your first opportunity to visit the Mojave Desert, you will see it as very few people get to see it. I would not pass up the chance if I were you. I'll rent you a horse, and you can leave the animal at the stable in Barstow. I'm going to Barstow next week, and I'll pick up the horse and ride it back. It will give me a chance to see the Old Indian Trail again. It's been seven or eight years since I've traveled it."

"Traveling by horseback is an idea I hadn't considered," Dan commented, "but I think I prefer to travel the trail by foot the same way the Indians did."

John McKay drove up in his Model T just as Dan finished his bit of the conversation. After passing amenities, Bill filled McKay in on the subject of their discussion. "I suggested he rent one of my horses for the trip, John, but he turned me down. He said he prefers to walk, what do you think?"

John smiled, "I don't want to beat you out of any business, Bill, but I think Dan has the right idea. I'm in favor of hiking. I think he will enjoy the hike and he will see a lot more."

"I think you are right, John," commented Bill without trying to push the suggestion of using a horse any further, "and my guess is, Dan, you've got a lot of things to do if you plan on leaving tomorrow morning."

John turned to Dan and asked, "What can I do to help? I don't have anything lined up for today, so the Model T and I are at your disposal."

Dan explained his need to send the telegram and to ship the ore samples and his personal items to San Francisco.

"OK, Dan, I'll take you up to the boarding house, and we'll pick up your things and haul them to the train station. You can tell the agent what you want to be done, then we will return to Randsburg and visit the general store so you can pick up the things you will need for the trip. How does that sound to you?"

"It sounds great to me, John, and I do appreciate your help." Dan shook hands with Bill Cole and said goodbye then climbed into the front and only seat of the topless Model T. They drove up the hill to the boarding house where Dan picked up the ore samples and his personals, he had packed the night before.

The trip from the boarding house to the railroad station in Johannesburg took about fifteen minutes.

The Santa Fe Railroad provided passenger and freight service to the Rand Mining District communities of Atolia, Red Mountain, Johannesburg, and Randsburg. Because of the terrain, the branch line had not been extended to Randsburg. The train originated in Barstow and usually consisted of five or six assorted freight cars, a combination passenger, baggage, and mail car, pulled by a steam locomotive. Now and then a caboose was attached for the convenience of the conductor and the brakeman. The train seldom left Barstow on time because of its low priority. When it finally received clearance to leave, it traveled the San Francisco mainline west for 30 miles, to Kramer Junction, stopping along the way to drop off and pick up passengers and freight. The train then switched from the San Francisco main line to a branch line at Kramer Junction that carried it north to Johannesburg. On its way to Johannesburg, it stopped at the Fremont railroad maintenance station, Atolia, and Red Mountain before reaching Johannesburg. The train terminated its trip at Johannesburg and returned the same route to Barstow. The round trip, a total of 110 miles, took about 12 hours. Despite the train's lack of priority, and that it required six hours to travel 55 miles, plus the discomfort the passengers endured sitting on solid oak seats without cushions, broiling in the summer heat with flies zipping in through the wide-open windows but unable to find their way out, and freezing in the winter cold with no heat in the passenger compartment, the people who lived in the Rand Mining

District were proud of their train. And why not? They had built and paid for the Randsburg Railroad, as it was called with its 25 miles of track, before being bought by the Santa Fe. John McKay was working at the Yellow Aster Mine during the conception and birth of the Randsburg Railroad and knew just about all there was to know about it.

McKay, knowing the train schedule and the habits of the station agent, was not surprised when they arrived at the train station to see a note on the clipboard attached to the depot door. He climbed out of the Model T and left the engine running while he walked over to read its contents. He returned to the pickup and explained to Dan, "The note says the agent has gone home and will be back at 3:00PM. That's not unusual. If things are quiet, he leaves around eleven and comes back about three. Apparently, he left a little early today."

"What do we do now?" asked Dan.

"I know where he lives, so we'll drive out to his place and talk to him. He's a really nice guy, and I'm sure he won't mind coming over and taking care of your business."

McKay backed the Model T away from the depot and turned off on a winding dirt road. They followed the road northeast for a half-mile, passing, along the way, a few isolated wooden frame houses and now and then a miner's shack. McKay stopped the Model T in front of a white frame house that looked like it had been freshly painted. A veranda extended along the south and east sides, partially shaded by vines. A white picket fence surrounded both the house and a shed attached to the house which sheltered a parked touring sedan. Apparently, the occupants had tried to grow grass within the boundaries of the picket fence, but the desert had won. Only a few scraggly clumps near the fence continued the struggle.

McKay had not had time to turn off the engine when the screen door was blown open by three children trying to see who could reach the car first. As the screen door banged shut, Dan heard a woman with a Midwestern twang yell, "Be careful or you'll knock the screen door off its hinges." They hit the wooden gate hinged to the picket fence with the same velocity, then they stood silently by the Model T with their hands held behind their backs smiling and looking up at John McKay.

As McKay reached over the back of the seat to pick up a small brown bag from the bed of the pickup, he said, "Hi Julie, Joshua, and Jason. Why aren't you kids in school?"

As if on cue, they all replied together, "It's Easter Vacation, Mr. McKay."

McKay pulled three lollipops from the bag and handed one to each of the children. Dan judged their ages to be between six and nine. As he watched the three healthy, vigorous children, he smiled and thought, they are one of the other reasons the grass struggles to grow in the yard.

The children were murmuring their thanks when a slightly stooped man, whom Dan judged to be in his mid-thirties, opened the screened door, and walked from the porch to the car.

"Hello, John, what brings you to our fair city?" he asked.

They shook hands, and McKay introduced Dan.

"Abe Carlton, this is Dan Sanders. Dan wants to express some luggage and boxes to San Francisco. He can give you the details, Abe. It's important to Dan that he gets the task out of the way this morning if at all possible."

Dan did not have to be told Abe Carlton was a station agent.

He wore black pants, a white long sleeve shirt with black

sleeve protectors covering his shirt sleeves from his wrists to above his elbows, and silver-rimmed glasses.

"Hey, John, it's my pleasure. I'm more than happy to help out a paying customer. It's a real pleasure meeting you, Dan. I'll back out the Chevy and meet you at the station."

McKay turned the Model T around and headed back down the dirt road while Carlton backed out his car to follow them.

During the trip back to the station, Dan asked, "Does Abe have any help in running the station?"

"Nope, Dan, he handles the whole operation himself. He operates the telegraph system maintaining communication with Barstow and Kramer Junction, sends and receives telegrams, helps with loading and unloading mail and baggage, manages the Railway Express operation, sells passenger tickets, sweeps out the station, cleans the toilets, and performs any other odd jobs that need to be done around the station."

"It must keep him pretty busy."

"Not really, not since the Yellow Aster shut down most of its operations about four years ago. The Kelly Mine over at Red Mountain is the busy stop now. If the train is late, Abe may have to work until 10 PM, or until the train gets back to Kramer Junction."

As they passed the scattered houses and shacks while bumping along the dirt road, Dan asked, "What is the population of Johannesburg, John?"

"Well," John thought for a moment and then replied, "if you count all the chickens, dogs and cats, and the two burros Fred Thompson owns, I'd guess about a hundred. It does have a combination hotel and restaurant, a small general store, and a garage and filling station, but that's about it. The town depends on the people traveling along 395 for most of its support, plus the activity of the railroad terminal. Route 395 doesn't pass through Randsburg so travelers must stop here, if they intend to stop, before going on towards Reno."

By the time McKay had finished his dissertation on Johannesburg, they had reached the depot. McKay pulled the Model T alongside the building and turned off the engine. Carlton pulled up in back of them and helped Dan unload the luggage and the ore boxes. When Dan had finished his business with the agent, including having his return passenger ticket checked, he thanked Carlton and climbed into the Model T where McKay had been waiting. During the three-mile ride from Johannesburg to Randsburg, John talked about Dan's trip across the desert. "Last night, Dan, when we were discussing the Old Indian Trail, we mentioned Jim, the old prospector, who has a claim about five miles southeast of Fremont Peak. If you look closely, you can see the mine dump about a half-mile to the east of the trail. It won't be much out of your way to stop there for the night. If you are lucky, you might find Jim working on the claim. If not, you can sleep in the tunnel. The next morning when you leave the claim look for the path Jim uses to reach a spring which is located about a mile south of the claim. The spring is only a hundred yards or so from the Old Indian Trail, and you can refill your canteen on your way out. The spring should be overflowing with all the rain we've had, plus the heavy snowpack in the San Bernardino Mountains."

When they arrived in Randsburg, McKay drove directly to the general store. They looked over the merchandise and John suggested Dan buy two blankets and a piece of canvas for ground cover, a canteen, and a knapsack. Dan added a hunting knife, a new set of batteries for his flashlight, and a small box of matches. In lieu of buying food, Dan said he would ask Mrs. Reese to fix sandwiches and throw in a couple of apples. John agreed and suggested Dan ask Mrs. Reese to add a small bag of coffee. "Even if Jim isn't at the claim, you shouldn't have any difficulty finding a tin can to brew some coffee."

When Dan finished his shopping, they walked out to the Model T. Dan tossed the supplies he had bought on the truck bed and then cranked the engine for John. When they reached the boarding house, Dan removed his supplies and thanked McKay for his help. "Glad I could help, Dan. I'll see you at supper."

Dan carried the supplies up to his room and laid them out on the bed, then he packed everything in the knapsack except the toilet articles and his razor which he would be using that evening and the next morning. When he finished packing the knapsack, he picked it up by the backstraps and hefted it. He thought when I tie on the bedroll, including things I can't pack tonight, plus the canteen, and my revolver, I'll be carrying about fifty pounds or better. He rolled his blankets together, with the canvas cover on the outside, and tied the roll together with a piece of rope left over from packing the items he had shipped. Tomorrow morning, he thought, I'll shape the roll in the form of a horseshoe and tie it to the knapsack.

Now to check with Mrs. Reese about the sandwiches.

Dan found her in the dining room setting the table for the evening meal and asked her about the sandwiches and the coffee. "I'll be leaving at five-thirty in the morning, and I hope I'm not imposing on you, Mrs. Reese. I feel guilty asking you for another favor."

"So, you have definitely made up your mind. I think that is wonderful and don't worry about a thing. We will have breakfast together, and I'll see that everything is ready to go when you are. Now you go back upstairs and finish getting your things together, and I'll see you at supper time. OK?"

"Mrs. Reese, you make everything sound so easy, again, thank you."

Dan returned to his room, inspected his revolver, and changed the flashlight batteries. Now, he thought as he lay back on the bed, I'll relax for a few minutes before I clean up for supper.

I wonder if I've forgotten anything. He reviewed the events of the day, the things he had bought, the items he had packed in the knapsack, and his conversation with Mrs. Reese. What a wonderful woman, he thought, I felt like giving her a big hug, but I haven't known her long enough to get too personal. She would have made a great and understanding mother. Well, he thought, everything seems to be in order. It's four o'clock and time to wash up and get ready for supper.

Dan walked down the steps and into the dining room. The other boarders had arrived and were getting ready to sit down to eat. When he saw McKay, he moved around the table to a vacant chair next to him and sat down.

A few of the boarders had heard of Dan's plans before arriving, and when Dan walked into the dining room, they began passing the word around. Now, as they began settling into their chairs around the table, the focus was on Dan with questions, comments of envy, and well wishes. But not for long. Someone started passing the steaming bowls of hot food, and the conversation and the attention of the boarders changed immediately.

When the food passing slowed, and the plates had been filled to the point where they appeared to be in need of sideboards, Dan turned to McKay and asked, "John, where is the best place to pick up the Old Indian Trail?"

"I think your best bet is to start where it crosses the road that connects Johannesburg and Trona. I'll take you out there tomorrow and show you what to look for."

"You've already done enough for me, John. I can't continue to impose on you."

"Forget it, Dan, I volunteered, didn't I? Now, just listen. I don't think you will have any trouble following the trail once you know what to look for, and tomorrow morning I'll show you the signs."

They continued their conversation until everyone had finished eating. When people began to rise to leave, Dan thanked McKay and shook hands with the others, then left for his room.

The next morning, Dan woke up at 4:30. He washed, shaved, dressed, and finished packing. After carrying his gear downstairs and leaving it in the parlor, he joined Mrs. Reese in the dining room. She had placed his breakfast on the table and was in the process of pouring his coffee when he entered.

"Good morning, Dan," she said. "Did you sleep well last night?"

"Like an animal in hibernation," he replied. "It must have been all the running around I did yesterday. My guess is it wore me out, that, and all the excitement a person experiences when he is anticipating a new adventure. I don't think I had been in bed more than three minutes before I was sound asleep."

"I'm glad to hear that," she said. "There is nothing like a good night's sleep to get one started for the day, and today is the big day. I hope everything goes well for you."

"Thanks," then smiling, he said, "I may need your well-wishes. I noticed the calendar shows today is the first day of April. I sure hope Mother Nature doesn't have any pranks stored up her sleeve; she plans to play on me."

"For Heaven's sake," she exclaimed, and a slight expression of concern appeared in her eyes, "I had forgotten today is April Fool's Day."

"Are you superstitious?" He asked.

"I think all Irish are a little superstitious," she replied. "My parents told me the Little People of Ireland are always playing jokes on human beings. I hope you don't meet any of those strange little fellows on your trip."

"Now, don't worry, Mrs. Reese, everything is going to be all right."

They continued their conversation while eating. When they had finished, Dan told her how much he had enjoyed his trip to Randsburg and how he appreciated all the things she had done for him during his stay at the boarding house.

He heard John McKay's Model T pull up in front and got up to say goodbye. He held out his hand, but she quickly grabbed him and gave him a big hug. Tears moistened her eyes as she said goodbye. Perhaps she saw in Dan, the son she had never had. Dan picked up his gear, including the brown paper bag of food Mrs. Reese had prepared for him and hurried out to the car.

"Good morning, John," said Dan, and tossed his gear into the back of the pick-up.

McKay returned the greeting as Dan climbed over the door of the topless Model T. Dan had barely settled into his seat when McKay pushed the clutch to the floor and pulled down the gas throttle. The Model T jumped ahead when McKay released the clutch and gave a few convulsive jerks before settling down into its fifteen mile an hour gait over the dirt road.

While driving from Randsburg to Johannesburg, Dan and McKay exchanged bits of information about the weather and the area around Randsburg and Johannesburg. McKay turned left on to the road connecting Johannesburg with Trona.

Approximately five miles east of Johannesburg, McKay pulled the pick-up over to the side of the road and turned off the engine.

"Well," he said, "there it is."

Dan, still sitting in the pick-up, looked in the direction McKay was pointing but saw nothing but sagebrush and rocks. He climbed out of the car and looked at McKay somewhat apprehensively. "Where?" he asked and feeling a little bit foolish for asking.

McKay laughed, "Everyone always asks the same question. You won't find any footprints, except maybe mine. I mentioned the other evening I hiked to Red Mountain, but that's not the point. The Indians seldom used the trail after they were put on the reservations. But the desert doesn't heal rapidly, as you may already know. Scars, in the form of stunted sagebrush and displaced rocks, stepped on and kicked by thousands of feet over thousands of years, have left a trail eight to ten feet wide, and that is what you look for. Get your gear, and I'll walk with you a ways and show you what I mean."

Dan removed his gear from the pick-up, strapped on his revolver, and shouldered his pack and canteen. He followed McKay for about a quarter of a mile while McKay explained to him what he should look for. The not too obvious outline of the trail would be covered with stunted sagebrush and be fairly smooth when compared with the surrounding area. Dan began to notice the difference and nodded his understanding as McKay explained.

"If you lose the trail, and I'm sure you will, keep moving in a southeasterly direction, and you will find it again. Skirt west of the base of Red Mountain until you've passed it, then from the high ground, you will see Fremont Peak. Use Fremont Peak as the guide for your next leg. The trail passes about a mile east of Atolia, and the Tungsten mill will be visible from the trail. Five miles southeast of Fremont Peak you should spot the ore dump of Jim's claim. And as I said before, when you leave the claim the next morning and if Jim isn't there, walk south, and you will find the trail Jim uses to get to and from the spring."

McKay continued, "You will find the Old Indian Trail about a hundred yards west of the spring. Follow it in a south-easterly direction until you get to the railroad tracks. They run east and west, and it's about a twenty-mile hike. I suggest you follow the tracks to Barstow because I doubt if you can cross the Mojave River. The heavy snowpack in the mountains is melting, and water is flowing down the usually dry riverbed for the first time in seven or eight years. You may have to leave the tracks where they cross the river. If you do, stay north of the river until you come to the bridge that handles the traffic traveling to and from Las Vegas. It's only a couple of miles out of your way. That's about it, Dan. Have I confused you, or do you think you can make it?"

"You couldn't have done any better if you had given me a road map. You will never know how much I appreciate all you have done for me, John. At the moment I can't think of how I'm going to repay you, but I guarantee you, I will. And again, I thank you."

"No thanks necessary. I enjoyed doing it. Keep to the left of Fremont Peak, and you will be OK. Good luck, and I hope we will meet again. If you see Jim, say Hi to him for me."

They waved to each other, and Dan turned away and started down the trail.

John watched Dan's long quick strides as he moved down

the trail. His tall frame, over six feet, and slim 180 pounds, easily carried the fifty pounds of equipment.

I wonder if he is part Indian, thought McKay. The light, tan-colored skin, hawk nose, black hair, the brown eyes, and the way he walks, leads me to believe he may have some Indian blood. He sure is a handsome young man, and he has a great personality, too. John took one more look down the trail just as Dan turned and waived then disappeared behind a small hill. McKay stuck his hands in his hip pockets and began walking slowly back to his Model T.

Dan enjoyed the cool crisp morning air. He had walked less than a mile when he crossed over a small knoll and saw ahead the reddish hue of the oversized hill called Red Mountain. I'll pass it within the next hour, he thought.

The time and distance passed quickly. When he reached the south slope, he stopped to look back up the mountain. He stood several seconds, staring in amazement at the incredible sight before him. One solid field of asters blanketed the southern half of the mountain exactly as McKay had described. The sun by now had risen above the horizon, shining on the field of asters, adding to the magnificence of the spectacle.

Dan took in a deep breath and sighed. "There are millions," he whispered. "It is amazing how the seeds are able to remain dormant year after year and only bloom with such splendor when the desert moisture during the winter months is double the average or more." But there are many things about the Mojave Desert we don't understand, he thought. I remember the story about the shrimp in dry lakes that hatch out when heavy thunderstorms fill the lakes with water. The lakes dry out within a very short period of time, but the shrimp go through their complete life cycle of hatching, maturing, and laying their eggs in preparation for the next time the lake fills which may not happen for ten years or more.

Dan turned back to the task of following the trail. So far, it had not proved difficult. In many places, thunderstorms had washed away the trail's outline where it crossed arroyos, but he had been able to pick up the signs McKay had shown him when he reached the opposite side.

The town of Red Mountain, named for the mountain Dan had just passed, lay a mile west of the Old Indian Trail. The town had sprung up almost overnight around a mother lode of silver discovered the year before. As Dan hiked along the trail, he noticed how the huge steel derrick constructed over the mineshaft of the discovery, dominated the landscape and the town.

The strike had been named the Kelly Mine, and news of the discovery had quickly spread across the West. Dan had read about it in one of the San Francisco newspapers. The amount of silver being hauled to the surface from the shaft and the tunnels read like a story from the Arabian Nights. The amount would soon reach a million dollars, and no one could guess how many more millions lay below. While the fame of the Kelly mine had spread, the notoriety of the town that had grown up around the mine was also getting its share of publicity. Wild and wooly from what I've heard, Dan thought. A half dozen saloons sell bootleg whiskey across the bar by the drink or by the bottle. Professional gamblers and prostitutes operate in the saloons with no visible control by any law enforcement agency. There must be a big payoff to somebody pretty high up, he thought. Add to that, he thought, the shootings, the knife and fistfights, and you have a town that makes the Barbary Coast seem tame. No wonder they call it 'Sin City.' I'm not interested in the town, but if I come out this way again, I'm going to ask the boss if he can pull a few strings and get me permission to visit the mine. It should be an interesting experience to see what kind of rock formations yield that much silver.

Dan set aside his thoughts about the Kelly Mine and the town to concentrate on the Old Indian Trail. He passed fields of lupine and patches of desert candles, called squaw cabbage by the natives. I've heard the Indians used to strip the green leaves from the stalks of the desert candles and eat them raw or cooked, he thought, I wonder what they taste like? He reached down and pulled one of the leaves from below the purple blossom and chewed it. It tastes like spinach, he thought. I wonder how many more edible plants grow in the desert.

He found he could identify some of the flowers by their shape and color or because they resembled their domestic cousins. The curved blossom of the fiddleneck, for example, looked like the miniature neck of a violin and he didn't have to stretch his imagination to see the similarity between the flowers of the primrose and the larkspur, and those his mother grew in her flower garden. Then Dan stopped because he thought his eyes were deceiving him. It's hard to believe, he thought, that California Poppies grow in the middle of the Mojave Desert. He stared at the lacy leaves of three plants and the long stems rising from the center of each plant supporting the buds. The buds, closed during the night, were just beginning to unfurl their golden petals to greet the morning sun. Convinced he had properly identified the plants, he turned to look back up the trail before moving on. What a sight, he thought. The asters cover the south slope of Red Mountain like a huge colored canopy. It doesn't seem right, he thought, that in three or four weeks the hot desert winds will begin to blow and all of these marvelous desert plants will disappear and may not appear again for five or six years. During that time only the hardy sagebrush, cactuses, and the greasewoods will be able to withstand the heat, the harsh winters, and the desert winds.

Dan crossed a ravine, and when he climbed up the bank on the other side, he saw his next landmark off to the right, the tungsten mill in the town of Atolia. Dan recalled his trip to Atolia shortly before the United States entered the War. He had been sent there as a consultant to assist in the installation of new machinery in the mill. The mill operated 24 hours a day, seven days a week. Taking the mill out of production for any reason interrupted the steady flow of tungsten to the steel mills producing armaments, and huge profits from flowing into the pockets of the owners. Dan recalled, too, the ghostly silence that hung over the town during the period the mill had been shut down. The roar of the shot-put size steel balls, rolling and crushing the tungsten ore in giant steel pans, could be heard for miles. It was said that when the mill shut down, the people of Atolia talked in whispers in the eerie silence. Now that the War had ended, the tungsten mill, once a symbol of America's might and dedication to the War effort, lay idle. Atolia was rapidly fading into oblivion, and the corrugated sheet iron covering the mill appeared to be bleeding as the rust slowly ate the sheeting away, while broken skylight windows added to the mill's look of despair.

After passing Atolia, Dan continued his steady pace toward his next landmark, Fremont Peak. The Old Indian Trail wound between low hills, which once were hot lava flows, at times blocked his view. Two miles southeast of Atolia the trail moved out of the hills, and he could see the top of Fremont Peak about ten miles away. I should be east of Fremont Peak by one o'clock, he thought. It will be a good time to rest and have lunch before continuing on to the old prospector's claim.

The temperature had been rising steadily while the sun had

been moving toward the noon hour. Dan began to perspire and feel the effects of the desert heat. There is no point in wearing myself out, he thought. And he slowed his pace. I'm, roughly halfway to the claim. And if I do hurry, I may miss something worth seeing.

Dan passed several species of blooming cactus. The blossoms varied in color from the creamy white of the yucca to the rose of the tiny fishhook. Some yellow and orange blossoms appeared to be transparent. The blossoms are so delicate and beautiful, he thought, and most only last for a day. Yet, thousands of years were required by Mother Nature to develop the delicate but showy cactus blossoms.

He stopped to examine a snakeskin attached to cactus thorns.

I've heard, Dan thought, when snakes come out of hibernation and begin shedding their skins, they rub against cactus to help remove the skins. It may be true, but I doubt it. It seems more likely the snakes shed their skins, and when the wind blows they catch on the cactus. Perhaps, he thought, I should watch my step. From the stories I've read, snakes, and especially rattlers, are not very sociable when they are shedding.

The desert plant life had so absorbed Dan's attention, he did not realize he had wandered from the Old Indian Trail. He kept looking in the area where he thought it might be but gave up and checked his location by using Fremont Peak as his coordinate. He found he had moved too far west and began zigzagging in an easterly direction until he found the trail a quarter of a mile away.

It's a little embarrassing to lose your direction when you are an engineer, he thought. It may help if I'm a little more alert the rest of the trip. Then Dan smiled, there may be more to the 'Little People' Mrs. Reese talked about than I'm willing to admit. He slipped the canteen from his shoulder and drank a small amount before moving on.

Dan estimated two more miles should bring him to the north slope of Fremont Peak. He looked to the west, and seven miles away, he could see the tiny buildings of Fremont Station, the location of the railroad maintenance facility. He recalled the train stopping at the station to drop off supplies during his trip to Johannesburg. When the train pulled away from the station, the foreman, his wife, and a small boy waved goodbye.

I waved back, he recalled, and as I waved, I could not help thinking how lonely they must feel at times. Only three buildings, he thought, and one of those house the Mexican track workers who probably don't speak English.

The trail began to swing to the left and to the east of the mountain as Dan approached the north slope. Looking ahead, he spotted a huge boulder. It should provide a nice shady spot to rest and have lunch, he thought.

When he reached the rock, he found the winds had piled sand on the shady side. He removed his hat and gear and lay back on the sand for a few minutes to stretch his legs and rest his shoulders before eating. Leaning on one elbow, he opened his pack and removed one of the ham and cheese sandwiches Mrs. Reese had packed. He smiled as he thought of Mrs. Reese and her superstitions. Then he silently thanked her for all the nice things she had done for him. Dan finished his sandwich and ate an apple, then took a long drink from the canteen. I'll rest another fifteen minutes, he thought, then I'll hit the trail for the final jaunt to the old prospector's claim.

As he lay resting and looking across the tops of the sage and greasewood bushes, he saw buzzards circling in the area where he believed the old prospector's claim should be located.

He watched them soar and circle for a while. Then, he thought, I wonder if they have found something or are just searching.

I'll be over in that area before long. Maybe I'll find out.

He rose to his feet, shouldered his gear, and picked up his hat.

He saw two large desert tortoises as he walked toward the trail. They could not see each other because of the brush, yet they were lumbering toward each other. Their wrinkled necks, supporting their reptilian heads, were stretched skyward to the maximum as they walked flat-footed on their hind feet and pulled their bodies forward with their front toes and claws. Some instinct must be guiding them toward each other, Dan thought, how strange. The young engineer thought of them as turtles, the same used by the desert dwellers who loved these harmless reptiles, not tortoises, the name he had been taught in school.

Now, Dan thought, they are about fifteen feet apart and can see each other. They've stopped and appear to be glaring at one another. But it is spring, and it may be a look of love. Dan smiled. Are they going to fight or make love? I've never seen turtles do either. It should be interesting to see how they go about it with all that armor plate they carry around. I wish I had the time to stick around and find out. He gave his shoulder straps a tug and hitched his canteen to a more comfortable position, then resumed his trip.

Due east of Fremont Peak he crossed an arroyo and noticed mesquite bushes growing in the channel. Mesquite makes great firewood, he thought. I'll bet the old prospector gets his firewood from here. Picking up the trail on the opposite side of the arroyo turned out easier than Dan had expected. He followed it until he spotted the ore dump McKay had described.

There must be a side trail leading to the claim, Dan thought.

He reduced his stride and began watching for it. When he was about to give up, thinking that perhaps the old prospector had not always used the same route to get to his claim, he found it directly opposite the ore dump. I've found it, Dan thought, but it doesn't show signs of being used recently. He followed the trail to the claim and stopped at the foot of the ore dump. Cupping his hands together to form a megaphone, he put them to his mouth and shouted, "Hello, there." The place looked deserted, so Dan wasn't concerned when no one acknowledged his greeting.

He removed his gear, and as he was setting it down, he noticed a stake with a rope attached. It looks like a tether, Dan thought. His eyes automatically followed the rope, partially covered with dirt and sand, to a halter tied to the end of the rope. That's strange, he thought, halters are usually left on the animal. He walked over to the halter and picked it up, examined it, and saw the neck strap was broken. What could have happened? he thought. While studying the break, he rubbed the broken strap between his forefinger and thumb as if the feel of the worn leather might offer a solution. Frowning, he tossed the halter aside.

Still thinking about what he had seen, Dan walked back to his pack and pulled out his flashlight. He checked it to be sure it was working and walked up the ramp toward the tunnel entrance. Noticing the coffee pot on the stove, he stopped and lifted the lid and looked inside. The dry pot and the shriveled grounds told him the pot had not been used for a long time.

He turned and walked to the tunnel entrance and looked inside.

Rocks, large and small, littered the tunnel floor. Just inside the tunnel entrance lay a packsaddle and a set of saddlebags next to the tunnel wall. These and other supplies near the tunnel wall were half-buried under rocks and dust. Dan turned on his flashlight and began picking his way slowly through the rubble, flashing his light along the walls and the tunnel floor. The rocks increased in size and number as he worked his way deeper into the tunnel. His footsteps and the rocks he accidentally kicked echoed from the tunnel walls and the rear of the tunnel.

As he advanced, the beam of light began to pick up pieces of shattered timbers in the rubble. The young combat engineer's experience in France told him the debris scattered over the tunnel floor was the result of a strong explosion.

About thirty feet from the tunnel entrance a pile of rubble, mixed with splintered boards and broken timbers, blocked Dan's advance. He flashed the light over the mound and then across the top of the tunnel. The light exposed a cavity three feet wide and ten feet long in the top of the tunnel, directly over the mound. I can't tell much about the explosion from what I see here, thought Dan, except that it was a hefty one.

Knowing the explosion had weakened the tunnel ceiling, and any vibration could cause rocks to fall, Dan moved cautiously forward, running the light beam over the pile of rocks and timbers as he advanced. Now, only a few feet from it, the light found something near the base of the mound which had the appearance of being the sole and heel of a heavy shoe. A slight shiver ran through the young engineer's body. What could have happened? he thought. An accident? Suicide? Perhaps murder?

"Don't let your imagination get the best of you, Dan," he whispered. "It is probably just a shoe."

Dan stooped down and began to carefully remove the rocks

and shattered pieces of timbers covering the shoe. When he gently brushed away the last bits and pieces from the top of the shoe, he exposed dry, cracked skin stretched over a lower leg bone. "My God!" he whispered, "There is a body buried beneath this rubble."

The young engineer had seen death before, but it was an experience that always shocked him and one he could not brush off lightly. Each time it touched him, he felt deep sympathy for the person whose life had been lost. I wonder what happened, he thought. It can't be the body of anyone except that of the old prospector. It seems apparent because none of his equipment has been disturbed. There must have been an accident of some kind. But what about the broken halter and the disappearance of the burro? It is evident the old prospector didn't turn the burro loose. And most domestic animals will lie down and die when they become weak from hunger rather than trying to escape their confinement. Perhaps those saddlebags lying against the tunnel wall near the entrance contain the solution.

But I dare not disturb anything, I'll leave the solution to the authorities in Barstow. Dan began replacing the rocks and pieces of broken timbers over the shoe and leg to prevent any further damage to the old prospector's remains.

Dan completed the task and rose to his feet. He did not try to climb over the mound since he now thought of it as the old prospector's grave. It is strange how I feel about this since I have never met or known the old man, he thought. Dan flashed the light toward the back of the tunnel and judged it extended another thirty feet beyond the mound. He also estimated the amount of rock the old prospector had removed to advance the tunnel to that depth.

The old prospector had to work long and hard digging this

tunnel through solid rock, Dan thought. And from what I can see, the quartz looks very promising. He may have been on the verge of striking something profitable. Perhaps with my training, I could have helped him. How sad, his life had to end this way, Dan thought.

Before leaving the tunnel, Dan turned his light overhead to take a final look at the cavity blown out by the explosion. For the first time, he noticed the fault that cut through the tunnel.

It must be the fault John mentioned, Dan thought.

John said the old prospector had been in the process of shoring it up the last time he passed through here. It appears the explosion occurred under it and blew out the timbers that shored up the fault. The shoring had to be the source of the shattered timbers scattered along the tunnel floor.

But why, the young engineer thought, should an explosive charge that strong be discharged, or go off accidentally, directly under the fault? I don't think it would be wise for me to try to guess based on the meager information I have been able to gather.

While these thoughts were going through Dan's mind, he had been examining the huge cavity as well as the fault. The beam reflected a glitter from a point near the fault that caused him to take a second look. The glow reflected from the light startled him because he knew it was gold. He moved the light along the length of the cavity and saw the vein of gold ran from one end of the top of the cavity to the other, broken only by the fault. Although it disappeared at the end of the cavity, the young engineer knew it continued deep into the hill, how far could not be determined without further development of the claim.

He continued to stare in awe at the bright yellow gold glittering in the flashlight beam and tried to guess the amount of wealth the claim might yield. I'm positive it will develop into a rich strike, he thought. And I wonder who will inherit the claim? This much gold and the mystery that surrounds the old prospector's death is a combination that is bound to breed skulduggery.

Then he turned his light to the mound of debris and thought of the old man lying beneath it. His eyes blurred, and he said aloud as if he were calling someone to correct a grievous error, "If only he had started the tunnel three feet higher." His voice echoed, "HIGHER, higher," from beyond the old man's grave. The echoes sounded to the young engineer like cries of sympathy for the old prospector.

3

THE AUTHORITIES

Dan shook his head from side to side as he slowly picked his way through the rocks and shattered timbers toward the tunnel entrance. This has been the most unusual series of events I have ever encountered, he thought. First, the broken halter, then the evidence of a powerful explosion, the discovery of what I presume are the remains of the old prospector, and finally, the rich vein of gold exposed by the explosion. It seems unreal and incomprehensible the explosion that killed the old man could have, at the same time, uncovered the riches he had been searching for all of his life. It is unbelievable any one person could have had such terrible luck. How can fate be so cruel?

Dan stopped beside the canvas-covered cot he had noticed near the tunnel entrance. He shook off his depressing thoughts about the old prospector and examined the cot. Sleeping on this cot, he thought, will sure beat sleeping on this rock ore dump with nothing under me but a piece of canvas and a blanket. He reached down and turned the cot on its side and dumped the rocks and gravel blown there by the explosion. Then he shook the cot to remove the dust and carried it outside the tunnel and set it next to the shoring.

I know I won't be able to block out all of my thoughts about the old man and the events that apparently took place inside the tunnel but sleeping out here will help.

After getting his bed ready, Dan walked over to the stove and noticed a short-handled shovel with a broken blade lying beside it. Using the shovel, he began cleaning out the firebox. When he finished, he looked at the shovel. It appears it has been used for this purpose before. He started a fire by shaving tender from a board splintered by the blast then adding dry sage bush roots. As soon as the fire began to blaze, he added mesquite wood from the small pile the old prospector had not used.

Dan recalled John's suggestion while cleaning the coffee pot that he ask Mrs. Reese to include a bag of coffee with his sandwiches. I did not realize how much I would be looking forward to a hot cup of coffee. It is sure to improve the taste of those cold sandwiches. He finished cleaning the coffee pot and walked over by his bed to get his canteen. When he reached down to pick it up, he spotted the old prospector's Dutch oven in a wooden box under a homemade table. He walked over and lifted it from the box. Why should I eat cold sandwiches when I can heat them in this Dutch oven? he thought. Then he thought, Should I feel guilty about using the old prospector's equipment? I am sure if he were alive, he would not mind. I have learned through the years that I have had the good fortune of knowing and working with miners and prospectors how friendly they are. I only wish I had had the opportunity of meeting this old prospector they called 'Jim.' I'm sure he had many experiences I would have enjoyed listening to.

I'll get the sandwiches ready while the coffee is heating, he thought. And since my water supply is limited, I hope I don't have to scour the Dutch oven. He removed the lid and smiled.

This is a surprise, he thought, if I wipe out the dust with one of the sandwich wrappers, it will be ready to put on the stove.

The old man must have been neat and well organized from what I have seen of his equipment. It is clean and stored out of the work area but easily accessible.

Dan glanced toward the West. The sun has just about done its job for the day, but not quite, he thought. Those clouds hovering over the horizon have the makings of another glorious sunset. Dan stood up, and as he watched, the sun slid slowly below the horizon showering the clouds with yellow, orange, and pink. Then the twilight deepened to dusk, and the colors slipped away like ghosts into the approaching darkness.

As Dan turned back to the stove, he caught the aroma of the boiling coffee. It doesn't take long for the desert to cool after the sun sets, he thought, and the coffee will be exactly what I'll need to dull the chill. I'll bet it will taste twice as good as it smells, too, he thought. I'll borrow one of the old prospector's tin cups, and while the coffee is cooling down, I'll get the sandwiches ready.

He decided on two roast beef. After cutting them in half, he Arranged them in the bottom of the Dutch oven, replaced the lid, and put the oven on the stove. Checking the remaining sandwiches, he saw he had one roast beef, two ham and cheese, and one strawberry, two apples and some oatmeal cookies. This evening, he thought, I'll have an apple and a couple of cookies for dessert.

Dan sipped his coffee while repacking the remaining food in the paper bag, checking the Dutch oven every minute or two until the sandwiches were hot. When they were ready, he carried the Dutch oven over to his bunk and set it on a nearby dynamite box. Now, he thought, I'll warm my coffee, get my apple and cookies, and I'll be ready to eat.

After eating, he wiped out the Dutch oven, put the sack of food inside, and covered it with the lid. Now, he thought, if there are any varmints around, they will have a tough time trying to get my food.

Dan turned his cot around so he could lean against the shoring. Then he poured himself a fresh cup of coffee and tossed some wood on the fire. It's too early to turn in for the night, he thought, so I'll stretch out for a while and relax. He removed his boots and lifted his feet up on the cot then moved back where he could lean against the shoring. After pulling a blanket up over his feet, he picked up the coffee cup and held it with both hands feeling the warmth and leaned back.

While sipping his coffee, his thoughts returned to the old prospector. I'll bet the old fellow sat here just as I am doing while watching the stars. I wonder what kind of thoughts he had. I wonder, too, what he would have done with all the wealth he would have received from this strike? It doesn't appear to be a mother lode, but from my superficial observations, it should yield a small fortune for someone. Once the word gets out about this strike, people will be swarming over these hills like flies over an open sardine can. And that concerns me, Dan thought. If I mention gold to anyone in Barstow tomorrow, the word will spread like the plague and do just about as much harm. Some could even beat the authorities out there. I'll give it more thought while I'm hiking to Barstow. But now, I feel very strongly I should not mention it, I should let the authorities decide when and what to do when they discover it.

My coffee is cold, Dan thought, as he took a final sip.

I'll slip on my boots and tend to nature before turning in for the night. As he stood on the side of the dump, the yip of the coyotes suddenly broke the silence. I've got company, Dan thought. He buttoned up his pants and turned and looked toward the southwest. They must be over by the spring. John said it was over in that general direction. The yipping and howling again split the cold night air. Dan felt a shiver run down his spine. I don't know of anyone who doesn't get goose-bumps when he or she hears a coyote tuning up. I hope they don't keep it up all night.

The Coyotes woke Dan up at dawn. I must have been worn out not to have heard them last night, he thought. However, I guess I owe them one for waking me up early. The desert mornings in the early desert spring can be pretty nippy, I hope I can get my clothes on without freezing to death. He quickly slipped on his shirt and pulled on his whip-cord trousers then pulled on his boots, laced them, and pulled his trouser legs down over the top of his boots. Hot coffee will never taste better than it will this morning.

While waiting for the coffee to boil, Dan removed the sack of food from the Dutch oven and selected a ham and cheese, and a jam sandwich, plus an apple for his breakfast. Then he closed the bag and placed it by his knapsack. He returned to the table, cut the sandwiches, and arranged them in the Dutch oven as he had the night before.

It will take another ten minutes for the coffee to boil, he thought. In the meantime, I'll start packing. I hope I can get to Barstow early enough this evening to make my report so I can catch the morning train to Oakland.

By the time he had finished assembling his pack, the coffee was boiling. The coffee and the sandwiches were ready at the same time. Dan filled the tin cup with coffee, picked up the Dutch oven and carried both to the table, and began eating.

When he finished, he used the last of his water to clean the utensils he had used, then he replaced them in the box and returned them to the location under the table where he had found them. Next, he moved the cot back into the tunnel. While I'm in the tunnel, he thought, I feel I should return and pay my final respects to the old prospector. But I won't because I might do something that could interfere with the investigation. He left the tunnel and began strapping on his gear.

Although somewhat dim from two years of desert winds, Dan easily found the trail leading to the spring. Burro droppings along the way added to the ease of following it. The old man must have packed in water every day to have left a trail this visible, he thought.

He reached the spring in less than 30 minutes and saw with some amazement, the stream of crystal-clear water about the size of a pencil, flowing into the basin and over the side then disappearing into the desert sand leaving only a small wet spot in the dry desert sand. Looking around, he saw and recognized fresh coyote tracks and stools. They were here last night, he thought. This must be their watering hole. I'll bet the old prospector heard them many times serenading the moon when they gathered here.

Dan set the empty canteen by the spring and removed his pack, then he filled his canteen directly from the stream flowing into the basin. John said the spring should provide plenty of water, and it will, Dan thought. He looked at the moss. Whoever comes out here to investigate the death of the old prospector, will have to come by horseback. I don't think they can make it in one day, so the horses will need water. My guess is that under this moss lies a foot of mud. If I can find something to scoop it out, it should provide the officials with adequate water. After searching for two or three minutes, he found a rusty coffee can beneath a greasewood bush. But before disturbing the water, he removed his jacket and shirt and washed his hands, arms, and face. Then he began cleaning out the basin. By the time he had finished, his watch had shown a few minutes after eight. I hadn't planned to lose this much time, he thought, but I think it was time well spent. Now, to strap on my pack and get started.

An hour after he left the spring, the decaying volcanic hills and the greasewoods had disappeared leaving the desert more barren and desolate, broken only by gently rising sandhills formed by the strong desert winds. A few low, round sage bushes, the same color as the sand, scattered among the sandhills, struggled for survival. Now and then a spiny cactus could be seen which had joined the struggle.

The winds have blown away the Old Indian Trail, Dan thought. When I lose it, I am spending too much time looking for it. The situation has changed since I discovered the old prospector, and my priorities have also changed. Hiking the Old Indian trail doesn't seem as important as it did yesterday.

At the rate I am· going, it will be dark when I reach Barstow. I've got to strike out on my own. I'll hike in the general direction I think the trail should follow, and as long as I keep going, I'll eventually come to the railroad tracks. I'd like to have a compass, but the sun will do. It is 1:15, and I don't know how many miles I've traveled. I do know I have lost at least an hour doubling back and forth trying to find the Old Indian Trail when I have lost it.

The heavy sand shortened Dan's stride and slowed his pace.

An hour after striking out on his own, he crossed over the

top of a small rise and looked down on what appeared to be a large lake directly ahead. He judged it to be about five miles away. I don't recall John mentioning a lake, Dan thought. Perhaps it is a mirage. It is hot, and the sun does strange things to your vision in the desert. He lowered his pack and unscrewed the lid from his canteen. While looking at the lake, he took a long drink then lowered the canteen and replaced the lid. Since I have stopped trying to follow the Trail, it is hard to say how far I have wandered from it. I'll have to presume it is just another dry lake and John didn't think it was important enough to mention it. The Trail may cut directly across it. The best way to find out is to hike down there and have a look.

As he drew near, he could see it was a dry lakebed, but he could not tell if the lake contained water or if he saw a mirage. Now he was near enough to see the cracked curled chips of dry clay, but a hundred yards from the edge of the lake, the clay chips turned to mud, and beyond the mud, water covered the center of the lake. And as Dan watched, the desert winds pushed tiny waves over the shallow water.

This is a big dry lake, Dan thought. It must cover over ten square miles. I wonder how long it will be before it completely dries up. I wish I had more time to spend here, it would be a good place to eat lunch, but I have to get moving. I'll wait until I reach the railroad tracks before I stop to eat. Now, which way should I go to get by the lake? My best bet is to go south toward the railroad tracks. The sooner I reach the railroad tracks, the sooner I will get out of this loose sand, and I can make better time.

Dan headed south and a half an hour later, he heard a train whistle. He walked up on a small knoll and saw the toy-like train, about four miles away, traveling toward Barstow. As Dan's eyes moved ahead of the train, he spotted a group of trees about six or seven miles to the southeast, equally divided on both sides of the tracks. I not only see trees, Dan thought, I can also make outbuildings scattered among them. It has to be the town of Hinkley. It was the only place the train stopped between Barstow and Kramer Junction on my trip to Johannesburg. I'll set my sights on Hinkley instead of hiking south to the train tracks, but I'll have a drink before I start.

As Dan picked his way through the sage bushes, the afternoon winds spawned mini cyclones called whirlwinds by the natives. Although harmless, they carried considerable energy. Observing them as he hiked, Dan thought, They push the dust and dried twigs from the sagebrush thousands of feet into the air. I wonder how they generate that much energy?

When Dan finally reached the road that led through the center of town, he checked his watch. It's 3:20, he thought. I'll stop and have a sandwich and then continue on. Maybe I'll get lucky and catch a ride on the way in. If I don't, I doubt if I will get there in time to make my report.

As he approached the first house, a large mongrel dog with characteristics that claimed no heritage, trotted out emitting halfhearted barks. A smaller, more aggressive white terrier with one black ear, bounced up and down but stayed behind the larger dog while pouring out a continuous barrage of high-pitched yips, then other dogs in the neighborhood felt the need to join in the chorus. Dan glanced at the apparent home of the two dogs and caught a glimpse of a woman's face just as she pulled together her window curtains, however, she made no effort to call off the dogs. Dan did not break his stride, and eventually, the dogs became bored and turned back.

He continued along the dirt road until he came to a wooden building with a General Store sign painted on the false front. He stopped by one of the posts supporting the wooden cover and stepped up on the boardwalk. Two elderly men sat on a bench facing the road next to the store entrance. One of the men looked up and said, "Howdy." The other glanced up at Dan's campaign hat but did not speak. He stood up, walked over to the edge of the boardwalk, squirted a stream of tobacco juice out on the dirt road, and returned to the bench and sat down. Ignoring Dan, the two men resumed their conversation.

In the meantime, Dan had set his canteen on the boardwalk next to the store entrance, slipped off his shoulder straps, and was about to set the backpack down next to the canteen when a half-grown pup with short yellow hair came squirming around the corner of the store and sidled up to Dan, wagging his tail and rubbing against Dan's leg while eyeing his pack. Dan looked down at the dog and decided it would be a mistake to leave the pack outside. He slung the canteen back over his shoulder, opened the screen door, and stepped inside. Blinded momentarily in the dimly lit store, he stopped inside just as a voice from the rear yelled, "Get out of here, you yellow mongrel!"

Startled by the voice and something pushing hard on his legs, Dan looked down and the yellow dog banging his head against the screen trying to get out. Dan's eyes, now adjusting to the light, saw the source of the yelling getting up from a desk in the back of the store, a man of medium height, bald, and wearing glasses.

"I'm sorry, stranger, I didn't mean to startle you. That dog seems to know when anyone anywhere near this store is planning to come inside. I feel sorry for him, but he is a pest, I keep hoping someone will adopt him and get him out of my hair." He rubbed his bald head and laughed, "Not that I've got much left. Now, what can I do for you?"

Grinning, Dan replied, "When you yelled, for a moment I

thought I was the yellow dog, then I felt something banging against my leg and saw it was the dog trying to get out through the screen door." After letting the dog out, Dan walked over to the counter and replied, "I came in here to buy a cold drink, a Coca-Cola if you have one."

"Sure thing, right off the ice." Walking over to the large icebox, he asked, "Did you come in from Bakersfield or Barstow?"

"Neither, I hiked in over the Old Indian Trail from Johannesburg."

"I've heard of it but often wondered whether it really existed. A person hears so many stories about Indians and gold mines, I find it difficult to separate the real McCoy from make-believe." Holding up the Coke, he asked, "Do you want it opened?"

"Yes, please." Dan had set his gear on the floor next to the counter, and he reached over the counter for the bottle.

Then the man behind the counter introduced himself. "My name is MacDonald, but everyone around here calls me 'Mac.'" He held out his hand and continued, "I know it is none of my business, but what induced you to hike all the way from Johannesburg and I won't be offended if you say that your reasons are personal."

Dan replied without getting into any of the details. "The reason, as someone said, 'Because it is there.' A couple of people whom I met while I was in Randsburg on an engineering project, suggested that if I were interested in making the trip, this was one of the best years and the best time of year to travel it. And that is the reason, Mr. MacDonald. By the way, Sir, I haven't eaten since this morning. Do you mind if I grab a sandwich out of my bag and wash it down with this Coke?"

"Not at all," he replied. A woman had just opened the screen door kicking the dog outside as she entered, and MacDonald excused himself to wait on her.

While eating his sandwich, Dan looked around the store and saw two Coleman gasoline lanterns hanging from the ceiling. Enough, he thought, to light a store of this size.

Checking the merchandise, he noticed the store's stocks consisted mostly of staples and these only in small quantities. But he could also see tables along the walls with small stacks of Levi pants, blue work shirts, straw hats, and a limited supply of other dry goods.

Dan had finished his sandwich and was munching on an apple when MacDonald walked up. Before taking another bite, Dan commented, "I had better get going if I intend to get to Barstow before everything closes down. I have business I want to take care of today because I need to catch an early train tomorrow morning for San Francisco. If I don't get it done today, it means I'll have to wait and do it tomorrow morning." Dan slid off the counter where he had been sitting and started to pick up his equipment.

MacDonald interrupted Dan's thoughts by saying, "Dan, if you don't mind waiting around for about 20 minutes, you are welcome to ride into Barstow with me. I have to pick up some supplies and a few special orders for people living in the neighborhood, and we should arrive there shortly after four."

"I certainly would appreciate a ride, Sir. Unless I am lucky enough to catch a ride along the way, I doubt if I can get to Barstow much before six. What about your store, do you close it before you leave?"

"No, my wife takes over. Normally, I leave in the morning and get back before noon, but my wife had to attend a town meeting this morning, and I am not much of a meeting man.

She loves it, so everything works out for both of us. She won't be alone; we have a high school boy who helps us in the late afternoons."

A few minutes later, MacDonald's wife arrived, and he introduced her to Dan. While MacDonald was getting the car ready, she inquired about his business, where he lived, and what he was doing in this area. Dan could tell by the way she walked and the way she talked, she had twice as much energy and curiosity as two people, but he found he liked her and enjoyed talking to her. Before he could finish answering all of her questions, he heard the car drive up, so he excused himself, picked up his gear, and said goodbye.

When he opened the screen door, he pushed the dog aside, and looking up, he saw MacDonald pumping gasoline into a Model T pickup from a hand-operated pump in front of the store. He tossed his gear into the back of the pickup then walked over to the gasoline pump just as MacDonald withdrew the nozzle from the tank and hung it back on the pump.

"We will be ready to go as soon as I check with my wife for any last-minute instructions."

"I'll replace the cap and the seat," Dan offered. "Thanks," MacDonald replied.

After replacing the cap and the seat, Dan moved to the front of the truck to crank the engine when MacDonald returned.

Dan did not mention the old prospector or the mine on their way to Barstow. The fewer people who know, the fewer problems the authorities will have, he reasoned. He opened the conversation by commenting on the large number of small farms they were passing. "I never noticed all these farms when I passed through here by train. It must take a considerable amount of water to irrigate all of the crops."

"It does," replied MacDonald. "The water comes from the underground river that generally follows the dry Mojave Riverbed. Normally, the farmers strike water at about fifty to a hundred feet, but the water level is higher now because surface water is flowing down the Mojave Riverbed."

"John McKay, an elderly man whom I met in Randsburg, told me he had heard the news about water flowing down the Mojave River," commented Dan. "He also said surface water flowing down the Mojave is so rare, people flock down to the banks of the river to watch it flow by."

"Yes, they do. The river is vital to the farmers, and to the communities as well, which have sprung up nearby. During long droughts, the water level drops, and when it does, the farmers suffer the most because it costs them more to pump water. Alfalfa hay is one of their major crops, and growing alfalfa requires lots of water. Yes, Dan, people who live along the river really get excited when the Mojave River flows because they know their water supply is being replenished."

"I noticed quite a few tank cars parked on the railway sidings at Hinkley. Are they used to haul water?" Dan asked.

"Yes, Hinkley supplies water to the railroad maintenance stations up and down the railroad line for hundreds of miles that do not have wells. Supplying water is what keeps Hinkley alive, that, and the maintenance we do on the water tank cars." MacDonald laughed, "And it keeps my family alive, too."

They passed a school bus parked by a road leading to a farmhouse. The bus had just dropped off a student who was walking up the road toward the farmhouse. MacDonald remarked, "That is the Barstow High School bus returning students to their homes along the route from Barstow to Hinkley."

The two men continued their light conversation until they

crossed the Mojave River bridge on the north side of Barstow. Dan commented on the amount of water flowing under the bridge.

Then after crossing the bridge and traveling another half mile, they crossed the viaduct which carried them over the railroad tracks into the business section of Barstow.

Dan asked MacDonald to drop him off at one of the hotels.

"I'm not particular which one as long as it is clean, and it has a bathtub. I feel like I haven't had a bath in a month."

MacDonald acknowledged the request and drove the pickup up the main street and parked in front of a two-story building. An overhead sign identified it as a hotel. "I think they will take care of you here, Dan. I send them a customer occasionally."

"Thank you, Mr. MacDonald, please let me pay you for your trouble." Dan had pulled a five-dollar bill from his shirt pocket and held it out to MacDonald.

MacDonald held up his hand with the palm facing Dan. "No, Dan, I had to make this trip, and I enjoyed our chat. If you are out this way again and have the time, please stop by for a visit. We are located off the beaten track. Consequently, we seldom have the opportunity to visit with someone from one of the big cities. Good luck on your return trip."

Dan returned the bill to his shirt pocket and thanked him as they shook hands. Then he stepped out on the sidewalk, removed his gear from the truck, and waved goodbye.

When Dan entered the hotel lobby, a middle-aged man with thinning hair, slightly on the heavy side, and wearing glasses, greeted him from behind the hotel desk. "What can I do for you, Sir?"

"A room with a bath." The clerk eyed Dan's pack as he walked over to the desk, then turned the register around for

Dan to sign. While signing, Dan asked, "Where is the police station located?"

An inquisitive look crossed the clerk's face, but he immediately regained his composure. Pointing in the general direction where he wanted Dan to go, he said, "when you walk out of the hotel, turn right and walk to the second intersection and again turn right. Keep walking toward the railroad yards until you see a sign hanging over the constable's office door."

The clerk turned the register and glanced at the signature and address. "San Francisco." He selected a key from one of the pigeonholes and said, "This way, Mr. Sanders," and began walking up the stairs but did not offer to carry Dan's pack. When they reached the room, the clerk unlocked the door, and Dan stepped in. He thanked the clerk but did not offer him a tip. He closed the door and set his gear against the wall. The clerk had turned on the electric lights but had not offered to pull the window drapes. Dan walked over, pulled opened the drapes, and raised the window. Nice view, he thought, the railroad yards, the passenger depot, and beyond that, the Mojave River.

He turned away from the window and walked into the bathroom. The bathtub looks inviting, he thought, but I don't have the time. Since I don't know how late the constable's office stays open, I'll put on a clean shirt and bathe later.

It took Dan about fifteen minutes to find the constable's office. He pushed the door open and stepped inside. A low varnished wooden rail fence separated the visitors' area from the three desks behind the fence. A heavy-set man with a dead cigar stub clenched between his teeth in the corner of mouth sat at one of the desks. A star-shaped badge marked, DEPUTY, hung from his shirt pocket. The other two desks were not occupied.

The deputy looked up as Dan approached the fence. "What can I do for you?" he asked.

"I would like to speak to the constable," Dan replied. "The constable is out of town and won't return until tomorrow. If it is not too personal, perhaps I can help."

Since the deputy had not removed the cigar from his mouth, Dan had difficulty understanding the words hissing through his clenched teeth.

"What I have to say is not personal. It pertains to a human body I found on my way here from Randsburg."

The deputy immediately removed the cigar from his mouth and placed it in an ashtray stacked with several other stubs. He pushed his heavy body from the chair and stepped over to the fence and opened the gate for Dan. "Step inside and have a chair. I'll have to get a statement from you and fill out a form for the investigation." He pointed to a chair next to his desk where he wanted Dan to sit. Then the deputy sat down and removed a form from one of the desk drawers. "Now," he remarked, "let's get started."

The deputy identified himself as William Lomac. He lit another cigar and began asking Dan questions and filling out the form. When he had completed the task, he asked Dan to review it and sign it. Dan reviewed the document, signed it, and handed it back to the deputy.

"Now I will need a map," the deputy commented. "I want it to be as accurate as you can make it of the claim's location. Since we do not have jurisdiction outside the limits of Barstow, the constable or I will contact the sheriff's office in San Bernardino tomorrow and turn the report over to them. A map will be a big help and save time."

"I have included the location of a spring," Dan said, as he handed the map to the deputy. "It is about a mile from the claim. Since there are no roads, I cleaned out the basin at the foot of the spring because the claim can only be reached by walking or by horseback. I'm sure horses will be used, and they will need water. I believe it will take at least two days to ride out, make the investigation, and ride back. I assume those who make the trip will also take a pack animal. The spring should provide ample water for two men· and three animals." Then Dan asked, "Is there anything else I can do, or is there any other way I can be of assistance?"

Before replying, the deputy examined the map. "No, not a thing at the moment. I have your address, if I need you, I'll let you know. That will be all for now." He thanked Dan, but without enthusiasm, and he did not offer to shake hands.

He isn't the friendliest person I have ever met, Dan thought, as he pushed back his chair and stood up. He turned and walked through the fence gate then through the office door without looking back.

He returned to the hotel and took his long-overdue bath.

By the time he had finished, it was after six o'clock. I'll walk over to the train station and verify my train time and eat at the Harvey House. As I recall, the train leaves about seven o'clock. If the train has a dining car, I'll have breakfast on the train and kill some time. It is a long ride, he thought.

That evening, he repacked his equipment to form a satchel using the rope to make a handle. A satchel will be easier to store on the train, he thought.

The next morning, he woke up a 5:30, dressed, and walked to the train station. His train had arrived, and the early rising passengers were having breakfast at the Harvey House. He checked with the train attendant and verified the train included a dining car. I'll board now, he thought, and get settled down before the other passengers return then I'll wait until the train has been on the road for an hour before I have breakfast.

He had finished storing his gear in the overhead rack before the other passengers began returning. A short time later the train began to move and snake its way through the railroad yards and onto the San Francisco mainline. He recognized Hinkley when the train flashed by. A busboy passed by ringing his chime and announcing breakfast was being served, but Dan decided to wait a while longer before eating. The train passed through Kramer Junction and was well on its way to the town of Mojave before he decided he had waited long enough. He checked his luggage to be sure it was secure then he walked through the swaying passenger cars to the diner. The head waiter greeted him and led him to a table next to a window. The table had not been completely cleared, and he apologized to Dan for the few seconds he had to wait. A waiter stood by until Dan had been seated then he handed Dan a menu and waited for Dan to order.

While waiting for his breakfast, Dan's thoughts returned to the old prospector and the claim. I'm sure I did the right thing by not mentioning the gold to anyone, but only time will tell, he thought. In the meantime, I'll keep in touch through the newspapers. Something should show up in a few days. In addition to the Chronicle, I'll also pick up the Examiner. I'm sure Hearst will never let a gold discovery slip by unreported regardless of how insignificant the strike might appear. He will never forget the Hearst fortune started with the Comstock.

After breakfast, Dan bought a newspaper from the butcher and returned to his seat. I'll sit down and relax for a while and catch up on the news.

Although the route Dan traveled was generally referred to as the San Francisco route, the San Francisco passengers terminated their trip in Oakland. The passengers then boarded the ferry at the Oakland Ferry Terminal and were transported across the bay to the San Francisco Terminal where streetcars, buses, and taxis carried them to their final destination. Dan called for a taxi to carry him to his bachelor's apartment.

After climbing the steps to his door on the second floor and setting his equipment inside, Dan walked directly to his phone and called his supervisor, Dick Hammeric. He listened while the operator dialed the number then heard the click of the receiver being picked up, followed by Hammeric's voice, "Hello?"

"Hi, Dick, this is Dan."

"When did you get in, Dan?"

"I haven't been home for more than about two minutes, but I arrived in Oakland about two hours ago. As usual, I came over by ferry. I called to tell you I'll be in the office tomorrow morning at the regular time. Did anything important happen while I was away?"

"No, nothing around the office; however, a cave-in occurred at one of the big mines near Auburn. One miner was killed, and another received a broken leg • The shoring collapsed in one of the tunnels. We were asked to send someone up to inspect the shoring in the other active tunnels, so we sent Jerry. He should finish up by tomorrow. Most of the new jobs coming in have been small, requiring no more than three or four days. As you know, our big project is the new gold ore reduction mill we have in the works in South Africa. We are trying to meet our mid-May target date for completing the design and engineering package and sending it to their corporate headquarters for evaluation. We may have to burn a little midnight oil on it, so we plan on assigning you to the project as soon as you have wrapped up the Yellow Aster

Project. Speaking of the Yellow Aster, what is your opinion of the Yellow Aster dump? From the pictures I've seen, it is big enough but is there any way we can profitably extract mineral from it?"

"Not unless the assays from the ore samples I shipped into you before I left turn up something. Any time or money spent on the project would be about as profitable as pouring money into a salted mine. I climbed over the dump from top to bottom and from one side to the other. And as you said, 'It is BIG.' From what I could see, it is rock, and nothing but rock. Granted, a few pieces of good ore may have slipped by but very few. A twenty-unit stamp mill is located on the perimeter openings of the shafts and the tunnels. From what I saw and from what I heard from the mine superintendent, his skeleton crew, and any of the old-timers who were still around who had worked for the Yellow Aster, any rock that looked like it might contain mineral was tossed into the stamp mill when the mine shut down. I may be exaggerating a bit, but I'm sure you get the point." Hammeric comments that he gets the point and Dan continues. "There is a possibility that ore of some value may lie beneath the dump. Before the stamp mill was installed, the ore had to be shipped out for milling, and as you know, shipping ore is expensive. Consequently, the owners were more concerned with shipping the higher grade than the lower grade. Therefore, the lower grade may have wound up in the dump. There is no way of knowing unless we run expensive drill tests or physically remove the rock. Either way will cost money. I'll calculate the costs and include them in my report. I'll wind up my report on Monday, and if you can arrange it, I'll brief the staff on Tuesday."

"It sounds OK to me, Dan; and by the way, in your telegram, you asked for a delay in route. Since you did not explain why my curiosity has been out of control. If it is not too personal, would you mind filling me in? My first thought pictured you being snared by a beautiful desert queen. My second thought told me I was probably wrong because most of us have come to the conclusion you are a confirmed bachelor."

Dan laughed, "Unfortunately, I did not meet a desert queen, and don't make any bets I am a confirmed bachelor. My delay en route is a long story, Dick, but I'll try to make it short. While working in Randsburg, I heard about an old Indian trail that originated up on the east side of the Sierras and ended at the Mojave River west of Barstow. Most of it has disappeared, but some of it is still visible between Johannesburg and the Mojave River, and I decided to hike it. It turned out to be a trip I shall never forget. Someday, I'll fill you in on the details, but you will have to be in the mood for listening. Just to whet your appetite, I found the body of someone near the trail, and I am quite sure it was the body of an old prospector. The old-timers in Randsburg who knew him had suggested I stop by his claim and spend the night. Finding the body deeply disturbed me because I had been looking forward to meeting him."

"Yes, Dan, I am sure it was disturbing. Sally and I will have you over for dinner some evening, and you can fill us in on the rest of the story. What a trip that must have been. I know you are tired so I'll say goodnight, and I will see you in the morning. Thanks for calling, Dan."

Dan replied, "My pleasure, Dick," and hung up the phone.

"It is getting late," Dan thought, "but I'm hungry. I'll clean up and catch the trolley down to the bay. I've missed having a good seafood dinner."

Officially, the consulting firm's offices opened at 8:00AM and closed at 5:00PM. Because of the staggered hours the engineers worked, each one carried keys to the office building and to the entrance to the consulting firm's offices which occupied most of the third floor.

Dan arrived and entered the firm's offices shortly before seven. Following the custom of the first person to arrive, Dan set up the coffee urn. He had poured his first cup and had started sorting and reviewing his notes when the other employees began to trickle in. The engineering firm's payroll averaged 30 engineers, 10 draftsmen, and 10 clerical personnel. Consequently, all knew each other and most of each other's personal business. Those passing by Dan's office, which was seldom closed, stopped to welcome him back and inquire about his trip. Joel Blake, one of the engineers, stopped and extended his mug of coffee towards Dan. "You make a great cup of coffee, Dan, it is a pleasure to have you back." He grinned and started to leave.

Dan laughed, but before Joel could turn away, Dan returned the barb loud enough for his neighbors to hear, "Someday, if we should live so long, maybe we will have the great honor of tasting a cup of your coffee." Dan looked back at his notes and slowly shook his head from side to side. His smile lingered, and he thought, sometimes I wonder about this place.

The firm officially closed at noon on Saturdays, but Dan continued working until 3:00PM. I haven't seen my parents for over a month, he thought. I'll run by the apartment and give them a call, and if they are in, I'll catch the train to Sacramento and spend the night with them.

Dan returned to San Francisco Sunday evening. Monday morning, while drinking a cup of coffee, he searched the Chronicle for news about the old prospector and the gold strike. It is a bit early, he thought. The news may not appear before Wednesday. However, on his way to the office, he picked up an Examiner but found nothing. Tuesday morning, he followed the same routine with the same results.

By 9:00AM Tuesday morning, Dan had finished his report and briefing charts and notified Hammeric he was ready. The briefing covered in detail the summary he had given Hammeric over the phone; his conclusions and recommendations were the same.

After Dan had finished his briefing, George Conrad, the president, and owner of the firm congratulated Dan and instructed him to put a package together which would include copies of the report, the briefing charts, and a letter of transmittal to the company that had contracted for the study. The letter, thanking the company for their business, would include an offer to send Dan, if requested, to brief and answer questions concerning the project which may not have been answered to their satisfaction in the report.

The next morning Dan hurried downstairs and picked up his paper. There should be something in here today, he thought. He unfolded the paper while walking slowly up the stairs and glancing over the headlines. When he reached the kitchen, he poured himself a cup of coffee, and drew a chair to the small table. After turning the paper's pages to the business section, he began checking each news item but found nothing. On his way to work, Dan picked up an Examiner, but again, he found nothing.

As soon as Dick Hammeric had completed his morning assignments, he called Dan into his office and brought him up to date on the South African Project. "As you know, Dan, the new mineral extraction and recovery system we are installing in the mill has never been tested commercially, but it looks great on the drawing board. We have decided to put your training and experience in metallurgy to work on the project.

Your task is to review all the prints, the tests, the procedures used in the tests, and the results of the test. Look for flaws in all of these areas and be especially alert for any assumptions that may have influenced the test results. When we put this system online, we cannot afford to suddenly find ourselves jousting windmills. So far, this is the largest foreign contract, monetarily, we have ever won over the competition. Naturally, we are eager to get more. And that's about it, Dan. I hope we both luck out, and you find everything okay."

"Dick, I appreciate the opportunity, and I know how important the project is to all of us."

Both rose from their chairs, and Dan followed Dick to the enclosed area where the personnel assigned to the project were working. Since they all knew Dan, they greeted both Dan and Dick when they arrived. After briefing the project personnel on Dan's assignment, Dick left.

After passing amenities, Dan asked each of the engineers to cover in detail the current status of their assignment on the system and any problems they had encountered in interfacing the recovery system with the other systems. Because of the complexity of the system, the short deadline, and the importance of the project, not only to the company but to each person working for the company, the engineers welcomed Dan's review, jokingly calling it "The Sanders Inquisition."

Dan worked long hours checking and rechecking the engineering on the new system, but he could not forget the old prospector and his claim. Each morning while eating breakfast, he always turned to the business news before reading the rest of the paper. And each morning on his way to work, he stopped to buy an Examiner, but not a single paragraph had appeared.

Two weeks slipped by, and one Sunday morning after he had finished reading both the Chronicle and the Examiner, he set them aside then placing one hand on each thigh he looked up and thought, Nothing is going to be published. I wonder what happened? I am sure I did not miss the article because I checked the papers thoroughly. Perhaps the editors considered the strike too insignificant to publish. But that I can't believe. From what I saw, a half-million dollars can readily be recovered, and I am sure it will be more. I believe it is highly unlikely it would not have been picked up by the papers. So What? I turned the problem over to the authorities in Barstow. Naturally, I am interested in the outcome of the discovery, its disposition, and the cause of the old prospector's death. But it is none of my business; therefore, the best thing for me to do is to remember it as an interesting story.

Next morning, as usual, he picked up the paper, and as usual glanced at the headlines while walking up the stairs. When he sat down to drink his coffee, he found himself turning to the business section and checking the mining news. It must be from habit, he thought. And on his way to work, he bought an Examiner. I don't know why I'm doing this, he thought. Perhaps my interest is greater than I am willing to admit. Is it curiosity or concern, or both?

Being single, without any specific obligations, Dan continued to arrive at the office early, set up the coffee, and scan the Examiner until the coffee brewed, then filled his mug and began concentrating on his recovery and reduction system assignment.

On Monday of the fourth week, Dan called Hammeric and asked for permission to brief him on his progress. Dick agreed and set up the briefing for the following morning.

Dan opened the briefing by complementing the personnel assigned to the project. "It is my opinion, Sir, everyone working on this project is doing a super job. I know my assignment does not include spying, nor am I trying to butter you up."

Hammeric presented a half-smile but did not comment. Dan continued, "I must give credit where credit is due. I hope you share my opinion. I have received full cooperation from everyone, and as a result, I expect to complete the review and submit my final report within the next four days."

Dan turned to the first page of his charts and began by showing sketches of the segments of the systems he had checked and explained what he had been looking for and what he had found.

When Dan finished the briefing, he said, "As you can see, Sir, I found no major discrepancies and only a few minor ones. We immediately corrected the ones we found and sent corrected blueprints to the contractor. And that is about it, Sir," he concluded, then he pulled down the briefing charts.

"I am pleased there were no surprises," Hammeric commented, as he unfolded his arms from across his chest and laid them on the desk.· "I'm sure I would have been notified if you had found any major problems that could have had a major impact on the project. As you know, I kept an eye on things by looking over your shoulder, and from what I saw, and what I heard, I got the feeling all was going well. And now you have confirmed that feeling. Many things can and do go wrong on a project of this magnitude. Thanks, Dan, for a job well done. Do you have anything else to bring up?"

"Yes, I do, but it is personal. When I have completed this project, I would like to take a couple of weeks leave. I know it is earlier than usual for my vacation, but I have some personal matters I would like to take care of, and I would like to tie them in with my vacation."

"I'm sure we can arrange it, Dan. In fact, your idea of an

early vacation fits in with my future plans. I may want to send you to South Africa in eight to ten weeks. The building construction is already under way, and as you know, we have engineers on sight overseeing that part of the project. All the standard machinery has been purchased and is being modified to our specifications. About half has been completed and shipped. The balance, including the recovery and reduction components, should be completed and shipped within the next 90 days. All of the equipment is being shipped out of New York City. We believe it is logical to send you for the reason we selected you for the task of double-checking the engineering on the reduction and recovery systems, your training and experience in both mining engineering and metallurgy."

While Hammeric had been talking, his hands and elbows had been resting on top of the desk with palms down, now he turned his palms up in a gesture to Dan. "Well?"

Dan looked at Hammeric for a moment before answering. "I am grateful for being selected. Thank you. Other than saying that, I am speechless. I will be ready to leave when you give the word."

Dan noticed Hammeric getting ready to push himself up from his desk and rose, too. Again, he thanked Hammeric, removed his charts from the stand and left.

Dan finished his report early Friday afternoon of the fourth day. He called Hammeric and asked permission to review the report with him. After discussing the report over the phone, Hammeric decided a joint review would not be necessary but asked Dan to drop it off in his office.

After saying his goodbyes, Dan left for his apartment and began packing for his trip to Barstow. I'll take part of the equipment I used on the Old Indian Trail. If I am not satisfied with what I hear at the constable's office, I may decide to visit the claim. I hope my curiosity doesn't get the best of me, but I will be forever haunted by my imagination if I don't find out the results of the investigation. If I do visit the claim, I shouldn't have any trouble renting a saddle horse.

Dan finished packing and checked his watch. It is 2:45 p.m., and as I recall, the train leaves Oakland for Barstow at 6:00 p.m., and I should arrive in Barstow about 7:00 p.m. And before forgetting, I'll call Mom and Dad and tell them I'll be out of town for a couple of weeks.

Dan arrived at the depot an hour before the scheduled departure time. He picked up his tickets and checked his luggage, then looked at his watch. "I'll have time to eat," he thought. "After dinner, I'll pick up a newspaper before I board the train and read until the porters start making up the beds."

Dan had only been seated a few minutes when he felt the train begin to move. Watching the last passenger who had boarded walking down the aisle, he thought, I often wonder if the train left someone at the station.

The train was an hour late when it pulled into Barstow.

Dan had dressed and was ready to leave as soon as the brakeman raised the hinged steel door over the steps and set down the stool. I'll eat first then worry about finding transportation uptown to the hotel. When he finished his breakfast, he walked to the passenger waiting room and up to the ticket window.

The ticket agent came to the window and asked, "How may I help you, Sir?"

"Is there any transportation available to take me uptown to a hotel. I have luggage, and I don't relish the idea of dragging it over the viaduct and up the hill to Main Street."

Dan smiled while talking to the agent.

The agent, returning Dan's smile, replied, "I'm sorry, Sir,

our taxi service isn't the best, but you can catch the courier who picks up and delivers packages from the express office to the local merchants. He should be making his first morning run about now. He charges a quarter and ten cents for each piece of luggage, and he will pick up anyone waiting at the express office."

Dan thanked the agent and hurried to the express office with his one piece of luggage. When he arrived, the agent was busy checking incoming and outgoing packages. Dan stood behind the half door which kept the customers from entering the working area and asked, "Pardon me, Sir, can you tell me when the courier will arrive?"

The agent looked up and replied, "He hasn't arrived yet, but I expect him any minute. He called earlier and asked if I had anything for him. I told him I did. Are you looking for a ride uptown?"

"Yes, I am. Will he have room for me?"

"Sure, so far you are the only passenger, and I only have a half dozen packages for him." The agent turned his head, slightly, and looked beyond Dan. "Here he comes, now," he said.

Dan turned and saw a small, skinny, bareheaded man with shaggy grey hair, wearing a rumpled blue shirt and Levi's, walking toward the express office. He walked past Dan and spoke to the express agent. "Hi, Tom, did you say you had six for me."

"That's it, Jerry, only six, but I've got a passenger for you."

"That will help, but you've got to drum up more business for me or I'm going to have to find another job."

Without waiting for the agent to comment, the courier turned to Dan and asked, "Where do you want to go, Mister?"

"Uptown to the hotel," Dan replied.

"OK, that will cost you a quarter and a dime for each bag, and you carry the bags."

The courier loaded his packages on a dolly and began pushing it toward the rear of the depot without asking Dan if he also wanted to load his luggage. Dan followed him to a Model T pickup and tossed his luggage onto the truck bed.

This courier is about as friendly as a rattlesnake, Dan thought. But transportation is transportation and it doesn't seem very plentiful around here. I may need his help later on.

When they arrived at the hotel, Dan handed the courier a dollar bill. The courier reached for change, but before the courier's hand could reach his pocket, Dan held up his hand and said, "Keep the change."

The courier's hand hovered over his pocket for a moment as if he could not believe his ears. Then his face cracked into a broad smile showing tobacco stained teeth and a gap where a tooth should have been. "Thanks, Mister, I don't get many big tips like this one."

"There is a catch," Dan said. "There is a chance I may want to hire you later on. My name is Dan Sanders."

"I'm mighty glad to meet you, Mr. Sanders. I'm available except when I'm making pick-ups and deliveries, and that only takes about 30 minutes. If you want to get in touch with me, check with Clyde across the street at the hardware store. Just tell, him you want to see 'Jerry' Thanks, Mr. Sanders. Let me help you with that luggage."

Dan declined the offer and removed his luggage from the back of the pickup and walked into the hotel. He did not recognize the clerk and assumed they had switched shifts. The clerk yawned when he greeted Dan and turned the register toward Dan to sign.

"Since I am not sure how long I'll be in town, I'll sign up

and pay you in advance for three days. If I don't show up during either the day or the night, don't be concerned. I have some out of town business that may detain me, and I plan on using this hotel as my point of contact."

The clerk nodded and said, "Yes Sir," then picked up Dan's luggage and carried it up to Dan's room. Dan tipped him and immediately began unpacking his suitcase.

By the time he had finished, it was 9:30. Well, he thought, it is time to get on with it. He walked downstairs, nodded to the clerk, and continued through the lobby, and out on to the sidewalk. He felt himself hurrying, and thought, I've got to slow down and remain casual, and look unconcerned.

Something is wrong but I don't know what, and it is time to check with the constable and find out.

As he drew near the constable's office, again he had to force himself to slow down. You came down for a vacation and you dropped by the constable's office for a casual visit, Dan thought. When he reached the door, he took a deep breath and slowly exhaled before entering.

Dan opened the door and stepped inside. Lomac, the deputy constable, sitting at his desk, looked up from his paperwork. But before Blake could greet him, Dan removed his hat and said, "I am Dan Sanders. About a month ago, I reported finding a body in a mine tunnel in the vicinity of Fremont Peak. I'm out here on vacation. Since I had a little time to spare, I stopped by your office to find out if anyone identified the body and what happened to the remains. For some strange reason, I can't forget what I saw in that mine tunnel. When I walked through your door, I was hoping you might have a few minutes you could spare to tell me what the sheriff's office reported."

The deputy had listened to Dan without attempting to

interrupt him. When Dan finished, Blake almost smiled as he pushed away his chair from the desk and heaved his body from the chair that seemed too small for him. "I remember you," he said. "It is hard to forget a person who comes in here and tells us a story about finding a body. Come in, Mr. Sanders, and sit down." He opened the wooden gate and pointed to a chair next to his desk. Both sat down at the same time.

"There isn't a whole lot to tell. I briefed the constable when he returned the next day, and then I called the sheriff's office and read the report to one of the clerks. A couple of days later, two deputies, one named Max Schuleman, and the other, Fred Olsen, drove in dressed up in their riding gear. After briefing them and passing on your recommendations, and giving them the map you drew, Max, the spokesman for the two, said they planned to rent two saddle horses and a pack animal and ride out to the claim that same day."

Lomac stopped momentarily and pushed back his chair, "How about a cup of coffee?" he asked.

"Yes, please. I usually have one about this time." Then he added, "Black."

Lomac picked up his empty coffee cup as he rose from his chair and waddled over to a small wooden stand at the rear of the office. An electric coil on top of the stand kept the coffee pot hot. The deputy selected a clean cup from the shelf below and filled both cups. After handing a cup to Dan, he sat down and continued his story.

"They were gone for three days," Lomac said, "and did not return until late in the evening of the third day. For some reason they drove out of town without contacting either the constable or me. The next morning, when the constable found out they had left without leaving a message, he called the sheriff's office and registered a complaint. He told the sheriff he was holding an incomplete file on the case and wanted to close it. The sheriff apologized and promised to mail a copy as soon as the report had been finalized. We received a copy two days later. As I mentioned earlier, there wasn't much to the report. They arrived at the mine tunnel and found the body where you described it would be. After uncovering it, they moved it to the front of the tunnel to examine it. Nothing much remained but the skeleton, and it was so badly mutilated from the explosion, they had difficulty making a determination as to exactly what happened. They could not find the skull and parts of the lower neck were missing. The lower extremities were intact, but the left leg was totally incased, in what appeared to be crude wooden splints tied together with lashing ropes. They removed the splints and saw the thigh bone had been shattered. Based on these findings, the deputies concluded the person had been involved in an accident, and rather than die of thirst or starvation, had chosen suicide. Apparently, he had placed dynamite under his head or neck and lit the fuse. They also concluded the mutilated remains could not be identified without the missing parts, so they buried the remains near the claim. The deputies report used the pseudonym, John Doe, to identify the remains."

The deputy's arms had been resting on the top of his desk while he had been talking. Now he turned the palms of his hands up and said, "Well, Mr. Sanders, that's about it."

"I gather from what you have told me, Deputy Lomac, they did not find any papers, letters, or any other bits of information which could have positively identified him."

"Not according to their report," Lomac replied.

Dan slowly shook his head from side to side and looked at his hands clasped tightly together in his lap. The saddlebags, he thought. What happened to the saddlebags? Finally, he said, "I wish I had had an opportunity to talk to them."

"I'm afraid it is too late, now, Mr. Sanders."

Dan quickly turned his attention from his hands to the deputy, and without giving Lomac a chance to continue, asked, "Why?"

Blake appeared slightly annoyed at Dan's interruption, but went on. "About a week after completing the investigation on your report, the same two deputies, Olsen and Schuleman, were sent out to check on a report by an informer about a bootlegger operating a still along the Mojave River 40 miles east of here. They stopped here to report, then they headed east in their big touring car. The next day, Schuleman returned with two bodies, wrapped in canvas lying in the back of the car."

"According to Schuleman's report, Olsen and he found what they believed to be the location of the still based on a sketch of the location provided by the informer. The still lay hidden among cottonwood trees and willows growing along the banks and shallows of the Mojave Riverbed where it surfaced for about a quarter of a mile. What they saw jibed with the sketch."

"Knowing that bootleggers were unpredictable, they parked the car and proceeded on foot with their sidearms and rifles. Nothing unusual happened until they reached the trees and began working their way through the heavy brush. Then, without warning, they found themselves pinned down from the fire of a high-powered rifle. They ducked down and began moving out of the line of fire. Schuleman reported they believed they must have triggered some kind of an alarm system."

Lomac stopped paraphrasing and began reading directly from Schuleman's report. "Olsen began shouting, 'Sheriff Officers. Lay down your arms.' The rifle fire stopped momentarily but then began again. We returned the fire for several minutes without making any progress. He knew where we were, but we did not know his exact location. When the firing died down, Olsen said he would circle around to the right of the bootlegger and outflank him. I told him to give it a try, but he was not to take any unnecessary chances. He moved off to his right and made good progress until he came to the break between the trees and the brush. I began firing in the direction from where I thought the bootlegger was firing hoping to distract him, but the bootlegger's bullet struck Officer Olsen while he was running across the break. I saw him fall and immediately pulled a white handkerchief from my hip pocket and tied it to the barrel of my rifle then waved it over my head. I heard the bootlegger yell, 'What do you want?' I called back, 'My partner is down and needs help.' He shouted back, 'OK, stand up and drop your rifle.' I saw him step from behind a camouflaged tree about two hundred yards away with his rifle raised. I started to raise up but before I could drop my rifle, he took a pot shot at me. I jerked my rifle waist high and snapped off two quick rounds before he had a chance to fire again."

"I saw him fall and ran over to check on Olsen. Olsen lay on his back clutching his chest with both hands, but when I checked his pulse, I knew he was dead. I picked up my rifle and began moving in the direction where I saw the bootlegger fall. I moved cautiously because I did not know how badly he was wounded, nor did I know if he worked alone. I decided to circle and come in near the river where I suspected he had located his still. I moved west and then south until I came to the river, then east. Suddenly, in a small clearing directly ahead of me, I spotted his camp. It consisted of a lean-to constructed from limbs and branches covered with a large piece of canvas that hung down the back and over the sides. Several five-gallon cans were scattered around the camp, which I presumed were used for water, and I could see the copper still about 50 feet from the lean-to. I waited and looked for signs of other inhabitants, and after about five minutes, I moved in with my rifle ready. I saw none and moved cautiously on through the camp toward the location where I thought the bootlegger had fallen. I continued walking slowly until I spotted him lying face down about 50 yards ahead. I watched and waited but he did not move. I approached him with my rifle cocked. When I drew closer, I could see the back of his head caked with blood. I shoved him over on his back with my foot and looked into the open glazed eyes of a dead man. The bullet had struck the bootlegger just above the left eyebrow and exited through the back of his head. What a lucky shot, I thought. I walked up to the location where we had parked the car and, fortunately, found I could drive within a few feet of the bodies. I wrapped the bodies in canvas covers we carry in the vehicle for that purpose, loaded them in the car, and returned to Barstow. I reported to the local constable and asked for his assistance in arranging with the local funeral parlor to transport the bodies to San Bernardino."

Lomac laid down the report and said, "Of course there is more in the report but none of it would be of interest to you." Dan had been listening closely to the report. Now he looked at Lomac and I asked, "What kind of a rifle was Schuleman using?"

"A 30-30 lever action Winchester. The bootlegger had been firing an Army surplus Springfield 30 caliber bolt action rifle. That is why Schuleman got two quick shots off before the bootlegger could get another round in his rifle chamber and fire."

Dan decided not to comment on Schuleman's lucky rifle shot.

Instead, he asked, "What happened to Schuleman? You inferred something had occurred which would prevent me from contacting either one of them."

"Schuleman quit his deputy sheriff job a few days after the bootlegger killed Olsen. He said he could not get over the loss of his partner and felt, that because of his grief, he might endanger the lives of some of the other deputies if they came under fire. Rumors have filtered down that he is now working as guard at the big Kelly mine at Red Mountain. I also heard he fills in as a bouncer at one of the local saloons."

Lomac had been resting his hands on the top of his desk.

Now, he removed them, and while looking directly at Dan, slapped his huge thighs and said, "That's about it, Mr. Sanders." The look implied the meeting was over.

Dan rose to his feet and said, "Deputy Lomac, you have used a lot of your valuable time to bring me up to date. I appreciate the time you have spent with me and I thank you."

"No problem at all," Lomac commented. "If you are out this way again, drop in for a cup of coffee."

They shook hands and Dan left the office. While walking up the dirt road toward Main Street, he kept thinking about Schuleman and the saddlebags. Was it a coincidence that Schuleman found a job at Red Mountain, or did he have a specific reason in mind, the old prospector's mine, for instance? I came prepared to visit the old prospector's claim, he thought, and now with all the unanswered questions, the sooner I find the courier, the sooner I can get going and, hopefully, come up with some answers.

When Dan reached Main Street, he spotted the courier's pick-up parked in front of the hardware store and when he entered, he found the courier inside. "I need your pick-up for about an hour," Dan said. "How does five dollars sound to you?"

"You can have us for the rest of the day for that much," the courier replied, giving Dan the missing tooth smile. "Everybody calls me Jerry, and I will feel honored if you will call me Jerry, too. Now, where do we go from here?"

"My name is Sanders, Jerry. The first thing I have to do is buy a canteen. Then we will stop by the hotel and pick up some of my belongings. I'll explain to you later the rest of my plans. We will be stopping by the depot and you will have time to drop off any parcels if it is convenient for you."

"Thanks, Mr. Sanders, I'll make a quick check while you are buying your canteen."

Jerry was standing by the pick-up when Dan walked out of the store. He asked Jerry to turn the truck around and park it in front of the hotel while he walked across the street and picked up the things he planned to take on the trip. Before stepping into the lobby, he checked his watch. It is 10:15, I'll try to be on my way in an hour, he thought.

When he stepped into the lobby, the clerk who had been on desk duty during his last visit greeted him. "Good morning, Mr. Sanders. Welcome back."

Dan did not give him an opportunity to continue. "Thank you. I'll be leaving this morning; I may be back tomorrow evening or the following day. It will depend upon the circumstances. I will be taking part of my belongings and leaving the rest here. I'm sure that will be satisfactory with you."

"Oh, certainly, Mr. Sanders."

Dan had not waited for the reply. He hit the steps running, taking two at a time. It took him less than ten minutes to gather his gear and meet the courier in front of the hotel. He tossed his gear on the pick-up bed and climbed over the door and into the seat. "Next stop, the depot," he said.

After parking at the depot, Dan said, "I'll be in there for about 15 minutes. You will be on your own while I'm gone."

"Fine, Mr. Sanders. I have a couple of packages for the Express Office, and I'll also check for any incoming. Don't worry about your equipment, I'll only be gone a couple of minutes."

Dan had already climbed out of the pickup and had to turn to thank him while walking away. He headed for the Harvey House and asked for their prepared sandwiches and fresh fruit to be packed for carryout. Back at the pickup, he checked his watch. It read 10:40.

Jerry, feeling the energy radiating from Dan, had the pickup running before Dan climbed in. "Where to now?" he asked.

"I need a good saddle horse, Jerry, one I can rent for two or three days. I'm depending on you to tell me where I can rent one."

"There are several places, including a couple of dude ranches, but I think the stable about a quarter of a mile north of the of the river has the best selection. If it is OK with you, we'll try it first."

"Let's go," replied Dan.

Fifteen minutes later, Jerry parked the pickup by the barn and got out. In the meantime, Dan had opened the pickup door and was about to walk over to the corral when he heard Jerry say, "Howdy, Tim, I've brought you a customer."

"Thanks, Jerry, how is everything with you?" Jerry replied, "OK, Tim."

In the meantime, Dan had walked around the Ford toward the man Jerry called Tim.

Jerry turned toward Dan and said, "Tim Slocum, this is Mr. Sanders."

They exchanged greetings, and Slocum asked, "What can I do for you, Mr. Sanders?"

"I need a good saddle horse for a couple of days, maybe three, and if you have what I want, I won't quibble over the price."

"I think I have what you want. I don't rent him to every stranger that comes along because I consider him kinda special, but you sound like a man who knows horses."

Dan did not comment as they walked to the corral.

"I don't want to seem nosey," Slocum said, "but I would like to know how far you will be traveling. It is a question I ask of all horsemen who plan to stay overnight."

"Between 25 and 30 miles, according to my hand drawn map. About three years ago, a friend of mine filed on some claims out in the Goldstone area. Since I'm a mining engineer, and I happened to be traveling out this way on a vacation, he asked me to take a look at them and see if I thought they were worth spending the time and money to do the assessment work." (There are many holes in that lie, Dan thought, because I'm not very good at it. However, after what I heard today, I don't trust anyone, and it will have to do)."

Then Dan heard Slocum say, "The horse I am recommending can handle your trip, but what are your plans for feed and water?"

"There is a spring in the area, and I bought an extra canteen. I also plan to pack enough oats for a couple of days."

The stable owner had opened the gate and the three men stepped inside. He pointed to the far corner of the corral where four horses were standing close together brushing flies from each other's backs. Dan glanced around as they walked toward the horses and guessed the corral contained about a dozen animals, including two burros. All appeared healthy and well groomed. This man loves his horses, Dan thought.

"The bay gelding is the one I recommend," Slocum said.

Dan spotted the animal and Slocum continued, "He isn't the biggest horse in the corral, but he is strong and has a smooth fast walk. Unless the going is extremely rough, he should make the 30 miles in less than six hours."

The horses watched the men as they approached but they did not shy away. Slocum slipped between them and snapped a lead rope on the bay's halter then led the bay to where Dan and Jerry were standing. When Slocum spoke, his voice revealed his pride, "Mr. Sanders, this is Socks." Then Slocum stroked the shiny red coat along Socks' arched neck, the red coat marred only by white bands around his fetlocks on his forelegs. He turned to Dan and asked, "Well, what do think?"

Dan, who had been watching the quick powerful movements of the bay, could think of only one word to describe the horse, "Great! I'll take him." Then he added another compliment, "From what I can see, he would have made a great stud. It seems unfortunate he has been gelded." Dan cut off further conversation because of his desire to get started. He said, "Mr. Slocum, you can save me a trip back to town if you can provide me with the few things I will need for the trip. I will gladly pay you."

"If I've got them, I'll supply them. What do you need?"

"A tether, oats, a pan to water the horse, a hatchet or a small axe, a short handled, shovel; and another canteen."

"I've got them. I'll throw them in with the horse and saddle for ten dollars a day."

"It's a deal," Dan replied.

"Good, I'll get the horse ready. And, Jerry, you know

where I keep the supplies, would you mind getting them together?"

"Be glad to, Tim,"

Dan removed his gear from the Model T, set it by the barn where Slocum was saddling the horse, then removed his revolver and strapped it on. Now, he thought, by the time I get the canteens filled, Slocum and Jerry will finish their tasks, and I can be on my way.

The three men completed their tasks at about the same time. Dan hung the canteens on the saddle horn and tied the supplies on the back of the saddle. Then he stepped back from the horse, pulled out his wallet, paid both, and thanked both at the same time. Turning to Jerry, "I may need your services when I get back."

"Sure thing, Mr. Sanders, it will be my pleasure whenever you say the word."

Dan mounted the bay and reined him toward the road leading from the stable. The bay immediately broke from a trot to an easy lope. When they reached the crossroads, Dan turned north. The bay continued the easy lope for another 100 yards, slowed to a trot, then settled down to a fast walk.

Dan did not look back. He checked his watch. It is 11:35, he thought. I'm getting a little later start than I would like, but I have a good horse which is a major plus.

He reached over, patted the bay on the neck and said, "Socks, I'll soon know if you are the horse your master thinks you are." Dan reached down and placed the palm of his hand on the shoulder of the bay and he could feel the ripple of the powerful muscles keeping pace with his smooth stride. Then again Dan said aloud, "I think you are."

He checked his watch again and saw they had been on the road for an hour and estimated they had traveled about six miles. He had been watching for a road or trail that branched off to the west, and now he could see one about 300 yards ahead. As he drew near, he thought, It doesn't appear to be used very often, but it is heading in the right direction. Looking back, he could see they had been climbing a slight grade, and when he turned the bay west on the lateral road, he saw the road passed through low hills five or six miles ahead.

The bay continued at a good pace but began to slow when they approached the hills and the grade grew steeper, and then he began to lather. Dan pulled up the bay and said aloud, "It is time for me to get my fanny out of this saddle and lighten your load, Socks. We still have a long way to go."

Dan dismounted, flipped the reins over the bay's head and began leading him. Then he said aloud, "It's getting pretty warm and I don't know how long we will be climbing this grade. I do know, I can't take any chances of wearing you out."

Now, he could see Joshua trees ahead. An hour later, they began passing through the Joshua trees and arrived at the summit. Dan knew they had climbed several hundred feet since leaving Barstow because the strange looking Joshuas grew only on the higher desert elevations.

After mounting, the bay immediately picked up his smooth fast walk. The bay followed the old dirt road through the Joshua trees for several miles, then the road began its decline. And as the elevation dropped, the Joshuas began to disappear leaving only singles and groups of twos and threes. Now sagebrush and greasewoods dominated the landscape with a scattering of a few wildflowers, remnants of the wet winter.

Over the years, the ruts of the old road had filled with dust and sand providing the bay with a smooth soft surface for the bay to travel.

Dan looked at his watch. It read 3:10, then he said aloud to the bay, "We have made good time, Socks, since we crossed the summit. We will stop in a few minutes and I'll have a sandwich and you can have a pan of water."

Later on, while looking down the road, Dan could see a clearing with three huge Joshua trees growing near the east edge of the clearing, the last of the Joshuas on the slope. As he drew near he recognized it as an abandoned mining camp.

Dan guided the bay past the ore dump and dismounted near one of the Joshua trees. Checking the area, he said aloud, "It seems our road ends here, Socks I'll give you some water and you rest while I eat."

After loosening the saddle cinch and watering the bay, he removed a sandwich from the bag and sat on a nearby rock relaxing while eating his sandwich. Which way from here, he thought? Fremont Peak is northwest from here, but my view is blocked by the hills directly ahead. My best bet is to skirt to the left of the hills and pick up the Old Indian Trail.

It should be five to seven miles due west from here. The route will be a little longer, but it will be easier on the horse.

After repacking the pan and cinching the saddle, he mounted and reached over the saddle horn to pat the bay on the neck, "No road or trail now, Socks," he said aloud, "all we can do is head west and hope we hit the Old Indian trail.

It had been 3:45 when they left the abandoned mine.

They passed to the left of the hills and Dan turned the bay to the northwest. A breeze blowing in from the west kept the afternoon temperatures to within a comfortable range, but in changing their route to the northwest, Dan had increased the miles for an early interception of the Old Indian Trail.

As a result, it was well over an hour before he began to recognize signs indicating they had converged with the Old Indian Trail.

Now he could see Fremont Peak about ten miles ahead. He reached over and patted the bay on the neck and said aloud, "We are on the final leg, Socks, and we will be there soon."

Although the bay had picked up his pace slightly since joining the Old Indian Trail, Dan knew by the arch of the bay's neck he had begun to tire. But when Dan had spoken to him, he had raised his head a bit, as if to say, "Don't worry, I'm OK."

They arrived at the spring shortly after six. Dan immediately removed the saddle and gave the bay a good rubdown before leading him to the spring for water.

As he watched the horse drink, he also noticed the clean basin and thought, Someone has been using the spring and keeping the basin clean. And I hadn't noticed before, but now I see horse tracks that are fairly fresh, and they are not Socks. As soon as I stake out Socks and feed him, I'll look around and try to find out where the tracks lead.

Satisfied that he had safely tethered the bay and given him more than an adequate ration of oats, he began circling the spring to find the direction from which the tracks came. A couple of ever widening circles around the spring and he found the tracks joined the trail leading from the old prospector's claim.

Dan looked at his watch. It is seven, he thought, too late to check on the claim this evening. I'll eat, get my pallet ready, and call it a day.

After eating, Dan carried his ground cover and blankets to the tether stake and spread them out then set the saddle at the head of the pallet and stretched out. He watched the bay lying a few feet away from him for two or three minutes and dropped off to sleep.

Dan woke up at dawn, watered and fed the bay, then began looking and found the can he had used to clean the spring.

It is a little rusty but good enough to brew a couple of cups of coffee, he thought. Since he was not eager to advertise his presence, he made a small fire from dry sage bush roots. After his breakfast of hot black coffee and cold sandwiches, he checked the tether, patted the bay on the neck, and began walking down the trail toward the old prospector's claim with a canteen and his revolver.

He spotted the ore dump about half the distance from the spring, and as he drew near the claim, he stopped and began looking for signs of life. It looks deserted, he thought. I heard some strange stories yesterday, and when I fit those stories with what I knew before I heard them, I can't be too careful. Dan pulled his revolver from its holster and checked it before proceeding.

Keeping his body low, and using the greasewoods as a shield, he moved cautiously, circling to the north until he reached a point due west of the dump, then he stopped again. I can't see the tunnel entrance because the dump is too high, he thought, but I don't see signs of life. What I do see does not appear to be the same as I remember it.

It is time to move in, he thought. He unbuckled the flap of his holster and drew his revolver, then he began moving in a crouched position toward the ramp. When he reached the ramp, he moved slowly up the ramp until he could see over the top of the ramp and stopped.

"I can't believe it!" Dan said aloud. "They have dynamited the tunnel entrance!"

He walked to the top of the ramp, replacing the revolver in his holster as he walked, to the pile of rock that blocked and completely closed the tunnel entrance. It is unbelievable, he thought. They must have used a complete case of dynamite to bring down this much rock. The two deputies did this. They saw the gold, no doubt about it. And the shoring, the blast shattered it and blew it over the sides of the dump, he thought while further examining the damage. The sight of the gold must have overwhelmed them, and they dynamited the entrance to protect it until they could figure out the best way to jump the claim.

What happened to the tools and cooking utensils the old prospector stored out here? Dan thought. Even the coffee pot is gone. He looked toward the tunnel, They probably carried or tossed everything in the tunnel before they dynamited it to lead people to believe it is just another abandoned prospector's attempt to find riches. Dan's eyes locked on the tunnel entrance and remained there for several seconds. I can still see those two saddlebags covered with dust leaning against the tunnel wall, he thought.

Dan sighed and turned away from the tunnel. I wonder where they buried the remains of the old prospector. Suddenly, Dan turned and again stared at the tunnel. Intuition or suspicion, he thought. Since I'm not long on intuition, it must be suspicion. I suspect the dynamiters removed saddle-bags from the tunnel before they lit the fuse. Why? Because they did not dare leave any incriminating evidence where it might be found.

Now the big question, what did they do with them, burn them? I believe their logical solution would be to burn them.

Where? Dan turned away from staring at the blocked tunnel and looked at the rock stove. He walked over to it and spotted the old shovel with the broken blade, the only tool in sight, and he began digging though the ashes. The buckles will not burn, he thought. If I can find the buckles, I will have satisfied myself they destroyed the evidence needed to identify the old man and his right of ownership to the claim.

He continued his search but gave up when he found nothing in the ashes except burned nails. What next? he thought. Did they take the bags with them? No, he thought, it would be riskier than leaving them in the tunnel. There is a chance they buried them, but where? I can't dig up every likely spot in the area. He looked up at the blue sky and closed his eyes. After a few seconds he opened them and watched a small devil wind spinning across the desert. Then the muscles in his jaw began to tighten, and he smiled and struck the palm of his left hand with his fist.

"The old prospectors grave," he said aloud.

He turned back to the old shovel and picked it up. Now to find the grave, he thought. But when I think back, I don't recall seeing anything that looked like a grave, including my walk around the dump. I can't think of a single reason why they should not have buried his remains near the claim, so I had better start looking.

I'll start at the bottom of the hill on the ramp side and walk out 60 yards, Dan thought while walking down the ramp. When I reach that point, I'll angle back, and continue angling back and forth all the way around the dump. Eventually I am positive I will find the place they buried him.

He began the search angling back and forth from the dump as he had planned. Two-thirds of the way around the dump, and about 40 yards from the dump, an unusually dense growth of greasewood bushes blocked his way. Dan started to circle around the bushes, but his engineering training prodded him into checking the growth in lieu of assuming it contained nothing to shield.

He pushed his way between two of bushes and saw that the

greasewoods sheltered a small cove about eight feet long and six feet wide. The area appeared level except for a rectangular depression about two feet wide and five feet long in the center.

It doesn't look natural, Dan thought, as he stepped forward.

Then he felt a slight shiver of anticipation run down his spine.

This has to be it, he thought. Apparently, they scattered the excess dirt and leveled off the area in an effort to conceal the grave, but they forgot that dirt settles and leaves a depression. I am positive this is it, but just to make sure, and maybe save myself a lot of extra work, I'll finish checking before I start digging.

Dan searched the remaining area but found nothing and returned to the location he had left. Now I am sure this is it, he thought. I am also sure the saddle bags are buried here. Otherwise, why didn't they mark the grave, and why did they try to conceal it? the young engineer thought. Apparently, no sandstorms have hit the area, if they had, it would have been a near impossible task to locate the burial place.

Dan, while thinking about the two deputies, had been removing his shirt. Now, he picked up the broken shovel, looked at it remembering the good shovel he had left at the spring, and began digging.

A half-hour hour later, he looked at his watch. It is 10:10, he thought. I'll venture a guess that I am about a third of the way there, and with this shovel, I'll have an hour or more to go. I am also going to guess the saddlebags were tossed in the middle of the grave. If I am wrong, I may be here another three hours.

He continued shoveling, concentrating on keeping the size of his excavation to within three by four feet, stopping every ten minutes to rest because of the heat. Two hours later, his shovel snagged on a blanket.

It is the blanket the deputies used to wrap around the old prospector's body, Dan thought. Now, which way should I shovel, east or west? I'll try west, he thought.

Ten minutes later, Dan pulled the saddlebags from the sand. After brushing them off, he felt the pockets. Lucky again, he thought, At least some of the contents are inside.

Dan tossed the saddlebags over the side of the grave climbed out with the help of his shovel. Now, to make the grave look like it did before I started digging, he thought. He filled the grave and leveled it off. Then he cut limbs from greasewood bushes and swept the area, Indian style, until he had eliminated all visible marks that the grave had been disturbed.

I can't leave a marker showing the location of the grave, he thought, but I can draw a sketch in my notebook which will serve the same purpose for future reference. Dan put on his shirt and removed the small notebook and pencil from his shirt pocket and drew the sketch.

After throwing the saddlebags and canteen over his shoulders, he picked up the shovel and the greasewood branches, and backed away from the grave site and up to the ramp, sweeping away any tell-tale marks that might arouse suspicion that someone had discovered the old prospector's grave. When he reached the rock stove, he smoothed out the ashes in the firebox and returned the broken bladed shovel where he had found it.

It is after one o'clock, Dan thought. When I get to the spring, I'll check Socks and decide if he is adequately rested. If he is, we will spend the night on the trail, probably, at the old abandoned mining camp. As of right now I can't get away from this place fast enough.

Checking again to insure he had left no evidence of his visit, Dan walked back down the ramp, and when he reached the end of the ramp, he turned and began walking backwards brushing away his footprints until he came to the path leading to the spring, then he turned, and with his long stride hurried back to the spring.

Dan set the saddlebags and the canteen down next to his other equipment and walked over to check on the bay. The bay looked at him when he approached but did not move. Dan patted the bay on the neck, and the bay returned the gesture by giving Dan a push with his muzzle.

"So, you are lonely and a little frisky, aren't you, Socks? How would you like to start back as soon as I can get the gear together?"

The bay moved his head up and down and pawed the ground with his left foot as if he agreed and wanted to get started.

"Ok, so you agree. Let's move over to the spring, and while you are filling up, I'll start packing."

Dan had the bay saddled and the gear, including the saddlebags, loaded and ready to go in 30 minutes. He made a final check of the area to be sure he had packed everything then mounted the bay. Dan reined the bay toward the Old Indian Trail, and Socks sensing they were headed for home, immediately broke into a gallop. Dan let the bay run for a couple of hundred yards then slowed him down to a fast walk.

Dan patted him on the shoulder and said aloud, "Socks, we have a long trip ahead, and some of it is going to be pretty tough going, so let's take it easy then we will both get there."

He reached down again and patted the bay on the shoulder and eased back into a comfortable position for the long ride.

Following the Old Indian Trail, Dan found hoof marks Socks had made on the way in. He guided him onto the tracks, and Socks sensing his wishes, began following them. Although the clear skies allowed the sun to beat down on them, the cool afternoon breeze kept the heat at a moderate temperature. The bay continued his steady pace without lathering until they began the slow steady climb leading to the old mining camp. Dan had been watching him, and when the bay began to sweat, Dan dismounted and walked the last two miles.

It was late afternoon when they reached the abandoned mine clearing. I don't see a better camping spot than the one by that huge, ancient Joshua tree where we rested on our way in, Dan thought. The sooner I get Socks rubbed down and watered, the sooner I can check the old prospector's saddle-bags. It is possible the two deputies took or destroyed the contents and replaced whatever was in the bags with rocks. I know they contain something.

Dan finished his chores and spread his blankets under the Joshua tree, then he carried the saddle and the saddlebags to the blankets. After setting the saddle where he could lean against it, he sat down on the blankets, Indian fashion, and opened one of saddlebag pockets then began removing its contents. He found each one neatly wrapped in oilcloth and tied. Good, he thought, nothing seems to have been removed. The old man was well organized, even to the smallest details.

Dan removed the last item from the bag. This feels like a revolver, he thought. He untied the string and removed the oilcloth. It is 32 caliber, and it is loaded, too, he thought.

Next, he unwrapped a hunting knife, then a package containing a razor, comb and brush, and a pair of scissors, and finally, a small tin box with four safety pins, needles, and thread. Dan then rewrapped the items and returned them to the bag. He unbuckled the straps on the other bag and withdrew a large tin box. Its contents were also wrapped in oilcloth. The first one he unwrapped held the original claim registration form of the claim near Fremont Peak which he had just left, and the papers showing dates he had completed and recorded the assessment work on the Fremont Peak claim. The recorder had registered the claim in the name of James Robert MacGregor.

Dan looked up from the form he had been reading and thought, This is the first time I can recall having ever seen or heard the complete name of the old prospector. It is strange everyone referred to him only as Jim, the old prospector. It is possible only a few close friends really knew him. I don't know. I wonder if anyone did.

The next package contained a leather purse with two pockets which opened from the top by twisting two snaps. One side contained three twenty-dollar bills, and the other side five one-dollar bills and some change. A savings account book on a bank in Barstow, also wrapped, showed a balance of $427.32.

Apparently, they didn't bother to open the saddlebags, or they would have taken the money, Dan thought. Gold causes some people to do weird and crazy acts, some even to commit murder. From what I have observed thus far, it appears that their only thoughts dictated the destruction of any evidence which might prove the gold strike was not theirs, and theirs alone. They buried the saddlebags assuming they would never be found. A bad assumption, Dan thought with a small smile.

The next package contained the old prospector's will showing he was leaving all of his earthly possessions, including the claim, to Alice Hazelton Holbrook, and subsequently to any of her offspring. Now only one package remained. The string tying the oilcloth around its contents appeared older and more frayed than those used on the other packages. He carefully untied it and unwrapped it. The contents appeared to be an envelope wrapped in a worn piece of tissue paper bound and tied with faded pink ribbon.

It must be very special, Dan thought. He untied the ribbon and removed the tissue paper seeing what he suspected, an envelope. It was so very, very old, he had difficulty in reading the addressee.

Mr. James R. MacGregor Comstock Mining Corp., Virginia City, Nevada Dan made out the return address to be:

Alice H. Holbrook
Box 74 Maple Street Terrace, Boston, Mass.

He opened the flap of the envelope, gently removed the letter, and unfolded the two pages, yellow with age.

Dan looked at both pages and saw the faded, but neatly formed letters of her handwriting. He looked at the date: February 1, 1865. I can't believe a letter which I am sure has traveled as much as this one has, is so well preserved.

He began reading, and when he had finished, he stretched out his legs and leaned on his right elbow but continued to hold the letter in his left hand while looking across the empty desert. I wonder what occurred to the two lovers during the intervening SO odd years? Dan thought. He continued gazing out across the desert for another minute or two, sighed, and finally folded the letter and returned it the envelope, then rewrapped it the way he had found it.

Again, Dan looked out across the desert but this time in the direction of Fremont Peak. What is my next move, he thought?

The easiest way out, is to bail out, forget what I know, what I have seen, and what I suspect. If my suspicions are correct, and I continue on the trail I am currently following, I may get my head blown off. Schuleman did not quit his job as deputy sheriff after the death of his partner. It was gold, pure and simple. I am convinced Schuleman is a very dangerous man. The more I think about the shootout between the two deputies and the bootlegger, the more I question Schuleman's report. Why, I keep asking myself, should a bootlegger stage a shoot-out with law officers, and risk 30 years in prison, or even hanging, when he knows that by getting caught and giving up, he probably will receive no more than a fine and a small jail sentence. I don't want to be a hero, nor do I want to be a heel, but Alice Holbrook is the legitimate heir, and I am the only one who can help her. How? a letter? If I try that, I would have to write a book, and even a book might be inadequate. Her letter tells me she is an intelligent person. But what if she has passed away and her heirs are in line to receive the inheritance?

It is possible the heirs, if there are any, would know nothing about the old prospector and his relationship with Alice Holbrook. Or perhaps, I should explain my thoughts to the authorities, turn over the saddlebags and the contents to them, and let them worry about it. But I tried that once and I cannot guarantee it will not happen again. On top of that, the chance they would believe my theory about the way the bootlegger and the deputy were killed is extremely remote. I doubt they would even bother to check it. Law officers are prone to believe their fellow officers when their stories conflict with those of outsiders. I believe my best bet is to sleep on all of the many thoughts I have been mulling over and, perhaps, the best solution will surface tomorrow before I get to Barstow.

Dan woke up the next morning with his decision. An urge

to tell someone prompted him to turn to the bay lying about 20 feet away and say aloud, "Socks, I'm going to Boston!"

Dawn had not yet arrived, but the bay turned his head toward Dan as if he were acknowledging his statement. He rose to his feet as if to say, "Let's go."

The young engineer dumped the rest of the oats into the feeding pan, and when Socks had finished eating, Dan took a drink of water from the remaining full canteen and poured the rest for Socks. While the bay had been eating, Dan had packed and had everything ready to load. He saddled the bay and looked in the paper bag at the sandwiches and the apple. I had planned to eat these along the way, he thought, but I am sure the wildlife around here will enjoy the sandwiches more than I will. I'll dump the sandwiches and munch on the apple. When I get to Barstow I'll have breakfast. He unwrapped the sandwiches, tossed them aside and mounted the bay.

"We have about five or six miles, Socks, before we reach the top of the grade," Dan said aloud, "then it will be downhill all the way."

The bay immediately broke into a trot. "Take it easy, Socks," Dan said aloud. After slowing the bay down to a walk, he said aloud, "We have about a three-hour trip ahead of us, and I don't want Slocum to ream me out when we get there because you are sweaty and worn out."

When they were about a mile from the summit, Dan dismounted and walked the rest of the uphill grade. When they reached the summit, he rested the horse for a few minutes before starting the decent. While the bay was resting, Dan checked the bedroll tied behind the saddle. I am pleased I had the foresight to roll the saddlebags up in the blanket, he thought. It will keep people from asking questions I don't want to answer.

It was near 9:30 when they arrived at the stable, When Slocum heard the horses whinny, he walked out of the barn and greeted Dan with a wave of his hand.

Dan dismounted and Slocum asked, "How was the trip?" "Excellent," Dan replied. "Socks is all you said he was and then some. I may try to talk you in to selling him. By the way, do you have a phone? I would like to call Jerry, the courier, for transportation to the hotel." Dan had been removing his gear from the saddle and setting it next to the corral.

"No need for that, Mr. Sanders. As soon as I groom the bay and put him in the corral, I'll take you. I have some things I have to pick up at the hardware store and it is just across the street from the hotel. Did you have any difficulty in finding the claims?"

"Some, but not much. I may want to go out in that area again, and I would like to leave the canteen with you. It will be cumbersome and hard to carry on the train. If I don't show up again, it's yours."

"Thank you, Sir. It will be here when you need it. And if you need any additional equipment, I have a pretty good assortment of pots, pans, two burner stoves, bedrolls, eating utensils, one- and two-man tents, and more canteens if you need them. During the spring and winter months, I get quite a few calls from visitors who want to go camping."

They continued their conversation until Slocum had finished rubbing down and grooming the bay. In the meantime, Dan had loaded his gear into the back of Slocum's pickup for the short trip to town. When they reached the hotel, Dan thanked Slocum then carried his gear upstairs to his room and dumped it on the floor.

Now, Dan thought, I'll clean up, change my clothes, and have some breakfast.

While he was shaving and taking a bath, Dan kept thinking about the claim. What rights would Schuleman have if he jumped and registered it in his name? At the minimum, it could cause a legal tangle requiring years to untangle. And if I can't find a legal heir during my investigation in Boston, he may be able to establish legal rights to the claim. The best and only move I can think of at the moment is to register the claim in my name. I can get the information I need from the original filing form in the saddlebags, and if I locate an heir in Boston, it will be an easy matter to transfer the claim to the original owner. My next move is to get out of this bathtub, get dressed, get packed, and try to catch a train to San Bernardino. If I can get there in time, I'll go to the U.S. District Land Office and refile the claim. As of right now, if I am lucky, maybe I can find Jerry and have him take me to the station.

Dan dressed and packed, and then he looked at his watch. It was 11:20. He carried his luggage downstairs to the lobby and called the passenger agent. He was advised the next train left for San Bernardino at 12:30 and arrived at 3:15. Now to find Jerry, Dan thought.

Dan walked out of the lobby and looked down the street toward the hardware store. Luck is running my way, he thought. That looks like his pickup parked in front of the hardware store. Dan did not hesitate; he returned to the hotel and carried his luggage across the street. After tossing it in the back of the pickup, he hurried to the hardware entrance and started to enter but the courier saw him coming and met him at the door.

"Welcome back, Mr. Sanders, did you have a good trip?"

"Nice to see you again, Jerry. Yes, I enjoyed the trip. Perfect weather, beautiful country, and a great horse. A person can't ask for more than that, can he, Jerry?"

"He sure can't, Mr. Sanders," Jerry replied. "I see you have your gear in the back of the truck. What can I do for you?"

"I took the privilege of loading it on without asking you because I am catching a train at 12:30 and I am hoping that you can drive me to the depot. Do you have the time to do it?"

"My pleasure. Hop in, Mr. Sanders. I'll crank Lizzy up and we will be on our way."

The courier helped Dan carry his luggage into the passenger waiting room where Dan paid and thanked him. After picking up his ticket and checking his luggage, he headed for the Harvey House and ordered steak, eggs, hash browns, a stack of wheat toast, and coffee. He drank half of his second cup of coffee when he noticed the crowded dining room had begun to thin out. Time to get moving, he thought. One more gulp and I'll be on my way.

Dan had reached the top of the coach stairs when he heard the conductor call out, 'All Aboard,' and he had only been seated a minute or two when the train began to move. The train stopped at Victorville to attach an engine to help pull the train up Cajon Pass. After dropping off the engine at the summit, the train continued down the mountain pass to San Bernardino.

When they arrived at the depot, Dan stored his luggage and hired a taxi to drive him to the U.S. District Land Office. When they arrived, he asked the driver to wait. Only one person waited at the counter when he entered. Thirty minutes later he climbed back into the taxi.

Now I can relax, he thought. I feel kind of numb, because I feel like I have been racing Schuleman to the Land Office. My guess is, he will not try to file on the claim for another two months because he is afraid of any attention he may draw, especially if it is associated with the claim, it might reopen the investigation of the deaths of his fellow deputy and the bootlegger. And the more I think about his story and compare it with information I have accumulated, the more I become convinced he murdered both. Pretty strong thoughts, Dan thought.

They were approaching the depot when Dan leaned over the front seat and said to the driver, "Cabby, I rode in on a train going to Los Angeles. I'll check but I doubt if another will arrive within the next two hours, and I've got to get to L.A. before 8:00 PM. Do you know of any other transportation available?"

The cab driver answered immediately, "Take the Pacific Electric. We call them the 'Big Red Cars'. One leaves every two hours. The next one leaves in about 45 minutes and the running time between here and L.A. is two hours."

That is good enough for me. Help me with my luggage and you can drive me to wherever I have to go the catch it. "

After paying the taxi driver and purchasing his ticket, he had 15 minutes to spare. A redcap helped Dan with his luggage to the loading platform where he joined between 30 and 40 passengers already waiting. A few minutes later, the conductor gave the sign and passengers began loading into two huge red, oversize, streetcars, connected together. The cars left exactly on time and quickly accelerated to the sixty mile an hour running speed. After four short stops the cars pulled into the Los Angeles station. On leaving the Pacific Electric station and arriving at the railroad depot, Dan inquired about a Pullman birth to San Francisco on the San Francisco overnight train. Upon being advised all births had been sold, he accepted a chair car seat.

The next morning after arriving at his apartment by taxi, he shaved, bathed and put on his robe then called Dick Hammeric. Hammeric answered the phone and Dan said, "Dan Sanders, Dick. How are things down at the office?"

"Great, Dan. Aren't you back a little early? I didn't expect to hear from you for at least another week. What's up?"

"I need to stretch my vacation an extra week. I'm going to Boston, and it will really crowd me to make the trip in ten days. Do you think you can spare me?"

"The same question, Dan. What's up?"

"I'll try to make it as short as possible. When I returned from my Yellow Aster assignment, Dick, I mentioned finding the body of an old prospector. Since then, the scene has been haunting me, so I decided to return. Surprisingly, I found some papers the authorities may have overlooked, or considered unimportant, perhaps intentionally. More important, the papers identified the old man, and the authorities said they could not identify him. The claim may be valuable, and among the papers, I found a will leaving the claim to a woman living in Boston. According to a very personal letter she had written over 50 years ago, they were lovers and she became pregnant. The fact that I could find no other correspondence between the two, lead me to believe they never saw each other again. I have her address and I feel obligated to go to Boston and report what I know to her, or her heirs, and turn over the papers and the letter. In the meantime, Dick, I will appreciate you not mentioning the mine or the reason for my trip until I return."

"Sure thing, Dan, things are running smoothly, and I have no objection to your taking an extra week. It all sounds very noble, but many things can and do happen over a period of 50 years. You may find on arriving that the interested parties have moved or passed away. However, I am sure you have considered all of the negative possibilities."

"I hope I have," Dan commented. "If the trip turns out to be a bust, I will at least have had the experience of visiting

Boston, one of our historical cities, and one I had put On my must list to visit someday."

Dan and Hammeric talked about the Company and Dan's trip to South Africa for another 20 minutes, then they exchanged goodbyes, with Hammeric wishing Dan good luck and a pleasant journey.

Now, Dan thought, I'll call Central Pacific and arrange for a round trip ticket and start packing, then I'll call Mother and Dad and let them know where I am going and when I'll be back.

4

BOSTON

The next morning Dan left early because he was not sure which train he would be taking to Boston. The ticket agent had told him he had a tentative cancellation on the A.M, Central Pacific for Chicago and he was trying to confirm it. In the meantime, the agent had said he would be checking for other possibilities.

When Dan arrived at the station, he immediately went to the ticket counter, located the agent, and identified himself. "What is the latest?" he asked.

"I have confirmed the cancellation on Central Pacific and reserved it in your name. It isn't the best because you must change trains in Chicago and New York City."

"I don't mind as long as I have a bed."

"Again, I apologize since the canceled ticket is for an upper birth."

"I'll take it," Dan said with considerable emphasis.

After boarding the train and getting settled in his seat, Dan gave a sigh of relief. I'm glad that is over, he thought. He changed trains in Chicago and New York City and arrived in Boston the evening of the fourth day. He hailed a porter for help to the taxi stand and later when the taxi arrived at the hotel, and after paying the taxi driver, Dan checked in and was escorted by the bellhop to his room. After bathing and changing his clothes, he called room service and asked that his soiled ones be picked up, then he took the elevator down to the hotel dining room.

While walking to the dining room entrance, he thought, A steak, maybe, with all the trimmings? Nope, when in Rome do as the Romans. I'll order oysters, lobster, and why not Boston Cream Pie?

Dan finished his pie and coffee then strolled through the lobby to the reception desk. The desk clerk greeted him. "Good evening, Mr. Sanders. How is your room, and did you enjoy your dinner?"

I often wonder how these clerks remember everyone's name, and how did he know I had just finished dinner," Dan replied, "No complaints about the room, and I enjoyed the dinner. The cuisine compares favorably with that of San Francisco."

The clerk replied, "I have never had the good fortune of visiting San Francisco. I have heard the food is excellent, and on my trip out west this fall, I shall make sure that I visit some of the restaurants in San Francisco I have read about. Now, Mr. Sanders, what can I do for you?"

"I'm looking for the Holbrook residence on Maple Street Terrace, and I thought possibly you could advise me on the general location and what would be the best means of finding it."

"I have a map of Boston and its suburbs," the clerk replied. He pulled the map from beneath the counter and spread it out in front of Dan. A guest approached the counter, and the clerk excused himself for a moment.

Dan turned the map to face him and began examining it.

He had glanced over it for only a few moments when the clerk returned.

The clerk turned the map so they could both see it, and then he commented, "I believe, Mr. Sanders, the area you are looking for is one of the oldest and most prestigious residential locations in Boston. It dates back in time to years before the Civil War. It is beautiful, and I am sure you will agree when you see it. But I can't help you with the party you mentioned, Holbrook, I believe. Sorry."

"Have you any suggestions for getting there? I am sure you have gathered by now that this is my first visit."

"I suggest you take a taxi. There are always three or four parked in front of the hotel. The doorman will help if you run into a problem."

"Thank you," Dan said, "you have not only been helpful, but you have also been courteous."

The clerk thanked Dan, and Dan returned to his room. I should not be sleepy because of the difference in the time zones, Dan thought, but I am tired, and as soon as I crawl in bed, I'll probably be asleep before I can pull up the cover.

Dan awakened and looked at his watch, "Seven o'clock," he said aloud, "I can't believe it."

I haven't slept this late in months, he thought. No reason to hurry, though, anytime between ten and eleven will be early enough to check the address. My primary interest is in finding someone home.

After breakfast, Dan returned to his room and began looking through the old prospector's personal possessions trying to decide what would be appropriate to show the heirs if he should be fortunate to find one at the address he was about to visit. Finally, he decided on the letter from Alice, the will, and the claim registration documents, both the old prospector's and his own.

As he passed through the hotel door, he nodded to the doorman and continued to the first taxi parked at the curb. The driver, standing by his cab, opened the door, then asked Dan where he could take him. Dan gave him the address, and without hesitation, the driver nodded and closed the door after Dan had settled down in the seat.

The driver acted as though he knows the area quite well, Dan thought. So far, so good. For some reason, though, I feel uncomfortable. Perhaps it is because of all the unknowns I am about to encounter, plus the thought of trying to explain my mission.

The driver headed west and crossed the Charles River.

Immediately the landscape began to change. The narrow-paved road began an almost imperceptible climb. Another quarter of a mile and he looked back. I can understand now why this area was selected for residential homes, Dan thought. The residents can see for miles, and they have a panoramic view of the winding Charles River and Boston.

A half-mile later they began passing private entrances leading to beautiful homes set three to four hundred feet back from the main road. Neatly trimmed shrubs, lawns, and flower beds lined each side of the driveways to the homes.

Dan noticed they had passed two crossroads since they had entered the residential area. The driver turned to the right on the third and drove past a half dozen houses before turning into one of the driveways, not unlike the others, which Dan thought hopefully, led to his destination.

The driver stopped in front of the residence, got out, and

opened the door for Dan. After stepping out of the taxi, Dan asked the driver to wait and began walking up toward the steps. While walking, Dan noted the structure was, indeed, very old with a stone base and heavy wooden sidings, rising two stories supporting a gabled roof with dormer windows. Dan stepped up on the covered veranda and tapped on the heavy oak door with the polished brass door knocker. A few moments later, a maid, dressed in black and white, opened the door.

"Yes?" she asked.

"I'm trying to find a lady whose name is Alice Holbrook. The only address I have for her is this one."

The maid stared at Dan for several seconds, then replied, "Please wait here a moment." She closed the door and left.

Dan waited for several minutes, then a well-groomed man of medium height with gray hair and a gray mustache, wearing a silk belted smoking jacket, opened the door and stared at Dan for a moment before greeting him with a question.

"May I ask what your interest is in Alice Holbrook?"

"I have a letter written by Alice Holbrook over fifty years ago to a man named James R. MacGregor. I also have a will signed by James R. MacGregor leaving all his possessions to Alice Holbrook or her heirs."

Dan watched the man's expressions change from suspicious, to interest, and finally, with his mouth slightly open, to amazement.

The man continued to stare at Dan with a trance-like look for a few more seconds, then he jerked his head slightly sideways as if to dispel the fog then he said to Dan, "Sir, will you come in, please?"

"Yes, thank you, as soon as I pay the driver."

Dan followed the man into a large library room and noticed law books filled half of all the shelves in the room.

Before asking Dan to sit down, the man said, "May I ask your name, please, and where you reside?"

"My name is Dan Sanders, and I live in San Francisco." The man held out his hand and said, "I am John MacGregor, and I thank you for coming in. As you probably observed, your comments startled me."

Now it was Dan's turn to be confused. MacGregor, he thought, I had formed an opinion that Alice Holbrook and the old prospector had never met again. Did they meet again and marry, or is it a coincidence this man's name happens to be MacGregor? Then Dan remembered the letter. No, he thought, it's highly unlikely they ever met again.

He heard MacGregor ask him to sit down. Although the fireplace was not lit, MacGregor pointed to two chairs, one on each side of the fireplace, and asked him to take one.

"Now, Mr. Sanders, will you please explain your mission. Are you a lawyer, and how did you get those papers?"

"Before I answer either of your questions, I need to know your relation to, or your connection with, Alice Holbrook. I am not trying to be rude, nor am I trying to pry or dig into something that is none of my business. The facts are that it is considerable at stake, and it involves a long story. Therefore, before I begin the story, I must know I am talking to the right person."

"Being a lawyer, Mr. Sanders, I can't criticize you for the position you are taking. Alice Holbrook passed away twelve years ago. I am her son. James R. MacGregor is, or was, my father. I don't know if he is alive or dead. That, too, is a long story, and if you are interested, I'll tell you the story. I have proof Alice Holbrook is my mother if you wish to see it."

"No, Mr. MacGregor, that will not be necessary." Again,

Dan remembered Alice's letter. "Your word is sufficient. Now for the story, but first, the answers to your two questions. I am not a lawyer, I am a mining engineer, and I work for a consulting firm in San Francisco."

Dan began the story with his trip to Randsburg and how he learned about the Old Indian Trail. He gave a detailed account of how he found the old prospector and the gold, and then he concluded with his return to the claim and the recovery of the saddlebags from the unmarked grave.

Dan continued, "Since I am positive Schuleman will jump the claim as soon as he thinks it will not arouse suspicion, and no one knows when that will be, I registered the claim in my name just before leaving for Boston. I will transfer the claim as soon as I find the rightful owner, and that appears to be you."

MacGregor had sat silently, concentrating on every word of Dan's story, his sharp blue eyes seldom leaving Dan's face, and then only for a moment as if to ensure he did not miss even the tiniest detail of the part Dan had been describing. Now he moved in his chair, clasped and unclasped his hands, looked at the floor, gazed at the ceiling, and finally looked at Dan.

"I am deeply touched by your story, Mr. Sanders, not only the story about my father, but also the personal sacrifices you have made to uncover a heinous plot involving possible murder, and then coming all the way to Boston to find the rightful heirs to a small fortune. A lawyer as old and as experienced as I am is supposed to be calloused and immune to the kind of feelings I am experiencing. It isn't often in a person's lifetime; one has the good fortune to encounter a person like you. You could have destroyed the papers, forgotten about the heirs, and kept the fortune for yourself."

At that moment, and before Dan could comment, he heard

a door open and heard a feminine voice call, "Hello there, is anyone home?"

Dan watched MacGregor's face quickly change from somber to the look of a little boy whose mother was about to hand him 'a sugar cookie. Looking over Dan' s shoulder toward the entrance, he replied, "In the library, Hillary."

Dan turned just in time to see a slender young woman who radiated energy, breeze past him with a nod of acknowledgment, then stooped down to kiss MacGregor on the cheek. "Hi, Dad, how are you feeling? You haven't started practicing law again, have you?" she asked. Then she turned to Dan and smiled. Her friendly smile caused Dan, who was now standing, to return the smile.

MacGregor, who had his arm around the young woman's waist looking up at her and also smiling, said, "No, Dear," then teasingly commented, "but I have been thinking about it." Then he turned to Dan and said, "Mr. Sanders, this is my daughter, Hillary."

The young woman immediately stepped from her father's side over to Dan, held out her hand, and said, "How d0 you do, Mr. Sanders."

No lily in that grip, Dan thought. Then he said, "Very well, thank you." He hesitated a moment and added, "Miss MacGregor, it is a pleasure meeting you." I must have addressed her correctly, he thought. She did not correct me.

"Thank you," she said.

MacGregor broke off any further conversation between the two by explaining the reason for Dan's presence. "Mr. Sanders traveled all the way from San Francisco to bring me information about my father."

MacGregor's daughter had stepped back to the side of her father's chair when he began talking. She gave Dan a puzzled look of amazement and doubt. "Your father! MY grandfather! The one no one has ever seen or heard from?" She shook her head in disbelief.

The grandfather clock began chiming, and MacGregor intervened. "Time has slipped away from us, and it is time to have a bite to eat. I'll do my best to pass on the story to you during lunch as Mr. Sanders told it to me, Hillary. In the meantime, please ask Nell to fix a cold lunch. Mr. Sanders, do you prefer coffee or tea?"

"Either will be fine with me." "Then we will have tea."

MacGregor's daughter excused herself and left. If she felt embarrassed by her candid remarks, she did not show it.

MacGregor turned to Dan. "You mentioned a letter and a will. Do you mind if I read the letter?"

"Not at all, they rightfully belong to you." Dan reached inside of his coat pocket and handed MacGregor a brown envelope. "Both are inside. I rewrapped them exactly as I found them in the metal box. Your father was a very meticulous person, the packet with the worn cord is the letter."

"Let's move over to the reading table where the light is better and where the packets will be easier to unwrap," suggested MacGregor. He was already up and moving, and Dan followed.

MacGregor removed the packets from the envelope as he sat down. He selected the one with the worn cord and noticed the oilcloth wrapping. He removed the oilcloth and looked at the faded ribbon tied around the tissue paper, then he gently untied the ribbon and unwrapped the tissue paper from around the envelope. He held the envelope closer to the light and reached inside the table drawer for a reading glass. After carefully examining the writing, he said, "That is my mother's handwriting." Then he carefully removed the letter from the envelope and began reading it with the reading glass. He read slowly and with great care, sometimes rereading a faded word or a sentence. When he had finished, he returned the letter to its envelope, rewrapped and tied it, and returned it with the will to the brown envelope. Then he removed his glasses, and while wiping them with a clean white handkerchief, he looked at Dan and said, "They must have loved each other very much. I knew Mother loved him, but I had doubts about my father, loving Mother. Now after seeing the letter, and the time and effort he must have spent preserving it, plus the faded ribbon tied with a bow, tells me he loved her equally as much. Mother told me she knew he had written, but my grandfather destroyed the letters. I have often wondered why he never tried to see her."

"We can only guess," commented Dan. "It could have been social status or money, perhaps a combination of both. It is obvious your grandfather had both because she mentions he knew men in high places, and he had brought his family to San Francisco on a business trip. Although I did not inquire into your father's background, I did conclude from the meager information I put together from conversations I overheard about your father, he was a miner working at the Comstock gold mine near Reno, Nevada during the Civil War. From the dates and the time-lapse indicated on the envelope inferred in the letter, we might deduct he may have been on leave in San Francisco during the Christmas holidays which could have been the time he and your mother met. I also gathered, that when he left the Comstock, he spent the rest of his life prospecting and only returned to work in the mines to accumulate money to continue his prospecting. I might add; apparently, he had few close friends and never stayed long in one place."

Dan continued, "After reading the letter and the will, and then trying to bring all I knew together, I came to the conclusion your father must have been on a mission, and that mission had one objective, 'Find Wealth', with the thought, perhaps, and again I am guessing, to gain the respect of your grandfather since it is obvious from the letter, your grandfather despised your father."

"As you said, Mr. Sanders, all we can do is guess. However, your theory sounds plausible. And here is Hillary."

"We have everything ready, Daddy. It is such a beautiful day, I helped Mary set up our luncheon on the veranda near the pool."

"Wonderful, Hillary, I am sure Mr. Sanders will enjoy it."

MacGregor's daughter led the way through the dining room and two open double glass doors to the oversize veranda that ran the length of the swimming pool. A tiled deck, ten feet wide, covered the area between the veranda and the pool, and the area around the pool. Flower gardens in full bloom lay at each end of the veranda, and beyond the flowers, Dan could see a variety of fruit trees. Hedgerows marked the property boundary lines. A beach umbrella, table, and chairs had been set up for the swimmers on the far side of the swimming pool deck. More flowers and trees growing beyond the swimming pool added to the pleasant view from the veranda.

A round table, covered with a white tablecloth, had been set for three. One chair faced the swimming pool, and the other two faced each other. MacGregor's daughter sat in the one facing the pool. Dan and MacGregor sat on each side of her.

Dan could not hide his admiration of the setting and the view. "This is something you only see in paintings." Dan directed his compliment to both of the MacGregors. Then he said, "My guess is, Miss MacGregor, you enjoy the pool and swimming is one of your favorite sports."

She laughed, but before she could reply, her father remarked, "You guessed right, Mr. Sanders, she loves swimming, but she also enjoys horseback riding, hunting, and fishing."

"Don't embarrass me, Dad or Mr. Sanders may think I'm a tomboy, or even worse, an Amazon of some kind."

While MacGregor and his daughter had been talking, Dan had been watching and listening to the banter between the two, he also noticed her slight tan which was unusual for someone with auburn hair, and now he noticed the small freckles bridging her straight, slightly turned-up nose. I've heard freckles are a sign of good health, he thought. I have to believe it when I look at her and after hearing her father's comments.

Dan's thoughts and observations were interrupted by the maid who had walked out from the kitchen and removed the cloth covering the food table which had been placed only a few feet from where the three were sitting. She held the serving Platters and bowls while the three selected from an assortment of neatly quartered sandwiches and a variety of salads and relishes. After serving from each of the dishes, she put each back on the serving table. Before leaving, however, she placed a large pot of tea on the table.

They had finished their sandwiches and salads, and Dan was about to ask for a cup of tea when the maid arrived with the dessert tray. When she set the plate in front of him, he saw it was heaped with strawberry shortcake and topped with an ample serving of whipping cream. The deep dark red strawberries were as large as any he had seen. Then Dan thought, When I was looking at her hair, I could not decide on the color of red. It is the same deep dark red as these strawberries.

MacGregor interrupted Dan's thoughts. "You arrived at the peak of our strawberry season, Mr. Sanders. We have our own strawberry patch and pick them fresh every day. I don't brag a lot, but I think you will agree these are some of the best you have ever tasted."

"Oh, I agree. We grow delicious strawberries in California, but these are as good as any I have ever tasted, and such a beautiful dark red color, too."

I had to bite my tongue to help keep me from saying, 'Just like the color of your hair, Miss MacGregor,' Dan thought. I am sure I would have embarrassed both of us if I had.

After the dessert, the maid cleared the dishes and poured the tea. While stirring his tea, Mr., MacGregor said, "If you have no objection, Mr. Sanders, I'll tell Hillary your story and then she will have a better understanding why you are here."

"I think she should know," Dan said. "At the moment I am sure she is curious and wondering why I came all the way to Boston to see you about her grandfather, a person she has never seen nor ever heard from."

"Thank you, Mr. Sanders. I am very curious. I'm listening, Daddy."

MacGregor began the story as Dan had, with Dan's trip to Randsburg, and with Dan's assistance finished the story, then he showed Hillary the letter and the will.

"I have read the letter," he said, "and I can verify the handwriting is your grandmother's. You may have the letter but not the will until I have looked it over, then you may have it, too. Now Hillary, what are your thoughts on the information Mr. Sanders brought us?"

"My first thought is to apologize to Mr. Sanders for my outburst when we were in the library. I'm sorry, Mr. Sanders, and doubly so, after learning all the trouble you experienced, and the time and effort you have expended trying to help us. Please believe me, I am normally a calm person and seldom let my emotions get the upper hand."

"No need for an apology, Miss MacGregor, it was an unusual situation."

"Thank you for being such a gentleman, Mr. Sanders. But before we proceed any further, please call me Hillary. When anyone calls me Miss MacGregor, I feel like a middle-aged spinster."

MacGregor broke into the conversation, "I don't know why you should feel like a spinster, you won't be 25 until September."

"Daddy!" she scolded, "You know women do not like to have anyone reveal their age."

They were all smiling, and Dan said, "I will call you Hillary if you call me Dan."

MacGregor had been following the exchange between the two. I like this young man, he thought. Then he said, "We have a big house with a half dozen bedrooms, and only three are being used. Since we have many things to discuss, I suggest Hillary drive you to the hotel to pick up your belongings, and you spend the rest of your visit here. What do you think, Hillary?"

She could not hide her enthusiasm. "I think it is a splendid idea, Dad. And, Dan, we will not take 'No' for an answer." She smiled and emphasized his given name as she used it for the first time. Then she asked, "When will you be leaving for San Francisco?"

"This is Saturday, isn't it?" Dan said, aloud. "I'm having difficulty keeping the calendar straight. I'll be leaving on Monday evening at 8:00PM. If all goes well, I'll arrive in San Francisco on Saturday morning. You are right, Mr. MacGregor, we have so many things to discuss and very little time to discuss them. If you are sure I will not be imposing, I will accept your generous offer."

The MacGregors turned and smiled at each other as if they had overcome a major obstacle. They rose from their chairs, and MacGregor said, "It is you who have been the generous one." He pulled his watch from his pocket. "It is 2:35. I'll tell Mary and Nell we will have a guest for the next two days. And, Hillary, if you have time, show Dan some of our historic sites." Then he turned to Dan and said, "I'm sorry, Dan, I forgot to ask you if you had been in Boston before, you may have already seen them."

"This is my first trip, and I had hoped I might find time to visit a few. We will let Hillary decide."

"I'm sure we will have time to visit some of them. It will be fun; I haven't taken the tour in years. I'll call Everett and tell him I won't be in Monday. He will be surprised; I haven't taken a day off in months. Dan, I'll freshen up a bit and meet you in front with the car."

Dan nodded to Hillary, and as soon as she left, Dan asked MacGregor for directions to the bathroom. A few minutes later, he walked out on the front veranda to wait for Hillary.

Dan had been enjoying the beautiful view when Hillary drove up in a late model Oldsmobile coupe. He opened the door and stepped in, and as soon as he was seated, she drove down the driveway and out on the street.

Dan noticed the ease and confidence with which she drove.

He relaxed and then asked, "You mentioned to your father you were going to take time off. Since it was on such short notice, aren't you concerned you might get in trouble with your boss?"

Hillary laughed, "Dad is the boss, but I try not to take

advantage of our relationship. My father inherited the law firm from my great grandfather, who founded the firm in 1848. He specialized in corporate railroad law, and I might add, he did quite well at it. He bought the land and the home where we now live in 1860 and completely remodeled it. Since Father is also a lawyer, I chose law as my profession. Unfortunately, law, like medicine, is the private domain of men. And when I make that statement, I say it without bitterness. It is a factual state-ment. My father pulled a lot of strings to get me into law school, and after getting my degree, he hired me to do research and write briefs. I enjoy my work, and I find it very fulfilling. I know; however, it is doubtful I shall ever defend a client in a court of law."

"I admit, Hillary, the prospects may look dim at present, but the War changed the way many people think about society. Women are becoming more and more visible in the business world, especially here in the United States, and their visibility will continue to grow as they expand their professional goals from teaching and nursing into law and medicine, and even into architecture and engineering. Madame Curie has demon-strated women are becoming a force in science. And I might add, Hillary, I admire you very much for bucking the odds in the law profession."

"Thank you, Dan, you are a very thoughtful person." She turned to him and smiled. "Not every male shares your views."

They rode in silence for a few moments, and then Dan looked at Hilary and said, "I am sure you haven't had time to read the letter your grandmother wrote to your Grandfather MacGregor that your father gave you."

"But I have," Hillary interrupted. "I went over it quickly while freshening up for our trip to town. I admit I had some difficulty deciphering some of the faded writing, and I'll go over it again. The letter said so much in so few words. And the ribbon, so faded and frayed, which tied the tissue paper around the letter tells me he must have loved my grandmother equally as much as she loved him. Yes, Dan, I read it, and I felt tiny chills run up my back. So sad, Dan, I could not help but shed a tear for both of them."

"Your father talked about the letter after he read it, and his thoughts and feelings were similar to yours. If I might add, mine was, too. Life, at times, can be very cruel, and I recall, I made that very same remark when, by chance, I discovered your grandfather had been killed by the same explosion which uncovered the fortune he had been seeking all his life. After discovering your grandfather's body, and then later finding the letter and reading it, I felt like a person who had read the last chapter of a love story and then read the first chapter. But when he decided to read the entire book, the pages in between were blank. Since finding the letter and reading the letter, I have often wondered what happened after your Grandmother Alice returned to Boston."

"That is probably one of the best-kept family secrets in Boston."

"I'm sorry, Hilary, I did not mean to probe into something that is none of my business."

"Now, it is my turn to apologize. You are not probing, as you call it, you deserve an answer because you already know more about the story than anyone else with the exception of Father and me."

"What I'm trying to say, Hilary, and I'm not doing a very good job of it, is that I am concerned about creating an embarrassing situation for you."

"That is not a problem. The whole thing happened so long ago that neither Father nor I have talked about it for years, and

I shall not be embarrassed because I believe you should know and I am sure Father does, too. Considering all you have done for us, Father and I owe you so much we can never repay you. The least we can do to show our appreciation is by sharing our secret with you." She turned her head from the road for a moment and gave him a small smile. Her blue-gray eyes said, "We like you, and we trust you." Then she began:

My grandmother told my father the entire story of her love affair with my grandfather, and on my 21st birthday, he passed it on to me. Since the letter pretty well sums up what happened in San Francisco, and since you have information about my grandfather, we were unaware of, I'll begin after their arrival in Boston.

Grandmother Alice did not tell her mother she was pregnant until the middle of March when she felt she could no longer keep it a secret. Her mother told her she was suspicious but had kept her concern to herself. Grandmother said she was surprised her mother took it so calmly. Her only response was a combined look of hurt and disappointment. Then her mother opened her arms and held her, and Grandma said she cried on her mother's shoulder. Then they sat down close together on her mother's bed and talked in whispers to prevent the household help from hearing. Neither knew how her father would react to Grandmother's condition since both were well aware of how furious he could become at times.

Her mother decided she should be the one to tell him.

Grandma said she did not eat dinner that night because she felt so tired and weary after the talk with her mother, and the fear her father might ask her if she were ill.

The next morning, she did not hear the usual sound of the horse and buggy leaving, so she knew her father had not left for work. She lay in bed longer than usual, and while dressing, gave special attention to her grooming, postponing the confrontation with her father as long as possible. Finally, she walked downstairs and into the dining room. He was standing with his hands clasped behind him looking out the window. When he heard her footsteps, he turned and looked at her. She saw his grim face, and his eyes seemed to bore into her. She felt frightened, but she did not cower. Then his face changed, and she saw in his eyes a question which seemed to be asking, 'Why did you do this to me?' Then he said, 'Get your mother and meet me in the library where we can talk.'

Grandma Alice and her mother walked into the library where her father was waiting. He closed and locked the door then turned and pointed to a table near the center of the room. Before sitting down, he said, 'Babe, you've got yourself in a hell of a mess, haven't you?' Grandma said it was the first time in all of her life she had ever heard him swear, and she expected the worst. But then he pulled chairs out for each one and nodded for them to sit down. Her father opened the conversation by expressing his concern about the inevitable scandal that would erupt as soon as word of the pregnancy reached the Boston newspapers. Then he said, 'Your mother and I discussed our situation thoroughly, and I see no point in discussing the whys and wherefores further. The problem now is to decide what we should do about it.' As I see it, we have two options: we can do nothing and face the problem head-on, or we can arrange for you to go to Europe, preferably London, for an extended period of time.

To make a long story short, they agreed the best solution

would be for Grandma Alice to go to London and enroll in one of the women's colleges in London's suburbs and rent a nearby flat, sufficiently large to accommodate a full-time maid, her father would contact his firm's London representative and ask him to make the preliminary arrangements, and hopefully they could plan on leaving the following week. Her father also said he would immediately send a priority letter to Mr. Beasly, his law firm's London representative, and ask him to meet them at the ship in addition to making the preliminary arrangements. In the meantime, the family planned to spread the word that Grandma Alice planned to get her degree in English Literature, and what better place to go than to a college in the vicinity of London.

The Civil War was rapidly winding down, and Grandma's father decided it would be better to book passage out of New York since European bound passenger ships sailed almost daily. They were able to book and leave within 10 days. All went well, and Mr. Beasly met them at the ship. And as soon as Grandma had settled into her flat, her mother and father returned to Boston. However, before leaving, my great grandmother informed Mr. Beasly of Grandma's condition, and after being sworn to secrecy, Mr. Beasly became Grandma's advisor.

A month passed, and during that time, Grandma wrestled with the thought of writing to Grandpa Jim, but each time she postponed it. Finally, she came to a conclusion she would only make matters worse for Mr. Beasly and herself, so she dropped the idea. However, she did decide to approach Mr. Beasly on the idea of getting her name changed to MacGregor. If he could arrange for a marriage certificate, even if illegal, she would accept it and lie about it if necessary, to protect her unborn child. When she approached Mr. Beasly, he appeared willing to take on the task but even though she was now 18, he said, he must first obtain approval from her father. It took over a month before he received a reply. Her father agreed, and his reply sounded almost enthusiastic about the idea. With the concurrence of her father, he proceeded to get the papers, and with the help of a few well-greased palms, had them signed and recorded. The marriage certificate bore the name of James Robert MacGregor.

She gave birth on September 16, 1865. Those who questioned her about her husband were told he was killed in a mining accident with no further explanation. She would change the subject immediately as if the subject was too horrible to discuss. Dan, little did we know you would bring news about my grandfather that would turn a white lie into a prophecy.

At the request of her mother and father, she returned home four years later with her son, John. His Grandfather Holbrook believed he needed a man's guidance and took over the male role model. My father immediately latched on to his grandfather, and when his grandfather was home, he, followed him wherever he went asking questions, and his grandfather never seemed to become irritated or tired of answering them. When the time came for him to enter college, his grandfather steered him into Harvard, and later into Harvard Law School. Dad joined his grandfather's law firm and soon became a junior partner. And when Great Grandfather Holbrook passed away, he inherited the law firm.

"WELL, Dan, now you have the story, and I finished just in time. I don't think we can get a parking place any closer, so I'll pull in here. The entrance to your hotel is just around the corner."

Dan had been listening so intently, he had been aware of the increase in traffic, but he did not realize they had reached the hotel. "A fascinating story, Hillary. Thanks for letting me share your family history. Are you coming into the lobby, or will you wait here?"

"I believe I will wait here and watch the people walk by. If I get bored, I'll come into the lobby. How long do you think it will take?"

"About 20 or 30 minutes if all goes well." He closed the car door and turned to leave.

"By the way, would you like to try out our swimming pool tomorrow, and do you have a swimsuit?" she asked.

He stuck his head back in the car. "'I sure would,' to answer the first part of your question and 'no' to the second part." Both laughed, then he turned and left.

Dan stopped by the desk and saw the desk clerk who had helped him the night before was on duty. "Thanks to you," Dan said, "I found the place I was looking for in the area where you directed me, and fortunately, the people. They have invited me to stay with them, so I'll be checking out."

"It has been a pleasure having you as our guest, Mr. Sanders. Your statement will be ready when you come down. If you please call when you are ready to leave, I'll send up the bellboy."

Dan thanked him and hurried to the elevator. His laundry and cleaning had been returned, so he removed his luggage from the closet and began packing. Twenty-five minutes late+, he and the bellboy arrived at the car, but Hillary was not there.

I may have missed her, he thought, and as soon as the bellboy and I have finished storing the luggage, I'll return to the lobby and check.

Just as Dan prepared to leave, he looked in the opposite direction and saw Hillary hurrying toward the car carrying her purse in one hand and a package in the other.

"I decided to do some shopping while you were gone. I hope I didn't keep you waiting."

"No," Dan replied, "we had just finished sorting the luggage. I thought perhaps I had missed you when I passed through the lobby." He turned and tipped the bellboy then continued. "I've got everything, even my clean laundry. I'm ready to leave when you are." He started to move towards the driver's side to open the door for her, but she had opened the door and climbed in before he reached the front of the car. He felt slightly embarrassed when he returned to his side and climbed in.

Hillary started the car and then commented, "We have about three hours to see the sites which means, of course, we can't spend much time exploring each one, so where do we start?"

"I have read and heard about the USS Constitution since my early years in grammar school. Should we take the time to visit the old warship?"

"By all means. 'Old Ironsides' is one of my favorites." Hillary pulled out of the parking place and drove to the Boston Naval Yard. They had to park quite some distance from the frigate's berth where she lay moored. Hillary got out and had moved to Dan's side of the car while he had been fiddling with the door latch. I must have been lucky at the first stop, he thought, as he finally climbed out. I wonder why this young woman makes me feel uneasy.

As soon as he had closed the car door, she put her arm through his as though she had been doing it for years and began guiding him down the walk. She looked at him and smiled, then she said, "It's about a quarter of a mile. It won't take long."

He smiled back and thought, I feel like I am being towed, but when she looks at me as if I am a V.I.P, I feel like I don't mind being towed. Noticing the way Hillary was walking and guiding him through the foot traffic, he knew it could not possibly take very long to reach their destination. She reminds me of the time when I was a small boy and on the way to see the carnival that had just arrived in town. She is so eager and radiates so much vitality, he thought.

Dan had been watching her, and she turned and smiled. "It is down at the end of this street." She pointed with the hand carrying her purse. "It has been at least two years since I visited the old ship, and I am looking forward to seeing it almost as much as you are. Are you familiar with her history?"

Dan smiled, "No, not really, I remember the story about her sailors seeing cannonballs bounce off her thick oak hull, and they nicknamed her 'Old Ironsides.' And as I recall, she and five other sister frigates were authorized to be built by President Washington to prevent the privateers operating along our eastern coast, and the pirates operating in the Mediterranean along the African coast from capturing and raiding our merchant ships. Other than that, my knowledge is very sketchy."

They reached the gate and were passed through by the guard to the gangplank and boarded the ship on the spar deck. Hillary pointed to the tall spars, "She can hoist an acre of sails, and with her 36 sails, she could outsail and outmaneuver any other warship on the high seas. She carried a complement of

450 men who could rig the sails in minutes." Then she pointed to the cannon on the spar deck. "The foreign frigates carried 38 to 44 cannon, usually 18 pounders or less on one deck. 'Old Ironsides' mounted 54 guns, 24 on the spar deck and 30 on the gun deck, outgunning enemy frigates, not only in quantity but also in size. Her cannon fired 24 or 32 pounders."

Hillary held Dan's hand and guided him through the other visitors and around the stacks of rigging while calling his attention to the features of the helm and the instruments used by the helmsman. They walked down the steps to the dimly lit captain's quarters, where the first commander of the USS Constitution, Captain Samuel Nicholson, followed by Captain Silas Talbot, Captain Isaac Hull, and other captains, lived and planned their strategies.

As they stood together looking through the dim light, Dan felt Hillary squeeze his hand and say, "I always get goosebumps when I come down here. I can't explain it, but I feel as though I am surrounded by the ghosts of all the brave men who met here and later lost their lives while serving their country." She looked up at Dan's face as if seeking understanding and support of her feelings.

"I believe most of us have feelings of being on a hallowed place the minute we step on to this ship, and as we explore it, those feelings grow. Yes, this ship is filled with ghosts of brave men who died in action."

When they reached the gun deck, they walked along the deck behind the guns and Dan noted the sand buckets near each gun, "The sailors used the sand to pour over blood to keep the gun crew from slipping. Flying wooden splinters caused more casualties to wooden warships than direct hits or shrapnel. Wars are a dirty business, Hilary, there are many ghosts of brave men in here, too."

"Yes," she said, "I can feel their presence, and when I picture the battle scenes this old ship has experienced, I smell the smoke from these big guns."

After finishing their tour of the ship and as they walked back to the car, Hillary said, "We won't have much time for the other places I want you to see, but we shall do what we can. Is that all right with you, or is there some special place you are interested in?"

"Lead on, MacGregor," Dan said teasingly, "you have done a great job this far."

Hillary laughed, "OK, I'll lead the way."

After reaching the car, Hillary said, "The Old North Church will be our first stop. From there, we will drive to the Old South Meeting House, Faneuil Hall, and the King's Chapel. I doubt if we will have time to go in except for a few minutes. Tomorrow, perhaps, if we can find the time, we will look over Bunker Hill."

They completed their tour and started back toward the MacGregor home. Dan thought about the events of the day, but most of all, about Hillary. I have never met a woman exactly like her before, he thought. She is so enthusiastic and so full of energy. She is independent, saying what she thinks, yet, tender, warm-hearted, and thoughtful. Intelligent, too.

Suddenly, his thoughts were interrupted by Hillary.

"You seemed to have slipped away." She turned her head, smiled, then asked, "Where did you go?"

Dan squirmed a second or two and replied, "I have been thinking about an enjoyable, well spent, very educational after-noon, accompanied by a very knowledgeable and personable young lady." Then he returned the smile.

"I enjoyed it, too," she said. "It was nice having someone

who shared my thoughts on our historical heritage. There are so many people who don't seem to care."

"I've noticed that, too. It seems to be a 'So what?' attitude. Apparently, they never consider the great sacrifices our forefathers made in human lives, human suffering, and personal wealth to give us our freedom. And through the years ensuring its perpetuation, so that we who followed could enjoy that freedom while creating a country which has become the envy of the world."

They rode in silence for a few minutes and then Dan said, "I have a question that intrudes into your family history, and again I have no right to ask it except out of curiosity. Please believe me when I say that if it is too personal, I will not be offended."

Hillary smiled, "Let's hear the question."

"While we were talking about your Grandmother Alice, I kept thinking about the letter she wrote to your Grandfather MacGregor. She said she was concerned, that if she was pregnant and her father found out, he might cause physical harm to be inflicted on your Grandfather MacGregor. Do you remember her comment?"

"Oh, definitely, I was a little surprised."

"It sounded to me, Hillary as if your Great Grandfather Holbrook was a violent man. Yet, when he was told his daughter was pregnant, he showed he was upset, but otherwise, he appeared to be only concerned with the welfare of his wife and his daughter. And the way he practically adopted his grandson, also surprised me."

"I agree with you, but I can't explain it. My great grandfather passed away before I was born. Consequently, I never had an opportunity for firsthand observations of his temperament. I know my father received all the love and care any father could have given him, and I have never heard of any violent act he may have committed from either my mother or my father. I can only guess, that during the conversation that ensued after my great grandmother told him their daughter was pregnant, she convinced him nothing could be gained through retribution, that they should support their child and go forward."

"Thanks, Hillary, trying to put a story together that happened over a half a century ago is not an easy task. Now, may I ask another question?"

"Fire away."

"Has your father been ill? When I arrived this morning, he appeared to me to be a little pale."

"Dad is not in the best of health. He had a heart attack two years ago shortly after Mother passed away. The attack forced him into semiretirement. Why do you ask?"

"I had hoped he might return to California with me and clean up the paperwork on the claim. It is possible to do it by mail, but it will take a lot longer. I am scheduled to leave for South Africa in about two months, and I would like to see everything in order before I leave. What do you think?"

"What needs to be done and how strenuous will the trip be?" "In addition to the paperwork involved in transferring the claim, I suggest new claims be marked and recorded around the original strike to prevent anyone from filing claims adjacent to your father's claim. If they do, they can tunnel into the main ore vein on your father's claim. The most strenuous task is the six-hour horseback ride to the claim. I walked and led the horse over the top of the hills, which must be crossed to reach the claim to be sure I did not exhaust him. However, my biggest concern is Schuleman. As I mentioned, he is a very dangerous man. If by some quirk of fate, he had shown up while I was at the claim, no one could possibly predict what might have happened, and I don't believe anyone can predict the outcome if he shows up on my next trip to the claim. The point being, of course, the trip will not be easy, and it could get nasty and turn into a very dangerous trip. I don't believe it is the kind of trip for a man who has had a heart attack."

"I agree, Dan, but r shall discuss it with my father and get his opinion on what we should do." Just then she turned into the driveway, and added, "Well, here we are safe and sound. I'll pull the car into the garage then I won't have to park it later."

Dan removed his luggage from the car and followed Hillary to the veranda by the swimming pool and into the dining room. Hillary then called Mary and asked the maid to show Dan to his room. "I'll meet you in the living room after I have cleaned up a bit and changed."

"I'll do the same," Dan said, and then asked, "What time is dinner?"

"Everything we do in Boston is based on tradition."

Then she smiled, "Dinner is served at eight." And with a slight hand gesture as she turned to walk away, said, "I'll see you later."

The maid led Dan upstairs to his room and showed him the clothes closet, the bath, and how to open and close the windows. Dan thanked her, and she left.

Dan looked at his watch, then he thought. It is 7:05.

I'll have time to unpack, bathe, and change my clothes. It has been an interesting day, he thought, while putting away his clothes. And I can't recall meeting two more interesting people than Mr. MacGregor and Hillary, they seem so grateful for everything I have done. I am glad I made the trip.

Dan walked into the living room 40 minutes later and immediately noticed the intense conversation in progress between MacGregor and his daughter. Since both were talking in low tones, he stopped and started to back away. This appears to be a private conversation, so I'll leave and return in a few minutes, he thought.

At that moment, MacGregor looked up and saw him and said, "Come on in, Dan, this conversation involves you." He pointed to a chair between his and where Hillary was sitting. Then he continued, "Hillary has been telling me about your tour of Boston and how much you seem to have enjoyed it."

"Thank you," Dan said as he sat down. "I enjoyed the tour immensely. Your daughter is a wonderful guide."

"She has also been telling me about your concern with the work which needs to be done on the claim from now until the time you must start your preparations for your trip to South Africa."

Dan raised his left hand with the palm facing MacGregor.

"It isn't all that serious." Then he turned toward Hillary, "I'm sorry I mislead, Hillary. I meant to imply it would be easier and quicker to get the tasks cleared away where the work is to be done rather than working by telephone and by mail."

Hillary immediately jumped into the conversation, "I know exactly what you said and what you meant. I know it isn't a crisis situation, but you have been carrying the entire burden of the claim on your shoulders long enough, and the time has come to provide you with some help. I have discussed the problem with Dad, and though he is not totally in agreement, I am going with you."

Dan had been following Hillary's conversation word for word because he sensed she was about to offer a solution to his problem, but he was not prepared for the solution she had presented. His jaw sagged, and momentarily he appeared to be in shock. He stared at Hillary as if he was trying to fathom what she meant. Yet, her words were clear. He looked at MacGregor as if to seek some kind of an explanation from him, "You heard what she said, Dan, I am concerned, but there is not much I can do about it. She is over 21 and entitled to make her own decisions. She mentioned you believe a return trip to the claim is necessary, and it could be dangerous. Why?"

Dan repeated the reasons for returning and the dangers he might encounter.

"Why don't you let the authorities handle the problem?" MacGregor asked.

"I did once," Dan replied, "and I created an even bigger problem. More important, everything I've told you about Schuleman is based on supposition and theory. I believe he is guilty, but I have no hard evidence and trying to convince an officer of the law that one of his fellow officers is a murderer is almost an impossible task. If I had the time, it would be possible to follow your suggestion. However, under the existing circumstances, I shall do my best to get the task accomplished, and if I am fortunate, without any unpleasant incidents. If not, I will cope with each one as it arises."

"Do you believe the claim is worth the risks you may encounter?"

"Materially, perhaps not. In my superficial examination of the claim, I estimated it should yield between a quarter of a million and a million dollars. However, the gold that it yields is not as important as seeing justice is done. I saw the amount of hard work your father put into that claim, and therefore, I easily visualized the amount of hard work he had put into other claims during his lifetime before he found his pot of gold. As a brother in the mining industry, I know of no other occupation more dangerous, nor any more physically strenuous than that performed by miners." Then Dan said in a low voice, "Regard-less of what anyone wishes to call it, I cannot stand by and let some unscrupulous character steal the fortune your father discovered after fifty years of searching and digging and digging and searching."

Both MacGregor and Hillary sat quietly for a moment, then MacGregor spoke, "I readily understand how you feel, Dan. I do not mean any disrespect to the three of us who are sitting here when I say that under the conditions you found my father, you probably feel closer to him than either Hilary or I do. And I want you to know I would gladly go with you if I did not believe I would be more of a burden than a help to you."

Hillary quickly followed up, "Dan understands, Dad. We discussed your physical problems on the way home. However, there is nothing wrong with my health, and I assure you, Dan, I will not be a burden. Pardon me, Dad, I did not mean to put you down, but I must convince Dan I can hold up my end of the load. It may help, Dan, if you know I have been on week-long fishing and hunting trips with Dad, and I can make camp and pitch a tent as well as any man. I can also saddle my own horse and load a pack animal."

Then MacGregor added, "She is also a crack shot and can gut, skin, and dress a deer as well as anyone. I am not in favor of her going, but she has made up her mind, Dan, and believe me, she will not be a liability." MacGregor looked up at the entrance to the library and said, "I don't know how long Mary has been standing there, but I am sure she is trying to let us know dinner is ready." MacGregor rose from his chair and asked of Dan and Hillary, "Are you ready?" and then added, "We can continue this conversation later."

MacGregor deliberately kept the conversation light during dinner. Dan did not inquire about the wine but decided the not too distant Canadian border provided the source. After dinner MacGregor suggested they go to the library where the lighting was better because he wanted their opinion on a document he had prepared.

After they had sat down at one of the reading tables, with Dan on one side and the MacGregors on the other, MacGregor asked, "Dan, do you wish to comment further on our conversation before dinner?"

"Yes, but only to ask Hillary to sleep on her decision. As I have said before, if my rational and conclusions are correct, the trip could become dangerous."

"I agree with Dan. Delaying your decision until tomorrow will give all of us more time to think about it."

Hillary smiled, "You don't leave me much choice, do you? So, I shall give you my decision tomorrow."

"Good!" MacGregor commented, and then he turned to Dan.

"Dan, while Hillary was showing you our famous city, I prepared a document I hope both of you will approve. "He looked at Hillary then at Dan. Puzzled, they both stared and waited. MacGregor continued, "I have drawn up a document making the three of us equal partners in the claim."

Dan turned his head from side to side while saying, "No, no." Then he stopped the head movement and looking directly at MacGregor said, "This is your inheritance from your father. I did not come here with the idea, or to suggest to you that you share it with me. I don't claim to be wealthy, but I am financially independent. You are not obligated to me in any way."

MacGregor smiled, "If you had taken a different position, Dan, I would have been disappointed. Being a lawyer, I am a pretty good judge of a person's character. I drew from our conversations you are independent, and I anticipated what you were going to say. Making you an equal partner with Hillary and me is not exactly a gift. I know nothing about mining and neither does Hillary, but you are an expert. The document spells out that the three of us will share equally in the development costs and equally in the profits. Dan, you are assigned the position of general manager, but you will not receive a salary."

Dan started to interrupt, but MacGregor held up his hand and continued, "More important, I know you are honest, and that Hillary and I can trust you. I also know you will be leaving for South Africa in about 60 days, but I am sure you have confronted like situations before, and you have overcome whatever obstacles you may have encountered." Once again, before Dan could interrupt, he turned to Hilary and asked, "What do you think of such an arrangement, Hillary?"

"I think it's an excellent idea, Dad. I know we cannot find anyone more qualified. He lives near the area where the claim is located; therefore, he can manage the operation much easier, and much better than you, Dad, who will be 3,000 miles away." Then she looked at Dan. "I think it is the very best arrangement Dad can make, and Dad and I will be forever grateful if you will accept."

Again, Dan felt himself squirm in the presence of his new friends as he looked back and forth from Hilary to her father. Slightly embarrassed, he finally smiled and said, "I find it very difficult trying to win an argument when I am opposed by two lawyers; therefore, I concede."

Hillary's smile grew bigger. She jumped out of her chair and gave her father a big hug. "Isn't this wonderful, Dad? This is the most exciting thing that has happened around here since we used to go deer hunting together." Then she turned to Dan and said, "Thank you very much for accepting Dad's offer."

She held out her hand to Dan. Dan rose and shook her hand then turned to MacGregor, who had also risen.

Dan offered his hand to MacGregor and said, "This trip has taken a twist I had not anticipated, and I can't say that I regret it. May our partnership, not only be prosperous but also increase the bond of friendship I sense is growing between us."

"I wholeheartedly endorse what you have said, and I could not have said it better. Now I suggest we review the document for any changes or additions that either of you believes are necessary."

MacGregor read the document aloud, explaining and interpreting the rationale he used in developing its contents. When he had finished, he looked at Hillary first, who nodded approval and then at Dan.

"I recommend a minor change in the title, Sir. Your father found the claim, registered it, and spent many years of hard work developing it. Please drop my name from the title so it will read: The MacGregor Mining Company."

Turning to Hillary, MacGregor asked, "What do you think of Dan's recommendation?"

"I like the idea, and once again it shows the thoughtfulness of our new friend."

Dan could feel the blood rushing to his face. He knew he did not become embarrassed easily, but Hilary seemed to have a way of making him feel uncomfortable without realizing it. He rubbed his face as if trying to rub away the redness, but neither Hillary nor her father seemed to notice. MacGregor's voice penetrated his thoughts.

"The majority rules, any other changes from either of you?" MacGregor looked at Hilary and then at Dan. "Since none seem necessary, I'll have the document typed so the three of us can sign it. Now, Dan, we need to discuss finances. Can you give us an estimate of how much we need to invest in getting the mine into production?"

"Fortunately, I have given the subject some thought. Our biggest expense at the outset will be wagons and mules to haul supplies in and the ore out. We can't use trucks unless we build roads, something we will look into and may decide to do later on. Fremont Railroad Station, our shipping and receiving terminal, is roughly ten miles from the claim, and a stamp mill is located at Red Mountain, twelve miles north of Fremont Station. We will also need a water wagon, tents, lumber for shoring and permanent quarters, tools, compressors, and other associated equipment, mess equipment, plus personnel. I estimate $30,000 will carry us until the mine can pay its own way."

"It sounds reasonable to me. I'll have the paperwork completed by Monday to establish the company and also a cashier's check made out to the MacGregor Mining Company. And, Hillary, you can repay me the next time you go to the bank. Where do you plan on establishing the mining company's account, Dan?"

"In San Francisco, which brings up another subject, if I may. I plan to discuss my ideas with my engineering consulting firm. If I can work out an agreement satisfactory to the three of us, we can have the firm run the operation while I am in South Africa. It is an old reliable engineering firm, and it has been in business since the days of the Gold Rush. It has managed many operations exactly like the one we are planning with great success, and it is licensed and bonded under the state laws of California. This is a subject I had to consider, and I will appreciate your thoughts on the idea after you have had time to mull it over. Getting back to finances, I will have my San Francisco bank issue a cashier's check, and we can open the account for the full amount."

"Having your firm manage the company while you are gone, Dan, sounds like an excellent idea," commented MacGregor. "But it has been a long day, and I am not as young as you two. So, if you don't mind, I'll call it a day, and we shall continue our discussion tomorrow."

MacGregor pushed himself up from the armchair, and Hillary and Dan stood up at the same time. Dan held out his hand and said, "It has been a real pleasure meeting you, Sir, and I hope you sleep well."

"Thank you, Dan, and I hope you do the same." Then he leaned over toward Hillary, offering his cheek for his good-night kiss. She responded and at the same time, reached for his hand and squeezed it.

"Goodnight, Dad." They smiled, and no words were needed to explain the affection they held for each other.

Dan continued to stand until MacGregor passed through the door. "Your father is a remarkable man, Hillary. Even though I have known him only for a day, I can say without reservation, he has made me feel as though we have known each other for years, and almost as if am a member of the family. Meeting the two of you has been a gratifying experience. I am glad I came."

"Thank you, Dan. Knowing my father as well as I do, I know he feels the same way about you. How many men would travel 3000 miles to give a stranger a gold mine he could legally have kept for himself? We are both lawyers, and we meet all kinds of people. Of course, I haven't been exposed to the number and variety my father has, but I have been in contact with enough to know the kind of men, and women, too, who are honest and forthright like you, are as rare as diamonds in a coal mine."

Dan rubbed his face because he knew it was getting red for

the second time that evening. I wonder why I become embarrassed so easily when I'm with Hillary, he thought. He looked up and saw Hillary smiling.

"I'm sorry, Dan, I did not intend to embarrass you. However, I meant every word I said. Now, why don't we change the subject? Dad and I enjoy a game of cribbage, do you play?"

"Not since my army days. I know you will skin me, but I am willing to give it a try."

"Good. Look in the drawer in your side of the table, a deck of cards and a cribbage board should be in there somewhere."

Dan found both and handed them to Hillary. She set the board between them, and they set their pegs in the game holes. After cutting the cards, and Dan winning the deal, the game began. Since Dan had not played in over two years, both agreed they should play a few hands to refresh Dan's memory before starting a serious game. As they played, they exchanged comments and discussed the finer points of the game, replaying a hand when Dan questioned his own play.

When Dan said, "I'm ready," he knew he faced an opponent as skilled as any he had met in the Army. They had completed three games when the grandfather clock struck twelve.

Hillary had won two games, and Dan had eked out one.

"You played exceptionally well, Dan, considering it has been over two years since you have played. I think we should call it a day if you are agreeable."

"Yes, let's do, and I might add, you are a tough opponent. I haven't had to concentrate like that for quite some time. Maybe we can try it again before I leave. I really enjoyed the match."

"Thank you, I did, too. I am going to have a cup of tea before going to bed," Hillary commented while handing Dan the cards and the cribbage board to put away. "Would you care to join me?"

"Gladly, I am very fond of tea, but I prefer coffee in the morning." As they rose from the table and began walking toward the kitchen, Dan continued, "I usually have a cup or two and a light breakfast before I leave for work in the morning, that is because I am single and usually the first person to arrive at the office. And since the first person to arrive is responsible for cleaning the coffee urn and preparing the coffee for our forty-plus employees, I soon discovered I had become the number one coffee maker and all the bad jokes that go with the job."

They entered the kitchen just as Dan finished his story.

She laughed a very feminine lilting laugh while pointing to a small kitchen table. Then she commented as she began preparing the tea, "You sound as though you and your fellow employees have a warm, friendly feeling toward each other."

"Now that you mention it, I suppose we do. Sometimes we are exposed to dangerous situations, and it is nice to know we can depend on each other."

"Being the only female lawyer in our law offices has its assets and its liabilities. I never lack for attention but the male-female barrier, which we discussed earlier, is always there."

Dan knew a person as beautiful and talented as Hillary, must have friends, both male, and female, but he sensed from the tone of her voice and her discussions of her office and school experiences, she also must have occasional feelings of loneliness. It must be very difficult, he thought, to be as capable as the people with whom you work, yet never have the opportunity to prove it.

He watched as she sliced a lemon and asked, "Where do

you get your lemons, from the West Coast or from Florida? I hear Florida is getting into citrus in a big way."

"California is our prime source. However, we do receive some Florida shipments, and now and then a ship from the Middle East brings in a load." While talking, she had set the sliced lemon, sugar, and a small dish of tarts on the table.

When she returned with the tea, Dan asked, "Have you ever visited California?"

"No, not yet." Then she looked at him with a mysterious half-smile, and said, "But I hope to someday."

Dan's heart skipped a beat because he felt sure he knew what the smile implied. He decided not to pursue the subject further since it might cause her to reveal her decision before she discussed it with her father.

While they drank their tea, they continued their inconsequential conversation and munched on tarts, until they decided to call it a day.

When Dan woke up the next morning, he was surprised to see sufficient light seeping through and around the heavy drapes to permit him to read the time on his watch. It is after eight o'clock, he thought. I haven't slept this late since I don't know when. It must be the change in the time zones. I wonder what my hosts are thinking. Then he smiled because he remembered it was after one in the morning before he got to bed.

MacGregor used steam to heat the house, and Dan's room was not cold, but the hot bath felt good, and he took his time bathing. By the time he had finished dressing, he had heard the library clock chimes ring nine times.

Dan walked downstairs and out on the veranda just as Hillary jackknifed from the diving board into the pool. The white bathing suit matched the natural color of her skin which only became visible when shoulder straps on her swimsuit shifted, or the swimsuit pants and skirt pulled up from her lightly tanned legs when she dove from the springboard.

She saw Dan when she surfaced and swam over to the side of the pool. "Good morning, Dan. How are you this morning?"

"Great, I didn't plan to sleep quite this late though. I'll blame it on the time zone, I can't think of any other excuse. You seem to be enjoying your dip on this beautiful morning."

"The water is perfect. Dad always keeps the water a little warmer during these brisk mornings, and that helps. It can get pretty chilly this time of year. The box on the table contains a bathing suit. I think it will fit you if you care to join me."

Dan turned and saw the box Hillary was carrying when she returned to the car from shopping. "Wonderful," he said. "I'll join you in five minutes." He picked up the package, waved, and hurried into the house and up the stairs.

When he returned, he saw Hillary cutting through the water toward the end of the pool with smooth overhand strokes. He dove into the water from the side of the pool and swam beside her to the end of the pool. As he hung on the side of the pool, he turned to her and said, "Thanks for the swimsuit, it was very thoughtful of you."

"No thanks necessary. Since you are from California, I had a feeling you would enjoy a dip." She smiled and continued, "I also assumed you did not bring a bathing suit. I hope you like black."

"Right on all counts, but my curiosity is eating me alive. How did you know my size? Or maybe I shouldn't ask."

Hillary laughed, but the laugh did not seem quite natural to Dan. "I asked a clerk in the men's department who was about your size, what size he wore." Without looking at Dan, she turned and began swimming back to the other end of the pool.

Slightly surprised, Dan slowly pushed off and followed her.

I hope I didn't embarrass her, he thought. Then he said aloud, but not loud enough for Hillary to hear, "Me and my big mouth."

She was out of the pool and climbing on the diving board before he reached the end of the pool. Running to the end of the diving board, she jumped high into the air and arced into a graceful swan dive. After a smooth entry, she surfaced and swam toward Dan.

What a beautiful body and what marvelous control, Dan thought. According to her father, she does many things exceptionally well. No wonder he is so proud of her.

Dan was hanging on the ladder by the diving board when Hillary swam up. "Would you like to try it?" she asked, nodding in the direction of the diving board.

"No thanks," Dan replied, smiling. "Diving never was one of my strong points. I usually wind up with a belly flop."

Hillary laughed and then suggested, "Let's do four or five laps, more if you like, then get out and get ready for breakfast. "

They completed four and decided to do two more. Hilary's father, dressed in his smoking jacket, walked out on the veranda during their final two laps and watched as they swam side by side with smooth, strong strokes. He nodded with approval, then left and walked into the kitchen to check on the arrangements for breakfast.

Hillary's father was sitting in one of the veranda lounge chairs when Dan returned from dressing. He heard the screen door shut and started to get up when Dan said, "Don't get up, Mr. MacGregor." Dan leaned over and shook his hand then continued, "Hillary and I were up a little late last night playing cribbage. I hope we did not disturb you?"

"Not at all, not at all. This house is built pretty solid and absorbs most of the sounds. Are you a cribbage player?"

"I used to be when I was in the Service. It's about the old story in the Army, 'Hurry up and wait.' While we were waiting, my buddy and I played cribbage. Since there was plenty of waiting, we had plenty of time for cribbage."

Dan sat down in one of the lounge chairs next to MacGregor's. They continued to chat until Hillary arrived. Dan stood up and remained standing while Hillary greeted her father. MacGregor suggested they have breakfast, then Hillary left to tell Nell.

The table used for lunch the previous day had been set, and as soon as Mary had placed the covered serving platters on the serving table, the three, led by Hillary's father moved to the table set for breakfast. Mary had placed a bowl of the home-grown strawberries covered with whipping cream in front of each person.

They sat down, but before Dan had a chance to comment on the strawberries, Hillary's father spoke to Dan and said, "Dan, we are not religious fanatics, but Hillary and I have been so fortunate, I always give thanks to the Lord each Sunday morning for his favors. Do you have any objections?"

"No," replied Dan, "I welcome it." Dan bowed his head and placed his hands on the edge of the table.

With breakfast over and the dishes cleared away, Hillary had just taken a sip of her second cup of coffee when she looked up at her father and knew the tone of the conversation was about to change. He looked at her, and his face showed concern that had not been there before. He reached over and put his hand gently on hers, and speaking softly said, "What have you decided, My Dear?"

Both Dan and her father watched her as she replied, "I

have decided to go, Dad." She turned the palm of her hand over and squeezed his hand. Then she turned to Dan and said, "I don't think I'll be a burden, Dan." She continued with a weak smile, "In fact, I believe I can help. As you know, I am a lawyer. What I am not, is a jellyfish." Then she turned to her father and said, "And, Dad, you are not to worry."

MacGregor then returned her weak smile, "I will worry about you because I am your father. Last night, you will recall, Dan remarked during our discussion, he could not discount the danger you may encounter, and even though I will worry, I want you to know I am very proud of you." He turned to Dan and said, "We haven't heard what you think of Hillary's decision, Dan."

Dan looked at Hillary and then back to MacGregor. "I don't claim to be a psychic, our discussion last night led me to think she might not change her mind; consequently, I was prepared for her decision. In fact, I welcome it because of my commitment to the South African assignment. The two of us can accomplish so much more than I can alone. I have made notes of matters she can handle, which will save us many hours. Getting back to the dangers we may encounter; I can't say with any degree of certainty they exist. I say this because the dangers are all based on my personal theories and assumptions. For example, I have never met Schuleman, I can't verify he blew up the mine, I can't prove he killed his partner, and so on."

MacGregor held up his hand and broke into Dan's personal condemnation. "Dan, remember, I am a lawyer, and I believe I am a pretty good one. I listened to your story yesterday. Your theories and your assumptions lead me to believe your conclusions are correct. I also believe your little dissertation discounting what you truly believe was for my benefit. Don't do it. If you continue expressing such comments, you may begin to believe them and lower your guard, then you will be endangering Hilary's life as well as your own."

Dan realized he had just been reprimanded, and he knew he deserved it. It did not seem possible he had only known Hillary and Mr. MacGregor 24 hours, yet he had developed a deep respect for both. "You are right, Mr. MacGregor, and I apologize."

Hillary's father turned to her and said, "Tomorrow evening will be here quicker than you think, so I suggest you begin thinking about packing. You may have to do some shopping tomorrow, too. I am sure Dan can give you some ideas on the wearing apparel you will need for the desert." Then he shifted in his chair and spoke to Dan, "If you let me borrow your tickets, Dan, I'll see what I can do to get you and Hillary on the same Pullman out of New York."

"That will be great, and as you suggested, I will get together with Hillary on what she will need. It is warming up on the desert, and if a person is not properly dressed, it can be a bit miserable."

Hillary pushed her chair back and said, "You are right, Dad, time is slipping away. In addition to packing, I have notes to write, including one to the office trying to explain my unscheduled leave of absence." She excused herself and left.

Dan and MacGregor rose from their chairs at the same time. MacGregor excused himself saying, "I have a few telephone calls to make, Dan, and Dan, I am sure the changes in your original plans have changed your itinerary. You are welcome to use my telephone to call anyone you wish, and please don't worry about the charges. We shall consider them part of the business agreement. I'll see you later."

Dan thanked him and immediately turned his thoughts to

Hillary. Now that she has confirmed her intentions to make the trip, he thought, I have to decide where she should stay when we arrive in San Francisco. I'll send a telegram to the St. Francis and ask for reservations. I'll also ask for confirmation immediately by return wire.

Dan slowly pushed his chair back to the table. While walking up the stairs to his room, he began thinking, it will be lonely for a single woman in a strange city and in a strange hotel. Since we will stop in Sacramento, I'll call Mom and Dad and ask if Hillary can stay with them. Dan smiled when he thought of all the questions and all the explaining he could expect when he told his parents about the strange woman he was bringing home.

He reached the top of the stairs and decided to make the call as soon as a phone became available. He turned and walked down the steps and into the library. Seeing MacGregor on the phone, he stepped back to the doorway just as MacGregor looked up and motioned for him to come in. Dan walked in and sat at one of the tables he judged to be a discreet distance from where MacGregor stood talking on the phone.

It was several minutes before MacGregor hung up the receiver, walked over where Dan was sitting and sat down. "I've been working on your reservations, and fortunately, I caught an old friend of mine at home who is in charge of the reservations for the New York Central. I apologized for the short notice and gave him a brief explanation. He said not to worry, he would get the two of you on the same Pullman. He will let me know sometime tomorrow morning." MacGregor continued, "It is Sunday, and I feel lucky to have such a friend. I hope I did not interfere with his plans for today. Now, Dan, you have something on your mind."

"Yes, I do." Then he told MacGregor about his plan to call

Sacramento and arrange for Hillary to stay with his parents in lieu of making reservations in San Francisco to give her a chance to rest before they left for the desert. "What do you think, Mr. MacGregor?"

"Personally, I think it is an excellent idea, but it has been my experience that women like to make their own decisions on matters of this nature. I suggest you ask Hillary. Is there anything else?"

Dan felt a tinge of regret for asking when he thought he saw a half-smile, half-smirk, on MacGregor's face. Then he replied, "You are right. Sir, I will ask her. Since I will be on the phone for about 30 minutes, is it convenient now to call my parents?"

"Anytime you wish. Hillary has her own phone in her room, so you won't inconvenience her. In fact, you can call her now, and then call your parents. One long and one short will get her. I'm going to my room to lie down for a while. I suggest we meet out on the veranda by the pool about two for a light lunch. I'll let you pass on the word to Hillary if you please. And tell your parents I am very grateful to their son, and I can never repay him for all he has done for us." He rose from his chair and said, "I'll see you at lunch, Dan."

Dan looked at the phone and felt tongue-tied. Then he thought, It isn't every day you ask a young woman you have barely known for 24 hours to spend a few days with your parents who live 3000 miles away. Well, this is a business trip, and it is a must that Hillary get some rest before we tackle the Mojave Desert, an area entirely foreign to her. What other places can she stay and get some rest if she does not stay with my parents? None. Now, who should I call first, Mom and Dad, or Hillary?

Dan decided to call home first since his strategy depended

on his parents being home and not otherwise obligated. He walked over to the phone and called the long-distance operator. When she came on the line, he gave her the information, and the operator told him to stand by because it was Sunday and she thought she could get him through in about ten minutes.

Dan returned to the table and alternately thought about the things he planned to discuss with his parents and Hillary.

The phone rang, and when Dan walked over and picked up the receiver, to his surprise, Hillary was talking to the operator. He broke into the conversation, saying, "This is Dan, Hillary, I'm calling my parents."

"Oh, Dan, I'm sorry, I'll explain later," and hung up the phone.

The operator spoke, "Mr. Sanders, I have Mrs. Sanders of Sacramento on the line."

He thanked the operator and spoke to his mother. After the greetings, Dan told her about meeting MacGregor and his daughter and how wonderful they had been to him. He explained the MacGregors' relationship to the old prospector and how they insisted he become an equal partner in the claim. He also told her about MacGregor's bad health and consequently, could not travel. Therefore, MacGregor's daughter would be coming back with him to take care of any legal matters when they organized the company. She also wanted to visit her grandfather's grave.

It was then his mother wanted to know all about her, including her age, did she work, was she single, among other questions. When she had finished with the questions, and Dan with answers, she said, "That poor girl, I hope you are not planning to stick her in a hotel someplace. You tell her I want her to stay with us while you are taking care of your business in San Francisco. She will be tired and will need rest after that long train ride. And I am anxious to meet her."

Knowing his mother, Dan was not surprised by her comments and her instructions, but he wondered why she was eager to meet Hillary. Dan promised to send her a wire after he had talked to Hillary and they had firmed up their plans. After saying goodbye, he hung up the receiver and rang Hillary.

Hillary picked up the phone on the first ring. When Dan identified himself, she immediately began apologizing. Dan interrupted, saying, "I know exactly what happened, the phone rings in your room when it rings in the library, and you had no way of knowing it was my call. Please, don't be concerned about it, I had put in a call to my parents in Sacramento to bring them up to date on all that has happened since my arrival. I hope you don't mind?"

"Of course not, Dan, they need to know. How are they?" "Fine, Dad had gone for a walk, but I talked to Mother for a half-hour, and she wanted to know everything. I told her your father's health was not the best; consequently, you were coming with me. She immediately jumped on that and said you would be tired from the trip, and insisted you stay with them so you could recuperate while I tended to whatever business I had in San Francisco. I explained to her I planned to be in San Francisco for only two days. She said that was not a problem, she was anxious to meet you, and she would not take 'No' for an answer. Now, Hillary, before you answer, your father said we were having lunch on the veranda at two. And I might add, my mother is a very kind person, and she will be hurt and deeply disappointed if you turn down her invitation. Please, wait until after lunch before you decide. It will give you time to think it over."

"Dan, that was quite a speech. I don't need time to think

and decide if I should accept your mother's invitation. You tell her I appreciate her invitation, and I do accept, and I am eager to meet her, too."

For a moment, Dan felt slightly confused, then after absorbing Hillary's statement of acceptance, all he could say was, "Thank you, I am sure you will make Mother very happy." Then he thought, Why is Hillary anxious to meet Mother?

"One more thing, if I may, Hillary?" "Yes, what is it?"

"The list of desert wearing apparel I promised, do you have a minute or two?"

"Yes, I have a pencil and pad ready so let's have it." "OK, here goes: broad-brimmed hat, long sleeve light cotton blouses or shirts, hiking boots, riding skirt or jeans, bandanas or scarfs, and a pair of calfskin leather gloves. That should do it. Since you have hunted and fished with your father, I'll guess you have most of the items."

"I'm sure I do, but I'll have to check on their condition. And thank you, I do appreciate your help. If you think of anything more, don't hesitate to let me know. Also, let me know if you need anything."

"Thank you," Dan replied, "I'll see you at lunch." Dan hung up the receiver and walked up to his room.

It is time I started my packing, too, he thought. By two o'clock he had both pieces of luggage packed but left them open so he could pack the few things he was wearing and his toilet articles. He hoped to get his underwear laundered before leaving so he could pack that, too. Perhaps Hillary can arrange for the laundering, I'll speak to her about it at lunch, he thought.

Both Hillary and MacGregor were sitting at the lunch table

when he walked out on the veranda. MacGregor started to get up, but Dan asked him to remain seated.

While Dan adjusted his chair, MacGregor said, "Hillary tells me you contacted your parents, and your mother wants Hillary to stay with them while you are in San Francisco. It is obvious you have very nice parents. Please thank them for me."

Dan returned the compliment, "I told Mother I had never been treated better than you have treated me. It seems as though I have known you and Hillary forever, yet I have known you less than two days."

The three continued their small talk through lunch and their final cup of tea. Hillary told Dan that Mary would pick up his laundry, and since they had a drying room, he would have it back in the morning.

MacGregor vetoed Dan's invitation to take them out to dinner because he was not sure what train schedule his friend might arrange for them, and Hillary should get as much of her packing accomplished as possible and then identify the additional items she needed to buy.

Hillary excused herself and left for her room, stopping by to give Mary instructions for Dan's laundry.

Dan and MacGregor sat on the veranda for another hour talking about the claim, MacGregor's father, interwoven with their personal experiences, and their families.

MacGregor then retired to his room, and Dan decided to stroll around the estate. After his walk, he looked in the library for a newspaper and found the Boston Globe. He settled down in one of the big comfortable chairs and spent an hour catching up on the world news.

The next morning Dan was up at six. While dressing, he recalled how subdued the conversation had been at dinner the night before. As he had listened, he could feel the effort Hillary and MacGregor were putting forth trying to make small talk, but he knew their hearts were not in it. He could only guess they had suddenly begun to realize the separation they were about to experience. From conversations with, and between them, they had never been separated more than one or two weeks at a time. I felt sure they would like to be alone, Dan thought, and I decided to excuse myself without appearing to be rude. I wiped my mouth and laid my napkin on the table and said, "if you will excuse me, I have a few odds and ends to put together, and I must send a wire to San Francisco. If I send a night letter, it will be there in the morning. I hope you don't mind." I noticed that both Hillary and her father seemed to relax at the same time.

MacGregor responded, "Go right ahead, Dan. I hope you have a good night's sleep; it may be the last one you will get for a few days. I have never slept well on trains."

Then Hillary added, "Goodnight, Dan."

When Dan woke up at six the next morning, he thought, This is the day the great adventure starts. Perhaps I should have said, 'No' to Hillary since it may get very dangerous. All I can do now is try to avoid exposing her to any unnecessary trouble.

After bathing and shaving, Dan dressed for the trip. He decided to check with Mary about his laundry but found it outside of his door. He returned and finished packing then left a five-dollar bill on the dresser with a note thanking her for her help.

Dan looked at his watch and walked downstairs and into the dining room where Hillary and MacGregor were at the table drinking coffee. When they heard Dan, they turned to greet him, and Dan noticed Hillary's swollen eyes. He returned the greeting and thought, This must be one of the most trying ordeals either one of has ever experienced.

During breakfast, Dan asked, "Hillary, are you going to town today?"

"Yes," she said, "I have a few things I need to pick up. Would you be interested in going with me?"

"Yes, if you don't mind. I want to buy a few souvenirs for my parents."

"Good, I'll enjoy the company. I'll be ready to leave in about 20 minutes, and since we don't know what our schedule will be, we should try to be back by noon. What do you think?"

"I agree. I never like to rush to catch a train."

They had finished their breakfast, and Hillary had risen to return to her room when the phone rang. MacGregor immediately spoke up, "I'll answer it, I'm sure it is for me. "

Hillary left, and Dan continued to sip his coffee. In a few minutes, MacGregor returned smiling and sat down at the table, "Well, Dan, you and Hillary are all set. You will board the express to New York at 3:00 P.M. and arrive in New York at seven. Your train for Chicago and San Francisco leaves at 8:00 P.M. When you arrive in Chicago, your Pullman will be switched to the San Francisco train."

"Switching the Pullman sure beats walking to change trains," Dan commented. "With every major trunk line converging at Chicago, finding your train can become a nightmare. I'll thank you for Hillary and for me."

"Thanks are not necessary, Dan. I only wish I could do more."

"Mr. MacGregor, you have done more for me than I ever expected, and as for the claim, I'll be contacting you for legal advice. I am sure the legality of some of the things I have done will be questioned."

"I shall be grateful if you will seek my advice. Call or wire. Now if you will excuse me, I have a few things I must do before I drive you and Hillary to the depot."

"Yes, Sir, and I had better get upstairs and wash up. Hillary will be down here any minute."

Hillary selected one of the largest department stores in Boston to shop. "I think I can find everything I need without having to look elsewhere," she said. "Do you have something specific in mind for your parents?"

"Yes," Dan replied. "I am looking for a meerschaum pipe for my father and a cameo brooch for Mother. What are my chances of finding them?"

"Very good. This department store has a broad selection of just about everything."

They were back at the MacGregor residence shortly before noon and packed and ready for lunch by 12:30. By 1:45, they had loaded MacGregor's Cadillac and were ready to leave.

When they arrived at the station, Dan, the first one out of the car, flagged down a redcap. He also volunteered to park the car while Hillary and MacGregor followed the redcap to the ticket window to pick up the reserve tickets. After parking the car, Dan entered the busy station crowded with passengers waiting to catch the three o'clock New York Express.

He worked his way through the crowd toward the ticket windows and spotted MacGregor in the reserve ticket line. Then he saw Hillary standing with the redcap a short distance away. He approached Hillary and asked, "How is the line moving?"

"Surprisingly well. Dad should be at the window in three or four minutes."

When MacGregor joined Hillary and Dan, the redcap walked up to him and advised him that the train was loading, and did he wish to board. MacGregor said they did, and the three followed the redcap out to the train which was parked on the first track. The redcap led the way to their chair car and stopped at the steps. MacGregor showed the tickets to the conductor, and then he handed one to Hillary and the other to Dan.

Then MacGregor spoke to both, "I'll say goodbye here. I am not up to climbing the steps and being pushed and shoved by passengers getting on and off the train." Then he turned to Dan and held out his hand. They shook hands, and MacGregor put his other hand on Dan's shoulder. "Thank you once again, Dan, for all you have done for Hillary and me. Although I have known you for less than three days, it seems like a lifetime. It is trust, my son, trust, something we very rarely find these days. With that, I will say, 'Farewell,' my young friend. I know you and Hillary will have a safe trip. Now I will talk to Hillary."

"Thank you, Mr. MacGregor. Try not to worry about Hillary. I'll have her call you as soon as we arrive in Sacramento."

MacGregor turned to Hillary, who had been watching and listening to her father and Dan. Dan turned and climbed up the Pullman car steps and walked down the aisle of the car, leaving the two to share their last few minutes together.

Halfway up the aisle, Dan saw the porter stowing the luggage in the racks above the seats, and for the first time, he saw a long, slender, leather carrying case among the pieces of luggage. Instinctively, he knew it contained Hillary's rifle. As he looked at the case, he smiled and thought, She can't use it for much except to shoot jackrabbits. But if she can shoot like her father says she can, I'd rather have her for a friend than an enemy.

The porter finished storing the luggage, and Dan handed him two dollars, then he asked him to help with the luggage when they arrived in New York City. The porter nodded and thanked him.

When Dan heard the conductor's first 'All aboard,' he looked at his watch. I'll check on Hillary, he thought, the train will be pulling out in a few minutes.

He walked back down the aisle, and just as he reached the end of the aisle, Hillary stepped around the corner, wiping her eyes. Without saying a word, he reached for her hand and lead her back to their seats. They had only been seated two or three minutes when Dan felt the train begin to move. He had not looked at Hillary during the time they had been seated; he had been looking up the aisle and out of the windows on the opposite side of the aisle hoping to give Hillary as much time as she needed to compose herself.

5

RETURNING TO THE CLAIM

The train moved slowly through dozens of converging railroad tracks after leaving Boston Central, then joining the mainline leading to New York, it began to gather speed. It wasn't until then that Dan heard Hillary say, "I am sorry, Dan."

For the first time since they had been seated, Dan turned toward her and noticed she had renewed her makeup. "No need for apologies," he said. "Those who do not shed a tear under the same circumstances are not capable of loving and understanding, and the word 'empathy' is not in their vocabulary."

Hillary smiled with a smile he had never seen before, a pathetic smile that tore at his heart like that of a small child who had been mentally wounded and needed reassurance and protection. He wanted to take Hillary in his arms to soothe and comfort her, but he broke the spell by smiling and saying, "I asked the porter to help us with our luggage when we arrive in New York. He can flag down a redcap quicker than we can."

"I'm glad you did, Dan." Now she seemed more relaxed. She continued, "I haven't the foggiest idea how far we will have to walk. Dad and I have counted as many as ten trains waiting at the station on our arrival or when leaving. There may have been more."

"New York and Chicago handle more passenger traffic than any of the other cities in the United States, perhaps in the world. I thanked your father for arranging our schedule. Our Pullman will be switched from the New York Central to our San Francisco train when we reach Chicago, which means we will remain in our seats during the switching process. Great, isn't it?"

"Oh, yes. Dad is thoughtful and knows the railroad business. As you now know, he has been in it all of his life. When he can help someone who is having a problem with one of the railroad lines, he doesn't hesitate. In his law practice, he defends the railroads; therefore, you would think he would be on their side, but that isn't always the case. If he hears or receives a complaint, he calls one of the officials, and it is usually corrected without any fuss. The railroad officials seem to appreciate his efforts. Being a lawyer, he can if necessary, offer suggestions for resolving these problems before they become court cases. Dad's efforts also help the railroads improve their public image, which has never been too savory, but there have been indications it is improving."

"Does Mr. MacGregor ever become angry?"

"No, but he can be tough and direct, and anyone trying to deceive him is asking for trouble. One of the first cases Dad and I worked on together after I finished law school pertained to a man who was suing one of the railroad companies over an accident. He fell down the steps of one of the chair cars and landed on the steel step stool. He lay there until an ambulance arrived arid transported him to a hospital. The doctors examined him but were unable to find anything seriously wrong, except for a few minor contusions and abrasions. But he kept complaining about his back, his shoulder, and his neck, so the hospital decided to keep him overnight. As soon as the doctors left, he gave the nurse a telephone number to call. The number she called turned out to be a lawyer who arrived within an hour. As soon as the lawyer arrived, the patient, (let's call him, Jack)."

Dan broke into the story, commenting, "Jack the Ripper?" then offered a big smile, "Sorry, Hillary. Bad joke, go on with your story."

Hillary laughed and continued, "Jack asked the nurse to leave. At first, she said, 'No,' then the man explained he was the patient.' s lawyer, and he had the right to speak to his client alone. Of course, we have no way of knowing anything about the conversation which took place between the two after the nurse left. The next morning the doctor examined the patient and said to discharge him. But before the paperwork could be completed, his lawyer arrived and objected saying he wanted his patient to be able to walk before being discharged."

Hillary continued, "Now comes the strange part as told by the doctor and the nurse to Dad after being retained by the railroad company to defend the case. The lawyer asked his client to get out of bed and walk. He tried to sit up but kept falling over on his side. Then he rolled over and fell out of bed. When the doctor and the nurse tried to help him stand on his feet, the muscles in one leg seemed uncontrollable, and the muscles in his neck and back pulled his right side down and his head in the opposite direction. It appeared obvious he could not walk. Consequently, they put him back in bed for further tests and observation."

"Next, Dad called in the brakeman who was tending the passenger car the afternoon of the accident. Dad asked the brakeman what he was doing and where he was standing at the time of the accident. He replied that he was standing at the side of the footstool which was set at the foot of the steps to the entrance of the chair car unloading passengers. Dad then asked why he was there. The brakeman replied that he was helping the passengers as they stepped from the steps onto the step stool. Then Dad asked him if he saw the accident, and if he did, what did he see. The brakeman replied that he had helped a lady down the steps, then looked up just in time to see this big fellow apparently stumble and roll down the steps headfirst. He tried to stop him on the bottom step, but the accident victim was too heavy and knocked him over backward. Dad's next question pertained to the man's injuries. Had he seen the man strike his head, neck, shoulder, or thigh on the steps or any other part of the passenger car as he rolled down the steps? The brakeman replied that he had not, he said it was like watching a slow-motion movie, the man stumbled, lit on his hands on the second step, seemed to roll into a ball, tumbled down the third, and slid into a sitting position on the step stool. Then he rolled off the stool onto the asphalt moaning and groaning. It was then he decided to call an ambulance. The brakeman added that he could tell the man had a very powerful body when he tried to prevent him from being injured during his fall. Dad thanked the brakeman, but he did not comment on the brakeman's description of Jack's fall. The next day Dad hired the Pinkerton Detective Agency to investigate the background of Jack and his lawyer. While the investigation was in progress, Dad offered an out of court settlement which included doctor and hospital bills, and a substantial amount of cash, but Jack and his lawyer turned it down. They felt confident of winning a much larger sum with a jury trial. And as I heard later, they petitioned the Court to establish an early trial. Dad countered by asking the court for a minimum of two months to prepare for the trial.

"Six weeks slipped by before we received any news from the agency. The word was, 'Don't give up; We. are on to something' Two weeks later, the detective agency called saying they were ready to report. Dad said that the first thing the lead detective reported was, 'These two guys have been around!'"

"The detectives had traced the pair to Hollywood."

Hillary stopped and asked, "Are you becoming bored listening to all of this, Dan?"

"No! No! No!" Dan replied, "I love detective stories. Please go on. It's becoming more interesting by the minute."

Hillary smiled, "I'm not sure you are honest with me, however, since we have two to three more hours to spend on this train before we arrive in New York City, I shall continue. The detectives traced the pair to New York City, and after contacting several insurance companies, they finally found a hot one. It had not been more than four months since the insurance company had settled a case out of court with two men fitting their descriptions. It involved a pedestrian being struck by a car. The insurance company settled out of court because the car owner, a prominent politician, did not wish to be exposed to any adverse publicity. Because the insurance company believed the pedestrian was at fault, and they had witnesses to prove it, the victim and his lawyer settled for a nominal fee. The detectives asked for pictures of the victim and the accident which the insurance company willingly provided. The detectives also learned the victim and his lawyer were from the Los Angeles area.

"Now, the detectives had a picture of Jack and his lawyer,

and they boarded the next train for Los Angeles. While traveling, they discussed their strategy. Where should they look first? Should they try the insurance companies again? By now, they were convinced the accidents were rigged by a person who had the talent to fall down steps, get hit by automobiles, and perform other kinds of acrobatics without getting seriously hurt. And how about his appearance in the hospital as a man who had serious nerve damage? He must also be a contortionist. 'Hollywood!'

"It did not take long to find a motion picture studio where Jack had worked. He had been working as a stunt man at the studio for about a year when he showed up with a man who claimed to be a lawyer. The lead detective showed the man a photo of Jack's lawyer, and immediately, the man said, 'That's him.' About a month later, the stunt man quit work and left the studio. It was then the detectives decided it was time to start contacting the insurance companies.

"The detectives hit the jackpot at the third insurance company they contacted. The division manager recognized the photos and asked his secretary to pull the file. First, he showed the detectives a newspaper clipping with the story of the accident, then he outlined the salient points of the case. The stunt man and his lawyer selected prominent actors and motion picture moguls to swindle, the point being, the more prominent the individual, the more anxious he would be to settle out of court. The detectives soon determined that the method of operation used by the two swindlers in the Los Angeles area matched the method used in New York City.

"The insurance manager said they became suspicious when the insurance companies began to compare notes on the similarity of the newspaper reports of the accidents and the willingness of the victim to settle for less than the insurance companies expected. The manager also stated he thought the lawyer provided the brains for each operation because they picked a different insurance company for each accident. How they did this, he didn't know, but he guessed it may have been by bribing one of the servants since the top echelon of the Hollywood movie industry might have a dozen or more servants. The manager continued by adding that the insurance companies got together and convinced the next victim to let them take the case to trial, and all the insurance companies who had been victims would appear as witnesses against the two. It was a great idea, but it did not work because the two skipped town."

"Well, Dan, have you had enough?" Hillary asked.

"No, but if you want to stop, I have several questions. How about a question and answer session?"

"OK, fire away."

"Why did the stunt man and his partner suddenly ask for a jury trial when all of their previous cases had been settled out of court?"

"Their method of operation had been exposed in Los Angeles and in New York City, so they concluded time had run out for the old method, and it was time to try something new. Since they had never tried to swindle a railroad, and knowing that a large segment of the public did not like the way they were treated by the railroad companies, the two decided to pull a one-time deception on a railroad line and go for a large settlement with the preconceived idea a jury would render a verdict in the victim's favor. Then the two planned to quit, at least for the immediate future."

"How did they bungle the scheme?"

"As I mentioned earlier, Dad is a man who is difficult to deceive. The brakeman's story convinced him all was not what it appeared to be, and it was then he decided to call in the Pinkerton Detective agency."

"Did the case go to trial?"

"Yes, Dad had the insurance companies that had been defrauded, prepare depositions for each case showing its disposition and the methods of operation used by the pair."

"How did the trial end?"

"The railroad company won the case, but another case opened at the end of the trial."

"Intriguing. What happened?"

"Dad believed that with all the evidence the detectives had put together, he had an excellent chance of winning a felony charge against the pair, so he had subpoenas prepared for the two swindlers, hoping the judge would sign them and have the pair arrested before they left the courtroom. The judge signed the subpoenas, and the pair were held in jail while the charges were prepared, and then they were brought to trial. The two were found guilty of perjury and fraud. The stunt man received year in jail and a $5,000 fine. The lawyer received the same sentence and was barred from practicing law in the State of Massachusetts, and letter in New York and California."

"Your father sure did a job on those crooks, Hillary. He is the kind of man I am proud to know."

"Thank you, Dan, I am glad you feel that way."

They continued chatting about their lives and their experiences until the train pulled into the Grand Central Station in New York City. The porter arrived and helped them with their bags, and when they reached the passenger exit, he flagged down a redcap. They followed the redcap pushing his dolly loaded with their luggage to the ticket agent who verified their tickets. The ticket agent added that if they wished, they could board the train and avoid the rush. Hillary and Dan looked at each other and nodded to the agent.

The agent handed Dan the tickets then spoke to the redcap who led Hillary and Dan through the crowd and out to the train and to their Pullman car. After tipping the redcap, Dan handed the tickets to the car attendant, who in turn, handed them to the Pullman porter. The porter, carrying the luggage, walked to the head of the Pullman car and stopped in front of the first drawing-room, set Dan's luggage aside, and opened the door for Hillary. After setting the luggage on the luggage stands, the porter excused himself and said he would check back with her in a few minutes. He closed the door then picked up Dan's luggage and walked a few steps to the adjoining drawing-room. He opened the door for Dan and asked Dan where he should put his luggage.

Dan, a little overwhelmed by all this luxury, absentmindedly pointed to the luggage stands. And when the porter asked him if there was anything further, Dan looked at him as if he were waiting for the words to penetrate and then he said, "No." As the porter started to leave, Dan asked, "Will the dining car be serving dinner this evening?"

"Yes, Sir," the porter replied. "This train is made up here in New York City. We will announce dinner as soon as we get underway." The porter pulled out his gold-plated railroad watch and continued, "And that will be in exactly 26 minutes. The dining room will close at ten."

Dan tipped and thanked the porter, and after the porter left, he stepped next door to Hillary's room and tapped on her door.

"Yes?" the low voice barely penetrating through the oak-paneled door.

"It's Dan, Hillary."

"Just a moment, Dan." A few seconds later, Hillary, smiling, opened the door. "Are you settled in?" she asked.

"Hardly, I haven't unpacked a thing. I have been too busy admiring my new quarters, thanks to your father."

Still smiling, Hillary said, "I was unaware of your travel arrangements, but from your remarks, if I may guess, you must have slept in either a lower or upper birth." Then she dropped her smile and said, "Please don't think Dad is trying to be pretentious, he is not that kind of a person. I am sure he is trying to repay you for all of the trouble you have experienced in your efforts to help us."

Dan had been shaking his head from side to side, and when Hillary finished, he said, "I understand, Hillary, I know your father is a kind and thoughtful person. If I sounded as though I believed otherwise, I apologize."

"I am sorry, Dan, I think I owe you an apology."

Dan smiled, "Now that we have all of our misunderstandings resolved, the purpose of my knocking has to do with dinner. I talked to the porter, and he said dinner will be served as soon as we get underway." Dan made a slight bow and a gesture with his right hand while asking, "May I ask you to join me?"

"Most certainly, Monsieur," and returned his bow. "And at what time will you be calling?"

"The train leaves at eight. Will three-quarters of an hour after the hour be convenient?"

"I shall be ready and thank you."

Dan nodded and said, "Thank you, and I shall see you later."

Dan unpacked and put away the contents of one of his pieces of luggage. Then he washed and shaved and changed to fresh clothes. When he knocked on Hillary's door, she opened it immediately. He saw she had changed her traveling clothes for a beautiful, light blue, silk cocktail dress. A simple but elegant white shawl covered her shoulders. It, too, had been made from silk. Dan smiled and instinctively said, "What a beautiful dress and how marvelous you look this evening."

"Thank you, Dan, but I do have a problem. I don't know what I shall wear for an encore. This is the only party dress I packed."

Dan laughed, "I doubt if you will need more than one where we are going, formal and informal parties are a rarity on the Mojave Desert."

Hillary smiled and said, "I can understand that, shall we find the dining car?"

"Excellent idea." Dan gestured in the direction the train was traveling. "You lead the way."

The train had not quite cleared the greater New York City suburbs; accordingly, it continued traveling at a nominal speed allowing the passengers to move along the isles to the dining car with a minimum of swaying and vibration passengers experience when traveling 70 miles per hour.

When they arrived at the entrance to the dining car, they were greeted by the headwaiter and escorted to a window table for two. After handing each a menu, he motioned for the busboy who filled their water glasses while Hillary and Dan explored the menu. Hillary pleaded lack of hunger and said that she planned to order the Chef's Salad. Dan decided to wait for the waiter and his announcement of the special for the evening.

While they waited for the waiter, Dan commented on the efficiency of the dining car operation. "We will be traveling across the country at 70 miles an hour and eating excellent food from tables covered with snowy white tablecloths, using sterling silver service polished until it shines from the lights of the dining car, and served by personnel who would do justice to the finest hotels and restaurants in the country. I consider it American ingenuity at its best. Do you think I am stretching it a bit?"

Hillary could see how serious Dan felt about his comments, but she could not withhold a smile when she replied, "Well, almost. I vividly recall one incident when Dad and I were traveling by train to New Orleans." Hillary stopped when the waiter arrived to take their orders. After announcing the 'special' for the evening, Hillary ordered. After Dan decided on veal cutlets, Hillary continued, "We were having breakfast in the dining car, and by looking out the window, we could see the train was moving about as fast as the regulations permitted. Dad had started to reach for the coffee server when the busboy who was standing near, saw Dad and stepped over and picked up the server and filled Dad's cup. Then he turned to mine and picked it up with the saucer. Just as he started to fill it, the engineer, apparently, decided to brake for a crossing. Regardless of the engineer's reasons, the dining car jerked and threw the busboy backward spilling coffee all over me, my blouse, and my skirt. Immediately, or so it seemed, the entire staff, except the cooks and the dishwashers, surrounded me, wiping my clothes, my arms, and asking if I were hurt. I told them I was not and not to worry. The headwaiter called my porter, who followed me back to my drawing room and waited while I changed my clothes, took my soiled clothes, cleaned and returned them that afternoon. Do you see my point, Dan?"

"But Hillary, that proves my point. The busboy could not have avoided the accident, and the staff tried to express his concern by doing everything they could to help. I am sure the personnel at the Waldorf Astoria could not have done more. Do you?"

"But, Dan, I did not want any more coffee."

Both laughed, and by the time they had exchanged a few comments on the episode, the waiter arrived with their dinner, and by the time they had finished, the train had cleared the New York City suburbs. Now, the engineer having opened the throttle to the train's normal speed pulled the engine's steam whistle cord sending the eerie sound of the steam whistle floating back through the night air, telling the passengers they were well on their way to Chicago.

Dan and Hillary returned to their respective drawing rooms and listened to the clickety-clack of the steel wheels passing over the rail joints while they finished unpacking.

The train began slowing down in the afternoon near the suburbs of Chicago and pulled into the depot 40 minutes later. After unloading the Chicago passengers, the Pullman cars with passengers traveling west were switched from the New York Central to a train being assembled for the trip to San Francisco.

While the Pullman transfer proceeded, Hillary and Dan watched from their adjoining drawing rooms while they moved from track to track until their Pullman finally coupled with the San Francisco train. They continued their self-imposed seclusion until the train got underway and reached the outskirts of Chicago, then Dan decided it was time to check on Hillary.

When he knocked on the door, she responded with her usual, "Yes?"

"It's Dan, Hillary."

She immediately came to the door, opened it, and commented, "That was quite a little ride of bumps and stops we experienced traveling around the Chicago switching yards, wasn't it?" She noticed Dan was about to say something and held up her hand to silence him, then she continued, "I'm not complaining, Dan, I am well aware of all the walking and all the frustrations we would have encountered had it been necessary to change Pullman cars." She smiled and continued, "In fact, the more I think about changing oars, the more I am beginning to realize how much I enjoyed the scenic view of my journey around the switching yards."

Again, she smiled then she said, "Now it is your turn."

Dan laughed, "You can thank your father for arranging the trip, I appreciate what he did more than you realize. I don't believe I mentioned I had to change trains in Chicago on my way to Boston. I had trouble finding a redcap, and finally, I gave up and carried my bags into the station, which was a minor problem. I found out from the station agent I had to take a bus to another depot, and when the bus stopped, I had to walk a mile, carrying my luggage, to catch my New York City train.

"I think we should buy Dad a present and send him a nice 'Thank You' note."

"Good idea. You know his likes and dislikes, so you let me know, and I will pick it up Saturday in San Francisco."

"Don't I get to go?"

"I think it would be better if you stayed at my parents' house and rested. I want to leave for Barstow on Monday, and it is going to be a long grueling Monday and Tuesday."

Dan noticed a slight frown momentarily cross her brow then disappear but then she smiled and said, "I also have some laundry to worry about. Incidentally, we have been standing in this isle for about 20 minutes." Then she jokingly asked, "What will people think?"

Dan felt a slight glow creep over his face, but he laughed

and said, "After spending three hours touring the switching yards of Chicago, I thought a little exercise might be in order. Shall we look for the dining car, or walk back to the observation car?"

"Why don't we do both? We can walk back to the observation car for the exercise, and if we see one of the train crew, we can ask about the dining car."

"An excellent idea, Miss MacGregor. I suggest a light sweater may feel comfortable if we decide to stroll out on the observation platform."

"An excellent idea, Mr. Sanders," she mocked. "One moment, please."

Hillary returned with the sweater, closed the door, and said, "Shall we stroll?" However, the narrow aisle discouraged any thought they may have had of walking arm and arm. Hillary led the way and set the pace. They passed through several Pullman cars before reaching the observation car, which they concluded, put their car, again, up near the dining car. Hillary continued through the observation car, without stopping, out to the observation platform. She slipped on her sweater and said, "It isn't cold, but it is cool. What a beautiful evening."

"Yes, it is," Dan commented. "This is my favorite time of the day when traveling by train, especially when leaving a big city like Chicago and passing through many of the dozens of little towns which surround a big city. The street, business, and residential lights have been turned on, and the cars with their headlights shining are waiting at the railroad crossing with bells ringing and red lights flashing as the train roars by. The train travels at considerable speed through these villages, and it always seems to me the train barely leaves one village before it passes through another. But there are farms between the villages and lonely lights shining through the farmhouse windows, and I sometimes wonder what the people might be doing. And as we speed by the railroad crossings and through the residential areas, I wonder where all the cars are going. Woolgathering? Yes, I suppose."

Hillary had remained silent while Dan had been expressing his thoughts. Now she commented, "Call it what you wish, pleasant thoughts always prevail over unpleasant ones. I have had similar thoughts along similar lines many times, not only while traveling but also while Dad and I were on fishing and hunting trips. A person can gather tons of wool while lying on a cot in a tent at night in the woods."

They were passing through another small village when Dan said, "Well, Hillary, we are well on our way to California, I hope you don't become too bored. Train travel is not very exciting."

Hillary responded, "We can always play cribbage." "Where can we get a cribbage board?"

Hillary reached inside of her oversize handbag, fished around for a moment, and handed Dan a cribbage board. Even in the dim light reflected from the red safety lanterns hanging on each side of the observation platform, he could see it was the same one they had used before. Dan laughed, "Women have just found a new use for handbags. Great idea, Hillary, I can no longer drag up stupid ideas to keep you from beating me. I won't ask because I know you also have a deck of cards in that bag."

Hillary reached into her handbag, and with a knowing smile, held up a deck of cards, "I just happened to have one."

At mid-morning the following day, they started their daily cribbage marathon. They interrupted their play for a two-hour lunch and rest period, and they stopped early enough in the late afternoon to allow them time to dress for dinner. They also decided to end the game Thursday afternoon to ensure they had adequate time to pack for their arrival at 6 AM in Sacramento Saturday morning. During the discussion of their agenda and their itinerary Dan said he needed to talk over his plans for the rest of their trip, not only to Barstow but out to the mine and back, too.

They ended their match as scheduled, shook hands, and mutually agreed not to discuss who won how many, or who played the better game. After breakfast the next morning, they packed and decided to get together after lunch and discuss Dan's plans.

During lunch, Dan explained to Hillary he preferred to keep the discussion from being overheard by others. "If you don't object, I suggest we hold it in either your room or mine. If we leave the door open, the train noise will deaden and distort the sound of our conversation. Consequently, it seems very unlikely that passengers walking up and down the aisle will be able to hear us."

Hillary responded with! "We are both mature, and there will be little or no opportunity for gossip before leaving the train tomorrow morning. As for our discussion, I believe I will feel more comfortable in my room."

"Good, I will give you more specific reasons for the secrecy when we meet in your room."

"No further explanation is necessary, Dan, I am sure I already know."

After lunch, they returned to their rooms to wash up, then Dan joined Hillary. They left the door open and sat on the seats by the window, the farthest location away from the door. Hillary asked, "Do you think this will do?"

"I'm sure it will. The train noise will act as an acoustic barrier and sitting by the window will also help. Perhaps I am overly cautious, but I have noticed when the word 'gold' is spoken, it always draws attention and makes a person's hearing sharper."

"I have heard and read it does, too."

Dan continued, "I know of one person who was murdered over a gold mine, and over the years there have been thousands. But let's get on with what we want to discuss. I spoke to you and your father about being sent to South Africa. I expect to leave any time after the next six weeks; consequently, we have much to do during the next three to four weeks because I will need two weeks to prepare for the trip. I said I had hoped we could leave for Barstow Sunday night, now after reviewing what I have to do in San Francisco which includes meeting with all the personnel I must contact, finding out if Joel Blake will take over the mine management while I am in South Africa, and if he will follow us to Barstow a week later, and last but not least, putting a contract together, I don't see how we can leave before Monday evening. Basically, that is what I will be doing, now for the details, but before I get started, would you care to take notes? This is going to be rather lengthy."

"It can't do any harm, and it may help me to better understand your plans."

"Not only that," commented Dan, "you will have your notes for reference if something should happen to me."

"Heaven forbid, Dan, let's not get negative."

Dan smiled, "You never can tell, I might get run over by a train or bitten by a rattlesnake."

While Hillary and Dan had been exchanging quips, Hillary had walked over to a built-in desk and withdrawn a pad and pencil. She sat down and mockingly poised the pencil above the pad and said, "I'm ready when you are."

Dan grinned and began, "I am anxious to get together with

Dick Hammeric, the chief engineer, also my immediate supervisor. Although I sent him a long wire outlining the plan I had discussed briefly with your father, we have to talk about the details so we can prepare a contract. I think I can get that done tomorrow afternoon. I can catch a local into San. Francisco as soon as you have met my parents and we have had breakfast. The locals run every three hours."

Hillary interrupted and asked, "You don't expect to write the contract tomorrow, do you?"

"No, once we agree on the details and get the basic outline completed, we will turn it over to the legal unit and they will draw up the contract in the final form which may or may not be finished by Monday. Since I am hoping we can leave Monday evening, Dick can mail the contract or, send it out by Blake, our next subject for discussion.

"In my wire, I asked Dick to find out if Blake, one of our engineers, would be available to assume the management of the mine when I leave. He and I have worked together on several projects, a couple similar to ours. He is sharp and a good manager. And he has another plus, although he is married, his wife works, and they have no children. He doesn't mind these kinds of assignments as long as he is allowed to see his wife every other weekend. We can solve that problem by hiring a strong foreman, and they can alternate weekends off."

Hillary asked, "Mr. Blake seems to have all of the qualifications you need for the position. How sure are you he will accept it, and what will we do if he doesn't?"

"Good question. Although I haven't talked to him personally, I believe there is a 90 percent chance he will accept the position. Why? Because it offers independence, he prefers. If he does not, we will have Dick Hammeric send someone else.

We have several highly qualified engineers on our staff who can manage the operation."

"I now know Dad made a wise decision when he decided you should manage the MacGregor Mining Company. Dad and I thank you. Shall we continue?"

Dan smiled, "If everything goes as planned, Dick can send Joel out to Barstow to meet us a week from Monday. By that time, we will be back from the mine, and we can brief ham on what we have done. Although I plan to brief Joel at the same time I brief Dick and also bring him into the contract negotiations, many of the details which will not be a part of the contract must be discussed and worked out with Joel. We have to decide where to locate the camp, how many men we will need, including a cook, carpenter, and a teamster, and all the details about housing and feeding them. Most important, we must find a good foreman. In addition, we have to purchase mules, an ore wagon, a horse and riding gear for Joel, a water wagon and a water storage tank, plus feed for the animals. Then we have the mining equipment to decide upon, and lumber for housing and for shoring up the mine. Fortunately, we have bare bone lists of basic needs for most of these kinds of equipment and materials at the office, which should give us a head start. I must remember to pick up copies."

"I hope I am not boring you with all of these details, Hillary?"

"Not at all. Remember, I am a lawyer. Our profession totally depends on the details."

"Great. As you can see, we have plenty of them. I also want Joel to explore the possibility of finding a route which will permit us to build a road to Fremont Station that can handle a motorized vehicle. I believe I mentioned this to your father as part of our plan for future consideration. The more I have thought about it, the more I have thought the future is now. Five animals will require tremendous amounts of feed and water to be hauled a minimum of ten miles, maybe more. And as a sidelight which may help us in resolving this problem, I heard before I left Randsburg that someone is prospecting Fremont Peak. More importantly, he has scraped a road through the sagebrush from Fremont Station to Fremont Peak using a homemade grader pulled behind a Model T Ford. If we can build a road from the mine to join his, we can cut four or five miles from any road we might try to build directly from the mine to Fremont Station." Then Dan asked, "What do you think?"

"I think it is an excellent idea. I heard you mention the possibility of such a road to Dad, and I agree with you on all points, especially the thought that the time is now. And I would like to offer a suggestion if I may?"

"Absolutely, Hillary. No one has a monopoly on ideas in our organization. Let's hear it."

"If we have the time, I suggest we do some preliminary scouting while we are at the mine, then you can brief Joel on your findings."

"I think it is a great idea and we will do it. Do you have any thoughts on the rest of the plan?"

"No, but I can see we have plenty of work ahead of us to ensure we get the groundwork done before you leave for South Africa."

"I certainly can't disagree with you on that observation. When we arrive in Sacramento, we must call the train station and check on train reservations for Barstow. If at all possible, we will catch a sleeper in the early evening out of Oakland on Monday which should get us into Barstow early Tuesday morning. It will be a 12 to 14-hour ride then we can have our breakfast at the Harvey House and catch a ride to the hotel. I use the term 'catch a ride' rather loosely but with some authority, because there are no taxis in Barstow. A courier, named Jerry, picks up express packages at the train station and delivers them to the local merchants. He drives a Model T Ford pickup. If we are lucky, we will catch him at the depot, and he can drive us to the hotel. You ride with him on the seat, and I will ride in the back on the truck bed."

Hillary laughed, "I hope we don't lose you along the way."

Dan grinned and went on, "If Jerry has time, I'll hire him to help us shop for the supplies we will need for our trip to the mine and drive us to the stable. It is going to be a long day, Hillary, and it will not end until we reach the spring and set up camp. I'll pick up sandwiches at the Harvey House for our lunch and our evening meal and anything else you recommend we take along."

Dan continued to brief Hillary on his plans and what he hoped they would accomplish when they reached the mine. He also offered clothing suggestions and advised her on the kind of weather they could expect. The briefing and comments lasted another hour. And from the time Dan had entered Hillary's room to the time he was ready to leave, passengers had been passing by the open door. Some, more curious than others stopped, smiled, and looked in, while those who were timider, glanced in from the corners of their eyes. And there were those whose look revealed they were aware that Hillary and Dan had separate drawing rooms but were often seen together.

Shortly after Dan returned to his room, he decided to walk back toward the club car and buy a newspaper from the butcher boy. After finding the peddler and buying the paper, he started back, walking through four Pullman cars before opening the door and entering the one in which Hillary and he were riding. As he walked down the aisle, he saw a number of passengers standing up and craning their necks trying to see what was happening at the far end of the car. Dan focused on the same area and saw a man leaning with both hands against the door to Hillary's room. Hurrying forward, he saw Hillary caged between the man's arms trying to escape. Dan charged down the rest of the isle through the curious, jerked the man's arm away, and angrily asked, "What the hell do you think you are doing?" Dan caught the smell of bootleg whiskey.

"What's it to you," he growled, swinging a right fist at Dan's head.

Dan ducked under the swing then unloaded a rising left hook flush on drunk's chin. The drunk's knees buckled as he fell backward on the aisle floor, holding his lower right jaw.

Dan leaned down, grabbed him by the front of his shirt, and said, "If I ever see you touch, or even think of touching this young lady again, I'll have you thrown off the train at the next stop."

Someone had notified a train crew member, and a brakeman quickly arrived and asked, "What is going on here?"

One of the women passengers who had watched the affair develop volunteered her version, then others contributed theirs.

Dan had released the drunk's shirt and was standing glaring down at the man when the brakeman walked up. Dan turned to the brakeman just as Hillary walked over to stand at Dan's side. He put his hand around her waist and asked, "Are you all right?"

"Yes, Dan. A little upset. Nothing serious."

The brakeman looked at Dan's lips pulled into a thin tine, and he could almost feel the heat from his anger. "I am sorry this happened, Sir."

"Not as sorry as I am," Dan said. "I told him that if he even looks at my fiancé again, I would have him thrown off the train. I don't like drunks, and I hate men who molest women."

"You need not worry, Sir. I assure you he will not bother you or your fiancé again. If he causes a disturbance of any kind, I will personally see he is put off the train at the next stop."

Then the brakeman turned to Hillary and said, "I apologize for what happened, Miss, not only for myself but for all the train crew as well. I am sure the conductor will be around to see you and ask for your help in preparing the report for this incident. Now if you will excuse me, I'll run down the individual who caused this problem."

Dan suddenly became conscious he had not removed his arm from Hillary's waist. He gently withdrew his arm and said, "I'm sorry I had to refer to you as my fiancée. At the moment, it seemed the best way to justify my violent action against that jerk. When I realized what he was doing, I felt a strong mixture of fear and anger running through my body."

"I never became frightened because Dad warned me that someday I might suddenly find myself confronted with such a situation and taught me how to protect myself. But I was concerned Dan, the man was drunk, then I saw you, and I knew everything was going to turn out all right. And I felt very proud when you called me your fiancé."

They arrived in Sacramento at six the next morning. Dan's father met them at the train, and after being introduced to Hillary, led the redcap loaded with all their luggage, followed by Hillary and Dan to Mr. Sanders' touring, car.

The Sanders lived in a middle upper-class neighborhood.

Dan's father, now semi-retired from his transportation business, spent most of his time at home or playing golf with his friends at a course located within walking distance of the Sanders' home.

Mr. Sanders turned into the driveway and parked next to the cement walkway leading to the one-story, beautifully landscaped, red brick home. Before Mr. Sanders could turn off the engine, a beaming Mrs. Sanders stepped out of the doorway and walked rapidly to the car. Dan, who had been riding in the back seat with the luggage, was the first out of the car and gave his mother a big hug. Then he turned to help Hillary, but she was out of the car and walking around to the back when Dan joined her. He took her hand to lead her to his mother, but his mother stepped forward to greet Hillary.

"Mother," Dan said, "May I present my business partner and friend, Hillary MacGregor."

"You certainly may," she said, but she was looking at Hillary. Hillary held out her hand, but Dan's mother ignored it and threw her arms around Hillary's neck and hugged her. When she released Hillary, she held on to her arms and looked into her eyes and said, "Welcome to our home, My Dear."

Tears seeped into Hillary's eyes. She reached out and pulled Mrs. Sanders to her. "Thank you," she said in a low emotional voice.

A look of understanding passed between them. Hillary withdrew a handkerchief from her bag and wiped her eyes. To avoid embarrassing Hillary, Mrs. Sanders turned to her flowers and said, "Those flowers are camellias. Most gardeners considered them delicate to grow in this area. They were proved to be wrong, and now everyone who lives in Sacramento and loves flowers grows camellias."

When Mrs. Sanders had finished her story about flowers and turned to look at Hillary, Hillary had returned her handkerchief to her handbag. Mrs. Sanders hooked her arm through Hillary's, and they walked together to the front door.

While Hillary and Dan's mother were getting acquainted, Dan had carried Hillary's luggage into the guest bedroom, which overlooked a flower garden in full bloom. When Mrs. Sanders led her to the guest room, Hillary commented about the beautiful view. Then Mrs. Sanders showed her how the windows folded back from the screen so she could open them if the room became too warm. But when Mrs. Sanders showed Hillary the bathroom, she immediately thought how she would like to climb into it, and from it into the big double bed and enjoy a night's sleep without being subjected to the rocking and the clickety-clacking she had never quite become adjusted to while traveling on a train.

Dan had explained to his parents shortly after their arrival that he would have to leave for San Francisco as soon as they had eaten breakfast. So, while his mother and Hillary were preparing breakfast, Dan called the railway station for train schedules from Oakland to Barstow and confirmed a sleeper left Oakland at six in the evening and arrived in Barstow at seven in the morning. To ensure he would have adequate time to complete his work with his engineering firm, he decided to ask Hillary to meet him Monday at the Oakland Railway Depot in time to catch the six o'clock train.

As soon as they had finished breakfast, Dan apologized for leaving then said goodbye to everyone and asked his father to drive him to the train station. After arriving in Oakland, he boarded the ferry to San Francisco then flagged a taxi to take him to his apartment. When he walked into his apartment and turned on the lights, he dropped his luggage and took a deep breath. Then he walked to the lounge and sat down.

Suddenly I feel tired, he thought. So many things have

happened since I left here to go to Barstow, it seems I have crowded three months of events into three weeks, and I am not through.

Dan pushed himself up from the lounge, closed the front door, and carried his luggage into the bedroom. I'll unpack this evening, and when I have time tomorrow, I'll start repacking for the trip to Barstow, he thought.

I feel pretty crummy after that long train ride, Dan thought. Before I do any calling, I'll take a bath. He finished his bath and slipped on his robe. Ah, he thought, now I feel a lot better. I'll call Hammeric. Sally answered the phone.

"Hello, Sally, this is Dan Sanders. How is everyone?" "Fine, Dan. How was your trip?"

"Super. It was my first visit to Boston, and I was impressed. So much history. When we get together, I'll tell you all about it."

"I'll be looking forward to hearing about it. I know you called to speak to Dick, hold on a second and I'll get him. It is nice to have you back, Dan."

"Thanks, Sally."

A few seconds later, Dick came on the line. "Welcome back, Dan. I gathered from your wire you had a very successful trip."

"Yes, Dick, a very successful one, and a lucky one, too. You can't imagine how I felt when the people I traveled 3,000 miles to find, lived in the first house I stopped to check. And such wonderful people, they treated me like a long lost relative. How are things going at the office?"

"Other than being a little slow, I don't believe we can complain. My guess is, you are concerned and wondering if Joel will accept the management of the mine while you are gone."

"Yes, I am. What is the story, will he accept?"

"He wants to talk it over with you, Dan. However, if you sign a contract with the firm, and we ask him to go, I am sure he will not turn you down."

"I understand and appreciate what you are saying Dick, but I have too much at stake in this venture to assign a man to manage and perform the engineering on a project in which he is not interested. I am not surprised Joel wanted to know more about the offer before he accepted it. Having worked with him, I have found he is not the kind of a person to buy a pig in a poke without first seeing it. That is one of the reasons I want him to run this operation. And I don't believe I mentioned in my wire to you, Dick, I now own a one-third interest in the mine. But that is not the main reason I'm fussy about who runs the operation, my two partners are the son and granddaughter of the old prospector I found blown to bits in the mine tunnel, and they know nothing about mining, so we put up equal amounts of development money and asked me to manage and develop the mine. With that kind of trust, I can't let them down."

"Did you buy into the mine?"

"No, they said the least they could do after all the problems I had experienced in recovering the papers willing the claim to them, and then personally delivering the papers, would be to give me a share of the claim."

"You did all of it, and now I can understand why they insisted on sharing the mine with you. I'm surprised one of them didn't return with you to inspect the gravesite."

Dan squirmed a bit and then said, "The granddaughter did return with me. She is staying with my parents in Sacramento. We will be leaving for Barstow Monday evening."

Apparently, Dick had not detected any sign from Dan's

voice of his discomfort when he had replied. Now Hammeric asked, "Is she good looking?"

Dan, trying to keep ahead of Dick, replied, "Beautiful."
"How old is she?"

"Twenty-four."

"Is she married?"

"No.

Now Dick broke into a big laugh, and said, "Oh, oh. Wow!" Then Dan said, "I have only known the lady for a week, so don't presume too much, and don't let your imagination run away with you." Then Dan added, "She is a very nice person."

"I am sure she is, Dan, and I did not mean to imply otherwise. Now, getting back to Joel. I agree with you, and I'll let you handle it."

Dan asked, "When will it be convenient to discuss the contract?"

"I'm sorry, Dan, I can't discuss it this afternoon. I promised Sally and the kids I would take them out to dinner and then to a movie. Kids have a habit of reminding you when you don't keep a promise. Why don't you jot down some of the ideas you want to incorporate in the contract, and Monday morning we will get together and rough out what we agree upon, then turn it over to the legal people to finalize."

"It sounds great to me. Simple and easy. Before I let you go, and if you have no objection, I would like to get your permission to get in touch with Joel and get his thoughts on the contract."

"Sure, Dan, call him. This is your show, and as I see it, the Firm is only providing a helping hand. You are paying the bills, Anything else, Dan?"

"Nothing more. Tell Sally, goodbye for me, and I will see you on Monday morning."

After verifying Joel Baker's number, Dan asked the operator to connect him. Joel answered the phone. "Howdy, Joel, this is Dan Sanders, your favorite coffee brewer. Are you busy?"

"You don't need to tell me who you are, you old broken-down engineer. I'd recognize that voice if you were talking from the bottom of a forty-foot mine shaft."

"How are you and Judy doing?"

"Same old stuff. As you know, nothing much ever changes. Judy and I keep plugging along. What is this I hear about you opening up a mine on your own near Barstow?"

"It is true. The reason I called is to find out if you are interested in taking on the job of project engineer and manager of the mine while I am in South Africa."

"Dan, to tell you the truth, I haven't heard enough, nor do I know enough about the position to say yes or no, or even maybe. I would like to know more about it."

"Well, Joel, it is a long story, and it will take at least an hour, and maybe another, depending on the number of questions you ask. It will be just a bare-bones outline of the circumstances leading to my direct involvement, then I will get into the plans and how you will be tied in. Do you have the time?"

"I have about an hour and a half. Let's get started." "First, what I am going to tell you, is confidential. I am concerned that if the story leaks out, it will cause a stampede. So, say as little as possible on the subject, regardless of who the person might be. So, here is the story."

Dan told Joel about the claim and the conclusions he had reached concerning the blast and the old prospector's death. Knowing he was talking on an open telephone line, he deliberately avoided giving the exact location of the mine and using the word 'gold,' substituting the word, 'mineral.' Joel caught on to the subtlety of Dan's omissions and substitutions and followed Dan's lead. Dan also kept the details of the plan to a minimum and substituted Joel's and his personal experiences to highlight his ideas and give Joel a better understanding of his thoughts.

Dan concluded by saying, "The position of manager and project engineer includes the authority for hiring and firing all personnel in your crew from the foreman down to cook. We have worked together on similar projects, so you know approximately what personnel we will need, and I depend on you to locate a good foreman, hopefully, one with whom we have worked with before who is looking for a job. One of the provisions I plan to write in the contract will state that the manager and the foreman will alternate and schedule their workweeks in such way that each has a Saturday and Sunday off every other week. In other words, one weekend the foreman will have Saturday and Sunday off, the next weekend the manager. That is about it, Joel, what do you think?"

"I like it, Dan. I like it because it will give me an opportunity to gain some experience working on my own but being only a 12-hour train ride away from Judy, with two days off every other week is more important. Do you think you will run into any opposition from Hammeric?"

"No, Hammeric has agreed to assign you to the position if you are interested, and the Firm will only respond when asked for assistance. I have mentally kicked around the idea of turning accounting and payroll over to them, but I haven't discussed it with Hammeric or either of my partners. By the way, both of my partners are lawyers, but I assure you, Joel, they will be a help and not a hinderance. Don't hesitate to call them. The daughter, whom I mentioned, will be with us for the next two or three weeks, or until I leave."

"It is nice to know you have a couple of lawyers you can call on regardless of the kind of business you are in," Joel commented. "I am looking forward to meeting your partner, the one who is with you."

"I am sure you will be impressed." Dan said flatly, and he continued, "I will need your answer first thing Monday morning. What is your position now?"

"I fully expect to accept your offer. I am sure Judy will be happy to hear I will be located only hours instead of days from home. It could have been Nome, Alaska. As you know, we have only been married two years, and during those two years, we have been together a total of about one year."

"OK, Joel, I'll see you Monday morning. Please give my regards to Judy."

Dan hung up the phone and ran his hand through his thick black hair. I'll unpack now and put everything away, then call the family and find out how they and Hillary made out today, he thought.

After he had finished unpacking, he put through his call to Sacramento. His mother answered the phone.

"Hello, Mother, this is Dan. How did things go today?"

Knowing his mother, Dan knew he would get a full report.

"Oh, Dan, just wonderful. I enjoy Hillary so much. She is so bright and so thoughtful. After breakfast this morning, I tried to get her to lie down because I knew she was tired, but she insisted on helping me clean up the table and do the dishes. And while we worked, she told me all about her family and herself. She surprised me when she told me her father was the illegitimate child of her grandmother, who had an affair with the dead miner you found in the mine tunnel. It proves to me she wants to get everything out in the open and trusts me not to gossip about it. She is a very honest person. And, Dan, I am growing very fond of her, even though I met her just this morning."

"I am glad to hear that, Mother. As I told you, she is one of my partners; consequently, I am sure you will see a great deal of each other. Where is she now?"

"I finally talked her into taking a nap, and she has been asleep for a little more than an hour."

"Don't wake her. Tell her I called, and I will call again tomorrow. Now, I am going to eat. One more thing, though, before I hang up, tell Hillary I contacted both Hammeric and Joel Baker and had long talks with them. Everything looks favorable, and I will fill her in on the detail's tomorrow. Do you have anything else to add, Mother?"

"Nothing more, Honey, thanks for calling."

Dan dressed and took a taxi to the Fairmont Hotel. He had decided on Italian food which was served in one of the many restaurants in the hotel. Since he had not called for reservations, he had to wait for seating. While waiting, it suddenly dawned on him that he missed Hillary. We have eaten every meal together for a week, he thought, and it seems strange she isn't here with me. And while eating dinner, he felt the same way. Once, he caught himself about to turn and say something to her. Strange, he thought.

Dan returned to his apartment a bit upset with himself over his strange behavior, but he shook it off as being the result of his close association with Hillary while he was in Boston and on the trip back to Sacramento he put on his pajamas and his robe then went to his desk and began putting together the elements he wanted in the contract.

He woke up the next morning at 9:30. I think my time

schedule will require readjusting again, he thought. But I had a good night's sleep. I'll have coffee and shave and then call home. Since I left Hillary to stay with strangers, I feel a little guilty, and I am anxious to talk to her. I hope she isn't upset with me.

It was a few minutes after ten when he called. His mother greeted him with a cheery, "Good morning."

"How are you this morning, Mother?"

"Just wonderful, Dan. We finished breakfast about an hour ago, and while we were having breakfast, I asked Hillary if she cared to go to church with us and she said she would. She is getting ready now. Shall I call her?"

"Yes, if she can come to the phone. I don't want to interfere with her preparation."

"I'm sure she is presentable by now. She went to her room over half an hour ago. Wait, and I'll check."

Dan had been holding for only a minute or two when Hillary's voice came on the line. "Hello, Dan, how did your discussions go yesterday?"

"Very well, but before we talk business, how was your day?"

"Super. Your parents hovered over me all day like a mother hen with one chick. Both are such wonderful people. I felt guilty having people more than twice my age wait on me and who seemed to be trying to anticipate my every wish. I have never felt more welcome before in my life, and Mrs. Sanders practically ordered me to bed around four o'clock. And she did the right thing, I had not been in bed for more than five minutes when I seemed to slip away. It was two in the morning before I woke up. I got up, went to the bathroom, and crawled back in bed. The next thing I knew, it was 8:30. Your parents delayed breakfast for me, and during breakfast, your mother asked if I cared to go to church with them, and I said, 'Yes!'

"From the combined report from you and Mother, it appears there is no need for me to worry about how you and my family are getting along."

Hillary laughed, "No, you need not. I am sure any worries you may have had been teeny tiny ones because I am positive your mother can get along with anyone."

"True, Mother is a very caring person, and if she likes someone as you found out, she smothers them with her desire to please. Some people can't handle it, but you seemed to have enjoyed it, and for that I am pleased, to put it mildly."

"There was no pretending when she welcomed me into her home, Dan, and I shall never forget it."

Dan smiled, "I vividly recall how you and your father welcomed me into your home, and I shall never forget that, either."

Dan switched their talks back to his talks with Hammeric and Baker. When he had finished, and then clarified some of the points Hillary had questioned, he said, "It is time for me to hang up and let you finish getting ready for church. I am glad Mother asked you."

"I am pleased, too," Hillary commented.

"Before I let you go, Hillary, have Dad call the railroad station to find out what train you must catch to get you into Oakland by five o'clock. And then when you get to Oakland, if you get there first, wait for me at the ticket windows. If I get there first, I'll do the same. But more importantly, did you call your father?"

"Oh, yes, I called him right after you left yesterday morning. He said he was feeling well, but a little lonely, and he missed both of us. He wanted to know all about our trip, but I did not mention our encounter with the drunk. I'll call him again this afternoon around four."

"Give him my regards when you call. I have developed a great deal of respect for your father."

"Thank you, Dan. I know he feels the same way about you. And by the way, I missed you. I guess it was our close association together during this past week."

"I can understand how you felt because I had similar feelings. Well, if we don't hang up now, you will never get to Church. I'll see you tomorrow in Oakland. Goodbye for now."

"Thanks for calling, Dan."

Dan spent the rest of the day working on the contract.

Although what he had developed so far said little about purchasing supplies and equipment, except to say that the MacGregor mining Company would be responsible for purchasing and funding, he kept thinking about the mounds of paperwork if the company took on the accounting chores; If we have the Engineering Consulting Firm take on the task, Joel can funnel all the paperwork to the San Francisco office and have it do the accounting. Joel and the foreman can keep the payroll records and also send those along. The less personnel we house at the mine, the simpler the management task will be. I'll talk the proposition over with Hammeric tomorrow.

Dan kept jotting down notes, scratching some out, until he thought he had covered all parts of an agreement which would meet the requirements of the MacGregor Mining company while keeping the obligations and the costs to the Engineering Consulting Firm to a minimum.

When Dan arrived at the office the next morning, he began, as usual, preparing the coffee. He had just lit the jet under the coffee urn when Joel arrived, "Good morning, Joel. I'm sorry, but you are a little early for coffee. It should be ready in about fifteen minutes."

"No hurry, I had three cups before I left the house. I came early to let you know Judy gave me the green light. She said she may come down to visit me."

"That will be great. I plan on building separate tent houses for you and the foreman. Each one will be large enough for a stove, desk, table, chairs, and a cot, with adequate room for an extra cot."

They continued talking while the other employees began arriving in ones and twos. By the time Hammeric arrived; the coffee was ready. Hammeric had stopped by his office and dropped off his briefcase, and now he joined Joel and Dan at the coffee urn. After passing around greetings and filling their coffee cups, they returned to Hammeric's office, and he motioned for them to sit down.

Hammeric first turned to Joel and asked, "What have you decided to do, Joel?"

"If you have no objection, I will join Dan on the MacGregor Mining Company project. Dan and I have worked together on similar projects. We get along well together, and we have learned what we can expect from each other."

Then Hammeric turned to Dan, "I assume you have talked to Joel and any questions which may have existed between you have been resolved?"

"Yes, we have, Dick. Nothing major, for the most part, the questions were related to authority and responsibility. These will be spelled out in the contract."

"Good, let's get on with the contract."

Dan went over his notes while the two listened, commented, and offered suggestions. Some required minor debate but were easily resolved. They agreed the responsibility for funding and accounting should rest with the San Francisco firm, financed by the MacGregor Mining Company. The exceptions would be local petty cash expenditures and payroll records which would be kept by the MacGregor Mining Company Manager or his designee, then forwarded to San Francisco for incorporation in the master accounting and funding records. Payroll checks were to be issued each week by the San Francisco firm with blocks of funds being transferred, as needed by the MacGregor Mining Company to the consulting firm.

By noon they had completed the rough draft and had it ready to turn over to the legal unit for final preparation.

Dan signed the rough draft giving his approval for The MacGregor Mining Company. Then Dan said, "Thank you, Dick, for dropping your other work and helping me. I don't have to tell you I am squeezed for time to meet my South Africa commitment."

Hammeric smiled, "No thanks are necessary. Remember, our San Francisco consulting firm will not be doing the work on your project without compensation. You will be billed for our normal fee. The amount will be determined by our legal people and incorporated in the contract." Again, Hammeric smiled, "I'm sure you are aware of that, Dan."

"Oh yes," Dan replied with a broad grin. "I am only surprised someone didn't bring up the subject sooner. Be sure I get at least four copies."

"I will see to it personally. How soon do you expect Joel to report for work?"

"The sooner, the better, but no later than next Monday, Monday morning if possible."

Hammeric turned to Joel, "How long will it take you to clean up the projects you are working on?"

"I considered asking you to reassign one of my projects to one of the other engineers. I am sure someone would like to have the commission. I can finish the rest by Friday and report to Dan Monday morning."

"Good." Hammeric turned from Joel to Dan. "Anything else, Dan?"

"No, we have accomplished a good morning's work, and for that, I am very grateful to both of you. Now if you will excuse me, I have to get back to the apartment and get ready to catch a six o'clock train to Barstow." Dan rose from his chair, closed his briefcase, shook hands, and said goodbye.

Dan decided to dress in the clothing he used for fieldwork, including boots and his campaign hat. After packing two like sets of pants and shirts plus underwear and his personal items, he added his .38 caliber revolver and his hunting knife. Then he dressed quickly and looked at his watch. It is 2:30, he thought, time to call a cab.

He arrived at the station at 4:20 and carried his suitcase to the area near the ticket windows. Unable to locate Hillary, he checked the train schedule board and saw the next train from Sacramento would arrive at 5:10PM. I have about thirty minutes to wait, he thought.

Dan considered meeting Hillary at the train steps but decided he might possibly miss her in the large commuter crowd. He picked up an evening paper at the newsstand and sat down to read while waiting.

When the caller announced the train's arrival, he tucked the newspaper under one of his suitcase straps and stood up and watched until he saw Hillary following the redcap wheeling her luggage through the station entrance, then he began walking toward her, elbowing his way through the hurrying crowd. When Hillary spotted Dan, he saw the slight look of concern leave her face and turn into a smile. Quickly, she stepped up to the side of the redcap to greet him. Both gave each other a big hug like siblings who had been separated for a long time.

Hillary, looking up at Dan commented, "I hardly recognized you in that hat. It makes you look six inches taller."

As they followed the redcap toward Dan's luggage, he replied, "I feel very comfortable with it, it is the same one I wore in the Service. I have an extra, just in case that I bought at a war surplus store. How was the trip from Sacramento?"

"Not good, not bad, but about three hours too long." Both looked at each other and smiled.

Since insufficient time remained to eat before their train departed, they decided to board the train and eat in the dining car. When the porter led them down the Pullman isle, he dropped Dan's suitcase off in one of the seats and led Hillary to a drawing-room.

Dan explained, "Only one unreserved drawing-room on the entire train and tomorrow is going to be a very long hard day. You will need a good night's rest. I am accustomed to sleeping in upper and lower births, so you get the drawing-room."

"Dan, I too, can sleep in an upper or lower birth, and I want to be treated as an equal. But, Dan, thank you, you are very thoughtful." Hillary smiled at Dan and said, "I hope I don't overuse that phrase."

Dan returned her smile and said, "Never worry, you never will."

On their arrival in Barstow the next morning, Dan had a redcap take their luggage to the Railway Express Office. The same agent was busy behind the barrier gate sorting packages. Dan asked, "What time do you expect Jerry to show up?"

The agent quickly looked up, responding, "Say, I remember you. You were here about two weeks ago; your name is

Sanders. Jerry told me what a nice guy you are. Good to see you again. Jerry usually shows up about seven. Want a ride?"

"I sure do. Tell him I'll be over in the Harvey House having breakfast. Will it be OK to leave our luggage here?"

"Sure thing, Jerry is always anxious to pick up some loose change."

Dan thanked the agent, then he and Hillary walked toward the Harvey House.

When they ordered breakfast, Dan ordered 12 sandwiches of various kinds to take with them to the claim.

After they had finished breakfast, they were walking out the door when they met Jerry about to enter. Jerry stepped aside to let Hillary pass, not knowing Hillary and Dan were together. Hillary waited while Dan and Jerry shook hands. Jerry's toothless smile could not have been bigger.

"It's nice to see you again, Mr. Sanders. I've already loaded your luggage on the truck."

"Thanks, Jerry, I want you to meet Miss MacGregor." Jerry had not noticed Hillary standing behind him. He turned when Dan had spoken, and on seeing Hillary, grabbed his hat from his head and held it in both hands. He bowed and said, "Miss MacGregor, I'm glad to meet you, Miss MacGregor."

"Jerry, do you remember the old prospector who died in a mine explosion out near Fremont Peak? Jim MacGregor? Everyone called him Jim. This is his granddaughter."

"Glory be! Old Jim's granddaughter. What a surprise. Sure thing, Mr. Sanders, I met him in Barstow several times over the years when he came in to pick up supplies." Jerry had been looking at Hillary while pondering Dan's question.

Then Hillary spoke to Jerry, "It is nice to meet someone who knew my grandfather, Jerry. Unfortunately, I never had the pleasure of knowing him. Mr. Sanders and I are riding out to visit his grave."

When Hillary and Jerry had finished their conversation, Dan turned to Jerry, "I must make a call to Slocum. Is there a phone available nearby?"

"Yes, sir, Mr. Sanders. You can call from the express office. I'll walk over with you, so the agent doesn't give you any guff."

When Slocum picked up the phone, Dan told him what he wanted, and if at all possible, he would appreciate having it ready by ten o'clock. Slocum responded by saying that he thought he had everything, including the kind of horse he wanted for Hillary and a saddle scabbard for her 30-30 Winchester, and have everything ready by ten.

Hillary rode to the hotel in the front seat with Jerry, and Dan rode with the luggage. When they entered the hotel, and Dan asked for two rooms with baths and a room separating the two, the clerk looked up at Dan and started to smirk.

On seeing Dan's face and remembering Dan's previous visits, he changed his mind and turned the register for both to sign. Before going to their rooms, Dan asked Hillary how soon she could be ready. She responded with a guess of about forty-five minutes. He then asked that she meet him in the lobby.

Dan unpacked his clothes and after hanging them up, decided on a quick bath. Thirty minutes later, with his pistol strapped on, he walked down the steps and into the lobby. Not wishing to converse with the clerk, he dropped his bag into one of the chairs and continued through the lobby and out the front door. He looked across the street and saw Jerry's pickup parked in front of the hardware store.

Jerry has been a treasure to me since I met him, Dan thought. He and his Ford sure beat a taxi. I told him we would meet him at the hardware store, and there he is waiting. Dan looked at his watch. Hillary should be coming down in a few minutes, he thought. I'll go back in and wait.

When Dan walked into the lobby, the clerk asked, "How long do you expect to be in town this time, Mr. Sanders?"

"I have not decided," Dan replied. "I have paid you in advance for a week. I will be in and out. At the end of the week, I'll let you know if I decide to stay longer."

"And Miss MacGregor?"

"She is paid up for a week, too."

A few minutes later, Hillary walked down the stairs with a satchel slung over her shoulder and carrying her rifle.

She had dressed in riding clothes per Dan's instructions. Her blue denim split riding skirt, light blue long sleeve shirt, a broad-brimmed gray hat with a flat crown, tan-colored scarf, and boots, seemed perfect to Dan as he rose and joined her. The hotel clerk stared as they walked out the door and onto the sidewalk.

Dan pointed to Jerry's pickup across the way. "Jerry will be waiting for us inside the hardware store. We can buy you a flashlight while we are in there."

"I have one in my bag, but I should buy a new set of batteries, something I forgot."

"You are not alone, I forgot to buy some, too."

They crossed the street through the light traffic and entered the store. Jerry saw them coming in and walked over.

No laws barred people from carrying guns on the desert, and Jerry did not comment but asked, "What do we do first?"

Dan replied, "Miss MacGregor and I need to buy some flashlight batteries, and then we need to pick up a few groceries for our trip. Can you help us?"

"Sure can, I'll get the flashlight batteries and meet you over by the cash register." Before leaving, he turned to Hillary and said, "I sure like that outfit you are wearing, Miss MacGregor. You are a very beautiful woman."

"Thank you, Jerry, that is the nicest compliment I have had in a long time."

"By golly, you deserve it." And he hurried off to get the batteries.

After paying for the batteries, Hillary and Dan followed Jerry out the door, and two doors down, to the combination grocery store and meat market. They entered, and Dan said, "We should plan our food supply for three days. I always take too much, but I would rather be a little over than a little short. What do you and your father take with you when you go on your hunting and fishing trips?"

Hillary named a number of items including canned and fresh fruit. Dan agreed with the list and said Slocum had condiments left by other campers which he kept in special containers, and he and Hillary very were welcome to use them. When they had finished their shopping, Jerry helped Dan carry the food out to the pickup.

Dan checked his watch when Jerry pulled the pickup near the barn and parked it. It is 9:30, he thought. Hopefully, we can get everything packed and be on our way by 10:00.

Slocum walked out of the barn just as the three were climbing out of the truck. He approached Dan holding out his hand. "It is nice to see you again, Mr. Sanders."

"Thank you, Mr. Slocum." While Dan and Slocum had been passing amenities, Hillary had walked up to stand by Dan. Dan turned to Hillary and then to Slocum. "May I present Miss MacGregor, Mr. Slocum."

"How do you do, Miss MacGregor."

Hillary acknowledged his greeting by smiling and with a slight nod of her head.

Dan turned to Slocum. "Miss MacGregor is the grand-daughter of the prospector who died from a mine blast out near Fremont Peak. Jerry said he knew him, perhaps you may have known him, too. Jim MacGregor?"

"So that's who that was. Yes, I knew him. Everyone I know referred to him as 'Jim the Prospector.' There are very few people between here and Randsburg who did not know Jim. On the other hand, there are very few people who knew much about Jim, especially his private life. My guess is that very few people even knew his last name except postmasters and the bosses and payroll clerks where he worked. He never talked about himself, but now and then he might tell you of his experiences at the big Comstock Mine and Virginia City where he had worked and lived during most of the Civil War years. He talked in a low, quiet voice and never raised it. I considered him a friend because he always boarded his burro with me. I also sold him a few. He was a real horse trader. I don't think I ever got the best of him. He could make a minor blemish sound like the animal only had three legs, and darn near convince you. Everyone liked Jim, and I am going to miss him."

Hillary was smiling, but she could feel a tear in the corner of her eye. She thanked him for the information by responding, "When we have time, I would like to hear more about him, if I may. I never had the good fortune of meeting him. I appreciate every word you have contributed."

"I'll be looking forward to our talk, Miss MacGregor."

Then Slocum turned to Dan, "Mr. Sanders, I have everything packed and ready to load on the pack animal, and I selected a four-year-old mare for Miss MacGregor. As soon as we saddle the mare and Socks, and load the pack animal, you will be ready to ride. Shall we get started?"

"Yes," Dan replied. "Lead out the horses, and while you

load the pack animal, Miss MacGregor and I will saddle the horses. I didn't ask you for a list of what you packed, but if you don't have one, we will help you prepare one before you start loading."

"I know how difficult it is to scratch through bundles and bags trying to locate items, so I have a list of the essentials compiled in advance. I add the additional items the camper wants and scratch off those he didn't ask for. It works out pretty well. I number the bags to show the numbers on the lists."

"It sounds like a foolproof idea," Dan commented. Slocum asked Jerry to help him with the horses, and when Jerry led the sorrel mare out of the corral, Hillary showed little emotion, but as Dan watched, she walked over to the mare and took the lead rope from Jerry with assurance. Then she patted the mare gently on the neck, and the mare returned Hillary's show of tenderness by nuzzling her on the shoulder. Both seemed to be pleased with their new acquaintances, and Hillary seemed pleased with the name, Emmy.

Although the packhorse Slocum called, Sam could have carried all the supplies, Dan suggested that Hillary and he carry the groceries on the saddle horses. Slocum agreed, and he brought out four sacks which could be tied on the back of the saddles.

They left the stable shortly after ten o'clock. Dan knew Socks would be frisky for the first few minutes after leaving the stable, and he had to keep reining him in to prevent the packhorse from losing his load. Emmy also wanted to run, but knowing she might excite the other two animals, Hillary kept a tight rein on her, too. Dan recalled the steep grade they must climb that lay ahead, and his concern turned to the pack animal. Hillary and I can get off and relieve the saddle horses, he thought, but what can we do for the pack animal?

The two saddle horses must have realized they had a long way to go, and they had settled down to a pace which matched that of the packhorse. Dan held the lead rope of the packhorse in his right hand, and Hillary rode on his left side. Dan turned to Hillary and said, "We have a steep grade about an hour and a half ahead of us. What kind of hiker are you?"

"I have never won any marathons, but I shall try not to disappoint you."

"I asked because it will be noon when we get there and it will be quite warm. If we walk, we can rest the horses. But that won't help the packhorse. If we can switch part of his load to the saddle horses, I am sure the poor animal will be forever grateful. I wasn't paying any attention when Slocum loaded the animal." Then Dan's memory returned to Hillary's comment when she said that she would try not to disappoint him. He recalled her performance on the diving board and how high she jumped with seemingly so little effort, and how she controlled her body during those dives. No, he thought, I don't think she will disappoint me.

Hillary noticed that Dan seemed to be daydreaming, then she saw a slight smile appear and just as quickly disappear and wondered about his thoughts and the mysterious smile. She decided to interrupt his private thoughts. "When we reach the point where we start walking, we can examine the pack and perhaps find enough items we can remove without tearing apart the pack. What do you think?"

When Hillary started talking, it took Dan a second or two to catch up with the point of her comment. By the time she had finished, he had brushed away the cobwebs and responded, "I think that is a good idea, and I am sure it will work."

Dan turned in the saddle and looked over his right shoulder toward the southeast. He could see the outline of Ord Mountain perhaps 30 miles away, then he turned to the northeast and in the direction of Calico Hills but could see nothing because low hills lying in that direction blocked his view. Then he looked at Hillary and she, too, seemed to be absorbed in searching the horizons.

"Well, Hillary, you are looking at the Mojave Desert. It is vast, it is dangerous, it is adventurous, it is filled with hidden wealth if you can find it; it has many common and unusual plants and animals, and it is beautiful to some and ugly to others. I have been wondering if you have had time to form any thoughts about this strange and mysterious land?"

"Dan," then she paused as if she were having difficulty finding the right words to express her thoughts. Suddenly, she continued, "I have never been west of the Mississippi, and I am trying to fit together what I see with what I have seen. I see small round bushes that appear to be the same color of the sand in which they grow, a few larger bushes with long thin branches topped with tiny greasy looking green leaves, a clump of cactus now and then, barren hills with no visible trees, and an occasional lizard scampering across the road. I look back, and I see the town of Barstow, not very impressive, and the thin line of green trees marking the route of the Mojave River; and I wonder where it goes. Between here and the river and beyond the river, I see rocks and sand and sand and rocks. In contrast, I see wild strawberries and blackberry vines growing in lush vegetation and streams, some streams trickling through forests, others rushing through the forests to join the river to carry it to the sea. And I compare the barren rocky hills with low lying hills covered with trees and sage, birds nesting in their branches, and deer grazing in the meadows."

"Dan, I hope you are not disappointed with the way I compared the Mojave Desert with Massachusetts. I know you can't compare cabbages and carrots except that they are both vegetables, and using the same correlation, the Mojave Desert and Massachusetts are both part of the United States, so let us just say they cannot be compared. Each area has peculiarities unique to its climate and location. I am sure a person who has lived all his life within the confines of the Mojave Desert and suddenly woke up in the countryside of the New England States, would be shocked and in awe of what he saw, just as I was when I took my first good look at the Mojave Desert. Regardless of what you might be thinking, Dan, I am having a wonderful time seeing things I have never seen before. And I am sure that before this trip is over, I will see things I never knew existed." Hillary smiled and added, "Now it is your turn."

Dan's lips had been drawn into a straight line, that with his wrinkled brow, mirrored his concern about Hillary's remarks. Then as she began to expand on her thoughts, his face began to relax, and finally, a small smile appeared when she presented her closing remarks. "I have nothing to add," he commented. "You have covered your thoughts quite well."

Dan pointed up the road and said, "We will be turning off this road about 200 hundred yards ahead."

After turning off to the left on the side road he had used before, he checked for tracks but saw none except those made by Socks on his last trip to the claim. He turned to Hillary and said, "We will ride west for about five miles before we hit the grade, and we will have another mile before we reach the steeper incline."

"This isn't much of a road, is it?" Hillary commented.

"No," Dan replied, "I rode this way on my last trip to the claim. I doubt it has been used for many years. It leads to an old mining camp on the downside of the grade. We will stop there for lunch, and rest and water the horses."

Although they had been climbing a slight grade since leaving Barstow, the horses had not suffered because of the need to match the slow pace of the packhorse. Now they had reached the steeper incline which carried them over the hills. Hillary and Dan dismounted then tied the reins of the horses to a greasewood bush while they examined the pack.

After checking the pack, Dan asked Hillary, "Do you have any suggestions?"

"The sack of oats tied on the horse's rump is a possibility, and the canteens can be removed without disturbing the rest of the pack. What do you think the oats and the water will weigh?"

"Sixty pounds of oats and 40 pounds of water will be my guess."

"How much more do you think we should remove?" Hillary asked.

"Let's remove the two items and see how Sam carries the rest of the load."

By the time they had transferred the load, the horses had rested for 15 minutes. Dan said, "We have about a three-mile hike to the summit. After we have walked about a mile, I think we should stop again and check Sam and the pack."

They began their three-mile hike up the incline toward the summit. When Dan judged they walked a third of the way, he suggested they stop and recheck Sam and the pack. Both appear to be holding up well, he thought. He turned to Hillary, who was holding the horses and pointed up the winding road toward the crest of the hills and asked, "Do you see those strange looking trees up near the skyline?"

"Yes, and I have been trying to figure out what they are. They look more like tree stumps than trees. What are they?"

"They are called Joshua trees, a distant relative of the yucca family, which, in turn, belongs to the lily family. But don't cross-examine me because I am not a botanist."

As they trudged up through the hills, Dan continued his story about the Joshua trees. "Joshua trees only grow at certain altitudes, usually on what the natives refer to as the 'High Desert,' and as you can see, we are climbing into Joshua tree country. I have been told Joshua trees are native to the Mojave Desert, and I am sure you will become intrigued by this strange plant as we get closer."

"I don't see how a tree as large as they appear to be can survive without leaves."

Dan did not comment, and they continued their slow but steady climb up through the hills. When they reached a point about a quarter of a mile from the crest, the group moved into a clear view of the Joshua tree grove. Hillary said, "From a distance, Dan, a person can let their imagination run wild."

"What do you mean?" Dan asked.

"The Joshua trees, Dan," she replied, pointing, "I see such a variety of weird sights. The branches, I guess that is what you call them, can be imagined as a body with arms. Some seem to be bowing to each other, and others seem to be praying, while many appear to have their arms stretched toward the heavens as if they, too, are in a prayer stance. On a bright moonlit night, I should think the scene might be a little scary."

"It is strange you should notice and interpret the impressions you are having from seeing your first Joshua trees. As I recall, the Mormons, on their first trip to establish a colony in the southern part of California, crossed the Mojave Desert and saw for their first time these weird-looking trees. They, too, thought the branches looked like arms. Some tree arms pointed toward Heaven while others appeared to be pointed toward the promised land. As a result of what they saw, they named the weird looking trees after Joshua. And from that day on they have been called Joshua trees. And I might add, the Mormons did reach their destination, a small village called San Bernardino, where they built a fort. You will be registering our claims there, next Monday. The population of that small village is now 25,000."

"Dan, what an interesting story. How and where do you acquire all of this information?"

"One of the small dividends I receive from being a mining engineer is meeting and working with all kinds of people. Among the ones I enjoy most are the old-timers who always have stories to tell. I meet them at the mines, the restaurants, hotels, and boarding houses."

"How fascinating," Hillary remarked, then she questioned him concerning some of the old-timers he had met.

They continued the slow climb, talking as they walked and stopping to rest the packhorse until they reached the summit. Now they were surrounded by Joshua trees of all shapes and all sizes, and they could feel the cool breeze blowing across the summit of the hills from the west.

"Doesn't that breeze feel wonderful, Dan?" Hillary commented while tying Emmy's reins to one of the Joshua trees.

"Yes, indeed. While we were climbing up to the pass, the hills blocked the afternoon breeze from reaching us. We will benefit from it from now until we reach the spring."

"What causes the breeze?"

"It is a thermal action created by the heat from the desert. It causes the air to rise, and as it rises, it leaves a vacuum below which sucks in the cool air from the Pacific Ocean. As the crow flies, the Pacific Ocean is only about 200 miles from here."

"Amazing, Dan. It sounds like Mother Nature provided the Mojave Desert with a cooling system."

"True, but I suggest it is best you do not become too fondly in love with this cooling system because Mother Nature has a habit of turning it off during some of the hottest days in the year, namely, August and September. Now, the supplies—I suggest we repack the sack of oats on Sam but keep the canteens on the saddle horses. What do you think?"

"It sounds fine to me. What can I do?"

"You can hold Sam's reins while I make the transfer." After Dan had made the transfer and checked the cinches, they mounted and moved on down the road. "We will make better time now. The road has leveled off, and we should reach the abandoned mining camp in an hour or less. We will stop there and water and rest the horses and have lunch."

"After that hike, I am ready for lunch and a little rest, too," Hillary volunteered.

The old road wound through the Joshua trees for several miles then began to descend. When they reached the old mining camp, and before they dismounted, Dan pointed out to Hillary how the Joshua trees had thinned out. Then after dismounting and removing the sack of oats from Sam's pack, they watered the horses and sat down under the same Joshua tree Dan had stopped to rest on his return from the claim.

While Hillary sorted through the sandwiches to find the kind each one had decided to eat, Dan filled two of the tin cups with water, then when both had started eating, Dan remarked, "This is the place I stopped on my way back from the claim, and it was here where I opened your grandfather's saddlebags containing all of his personal belongings. After I had looked through the contents and read your grandmother's letter and your grandfather's will, I found myself undecided on what I should do. So, I decided to sleep on it."

"I woke up the next morning with my decision and an urge to tell someone. I turned to Socks and said aloud, 'I'm going to Boston.' He looked up and rose to his feet, as if he were saying, 'Let's go.'"

Hillary laughed and said, "I am glad you came, and I know Dad is, too."

They continued their conversation until Dan decided it was time to get the horses ready and prepare to leave. They followed Sock's tracks from Dan's previous trip until they reached the Old Indian Trail, and from there, on to the spring.

The sun had just begun to slip over the horizon when they arrived. Immediately, they began unloading the packhorse to locate the tethers, the tether stakes, and the short-handled axe Dan needed to drive the stakes. After tethering the packhorse, and unsaddling and tethering the saddle horses, Hillary helped Dan rub down the three horses. Then Dan led the horses to the spring for watering while Hillary located the feed bags and poured a ration of oats in each one.

Dan, carrying a canteen of water back from the spring for their personal use, walked over to Hillary and said, "Now that we have taken care of the animals, we can decide where we should lay out our camp. I have only one suggestion. Since this spring is the only source of water for all of the wild animals in this area, I believe we should locate it far enough away from the spring to allow them access without having to be concerned about safety. What are your thoughts?"

"I think it is a good idea. Anything else?"

"We have the horses tethered a little over halfway between the Old Indian Trail and the spring. We can set up your tent on one side of the horses, and I can sleep on the other. By having the horses between us, we will know if anything disturbs them. The arrangement will also provide you with some privacy."

"I like that idea, too. Now, what do we do with the supplies?"

"If we store them on the far side of the horses, away from the spring, there will be less chance the creatures coming to the spring will disturb our supplies, and we can also set up the stove, and the cooking and eating equipment there."

"I have been looking at the sky, Dan. How long will it be before darkness sets in?"

"It is June, so my guess is about 8:30. Since it is a little after seven, we have close to an hour and a half of light left. Let's get your tent set up. OK?"

"Dan, I can set it up."

"I know you can, but two of us can do it quickly and then you will be free to help me," Dan said.

"I don't seem to be winning very many, do I?"

"More than you realize." Dan had already started for the supplies when he answered.

In just a few minutes, it seemed to Hillary, they had located the components to her tent, carried them to the spot she had selected, had it erected, carried the rest of the equipment to the far side of horses, and started the task of sorting and storing it.

Dan said, "We are fortunate Slocum included a set of these empty storage cans within cans. Each of these becomes a separate can with a lid when they are separated." He held one up and showed Hillary how it worked.

"I don't recall seeing anything exactly like that in Boston. It is a sure way to keep mice and ants out of your food, especially when you can't find a tree from which to hang your provisions."

Dan laughed, "At least we don't have to keep rain umbrellas handy."

They continued to jest and poke fun as they sorted and arranged their supplies. Dan knew Hillary must be getting tired, and he also knew her pride would not allow her to admit it.

They finished, and Dan rubbed the palms of his hands together and asked, "What cuisine shall we serve this evening, Miss MacGregor: New England, Southern, Mid-Western, or Western?"

"A piece of shoe leather will taste like a porterhouse. Whatever you fix, I will eat."

"Ah yes, Miss MacGregor, then we shall have a Western pseudo-porterhouse."

Hillary smiled but did not comment as she lay relaxing against her saddle.

Dan lit the Coleman two-burner stove and placed a small pan of water on one of the two burners. Then he set the Dutch oven on the other burner and emptied a can of pork and beans into a skillet. When the Dutch oven had reached the temperature he desired, he removed it from the burner and replaced it with the skillet of beans. Next, he removed two beef sandwiches from one of the metal containers and placed them in the Dutch oven to warm. Then he rinsed out the cups they had used at lunch and put a teaspoon of tea leaves in each one, added boiling water, and carried the cup of tea on a tin plate with a wedge of lemon to Hillary where she lay relaxing.

She raised up, and with a surprised look said, "What a treat, Dan, how did you know I wished for a cup of tea?" She began stirring it, and after the leaves settled, she added the lemon. Dan had been watching her, and when she looked up and said, "Thank you," he thought he saw a tear in one corner of one of her eyes.

I wonder what caused that? he thought. She must be very tired. He turned and hurried back to the beans and sandwiches. He gave the beans a stir, checked the sandwiches, and put the Dutch oven back on the burner, then stirred the beans while sipping his tea.

A few minutes later, Dan asked, "Are you about ready to eat?"

"As soon as I wash my hands and that will only take a minute," Hillary replied.

Dan removed the Dutch oven from the burner and checked the sandwiches. They are steaming hot, he thought. I hope they didn't burn. I'll check one and find out. Ah, he thought as he lifted one with a spatula, a golden brown.

He replaced the lid, and while Hillary washed up, he moved his saddle directly across from Hillary's and spread a piece of canvas between them. Then with two clean plates, he ladled a healthy helping of beans into each dish and added two halves of sandwiches to each one. By the time he had finished, Hillary was standing beside him, offering her assistance.

"Do you mind carrying these to our dining area?" he asked.

"If you will, I shall bring the condiments."

"Thank you for your confidence," she joked. "I'll join you at our private table."

Both sat Indian style facing each other across their canvas tablecloth. Hillary bit into one of the halves, of her sandwich and said, "How did you learn to fix sandwiches this way? It is delicious."

"Strange as it may seem, in your grandfather's Dutch oven, It is a long story, and someday I shall tell you all about it. How are the beans? My special recipe, I want you to know."

Each had an apple, followed by another cup of tea. When they had finished, Hillary congratulated Dan on the wonderful meal he had prepared. They did not tarry; both were tired from the overnight train ride and the long day of riding and walking. And they worked together, quickly cleaning the dishes and cooking utensils. Then Dan carried Hillary's saddle to her tent, and on his way back, he picked up his saddle and moved it to the location he intended to use to lay his pallet. But prior to getting his pallet ready, he rolled the sack of oats up into the heavy canvas used to lash down the supplies on the pack animal.

The next morning, Dan woke up at dawn. The horses were lying down, but he could hear Hillary stirring. Not wishing to disturb her, he lay in his pallet a while longer. When he could no longer hear her, he put on his boots and walked out beyond the Old Indian Trail to relieve himself. When he returned, the horses were standing, and by the time he had watered two of the horses, he saw Hillary walking from around the horses carrying her saddle.

"Good morning, Dan, I did not have one bit of trouble falling asleep last night, nor did I have any trouble sleeping. How was your night?"

"If everyone slept the way I do, the word 'insomnia' would never have found its way into the dictionary. How do you feel this morning?"

"Oh, a little stiff and stove up but otherwise OK. It has been quite some time since I have had that much exercise. Now, what may I do to help?"

"We need more water for the horses and for our use. If you get the feed bags ready, I'll finish watering the horses and fill the canteens."

After they had finished watering and feeding the horses,

Dan asked, "How do pancakes, bacon strips, fried potatoes, and canned fruit sound for breakfast?"

"What are you trying to do, fatten me up to the point where I can't see?"

Dan laughed. "No, the kind of work you will be doing today will melt any fat you may even think about putting on like a block of ice sitting on a rock in the middle of the Mojave Desert in mid-summer."

Hillary compromised, "I'll have two small pancakes, two strips of crisp bacon, a very small helping of fried potatoes, and a double helping of canned fruit."

After finishing breakfast and cleaning up the campsite, Dan suggested they take a short walk and look for a patch of bunch grass where they could stake out the horses. "With all the rain this area of the Mojave Desert has had this year, we should be able to locate a nice patch nearby. When I was in Randsburg, I was told that the owner of the butcher shop runs a few head of cattle near Fremont Station when abnormal rains produce more than the usual amount of bunchgrass. Of course, that may only happen once in seven or eight years. We are exceptionally lucky it happened this year."

They had not walked more than a hundred yards toward the northeast when they found clumps of bunchgrass in a patch about one hundred feet across, surrounded by greasewood bushes. "We can't find a better spot than this," Dan said. "The grass is a foot high, and the greasewoods, although not as high as some I have seen, will offer some camouflage from prying eyes. We can't be too careful."

"You are concerned we may run into Schuleman, aren't you, Dan?"

"Sooner or later, I am sure we will. My only hope is that

you are not around when it happens." His nostrils flared, and he drew a deep breath then let it out slowly.

"Please, Dan, don't worry about me. I am here to help you, not hinder you. Remember?"

Dan looked at Hillary with a weak smile and said, "I remember, and I know you will help me, but I can't tell the worry to just go away."

Sensing Dan did not wish to discuss the subject further, Hillary commented, "It is strange the grass out here only grows in bunches, isn't it? I can't recall seeing grass growing like this before."

As they turned and started back towards the camp, Dan said, "Most deserts grow some kind of bunchgrass, but the bunch grasses I have seen are scragglier than those we see growing here. So, I assume we can safely say that bunchgrass is peculiar to deserts but may vary by the location. And of course, the reason it looks so lush is because of all the rain the Mojave has had this year."

"I am sure the horses will love it," Hillary commented. Having tethered the horses, and with Dan leading the way, they started their hike toward the claim, Dan carrying a canteen and shoulder satchel with the claim filing forms, and Hillary following with her rifle and a canteen strap hung across her shoulder. They followed the trail leading to the spring from the claim Hillary's grandfather had traveled so many times over so many years. Since they had been up since dawn, it was still early when they left. Dan turned to Hillary and said, "It is about a 30-minute hike, and by getting an early start, we should get a couple of claims staked out by noon, the coolest part of the day. Then we can return to camp, eat and rest, then ride out around Fremont Peak as we planned, to check the possibilities of running a road around the Peak to Fremont Station."

Hillary did not respond. They had been on the trail for several minutes, but Hillary had not spoken a single word.

Her silence began to disturb Dan, and he said, "A penny for your thoughts."

"I have been thinking about my grandfather, Dan. I have been trying to visualize him walking slowly down this trail leading his burro, but his appearance is so dim and shadowy, I am having difficulties because I have never seen him and unfortunately, I never will. I will visit his grave, and that makes me think about him, too. And I am also having difficulty sorting out my thoughts concerning the way I feel about him because of the beautiful letter my grandmother wrote to a man with whom she had fallen in love who apparently did nothing more than lead a burro around the Southwest most of his life looking for gold."

"I'm sorry, Hillary, I can't help you. However, you may have a better understanding of your grandfather after you have had an opportunity to talk to more people who knew him, and you have seen the evidence of how hard he worked trying to find his fortune. Surely, it was for only one purpose, that being to make your grandmother proud of him."

They remained silent for the rest of the way, and as they walked, they saw many of the desert creatures Hillary's grandfather had seen when he and Suzie traveled the same trail two years before.

When they appeared to be within a quarter of a mile of the ore dump, Dan began to scan the top of the dump and the area around the dump more intently, then Hillary saw Dan switch his shoulder satchel to his left shoulder with the canteen. And as she watched, he opened the flap of his holster and pulled the pistol out then eased it back into the holster. He slowed his pace when they were about 200 yards from the dump, then he stopped. He turned to Hillary and asked, "Have you noticed any activity or anything that looks suspicious?"

"No, the place looks deserted to me. What is your assessment?"

"I think it is, too. But we can't see the top of the dump. Do you think you can cover me while I do a little scouting?"

"Yes, where will you be going, and what do you want me to watch?"

"Stay hidden behind these greasewood bushes and watch the dump. If you see any movement, fire. I plan to work my way east, parallel to the dump and past it, until I can climb the hill in back of the claim where I can look down on the dump. If it is clear, I'll climb down the hill and beckon from the dump. Any questions?"

"Only one. If I should fire, how do I distinguish between friend and foe?"

"You don't. Keep yourself hidden until I give you the signal all is well. It will take me a good five minutes from the time I leave to each the spot where I can look down on the dump. Don't panic, and don't expose yourself. OK?"

"I understand I promise not to panic."

After leaving, Dan looked back, and he could see Hillary had stretched out and laid in a prone position behind a large greasewood bush with her rifle pointed toward the dump in a ready position.

A fair growth of sagebrush and greasewoods lay between the ore dump and the route Dan had selected to follow. Keeping the dump in sight, he ran low, crawling when necessary, until he was well past the claim. Then he turned and climbed the hill until he could see the tip of the west end of the dump but needed to see more. He began cautiously edging his way back along the side of the hill toward the claim with his pistol drawn. Now he looked directly down the hill and on the dump, but he could see no sign of human activity. Then he walked down and around the hill and onto the dump and scanned the area around the claim. Finally, he signaled Hillary to start for the claim.

They met halfway, and Dan noticed her slightly flushed face, but she seemed to be very much in control. He asked, "How did it go? Are you feeling, OK?"

"I am fine, but I worried about you when you were climbing along the side of the hill back to the claim. I was concerned you might slip and fall, then I would be stuck with a man with a broken leg." She looked up at Dan and smiled, then added, "It was quite an experience. Never before have I been asked to take a pot shot at a human being."

"I am sorry, Hillary, but as I said before, 'We can't be too careful.'"

"I understand, Dan, and I appreciate your concern and your caution."

When they arrived at the claim and walked up the ramp, Dan said, "Let's rest for a few minutes then I will show you where your grandfather is buried."

Hillary noticed a huge boulder that had been dislodged from the top of the tunnel and had rolled within a few feet of the stove. She set her canteen by the boulder and leaned her rifle against the stove. Then she remembered an empty dynamite box they had passed when they walked up the ramp. The box should make a good seat, she thought. She walked back to retrieve it and put it where she could sit and lean back against the boulder.

While Hillary had been getting her seat arranged, Dan had

been removing his satchel, and canteen and placing them by the stove as he gave a word picture of the tunnel before the blast. He had also found an empty dynamite box and placed it next to the stove so he could lean back against it with his head resting against the massive chimney. Now they were both seated, and Dan gave her his opinion of how the tunnel was destroyed.

Dan then removed the top from his canteen, took a long drink, and said, "When I look at the size of this ore dump," he turned and gestured with his hand, "I can't help but think of all the hard work your grandfather put into this claim. One of the men I met in Randsburg who knew your grandfather, told me he had been working on this claim, on and off, for 25 years. He said your grandfather was positive gold was hidden somewhere in this hill, and it was just a matter of time until he found it."

"Yes," Hillary responded, "I can readily understand the effort he expended simply by looking at all the rock he has removed from the tunnel. I assume he had very little modern mining equipment and very little hired help."

"From what I heard, he worked alone and never hired anyone to assist him. And from what I saw in the tunnel, his only tools were picks, shovels, drills and hammers to pound the drills, and a wheelbarrow to haul the loose rock to the edge of the dump. Are you ready now to walk down to the place where he is buried?"

"Yes," she replied and rose slowly to her feet. Looking toward Fremont Peak, she asked, "What kind of birds are those circling over there?"

"Buzzards," he replied.

"I believe they roost in the rocks up around the top of Fremont Peak, and they are now circling and soaring while using the air currents to push them higher than they will start looking for food. Buzzards are an integral part of the desert; they clean up the carrion."

Hillary and Dan walked down the ramp and around the end of the ore dump. About 50 yards from the dump, Dan pushed through a thick growth of greasewood bushes with Hillary following directly behind him. They stepped into the small clearing and Dan pointed to a slight depression in the center. He said, "This is where your grandfather is buried."

Hillary stood looking at the grave, gripping the barrel of her rifle with both hands while the rifle butt rested on the ground. Moments passed and then she said, "Not even a marker. What kind of animals are those people who buried him?"

"Yes, Hillary, they are animals, and one of them is dead. And as sure as I am standing here, the other animal killed him. It is for that reason I did not mark the grave when I dug down and found your grandfather's papers. If I had marked the grave, and he had returned and found the marker, I am sure he would have tried to find out who I was, then there is no way to tell what he might have done."

"I am sorry, Dan, I did not mean to imply that you should have marked the grave. I understand why. However, after resolving some of the problems we are working on, my first priority shall be to have his remains placed in a coffin and a carved headstone placed on his grave, and I shall also have a wrought iron fence built around it. Furthermore, when the mine is worked out, I shall have his coffin, the headstone, and the wrought iron fence moved to an established graveyard, and I shall have his remains reburied with a complete ceremony. I shall not allow this poor old man's grave to be vandalized and destroyed." She continued staring at the grave for a few seconds longer then she turned to Dan and said, "Are we ready to leave?"

Dan replied with a soft, "Yes," and led Hillary back through the brush to the ramp. He asked Hillary to wait while he climbed up the ramp and looked for the claim's boundary markers. "If we can find one, we should have no trouble locating the other three. There should be one on each side of the claim roughly about 600 feet apart."

After Dan had climbed up the ramp and walked down to the end of the ore dump, he began looking for one of the markers and spotted one on the south side of the claim and pointed in its general direction for Hillary. Then he turned and looked in the opposite direction and saw the other which marked the northwest corner of the claim. When he walked down to the marker where Hillary waited, she asked, "Why would my grandfather erect a marker out here in the flat which obviously is nowhere near the mouth of the tunnel or the location of the mineral?"

"Good question. If your grandfather had set the markers directly opposite on each side of the tunnel, he would not have an area on which to establish the campsite. The way he set up the markers, we have an area of about 300 by 600 feet for the campsite."

Dan turned to the marker and said, "Let's look and find out if the claim form is here." Dan began removing rocks from the three-foot-high marker until he saw a tobacco can. He reached down and fished it out without disturbing the rest of the marker and showed it to Hillary. "The Prince Albert tobacco can is the standard container used by prospectors for storing copies of claim forms in claim markers."

"What a clever idea," Hillary commented. "The cans appear to be waterproof, the right size, and they are free."

Dan opened the lid of the can and shook out the contents. It contained a paper form. He unfolded the form and said, "The form is dated December 1, 1918, and reads, 'I, James MacGregor, located this claim September 3, 1897, and I have filed this claim with the U.S. District Land Office in San Bernardino, Calif. It is located approximately five miles southeast of Fremont Peak on a hill about a mile long, 300 hundred feet high, and 500 hundred feet wide.' The form is signed, James MacGregor." Dan handed the form to Hillary.

"I feel a little strange seeing my grandfather's handwriting for the first time." Then she reread the information on the form, "There isn't much to it, is there?"

Dan replied, "According to the mining laws, only the name of the locator, the date it was located, and the location with some point of reference, is all that is required."

"Is it necessary to update the form?"

"It is a good idea because the information on the form fades over the years. And I think now is the time to relocate the claim and file it in the name of the MacGregor Mining Company. I'll give you a form, and you fill it out then sign all three of our names as our legal representative. When you finish, put it in the tobacco can, replace it where it was, and rebuild the marker. In the meantime, I will locate the other marker. After you have rebuilt the marker, join me at the other marker about 600 feet from here, to sign the form for that marker, too." Dan pointed in the direction he was going, handed Hillary the form and left.

After they had changed the claim form in the second marker, they walked along the north side of the hill until they located the third marker, then they crossed over the hill to the south side and found the fourth. "Now," Dan said, "when we get back to camp, we can make the extra copies we will need, two of which you will take with you to San Bernardino for recording the claims. We will refer to this claim as the Discovery Claim, and our other claims as Claim Number 2 of the Discovery Claim, and so on. We will build another marker next to the southeast marker of the Discovery Claim, and it will become the southwest marker Claim Number 2 of the Discovery Claim, then we will walk east 1500 feet along the side of the hill and set up another marker which will be the southeast marker for Claim Number 2, and so on until we finish. I hope we can set up markers for three claims by early tomorrow afternoon."

"What if we don't finish what we plan for today?"

"We will head back and finish up tomorrow. Will that be too much for you?"

Hillary looked up at Dan and smiled, "Let's get started," and she began picking up medium-sized rocks for the marker.

By noon, they had erected all the markers on the south side of the hill as they had planned. Hillary stood up and rubbed her back with both hands. Dan became concerned as he looked at her, not about her back but about her face. Her cheeks had turned a bright red. "Give me your rifle and your canteen."

Hillary did not argue, she handed him both. Quickly, he unscrewed the canteen cap and handed her the canteen. After she had taken a drink, he asked, "Have you ever had a heat stroke?"

"No," she replied and took another swig. "I feel a little flushed. If we can find a big greasewood bush where I can sit down and rest for a few minutes, I am sure I will be all right, I think stooping and picking up those rocks have caused me to get a little overheated."

"That may very well have been the cause," Dan said.

Then Dan leads her over to the cluster of greasewoods

surrounding her grandfather's grave. Both sat down in the meager shade and backed up under the overhanging branches. "It beats nothing," Dan said. He unscrewed the cap of the canteen and handed it to Hillary. When she returned the canteen, he said, "I'll walk back to camp and get your horse so you can ride back."

"Please, Dan, don't make me feel any worse than I do now. I insisted on coming with you, and I intend to do my share. I will be all right in a few minutes. Remember, I come from tough stock, my grandfather was a hard rock miner and a prospector."

Dan smiled, "You win. We will rest a few minutes then we will see how you feel."

While they rested, Dan discussed with Hillary their ride around Fremont Peak during the afternoon. He knew if he expressed any concern about her going, he would be asking for trouble. He decided that if he wanted to remain in her good graces, it would be better to let her make the decision.

Suddenly, Hillary said, "I'm getting hungry. Let's go." Dan turned and looked at her face. Although her cheeks showed a slight tinge of red, he decided it was caused by the sun and not from internal heat. He said, "Great, let me carry your rifle."

"No thanks, Illy canteen is less than half full. I feel fine, and I will be OK."

When they arrived at the camp, Dan asked Hillary to rest while he checked on the horses. Seeing they had eaten most of the bunchgrass within the length of their tethers, he pulled the stakes and led them back for water. In the meantime, Hillary had put coffee on the burner and opened a can of tomatoes and two cans of sardines. Then she spread a dishtowel over the open cans and joined Dan with the horses.

After tethering and watering the horses, Dan suggested,

"Lets spread one of the canvas ground covers between two of the larger greasewood bushes so we can have some shade while we eat."

"I'll buy that idea. I'll get the cover while you trim the bushes to hold it up."

When they sat down beneath the bushes to eat, Hillary remarked, "I did not realize what a cool breeze we have until we blocked out the sun."

"It does make a difference, doesn't it?" Dan commented. While they were eating, Dan suggested they leave around four o'clock. "It is a little after two now, and by four, the temperature should begin to drop a bit which will make the ride more comfortable for both the horses and for us. It will also give us time to rest before we leave. Building rock monuments is not exactly the same work as deciphering blueprints."

"The trip will be quite a little journey for the horses, will it not?"

"My guess is it will be between ten and twelve miles for the round trip, and I am planning on taking the packhorse with us."

"Why?" Hillary asked. "You are not planning to take supplies with us, are you?"

"No, he is a pretty strong horse, and he may get restless from being alone, or he may become frightened. If he decided to run, that stake would be about a useful as tying his tether to a matchstick. And once he started running, he would not stop until he got to Barstow. Well, what do you think, shall we clean up the kitchen and rest for a while?"

"I'm willing," Hillary replied, rising slowly to her feet then stretching and rubbing her back.

"Are feeling all right?" Dan asked.

"Yes, but a little stiff." She began gathering up the dishes and washing them while Dan dug a hole several yards from the camp and buried the cans and garbage.

They left shortly after four with Dan leading the packhorse. He set their direction toward the end of the southern slope of Fremont Peak. Dan explained that their route would take them in a southwesterly direction for about two miles, then west for a quarter of a mile before they turned north. He stopped several times along the way to check the depth of the sand with a short handle shovel. Fortunately, he found none deeper than four inches before striking solid ground, which, based on his experience, would not bog down a heavy truck with dual drive wheels. They found sandbanks piled high by the desert winds, but these could be avoided by routing the road around the sandbanks.

When they passed the south slope and headed west, they crossed the tracks of a four-wheel vehicle. Dan reined in Socks for a closer examination. He leaned over in the saddle and said, "They appear to have been made by a Model T Ford." Looking closer, he added, "There are two sets of tracks, one going south and one going north. My guess is the vehicle was driven south, turned around somewhere south of here and then drove north from where it came. Let's follow them."

"We are not as far from civilization as we thought, are we, Dan?"

"I agree. I believe I mentioned to you I had heard that a prospector and no one mentioned his name, is, or was prospecting around Fremont Peak. These tracks may have been made by his Model T. We should soon find out."

They followed the tracks as they moved between the sage and greasewood bushes while Dan continued to check the depth of the sand. Once Dan stopped Socks and pointed toward the northwest, "Do you see those buildings?"

"Barely, they must be a considerable distance from here."

"I'll guess about seven miles. It is the location of the Fremont Maintenance Station. The Station maintains the railroad tracks on the branch line running between Kramer Junction and Johannesburg. Fremont Station will be the receiving point for our supplies."

"It does not appear very impressive."

"No, but it is closer to the mine than any other railroad station, and the train stops there."

"If necessary, can we catch the train at the Station and ride to Barstow?"

"Yes, Barstow is the final stop."

They continued following the tire tracks until they joined a crossroad which they could see led west to Fremont Station and east to Fremont Peak. Dan turned right and followed the road to the foot of Fremont Peak. He pulled up Socks and said, "I can see a small ore dump about halfway up to the top of the mountain but no other sign of activity, Hillary, can you?"

"No, but I can see what appears to be the location of a camp. But it is obvious from the tracks in this road, the same vehicle that made these, made the same ones we have been following. Since we can't see a truck or a car nearby, I believe the person who lives there is away."

"I think so, too, and I would like nothing better than to go up and examine his claim, but I don't think it would be quite appropriate when the occupant is not there, and it is getting late, it took longer than I anticipated to ride out here. It has been a long day, and I think we should start back, plus we have a five-mile trip ahead of us. What do you think?"

"Dan, I hate to admit it, but I agree with you. I am getting tired even after an afternoon nap. Do you think this trip was worth the effort?"

Dan turned the horses around before he answered. "Absolutely, I have not found any piece of ground between here and the spring that cannot be graded and turned into a road adequate for a heavy truck to travel if it is equipped with dual solid rubber tires on the drive wheels. Before I jump off the deep end, though, I'll ride out here with Joel and get his opinion."

Suddenly, Socks broke up the conversation by breaking into a trot to show Dan he was anxious to get back to camp.

Caught by surprise, Dan almost lost Sam's lead rope. Quickly, he pulled Socks back to a walk and decided to give Socks a little more attention. Looking back at Hillary, following behind Sam, he saw her wave and smile and knew she was not suffering excessively from her strenuous day.

When they reached the camp, Hillary helped Dan unsaddle and tether the horses then she left to fix their dinner while Dan watered and fed the horses. Later, after finishing his chores, he joined Hillary in the cooking area, and Hillary handed him a cup of hot tea. She said, "The temperature drops so quickly when the sun goes down, the tea seems to taste better here than it does in Boston."

"The tea does taste excellent, and the weather may have something to do with it; however, it may have been the hand that brewed the tea."

They both laughed, "Don't put yourself down, you make an excellent cup of tea."

"You tasted your first cup of my tea last night. It is my considered opinion that as tired as you were, a cup of tea brewed by a Brazilian coffee grower would have tasted like the best cup of tea ever brewed in Boston."

Again, they both laughed, and Hillary said, "Dan, it was not that bad."

"Wrong choice of words, now I know it was bad," Dan smiled and said, "If I may change the subject," and pointed, "although the sun has dropped below the horizon, have you noticed the beautiful sunset this evening?"

Hillary, who had been facing east while talking, turned toward the west. "How gorgeous, Dan. I have read about the beauty of the desert sunsets, that they are equal to any in the world, but I never dreamed I would be lucky enough to see one except on canvas."

They stood together, and even as they watched, the colors grew darker, faded then reappeared and changed into different brighter colors as the magic brush of the Master Painter raced back and forth across the horizon creating another sunset masterpiece. They watched the sunset until dusk then shook their heads from side to side as if in awe of the beautiful scene they had just witnessed. Finally, Hillary summed up their thoughts, "Such splendor can be seen. It cannot be painted on canvas."

Dan broke the spell by asking, "What are we fixing for dinner this evening?"

Hilary replied, "A nice thick slice of fried smoked ham, hot green peas from a can, naturally, and fried potatoes and onions, and of course, subject to your approval."

"Perfect, we can top it off with a can of pears, and we can also bake a batch of biscuits in the Dutch oven if you are interested."

"Fried ham and hot biscuits go together like mashed pota-toes and gravy, but I will have to delegate the biscuit detail to you. I hate to admit it, but I don't know how to make them. Dad always made them on our camping trips, so I never both-ered to learn."

To this, Dan acceded, "I hereby accept the responsibility for making the biscuits, it makes me feel very important."

While they were eating and discussing their trip to the crossroad that joined Fremont Station and Fremont Peak, Hillary questioned Dan about the specific kind of truck he had mentioned they would need. "where are we going to find such a truck to meet our needs?"

Dan replied, "When my company sent me to Atolia to provide engineering assistance on the tungsten mill located there, trucks like the one I described were used to haul tungsten ore from the mines to the mill. Now, this was before our entry into the War, and when the War ended the mill shut down, and I don't know what disposition was made of the company trucks. Possibly, one is in storage somewhere in this area and is still operational. We must check and find out. Our best bet to get information will be Atolia which is now pretty much of a ghost town, but it is only about fifteen miles from here as the crow flies. We can ride over there and back in a day. When Joel arrives, the three of us can discuss the whole plan and get his opinion. If Joel agrees a satisfactory road can be graded to the Fremont Peak crossroad, and if we can't find our truck locally, we may have to order one. And that is it, and do you have any questions?"

"Your suggestions sound logical to me, and I have no questions. But I do know that as soon as we have completed our after-dinner chores, I am immediately going to crawl in bed."

After breakfast the next morning, while discussing their schedule for the day, Dan suggested they take a lunch since he did not know how long it would take to finish the task of locating the rest of the claims. And remembering Hillary's problem with the heat, he suggested they take the horses. Looking at Hillary, he saw her back stiffen, and her lips tighten, and he instantly knew he had said the wrong thing. Then she took a deep breath and seemed to relax.

"I will be all right, Dan, and I prefer to walk. The morning temperature is perfect, and the air smells so clean, I know I will enjoy the walk. And concerning the lunch, I like the idea. Eating at the mine will give us a chance to rest before we start back. Which reminds me, how early tomorrow morning shall we plan on leaving?"

"I am going to get as much ready this evening as I can without affecting our evening meal and breakfast. Hopefully, with what we can do this evening, we can get started by nine tomorrow morning and be at the top of the hill by noon. We will stop for a rest at the same spot among the Joshua trees where we stopped on the way down."

"Do you think we should fill the canteens tonight?" "Yes, if we wait until tomorrow, we may not have enough to water the horses and supply our needs."

"It all sounds good to me, Dan. Now, I'll fix our lunch, including a Thermos of coffee."

"Good, and I will lead the horses to another patch of bunch grass and tether them."

As they approached the claim, Dan asked Hillary to again watch the ore dump while he checked the area around the claim. When he gave her the all-clear sign, he looked at the area to the north, then began walking down the ramp toward her, and after joining her, they walked together back to the claim and around to the north side of the hill.

As they moved along the side of the hill, Dan said, "If we can locate two more claims, I believe we will have our vein protected; two more will bracket the hill and prevent anyone from penetrating it. Two more is one more than I had planned, but I believe the time and effort will be worthwhile." Hillary nodded in agreement but did not comment, and Dan knew better than to ask her if the extra work would be too much for her.

It was well after the noon hour when they walked up the ramp to the ore dump. Before Hillary sat down on her dynamite box, she rubbed her back then looked at Dan and said, "Another three days of this and I can qualify for this kind of work, but I am not sure I would care to do it the rest of my life."

Dan smiled, "It isn't exactly my idea of a career change I would relish either. And if I may add, even though we worked longer today than we did yesterday, you don't appear as exhausted."

"That is a compliment, and I thank you. Shall we have lunch?"

They had decided to eat on the top of the ore dump to get the full benefit of the breeze blowing in from the west. Hillary sat down on her dynamite box and leaned her rifle against the front of the stove then she leaned back against the huge boulder, unscrewed the cap of her canteen and took a long drink. In the meantime, Dan had selected the south side of the stove for his backrest, but he removed the satchel and his canteen before sitting down.

Hillary, sitting comfortably on her dynamite box, removed her gloves, and showed them to Dan, "These were a perfectly good pair of gloves before I started building rock piles, now look at them. The leather is so thin you can see through it." Then she stuck her little finger through a hole in one of the thumbs and said, "See?"

Dan, not sounding very sympathetic, responded, "Can you imagine how your hands would look if you had not worn gloves."

They continued their trivial conversation for a few minutes before Dan opened the satchel and fished out their lunch. "What have we got in here?" Dan asked.

"There are ham and cheese sandwiches, strawberry jam sandwiches, cookies, apples, and a Thermos of coffee."

"And what will you have?" Dan asked.

"A ham and cheese, half of a strawberry, one cookie, and an apple. Coffee later."

Dan reached over and handed her the food and removed the wrapper from a ham and cheese and took a big bite. After chewing and swallowing it, he said, "Great ham and cheese sandwich, Hillary."

"Thank you, it is difficult to make a bad ham and cheese."

She finished her sandwich and asked, "May I have a cup of coffee before I start my strawberry half?"

"One cup of hot coffee corning up." Dan poured the coffee and reached over to hand Hillary the tin cup. She pushed back her hat and leaned forward to take the cup just as the bullet struck the boulder behind her head showering her with splintered rock, then screamed off to the southwest.

Dan dropped the cup of coffee as he rolled off the dynamite box and grabbed Hillary by the front of her shirt and jerked her down on his chest behind the stove just as another bullet struck the rock where Hillary had been resting, then two more battered the north side of the chimney hurling shipped rock and mortar over their heads. Hillary tried to raise her head, but Dan held it firmly against his chest. Turning her head to the side, she stammered, "Dan, what is happening?"

"Someone is shooting at us!" Dan barked.

"What are we going to do?" Hillary asked.

"Think!" he said, as he lay bareheaded holding Hillary. After the four shots, the shooting stopped, and Dan rolled

Hillary off his chest over to his west side below the chimney. Then he said, "Keep your head down," and asked, "Where is your rifle."

"Leaning against the front of the stove."

Dan reached around the front of the stove until he could feel the rifle then he slowly drew it to his side. Easing the rifle over the top of the stove without raising his head, he pointed it in the general direction from which he had heard the shots fired, then he quickly raised up and fired twice. The rifleman immediately responded with two shots then two more. All four struck and jarred the stove.

Hillary appeared to have calmed down. She turned over on her side, facing Dan and asked, "How bad off are we, Dan?"

"Very bad, that has to be Schuleman. I blame myself for not being more alert and allowing us to get into this trap. And I am doubly angry for exposing you to this danger. How do you feel?"

"Afraid, but back in control. What can I do?"

"Hold on, I am going to let him know we are still here."

Dan eased the rifle back to his side and rolled over the edge of the front of the stove. After slowly slipping the rifle around the front of the stove, he raised it and fired one shot once again, the rifleman responded, this time with three shots that struck the stove.

Dan said, "More bad news, I am positive he has an Army .30 caliber Springfield like the kind we used during the War. Army surplus is my guess. The significance is his firepower. He can hide four to six hundred yards away and still outgun us. Simply put, his rifle is much more powerful than ours. We can't fix the gun problem, but I think we have a good chance of evening the odds. Based on the sound of the rifle shot and the bullet striking the stove, I estimate he is about 300 yards from here, and we can't just lie here and let him bang away at us. Consequently, I think you will agree we have to do something. While we have been talking, I think I have come up with a plan. The execution of the plan depends upon your answers to two questions. The first is, how many shells do you have in addition to the three in the rifle?"

"I only brought six, Dan, and they are in my pocket." "Good, I was concerned you may not have brought any. Six is plenty."

Two more bullets struck the stove. One hit the chimney, glancing off the side. Dan did not return the fire. He asked Hillary, "How do you feel?"

"I have never been shot at before, but I had a few whiz by me when Dad and I were deer hunting. I am all right now, Dan. Let's hear your plan."

"This guy is clever, and he is not going to be satisfied with just keeping us pinned down, so eventually he will try to outflank us. My plan is to outflank him which means I will be gone for a short time, and in the meantime, you must keep up the pretense we are both here behind the stove by firing your rifle approximately every minute. It will take me from five to seven minutes to get behind Schuleman. Well," Dan asked, "What do you think?"

"I have listened to everything you have told me about Schuleman, and I don't think we have any other option. I came here to help you, and I shall help you. When do we start?"

"Right now. First, remove your scarf and tie it around your hair, so it doesn't show." Dan reached around the stove and into the firebox and removed a piece of charred wood.

He handed it to Hillary, "Smear some of this over your face and on your scarf, not too much, just enough to make you blend with the surroundings. Also, smear a little on your hands and on your sleeves. And be sure not to expose your head. When you fire, never fire twice from the same location, mix them up so he can't draw a bead on you." Dan put his left hand on her shoulder and asked, "Now, Hillary, do you understand all I have said, and do you have any questions?"

"Yes, Dan, and I understand why."

"Good. I will back out to the ramp on my belly then cut back into the brush about 20 yards before I begin circling. Before I start; I want you to fire a shot to distract him."

While Dan had been explaining the plan, Hillary had quickly spread the charcoal over her face, scarf, arms, and hands. Just as she finished, Dan leaned over and kissed her on the cheek, then he pulled his revolver, spun the cylinder, and thrust it back into his holster. "I am ready when you are," he said. He turned over on his stomach and waited for Hillary to fire.

Hillary, surprised, and a little flustered with Dan's show of affection needed a couple of seconds to recover. She slowly pushed the rifle over the top of the stove next to the chimney, then aimed it in the general direction of the rifleman and pulled the trigger. She ducked down just as two bullets struck the stove, filling the air above her head with splintered rock and mortar. She turned and looked at Dan just in time to see him sliding over the edge of the ore dump onto the ramp and disappear. Her heart raced, and the pulse in her throat throbbed, choking her. She coughed, and feeling faint, grabbed the canteen, quickly unscrewed the cap, and poured water over the back of her neck. Looking over the edge of the dump where Dan had disappeared, she had to fight the urge to follow him. Hillary, she thought, calm down or you are going to get both of us killed. She poured more water on her neck and took a long drink. That is better, she thought. Then she looked at her rifle and decided to replace the four shells that had been fired. Looking at the sights on her rifle, she thought, If I reset the sights at 300 yards, I will at least have a fighting chance of hitting him if he decides to charge me. Then after reloading and checking her sights, she thought, I am sure more than a minute has passed. And she eased the rifle over the top of the stove near the opening to the firebox.

Dan ducked down as soon as his feet touched the ramp, moved quickly to the edge and dropped off onto the soft sand below. He ran south, with his head down and his body low, keeping the ore dump between the rifleman and his position. When he felt sufficiently concealed from Schuleman, he turned west, running low and dropping down to crawl when the brush thinned. When he turned north, he listened for Hillary's rifle. He thought, it has been a minute, maybe two, what has gone wrong? His imagination began to race, then he heard her rifle followed by one shot from Schuleman, then two more. She is all right, he thought, and those shots gave me a good estimate of Schuleman's location. I keep thinking it is Schuleman and I am sure it is.

Dan changed his course from north to northwest until he reached a position he guessed was about 150 yards west of Schuleman then he again turned north. He heard Hillary's rifle fire two different times as he moved through the brush. Then, unexpectedly, he heard Hillary fire two more shots in quick succession. While on his hands and knees, he peeked over the top of a sage bush just in time to see Schuleman scrambling back into his shelter.

Dan whispered to himself, "She caught him in the open, and a deer can run ten times faster than he can! Good Girl! Good Girl! I'll bet he won't try that again." Then he thought, He must have been trying to reach the hill in back of the claim.

Dan heard Schuleman's rifle quickly fire five times.

Dan thought He must be so upset from nearly getting himself shot, he isn't checking his surroundings. It is time for me to get behind him. I'm almost due west from him now.

Dan bent over into a low crouch and began running toward the northeast, concentrating on keeping a low profile. When he estimated he had run half the distance, he dropped behind a sage bush to rest and check his location. He guessed he had another hundred yards to go to put him directly behind Schuleman. Then he heard Hillary fire one round, and again Schuleman opened up with another barrage. Dan thought Hillary must have fired to let me know she is all right. Now she only has three shells left. I can't wait any longer. Schuleman will be busy reloading, and I've got to get into a position where I can move in on him.

Keeping his low profile, Dan moved rapidly but carefully, avoiding loose rocks and running into sage bushes, until he could see Schuleman's cover directly south of him. After resting a few seconds, he began working his way forward. He had snaked his way toward the cover about 25 yards when he heard Hillary's rifle, followed by Schuleman's return fire. Immediately, he began running and did not stop until he was within 30 yards of Schuleman's hideout, then he dropped on a sandy spot behind a greasewood bush. By looking through the branches of the greasewood, he could see Schuleman reloading his rifle. Dan thought, If I can close in another fifteen yards, I'll call him.

Fortunately, the afternoon breeze coming from the west had picked up, minimizing what little noise Dan made as he slipped forward from bush to bush while watching Schuleman for any unexpected move he might make. Schuleman, however, seemed to be concentrating on the old prospector's stove 300 yards away. Seeing Schuleman raise his. rifle to fire, Dan, now near enough to compete with Schuleman's rifle, rose to his feet holding his revolver with both hands while pointing the barrel at Schuleman's back, Dan snapped, "Drop the rifle, Schuleman,"

Schuleman, dumbfounded by the sudden command, did not drop the rifle nor did he turn around.

Dan spoke again, "You have three-seconds, Schuleman."

Schuleman, holding the rifle with both hands, made a movement to toss the rifle, but suddenly spun around and fired. Dan felt a tug on his shirt just above the belt as he fired two quick rounds. Schuleman dropped his rifle and grabbed his shoulder while slowly sinking to the ground.

Hearing Hillary's rifle shot, Dan looked up just in time to see Hillary leaping down the side of the ore dump holding the rifle with both hands high above her head, her scarf missing and her hair streaming behind. She hit the bottom of the ore dump running full speed hurdling over sage bushes and cutting around the larger ones like a skier in a slalom race.

Dan kept his revolver pointed at Schuleman while slowly inching forward. It seemed less than a minute had passed when Hillary broke though the greasewoods and stood by Dan's side, her rifle trained on Schuleman.

"Are you all right?" she gasped.

"I'm OK," he replied and slipped his arm around Hillary's waist. Now they stood about ten feet from Schuleman.

Switching her rifle to her left hand, she moved her right arm to his side. Then she felt the tear in his shirt and the sticky wetness of the blood, "Dan, you've been wounded!" She exclaimed.

"Nothing serious, only a nick. Let's check Schuleman."

Both had moved over, and we were standing close to the wounded rifleman. Dan asked, "How do you feel, Schuleman?"

"My shoulder is killing me. Who are you, and how did you know my name?"

"My name is Sanders, and this lady is Miss MacGregor. She is the granddaughter of the old prospector whose claim you tried to steal. I am the person who found the old prospector and reported my findings to the constable in Barstow. If I might add, your shoulder may hurt, but your chest wound will cause you to die. You have a punctured lung, and probably your liver has a hole in it. You will bleed to death, and there is not a thing we can do about it."

"I remember you. You filed the report I read in the Constables' Office." Schuleman coughed, and bright red bubbles formed on his lips. "You saw the gold, or you would not be out here. Why didn't you report it?"

"Because this area would have been swarming with gold seekers the next morning, and whatever clues or information that might shed a little light on the old man's death would have been destroyed. Schuleman, I put my trust in the authorities." Dan looked closely at Schuleman's face then continued, "While I was in the War, I saw many men die from wounds like yours. You are bleeding internally as well as externally, and you have about ten minutes left. What do you want me to do with your body? I can leave it here for the coyotes and buzzards to fight over, or I can pack your body into Barstow and see that you get a decent burial."

Schuleman, holding his shoulder while the blood seeped through his fingers, squirmed at Dan's remarks, and said, "I know I am dying, pack my remains into Barstow." Then he added, "Please?"

Dan said, "I have a few questions to ask you before I'll

agree. The first is about Deputy Olsen, I know you killed him. Why?"

Again, Schuleman shut his eyes, rolled his head, and squirmed before answering. "On our way to arrest a bootlegger running a still down along the Mojave Riverbed, he told me he was going to report we had found gold on the old prospector's claim. He didn't ask me, he told me he was going to do it. I argued with him, but it didn't do any good. While we were stalking the bootlegger, I got madder and madder, and when the opportunity came, I shot him."

"You also shot the bootlegger, why?"

"I was sure the bootlegger was watching when I shot Swede, so I had to shoot him, too." Then Schuleman asked, "Have you got any water? I'm burning up."

"Sorry, Schuleman, we don't have any with us."

For the first time, Hillary spoke up, "Dan, I'll run up to the claim and bring back a canteen."

Before Dan could answer, she started off in a dogtrot toward the claim. In the meantime, Dan stood over Schuleman, trying to shade him. But before Hillary could get back, Schuleman started coughing up blood and choking. He died just as she stepped around Schuleman's shooting blind.

"He's dead, Hillary." Dan reached down and closed Schuleman's eyelids.

Looking down at Schuleman as she slowly moved her head from side to side, she said, "How sad, Dan, that we have men who are as mean as Schuleman. How wonderful the world would be without them?" She took one last look at Schuleman, turned to Dan and handed him his hat saying, "I brought your hat, what do we do now?"

"We have to find Schuleman's horse."

"Before I ran down the side of the ore dump, I saw it about

200 yards north of here. It appears to be a dappled gray and is hidden in a ravine or a wash. Since the brush obstructed my view, and I was worried about you, I didn't take the time to take a second look."

"You know where the horse is hidden, so you lead the way."

They walked side by side when the sagebrush permitted, discussing the changes they must now make in their plans. Dan said, "I'm sure you are aware we must break camp and leave today."

"Yes, I have been thinking about it. Schuleman's horse will not have the stamina to carry a body of that size for any distance after the trip from wherever Schuleman rode the horse."

"You are right. The closest stable is Randsburg, and it is about 25 miles from here. When we get to camp, I'll unsaddle the horse, water and feed it. While the horse rests, I'll tend to the other horses, then we will eat before breaking camp and getting the horses ready to travel. I believe the most sensible way to carry the body is to put Schuleman's saddle on the packhorse and load the body on the saddle. And since we have a much lighter load, we can substitute the gray for the packhorse."

"Do you think the gray will accept the pack saddle?" "He may object for a few seconds, but he will be too tired to object for very long."

As they walked toward the horse, Hillary asked, "How is your side, Dan, do you mind if I look at it?"

"No, if it will help relieve your concern." Dan stopped and laid his canteen down, then began loosening his belt and pulling out his shirt. In the meantime, Hillary had leaned her rifle against a sage bush.

Dan held up his shirt while Hillary examined the wound and explained her observations to him, "The bullet broke the skin, but an excellent clot is forming over the wound. Some seepage is visible, but I am sure it will soon stop." Then with her fore and middle finger, she began to gently probe the area around the wound. "Do you feel any pain when I press?"

"It is sore but nothing serious."

Hillary concluded, "It looks good, and when we get back to camp, I'll bind it with a strip from one of my undergarments to keep the waist of your trousers from chafing the wound. However, I think you should have a doctor check it tomorrow." She looked up at Dan and said, "If I may now change the subject, what will we use to wrap the body?"

Dan answered while pushing his shirt back in his pants, "I'm sure Schuleman tied a blanket and ground cover on the back of his saddle before leaving this morning, and hopefully, a canteen or two. We will need extra water for the extra horse which I am sure will require us to draw some of the canteens direct from the spring. It could slow us down a half hour or more in leaving." Then Dan looked at Hillary and asked, "How are you feeling?"

"A little weary but nothing a good cup of hot tea can't fix." Trying to discount her true feelings, she continued, "I was rudely interrupted and missed my lunch hour coffee." She gave Dan a feeble smile.

Dan reached over and put both hands on Hillary's shoulders, "You are the most remarkable woman I have ever met. When you caught Schuleman out in the open and drove him back to cover, I could feel pride creeping over me. I wanted to stand up and wave my arms like a college freshman at a football game. And I felt your tenderness, and how you put your concern over me above that of your own. I have become very fond of you, and I need to have you around me for a long, long time. And I want you to consider sailing to South Africa for our honeymoon."

"Oh, Dan, I think that is a wonderful idea! I've been hoping you would ask me. Now there is no way you are going to get on that ship without me. Although he never said so, I know Daddy was sure I would become an old maid, but I was only waiting for the right man to come along, and he did." Dan's hands were still resting on her shoulders, so she slipped her hands up through his arms and put her hands behind his neck and pulled his head down then gave him a long loving kiss while tears trickled down her cheeks. When she released him, she felt Dan's arms around her waist holding her very close.

After releasing Hillary, Dan looked in the direction where they had left Schuleman's body, then he looked upward at the sky above the body and pointed, "Buzzards. We had better hurry and get the horse."

The End

ACKNOWLEDGMENTS

There are additional pictures on the web, with more historical information; you can view, by typing in any of the towns mentioned, Daggett, Atolia, Randsburg, Red Mountain, and Johannesburg, as well as the city of Barstow. Desert Historical Museum and staff. Fees to purchase any of these pictures of this era are minimal. Photos included in The Prospector book, are generally from the Jones family archives, contributed by relatives and friends.

Many thanks to the Jones family and friends who provided background, research, stories, and photos, for this book, and added help from the various historical societies in the area.

My thanks to Dave Dickson, who acted as the intermediary with the publisher. Thank you, Dave. And thank you, Rick Lakin, at iCrew Digital Publishing, for your patience and diligence, in publishing my Dad's book